HEARTS IN DEFIANCE

ROMANCE IN THE ROCKIES BOOK 2

HEATHER BLANTON

RIVULET PUBLISHING

Hearts in Defiance

Book Two

By Heather Blanton

Published by Rivulet Publishing

Cover DESIGN by http://ravven78.deviantart.com/

Scripture taken from the HOLY BIBLE,

KING JAMES VERSION - Public Domain

A huge *thank you* to my editors and beta readers: David Webb, Kim VanDerwarker Huther, Vicki Prather, Heather Baker, Sally Shupe, Connie Bartley White, Carole Sanders, and Kimberly Buffaloe!

Heather Blanton

Please subscribe to my newsletter
By visiting my website
Authorheatherblanton.com
to receive updates on my new releases and other fun news. You'll
also receive a FREE e-book—
A Lady in Defiance, The Lost Chapters
just for subscribing!

Therefore, there is now no condemnation for those who are in Christ Jesus, because through Christ Jesus the law of the Spirit of life set me free from the law of sin and death.

Romans 8:1

FOREWORD

Dear Reader,

What an amazing journey I've been on these last several years, but especially the last two. I self-published *A Lady in Defiance* in February of 2012 and, by the grace of God, it became a best-seller. No marketing. No publisher. No PR. Just God and your word-of-mouth. I don't have the words to express my gratitude to Him for His grace, or to you for picking up a book by an unknown author and then telling your friends about it. Oh, thank you, thank you.

Against the advice of folks in the traditional publishing industry, I opted to write the sequel *Hearts in Defiance* for you, the reader. Aren't all books written for the reader? Hardly. Just like *A Lady in Defiance*, this is an ensemble piece. Publishers are leery of those. The plots are too complicated. And while *Hearts* is a stand-alone story, it picks up where the first left off. Again, not what publishers suggested. They wanted a new storyline with only slight references to the first book.

I couldn't do it.

I wanted to write the story *you* wanted to read. I hope and pray I have accomplished that. I've read your emails, reviews on

Amazon, and comments on Facebook; then I evaluated your desires for the sequel and tried to work them into this new story.

I also wanted to write a story that would show, no matter who you are or what you've done, God is waiting to forgive you, but you need to accept His forgiveness. Even after we take it to God, most of us hang onto our sin, letting it slither around us like an evil, constricting vine from the Black Forest. That's an illusion. Once we're forgiven, sin is only a thin, brittle piece of wood covered in dead leaves. Accept His forgiveness, raise your arms to heaven, and explode that vine! Rejoice as the dust settles at your feet. You are worthy of His love, you are redeemed, and you are free!

I hope in this book, gentle reader, you will hear the Father bending down to whisper in your ear, *"You're a new creation, beloved. No more looking back."*

Blessings, my friends!

PROLOGUE

*N*ever had the sound of galloping horses brought Chief Ouray anything but death and disaster.

Though his dreams were haunted by screams and the echoes of rifle fire, the hoofbeats of unshod ponies roused Ouray instantly from his afternoon nap. He sat up in the rocking chair and squinted at the riders emerging from the Ponderosa pines, coming hard. Dread squirmed in his heart. He rarely had visitors anymore, and when he did, they wanted only to argue and complain.

Soul-weary, Ouray pushed himself out of the chair and trudged to the edge of his porch. Six braves thundered toward him. The sun glinted off their fine, lean bodies, highlighting the dancing feathers and bright war paint covering them in intricate patterns.

Ouray recognized one of the riders and breathed a white man's curse. The brave leading the pack, One-Who-Cries, lived to cause trouble. Always had. One-Who-Cries had tried to kill Ouray more than once for trading too much away to the white man. But Ouray had seen the strength of the white man, their fine cities, their soldiers numbering greater than pebbles on a river

1

bank. They could not be defeated. Ouray had known early on that the best his people could hope for was mercy. But these young bucks would not accept this truth, and their blood burned with a killing fire.

The six horses pounded up to his house and skidded to a stop, kicking up dust. But Ouray did not flinch. Their paint told him they had not come to kill him. Someone else was their prey.

"How are you today, old man?" One-Who-Cries mocked him. "Do you rest peacefully in your *house* while the Utes at White River live in windowless boxes and use their ponies to pull plows?"

Bones creaking, Ouray drew himself up to his still-impressive height, folded his arms across his chest, and waited. He'd heard such complaints many times before. Responding to this sharp-tongued badger would change nothing.

Frowning, One-Who-Cries slapped his horse's reins back and forth as if pondering the old man's silence. His large nose and dark eyes had always reminded Ouray of a bear, but the child had always acted more like an ill-tempered porcupine. Much as Ouray loved the little ones, he had never found a place in his heart for this boy. And now the boy had grown into a dangerous warrior. It grieved Ouray that his only daughter had wed the hot-tempered renegade.

Through wasting time, One-Who-Cries shook his head and attempted to wither Ouray with a disgusted glare. "I come to tell you there have been attacks. A village on the Yampa. Men, women, children, the white man spared no one."

Ouray waited. He knew the young man was getting to the point, though at a wearisome pace.

"Three days ago, white miners came across a hunting party of Uncompahgre and slaughtered them, too. Took their meat, their furs, their weapons."

If Ouray had allowed himself a reaction, he would have spit on the ground and uttered another white man's curse. Every time peace was close, a short-sighted Injun or drunken paleface set fire to it. There were bad white men just as there were bad Indians. The result was the same. The Utes gave up more land.

"*More* gold has been found in the Uintah Valley." One-Who-Cries knit his brows together as if he couldn't understand Ouray's lack of outrage. "Whites are flowing in like melting spring snow. They are overrunning our lands, ruining our hunting grounds, taking our women—"

"You have not come to tell me this," Ouray interrupted him, more than a little perturbed by this strutting rooster. "What is it you plan to do?"

One-Who-Cries leaned forward on his black-and-white pinto, staring hard at the old man, dark eyes blazing with hate. "From this day forward, for every Ute they kill, I will kill *two* white men. For every squaw they steal, I will steal *two* white women." The young brave's voice dripped with venom as he hissed, "We will burn their camps, steal their horses, and shoot a hundred arrows into their backs. We will enslave their children, rape their daughters, and bury the white man on Ute land till they come no more seeking gold."

"Killing one white man is like dipping water from a rushing river." Ouray spoke from deep, painful experience. The whites were a wildfire engulfing his people, one that didn't know how to burn itself out. "The Utes are fading away, like the buffalo," he reminded the young warrior, "like the great summer hunts, like the valleys where no man has stepped." Regret for so many things tightened his throat. "What you do will only bring more misery upon our people."

One-Who-Cries' face tightened at the warning, his lips curling into a sneer. "This time, the white man will have the greater portion."

CHAPTER 1

*C*harles McIntyre sat down at his desk in his saloon and stared at his Bible.

He almost laughed out loud but in the silence, the sound would have been deafening. He knew plenty of people who *would* laugh. A former pimp, saloon owner, and gunman reading the *Bible*.

Do you really think you're worthy to come before Him?

The subtle rebuke pricked his soul. But he was determined and reached for the book. Naomi had said several times during his convalescence that all the answers to his questions would be found there. Rolling mental dice, since he didn't know exactly how to start, he opened the book and read the first words his eyes fell upon:

Let thy fountain be blessed: and rejoice with the wife of thy youth.
Let her be as the loving hind and pleasant roe;
let her breasts satisfy thee at all times.

McIntyre's eyebrows shot up. *That* wasn't what he was expecting. Intrigued, he read on.

And be thou ravished always with her love.

And why wilt thou, my son, be ravished with a strange woman, and embrace the bosom of a stranger?

He sat back and pondered the Scripture, chastised by it. He had spent a shameful number of nights embracing the bosoms of strangers, and it had never led to anything like what he felt for Naomi. Perhaps this was what God was trying to tell him. There would never be anything as passionate and pure in a man's life as loving and honoring the one woman whom God chooses for him.

That acknowledgement led him, unfortunately, to face a bigger issue.

God, what is the matter with me? Why can't I give You my life as willingly as I gave Naomi my heart?

He shifted in his seat, uncomfortable with the question. A man who had once preferred to rule in hell rather than serve in heaven, McIntyre admitted that making Jesus Lord of his *life*—well, that stirred up resistance in him.

Through his half-open door, he could see the length of his bar. Once full of rowdy, dirty, jostling miners, the place now was as empty and silent as Christ's tomb. No bawdy tunes pounded forth from the player piano. No siren call of female laughter tempted men into sin. No shady deals simmered in his brain, and he hadn't meted out any frontier *justice* in months. All of that was behind him. He was glad too.

But something was still missing.

Footfalls and a soft tap at his office door drew him back to the moment. Ian Donoghue slipped in, saluting him with his cane.

"Good morning, lad." The Scotsman tugged off his Balmoral bonnet, revealing a shock of unruly silver hair, and claimed the seat in front of McIntyre's desk. His deep blue eyes shone with amusement when he saw the book open before Charles. "Well, looks as though ye're starting your day off with the right priorities. I'm heartened to see it."

"It is . . ." *Shocking? Unbelievable?*

"Aboot time." Ian chuckled and laid the cane and hat across his ever-growing midsection.

McIntyre smiled at his friend's burr and its contrast to his own Southern drawl.

"Of course, I knew all along ye'd come to your senses. No God," he shook his head, "no path to Naomi."

Almost offended, McIntyre picked up the black leather-bound book. "Do you think I'm doing this just for her?"

"No, no." Ian patted the air with his hands, defusing the tension. "That's not what I mean at all. Having that crazy Mexican wench blow a hole in yer shoulder would give any man his come-to-Jesus moment." He smiled at McIntyre like a father approving his son's behavior. "It was the way ye stepped in front of the bullet —for her, for love. I knew ye had it in ye."

McIntyre touched his aching shoulder, the sling still in place. "Don't remind me."

"Aye, lad, ye'd run from God a long time, but I saw ye slowing down. Naomi was yer—"

"Salvation." The word leapt out of its own accord, but it felt right. One glance at the grieving widow last July *had* started McIntyre down this path to becoming a better man. He'd closed the Iron Horse Saloon and Garden, retired all his lovely *Flowers*, and made an effort to recruit legitimate businesses for Defiance. He'd even hired a marshal. All in a vain attempt to get Naomi Miller to love him. Nothing had convinced her Charles McIntyre might be the man for her until Rose pulled the trigger on the .44.

He'd taken the bullet to save Naomi, not because he was a hero or because he was a noble man, but because he *loved* her. And for an instant, he'd seen the heart of God and understood that no sacrifice was too great to save the ones you love.

McIntyre's sacrifice had finally brought Naomi around. But it had also brought his wretched past into brutal clarity. "Ian, I have to tell her things about myself." His friend's face clouded with concern. "She has to know. I suppose, in reality, I never thought I'd actually win her. These past two weeks I've spent with her," Charles laid the Bible back down on the desk and evaluated their time together. "She nursed me, body and soul. She's tried to make me understand grace and forgiveness."

With infectious passion, she had attempted to make him believe his sins were washed away, that he was a new man, and the past was in the past.

Only it wasn't.

He blinked and returned his attention to Ian. "My past only weighs heavier upon me. She deserves more than me, Ian, and she deserves to know who I was."

Ian leaned forward. "Exactly. *Was*. Ye're not the man ye were." He spoke with firmness and conviction. "I saw ye changing the moment Naomi and her sisters rode into town. I see no argument for parading all the skeletons from yer closet. They dinna matter anymore."

The skeletons that still had flesh on them might matter quite a bit. "There are *some* things I have to tell her. The passes are open, and the stages will start up again soon. I won't have her ambushed by the truth."

Understanding and regret dawned on Ian's face, and he nodded. "Aye, I suppose 'tis not so grand to be the cock o' the walk now, is it?"

———

*M*cIntyre fanned himself with his coal-black Stetson as he stood waiting in the lobby of the Trinity Inn. Dressed in a tailored grey frock coat, matching pants, green silk vest, and polished cavalry boots, he could be mistaken for any Southern gentleman making a Sunday afternoon call on his lady. The sling on his right arm and the .45 on his hip did, however, muddle the illusion.

"Good afternoon, Mr. McIntyre."

Naomi's greeting floated down to him from the staircase landing. He followed the sound, and his voice caught in his throat at the sight of her. Instead of the austere braid she always wore, loose golden waves of shimmering corn silk cascaded gently around her shoulders. The simple blue gingham dress hugged her curves and moved with her in beautiful, enticing ways.

The welcome in her wide jade eyes warmed him body and soul. A new experience for him. No woman had ever affected him on such a deep emotional level.

Naomi strode over to him, carrying a white lace shawl, her gaze unwavering and filled with determination. She always seemed to face things without flinching—but this was a bluff, McIntyre noted with pleasure. He could see she was nervous. Her flushed cheeks and the delicate mist of perspiration above her lip were signs a seasoned gambler like him couldn't miss.

McIntyre scratched his perfectly-trimmed beard in an attempt to hide a pleased grin. It took a lot to unnerve Naomi Miller. She had more grit than most men he knew.

"You are a vision, Naomi." He motioned to her hair, desperately wishing he could run his hands through it. "Are all of those glorious waves of spun gold just for a buggy ride?"

Giggles from the top of the stairs drew his attention upward. Naomi's sisters, Rebecca and Hannah, and his former Flower, Mollie, leaned over the rail, their faces alight with curiosity.

"She had assistance, did she, ladies?"

Naomi blushed like a new bride. "I think they got a little carried away."

"Hardly." He bowed in appreciation to the ladies above them and thickened his Georgia drawl. "I approve"—he inched a breath closer to Naomi and swung his gaze back to her—"whole-heartedly."

Her eyes widened, and she turned away. McIntyre savored the reactions she tried in vain to hide.

"She's a little out of practice, Mr. McIntyre," Hannah, the younger of the sisters, teased. Fair-haired and petite like Naomi, she was as bubbly as a mountain stream. "This whole courting thing is new to her, but we'll get her going in the right direction—"

"Hannah Marie Frink!" Naomi stomped her foot in mortification. "Not another word!"

McIntyre laughed, truly enjoying watching his spitfire squirm. If this afternoon's ride didn't go well, he'd just as soon walk off a cliff. In the meantime, he would revel in this familial teasing.

"Don't worry." He slipped his good arm around her waist and pulled her closer, savoring the feel of her. "I believe I can provide skilled and enthusiastic instruction."

Huffing with indignation, Naomi pushed him off as she flushed the deep red of Colorado sandstone. "If you cannot curb your tongue, Mr. McIntyre, you can take *them* on the buggy ride."

Charles cleared his throat and took an almost imperceptible step back. The girls, well aware Naomi did not make idle threats, scattered to their rooms. McIntyre waited till all was silent, and then surrendered, showing Naomi the palm of his good hand.

"You should learn to take a joke, princess. We all mean well." Losing the battle to keep his hands off her hair, he reached out and slowly lifted one soft, glistening wave of silky sunshine, wishing he could take much more. "I truly appreciate their efforts. The first time I ever saw you with your hair down, you almost left me speechless."

Her shoulders relaxed and her lips softened. "The first time we served you dinner here in the hotel. I wondered if you noticed. At the time I told myself I didn't care."

"You and your stubborn pride—"

"So how do you like being back in your saloon?"

He withdrew his hand, watching the gold threads slip away, and gave into the change of subject. "I hate it," he said flatly, surprised by his honesty. "I hate every moment I am away from you. I'm almost tempted to get shot just so you can nurse me back to health again." He smiled ruefully. "Almost."

Her soft pink lips twitched against a smile. He had a nearly overwhelming urge to take her into his arms and kiss her until her knees buckled, but Naomi was not a soiled dove. This was courting, something *he'd* never actually done before, and he was going to have to figure it out—if he went through with it at all. If he did, the amount of self-control required to keep the relationship honorable just might kill him.

Resigned, he reached for her hand and placed it on his heart, pulling her closer. "I miss you."

Had he just said that? In the last twenty years he had made a game of saying things so lewd to a woman they could blister the lacquer on a new barouche carriage. It was amazing how this woman affected him.

To hide his astonishment, he lightened his tone. "I miss the rattle of dishes and your sisters' laughter in the kitchen." He closed his eyes and inhaled. "I miss the smell of roast elk and biscuits baking . . ." The banter was no good. Charles McIntyre had turned into a romantic. He had to speak his heart and, strangely, the resolve made him feel stronger.

He squeezed her hand and said, "But it is you I miss the most. What about you? Are you glad I'm gone from your bed?"

Naomi's breathing hitched at the question and something in her eyes smoldered. Her reaction lit fires in the core of his being.

"You were a stubborn patient . . . but I miss you, too."

Her gaze traveled to his mouth and she tilted her chin up ever so slightly—the surest invitation to a kiss McIntyre had ever had. When he'd lain bleeding on the floor of her kitchen, she had kissed him. And when he awoke three days later to her at his bedside, they had kissed to seal promises for a future. Now, mesmerized by her, he leaned down to brush that inviting mouth once more. He paused, so close he could feel her breath. Groaning, he pulled away.

He'd made himself a promise and meant to keep it. Disappointment and confusion warring on her face, he stepped back, letting her hand slip from his. "I have something special to show you."

CHAPTER 2

cIntyre slid his hand out of its sling and took up a rein. Holding his breath, he snapped the leather and the horse jerked the buggy forward. The pain in his chest was brief, sharp, but gone almost instantly. A good sign, he assumed.

"Are you sure you should be driving?" Naomi asked.

"I think I can manage to take us an hour out of town." He leaned into her, unable to avoid a little teasing. "But if I feel the need to rest, I'll be sure to find us a quiet spot."

Blushing again, Naomi snatched her gaze away, but then slid closer to him and hooked her fingers around his arm. Her touch made him puff up like a rooster. He was proud to have a fine woman like Naomi by his side. Beautiful, courageous, decent.

And those virtues yanked his bit every time he started getting ahead of himself. Truth be told, she deserved much more than the likes of Charles McIntyre.

"Can you tell me where we're going?"

"No." He maneuvered their buggy around a freight wagon and pointed the horse toward the western edge of the valley. "I have to show you."

Naomi bit her lip and narrowed her eyes. "A secret?" She

tossed her hair over her shoulder and wagged her head. "For shame, I didn't think you kept any of those."

At first, their path angled upward through thick pines. An hour out of town, the buggy crested a ridge and the road flattened out. Aspens filled the woods on either side of them, their leaves quaking in the spring breeze. Naomi stretched and arched her back. "Are we almost there? And where is there?"

"Wagon seat wearing out its welcome, princess?" Grinning, he motioned forward with his chin. "Right around this curve."

Moments later, McIntyre steered the horse off the road, around a mammoth boulder, and brought the team to a stop.

A wide, majestic valley yawned open before them, going on for miles. Rugged, snow-capped peaks bordered a series of flat, grassy plains and rolling, wooded hills. Hardwoods and pines darkened the lower elevations and painted the sides of the wide green Animas River that meandered through the heart of the valley. Overhead, a hawk screamed, the sound echoing into the distance.

The view always made McIntyre feel as if he were gazing down from the edge of heaven. Naomi's silence, however, surprised and concerned him.

"Well?"

"It's beautiful."

"But . . .?" He glanced down at her and was startled to see her eyes shining.

"John's accident," she whispered. "He disappeared over a cliff like this."

McIntyre sucked in a breath and nodded. A wagon accident on the Million Dollar Highway had claimed her husband's life, thus stranding her and her sisters in Defiance. Had they recovered the body? McIntyre ached for Naomi, but he would be eternally grateful that things had turned out the way they had.

Should he say he was sorry for her loss? This struck him as somewhat disingenuous. "I am sorry, but I'm also glad it brought you to Defiance." That, at least, was honest.

She blinked and quickly wiped away the tears. "Me too. So, what am I supposed to see?"

"It's mine," McIntyre swept his arm across the vista, "all sixteen thousand acres."

She surveyed the view once again, looking appropriately impressed this time. "Are you going into the ranching business?"

He set the brake, tucked the reins away below his feet, and then jumped from the wagon. "I am planning on many things." McIntyre helped her down and led her to the overlook, stopping a few feet from the edge. The height was dizzying. He laced his fingers with hers and drank in the amazing vista as if for the first time. "I have, in fact, a lifetime of plans. I plan to build my ranch— my *home*—right down there on the river." He gazed down at her, his heart affected by her in a way he couldn't explain. "I *don't* want to do it alone."

God, I don't want to build a life without her.

He slid his good arm around her and pulled the other from its support. With a light touch, he tipped her chin, and this time went through with the kiss. He started to pull away, but his resolve failed him. Their lips blended and McIntyre's body jolted as if he'd been hit by lightning. Clutching her face between his hands, he kissed her deeply, with a frightening need.

Naomi slid her arms around his neck, tightening her grip as if she was holding on to a rescuer. The world vanished, and McIntyre held her tighter and tighter, desperate to savor her and this moment. He wove his hands through the gossamer softness of her hair like a man starved for beauty. Standing on the edge of this cliff, the taste of her, the hunger of her mouth, the months of not being able to touch her, made his head swim, his heartbeat roar in his ears.

She let her fingers comb through the black curls at the nape of his neck. She gripped his shoulders and clung to him, and he could feel her yearning. McIntyre understood for the first time in his life a need that went beyond his body and ignited a deeper desire.

But his hands, trained by years of encounters with willing women, slid around to the front of her ribs. Almost instantly, mercifully, he registered the depth of the temptation and released her as if she was a wildfire bursting to life.

He backed away, disgusted by what he'd almost done.

Her chest heaving, Naomi stared back at him, her eyes filled with fear and desire. His self-control hanging by a thread, McIntyre realized they were both fighting a raging blaze that stole his wits and fogged his judgment. He stood for a moment, hand outstretched to her in apology.

"I am so sorry, Naomi." Snatching off his hat, he turned away and ran his hand through his hair. "Forgive me. I swore I would never treat you like . . . one of my girls."

Everything has to be different with Naomi. She's my chance to start over.

"You kissed your Flowers like that?" She sounded both astonished and disappointed.

He almost laughed, recalling how he *had* treated his prostitutes. "No, I did not. I've never kissed any woman like that." Twirling his hat in his hands, he smiled from surprise. "Your kiss hits me like good whiskey—a jolt and a smooth burn." He reached up to rub his neck. "And it's been quite a while since I've had a, uh . . . *drink.*"

He took a deep breath and tried to clear his head. The feel of her in his arms had snatched the earth right out from under his feet, and his balance with it. *Focus*, he told himself. *Focus.* He worked his jaw back and forth and reminded himself of what needed to be said, no matter the consequences. "Naomi, when you were nursing me back to health . . . all that talk, about God's grace and forgiveness . . . Can you forgive as well, no matter the offense?"

"Yes, I think so," she said, her caution evident. "The Lord knows I've had to ask for forgiveness enough times."

"All right," he said more to himself than her. He took another deep breath, pinching the sweat above his lip. "Mine is a sordid past, Naomi, and I believe certain aspects of it may affect you directly. A man doesn't run a brothel for years without . . . well, without . . ."

He had made so many mistakes, and soon Defiance would throw them right in her face. She had to know.

"I've been with my share of women." He half-turned to her, but couldn't look at her. "I didn't realize until I met you that I'd never made *love* to any of them, never *been* in love with a single one."

He heard her swallow. "Charles, I don't think I need—"

He slapped his leg with his Stetson and straightened up. "Let me finish." Feeling like a man about to step before a firing squad, he took a deep breath and turned to her. Sunlight spilled through the aspens and shimmered over her hair like a lace tablecloth. She watched him intently, her catlike stare alert, but he saw fear there, too, and hated himself for being the cause of it.

"When I turned fifteen, my father took me to the largest brothel in Atlanta. We stayed for three days."

Naomi's jaw loosened. "Really, I—"

"That's the way it has always been with the women in my life, Naomi. I've used them, plain and simple. Treated them like a commodity, as you've so often accused me."

She held her features still, but the muscle between her eyebrows twitched almost imperceptibly. The knife was in. Now McIntyre needed to figure out how *not* to twist it.

"*You* are the first woman . . ." He took a step toward her as he searched for words. "You are the first woman I have ever cared for more than myself. I want you so much, it's all I can think about. And yet, I don't want to touch you until we're married." He lifted his face to heaven and fanned the air with his hat. "God knows I have *never* felt like that before. I had never even *thought* about denying my passion," His gaze dropped back to her, "until you."

Jamming his hat on his head, he marched toward her. His sudden, determined stride sent her back-stepping till she bumped into the wagon. McIntyre reached out and clutched the railing on each side of her, trapping her. "The stagecoach routes are opening up. People will be traveling again." A crease in her brow revealed her confusion, and he cursed himself for being so inept at this.

Just spit it out.

"There are women who may come to Defiance. Women who will expect . . . my hospitality." *In every sordid way imaginable.* "And that will hurt you." He tightened his grip on the wagon, the force turning his knuckles white. "If I could, I would take another bullet instead of putting you through that."

Naomi shook her head and stared down at her clutched hands, trying to get rid of the sick feeling in her gut. "Don't say that . . . I don't understand what you *are* saying, but please don't say *that.*"

"I'm saying we all gave ourselves to strangers . . ."

He tried to look into her face, but Naomi avoided him. She needed a moment. A lump forming in her throat, she wondered if he was saying good-bye. She couldn't bear to lose him too.

"It's the kind of thing that destroys people, Naomi, if they can't get past it. Ghosts come out of the woodwork, reminding you time and again of the terrible things you've done."

She looked at him then and was saddened by the guilt and shame playing out across his face. She'd once thought his black beard, always trimmed to perfection, gave him such a mischievous demeanor. Now, his sparkling brown eyes showed signs of defeat, and pain etched itself in his creased brow. His bravado gone, here was a man stepping up to give the devil his due.

Wishing she could take away his pain, she touched his cheek. "What are you saying really? That you don't think we can be together because of who you *were*? I've told you, your sins are in the past, Charles."

"No! No they are not." He shook his head, and softened his tone. "I deeply regret that you may be forced to deal with the things I've done, but my past is definitely not dead and buried. Most likely it will dog us forever. I need you to understand that . . . so you can choose."

Reeling from everything he'd said thus far, good and bad, Naomi dropped her hand and absently fiddled with the wedding band she still wore. He rested his forehead against hers, the movement pushing his hat back.

"Naomi, I don't want you to end up hating me."

Still spinning her ring around her finger, she bit down on her lip and ruminated on his confession. Or was it a warning? So what if a couple of these old flames showed up? What if they flaunted their past relationships with Charles right in front of her? What would she do?

Pull out some floozy's hair.

But more importantly, what would *he* do? She looked up. "Ghosts from your past cannot hurt anything but my pride." She laid her hand on his heart and spoke slowly. "*You* can break my heart. But still I wouldn't hate you." She grinned. "I might shoot you, but I would not hate you."

They laughed softly together, and then Naomi shook her head. "Seems to me the real question here is what *you* are going to do if any of these women show up."

"I am done with them." The uncompromising tone in his voice gave her hope. "I'm done with that life. I'll make it clear the moment any of them set foot in Defiance." He clutched her hand and moved a breath closer. "I give you my word I will honor you, Naomi, and what you mean to me."

She heard a fierce determination in his voice and prayed it was born of love and not fear that he would fail.

He brushed her bangs aside and searched her face. "You make me believe . . ." He shook his head, an incredulous smile tipping his lips. "You make me believe."

"Then let them come. I can take it."

———

*N*aomi gently showered the row of tiny green corn sprouts with the watering can. Never much of a gardener, she had to admit that the pleasant spring sun, the smell of damp earth, and the promise of corn ears dripping with melted butter did at least make the chore bearable. It also put her in a mind to reminisce.

Back home in Carolina, the weather broke quickly. Spring meant warm dirt between your toes, and quick cool showers that opened the door to suffocating humidity. She recalled several spring plantings, walking with John as he plowed the dark earth. Sleeves rolled up, her hair tucked in a straw hat, she would happily amble alongside him, hunting for arrowheads in the freshly-turned earth. He would steer his Belgian, Sampson, with skill and confidence, the big horse an equal to John's brawny build.

She let a wistful smile break. Simple, sun-washed days. Life with John had been peaceful and predictable. Her oak, he had covered her with his strength and steady love. Charles, on the other hand, made her feel as if she were standing in an open field, waiting for lightning to strike. When he turned those spellbinding, consuming eyes on her, the air around them thrummed with a charge that quickened her pulse. And when he touched her, she felt heat shoot from his fingers down to her soul.

"You're going to drown those sprouts, Naomi."

"What?" She blinked, saw the small river flowing down the row, and jerked the water can back. "Oh! Good grief."

Mollie laughed, and Naomi wondered at the sound. The girl had been a weak, pale, broken Flower in Charles' brothel, which he had called the Garden. Now a contagious smile radiated from her, and her pretty petite face, not downcast anymore, glowed with true peace. Naomi had seen God work in people, but in Mollie, he had created a fair-haired angel with a heart so full of Jesus, it was humbling to be around her.

Her sins, which are many, are forgiven, for she loved much.

"Good thing you came along when you did," Naomi said, hugging the watering can.

"That must have been some daydream."

Naomi started to wave away the thought, but it led to another and she peered sidelong at Mollie.

The girl took a step back. "What? I don't think I like that look in your eye."

Mollie had been somewhat forthcoming about life in the Garden, but she had shared more with Hannah. Now Naomi saw an opportunity to gain a little understanding of Charles.

"Do *you* think Charles has changed?"

The girl sucked in a breath as if Naomi had asked her to raise the dead. "Oh, I don't think I'm qualified to answer that. I don't know his heart. I just know what I've seen."

Naomi studied the corn at her feet and scratched her nose. "He warned me about women who might show up in town this summer. Women he's been . . . intimate with." Jealousy gnawed at her. Angry over feeling so vulnerable, she shifted her gaze back to Mollie. "He said if I couldn't bear up under it, under his reputation . . ." Naomi shook her head, groping for a way to explain his concern, and now hers. "He's afraid he'll hurt me. And he's worried I might end up hating him." Her jaw tightened as she imagined an encounter with any of his former lady friends. "I cannot imagine looking any of these women in the eye, Mollie." She—and probably Mollie—knew it wouldn't end well. Naomi wasn't exactly known for her patience or compassion. God still had quite a bit of work to do on both fronts, as far as Naomi was concerned.

Mollie pulled her long blonde braid to the front of her shoulder and clutched it with both hands. After a moment, she nodded. "I think that he loves you dearly, Naomi. And I also believe he's finished with other women."

Naomi shifted and hugged the watering can tighter. "But . . ."

"Personally, I think summer doves aren't going to be his biggest problem."

Naomi tilted her head. "I don't understand."

Mollie took a few halting steps down the row to Naomi, glancing around as if looking for eavesdroppers, then spoke in a quieter voice. "Before you got here—before he hired Marshal Beckwith—Mr. McIntyre ran this town. His word was law, and he had the wherewithal to back it up. He wasn't afraid to get his hands dirty, if you understand my meaning." She paused, her brow diving. "True, a lot of women have loved him, but I know a lot of men who hate him. If they hear about his finding religion and trying to be respectable, well . . ." Mollie shoved her hands in her pockets and shrugged. "Maybe I shouldn't say this, but I doubt all the tests of his faith, or yours, will be wearing skirts."

CHAPTER 3

*T*he man's big, meaty fist connected with Billy Page's jaw like a hammer blow. Pain exploded in his face, the force of the punch knocking him back onto the poker table. It shattered beneath him, gouging his back as he fell to the floor in a shower of beer, cards, and coins. His head buzzed and his ears rang with the disgruntled cries from the motley crew of card players angered over the destruction of their game. Billy attempted to scramble to his feet, but hands the size of bear paws grabbed his lapels and snatched him up.

He was now eye-to-eye with his attacker. Billy's opponent in the "friendly" game of cards glared at him with one glittering brown eye as the other hid behind a black patch. A bushy, matted salt-and-pepper beard covered most of the big man's jowls. Tobacco juice dribbled from the corner of his mouth. As high and wide as an Amish barn, the big man lifted Billy completely off his feet and shook him like a rag doll. "You think you can cheat me, city boy?" he growled in a gravelly voice. "You've just made the biggest mistake of your life."

Billy tossed his blond hair out of his eyes and blinked. His first thought was how sick and tired he was of being controlled. He'd left his domineering father, suffocating Southern society, and the addictive Page fortune to come after Hannah. He wasn't about to let this gorilla who didn't like losing at poker stop him.

Billy's better judgment snapped like a kite string. With all the force he could muster in his own substantially smaller frame, he brought his knee up hard, hoping to hit anything sensitive. The big man's face turned purple and contorted oddly, inflating as if someone had pumped a load of air into his head. He let go of Billy, clutched at his groin, and doubled over.

No, Billy had never been in a fight. But he did know how to box. In a flash he positioned his feet properly, curled his hands into tight fists, and delivered an uppercut to the man's jaw that just about sent him airborne. Billy felt the bones in his hand break, but he ignored the streaking pain as his opponent straightened with the blow, staggered, and then recovered. To Billy's amazement, the man balled up his fists, sneered, and threw a wild haymaker. The blow would have knocked a slower man across the county line, but Billy dodged, weaved inside, and tapped the man hard on the jaw with his remaining good hand. His opponent shook off the blows and threw another wild punch which nearly clipped Billy because he'd underestimated the man's reach.

But Billy had him now. This big, burly fellow didn't know how to box—he only knew how to use brute force. Billy raised his fists, hunched up his shoulders, picked a spot on the man's jaw to target, and—

Stars and pain exploded like fireworks in the back of his head. Something sharp and wet rained down over his face, and Billy nearly gagged from the stench of stale beer. His knees buckled with a jolt, and a black fog reached out to grab him as thunderous laughter rang out around him. He thought of Hannah. Was she living in a worse town than this one? He wanted to find the answer, but the mist quickly thickened into complete darkness.

*T*hrobbing, bone-deep soreness crept into his consciousness, but Billy didn't open his eyes. There was so much pain everywhere. He took a moment to determine if anything *didn't* hurt. His hand throbbed. His head pounded. His nose had its own heartbeat, as did his ribs. Something rough dug into his cheek. Gravel?

Billy blinked, trying to focus. A warped board filled his vision and weeds sprouted inches from his face. Confused, he tried moving his head. The motion caused a searing pain to shoot up his neck and down his arm. He realized he was lying on his stomach in the dirt, head twisted to the left, arms bent behind his back. Pushing through the pain, he slowly rose to all fours and carefully rotated his head to loosen the kink in his neck.

His hair fell over his eyes. Peering through it, in the faint, predawn light, he could see he was in an overgrown, trash-littered alley at the rear of two weathered buildings. Empty kegs and barrels loomed over him. He staggered to his feet and immediately fell against the closest wall. He figured he must be out back behind the saloon.

But how—

A nearby door opened and a rotund woman marched out, carrying an empty pony keg on her shoulder. She spotted Billy immediately and grunted. "One of the girls said I might find you here." She was a big-boned woman with weathered features and drab brown hair pulled back in a tight bun. She set the container atop another and wiped her hands on her skirt. "You check your pockets?"

Understanding slowly dawned on Billy, and he slapped his pants, rifled through his coat pockets, and searched his vest. All empty. The fight came back to him now, his own cockiness, the rap on the back of his head. He reached up and touched a pretty impressive goose egg. What had they hit him with—Montana? The possibility that the scoundrel would cheat had never entered

Billy's mind. And now he had nothing. He couldn't pay for his room, he couldn't eat, he couldn't get his horse out of the livery . . . and he couldn't get to Hannah. Wouldn't his father just love to be here to gloat?

"Listen, son," the woman said, draping her arm over a large whiskey barrel. "That there was Earl H. Goode and friends that whooped you. They scouted for Quantrill. You'd best watch yourself in Dodge. Better yet, light a shuck out of Dodge."

A man on the train had warned Billy that Dodge City was rough—almost as rough as Defiance, the meanest mining town in the Rockies. And Hannah was in Defiance, along with his son. He imagined her surrounded by men like Earl H. Goode. The thought twisted his guts and stirred up an urgency to get to her that rushed through his blood like lightning.

His trip west had started out at a leisurely pace. A few races in this town or that, wherever he decided to take Prince Valiant off the train and out for a little fresh air. Admittedly, he'd been dragging his feet, putting off his reunion with Hannah because he was afraid of her reaction. Now he was afraid *for* her. Earl H. Goode had put it all into perspective. If Dodge City was the wickedest little city in America, what did that make Defiance?

No place for Hannah and his son.

But how was he supposed to get to her without money? He almost laughed at the reversal in his fortunes as he raked a bloodied, swollen hand through his hair, clearing his line of sight. "Ma'am, I'd be happy to leave your warm and friendly community." Billy straightened and looked the woman in the eye. "Only, for the first time in my life, and now when it matters most of all, I have no money."

Maybe the lady barkeep got the joke. She chuckled, the action jiggling her frame like gelatin, and hooked her thumb at the barrels. "Tell ya what, son. If you can load those in a freight wagon and get 'em down to the warehouse, it's worth a dollar to me."

Billy eyed the barrels. They were stacked two and three high, and they lined the length of the saloon. 'Miserable' wouldn't begin to describe the chore, considering his present condition.

The woman seemed to read his mind. "You can start with fried eggs and a cup of coffee. Even *I* wouldn't ask a man to do that job on an empty stomach, especially one who's had the hound beat out of him."

Her sideways smile struck Billy as sincere. He nodded. "Your offer is more than agreeable, ma'am. It may be a lifesaver." At least he would be able to get his horse out of the livery.

The woman ushered Billy into a small kitchen at the back of the saloon and sidestepped over to a potbellied stove. She cracked two eggs and dripped them into a pan, then tossed the shells into a bucket. As if she could do this in her sleep, she scrambled the eggs with a fork in one hand, while the other snagged a mug hanging from a nail and set it in front of him. The sublime scent of fresh coffee filled the room.

"Name is Eleanor, by the way."

Stiffly, Billy sank into a ladder-back chair at a small table. "Billy Page. And thank you." The friendly whiff of breakfast brightened his spirits a little, and he thought there might yet be hope for the day.

"One of the girls was tellin' me you put up a pretty good fight last night." Eleanor slid the eggs onto a tin plate and passed it to him along with a fork. "A dollar's all I can give ya to move the barrels. Will it get you out of town?" she asked, filling his cup with coffee.

Billy shoved a bite of egg into his mouth and savored the warm yolk touched with a hint of salt. He hadn't realized he was so hungry. "A dollar will get my horse out of the livery. If I can line up a race for him today, I should be set to move on to the next town."

"That's mighty confident talk." He heard another egg start sizzling in the pan.

"I have a mighty fast horse."

She stopped stirring and turned to him. She gave him the once-over with a skeptical arch in her brow. "You look like a dude in those clothes." Billy raised a hand to his chest, defending his well-tailored, but filthy three-piece suit. "And even with the swollen nose, I can tell you're handsome, but you're pale as milk. You're, oh, what, a banker's son?" She didn't wait for a confirmation. Instead, she tossed him a biscuit from the bread warmer and kept talking. "Dodge City is just dying to chew up somebody like you and spit you out." She turned back to the stove and harrumphed her disapproval. "Might as well be wearing a sign."

Billy touched his nose gingerly, as if it might fall off any second. "Apparently I was wearing one last night that said, 'Kick me.'"

Eleanor's shoulders jiggled again, then she jerked her head up and stared at the wall. "You're the one with the thoroughbred."

Billy wondered how she knew but nodded obligingly. "He's as fast as lightning and as light on his feet as the wind. He's how I've been making my way out West, pulling together races. I shouldn't have any trouble making it from here to Defiance."

"Defiance?" She did turn then, eyes wide. "Why in Sam Hill would you want to go to that cesspool? Ain't Dodge mean enough for ya?"

Billy quickly went back to the remnants of the egg.

"Ooooh," She drawled out the word knowingly and went back to the skillet, "a woman. Well, let me tell ya, boy. If she's in Defiance, you don't want to find her."

"It's the only thing I *do* want." He heard the misery in his voice and hated the childish sound of it, but miserable he was. He might as well spill the whole story. "I ran off and left her . . . and she was going to have my baby."

Eleanor sighed and shook her head. She mumbled something about the foolishness of youth. "So it's your plan to go find her. And then what?"

Billy thought he detected a note of cynicism in the question.

28

Maybe he was young and foolish, but he had to try to piece things back together with Hannah if he wanted to call himself any kind of a man. "I was a coward and ran. My father had a lot to do with it, but that's all behind me. Nothing will stop me from at least asking her forgiveness—and seeing my son."

Eleanor slid her egg onto a plate and joined Billy at the rickety table. She settled into a seat, then hit him with a bold stare. "Defiance is—" She bit off the words and softened her expression. "Well, a girl alone there—"

"She's not alone," he cut in, understanding the implication. "Her two sisters are with her. I know what you're trying to say, but I know these girls. They've opened up a decent hotel and restaurant."

Eleanor sat quietly while Billy finished off his egg and scraped up the last of the yolk with the biscuit. Finally, she spoke. "When you take the barrels to the warehouse, the man will count them and give you back my deposit. Keep the money and place a bet for me on your horse."

CHAPTER 4

*P*rince Valiant pawed at the ground and snorted. Billy leaned forward and patted the horse's elegant black neck. "Hang on, boy," he whispered. Snatching a quick peek at his opponent, who sat atop a muscular but restless sorrel, he said more loudly, "I'll turn you loose in a second."

Seth, a young man with red-hair, freckles, and the mass of a bean pole, shifted deeper into his saddle. He was trying not to show any worry, but uncertainty wiggled around a twitching brow. Prince Valiant was an animal of grace, balance, and stunning conformation. You'd have to be blind to miss what he was—an animal built for speed. As Billy casually rewrapped the bandage on his injured hand, he winked at his opponent.

Seth's face reddened and he straightened indignantly. "Y-You're just tryin' t–to rile me." He swallowed against whatever it was that caused the stutter to cling to his words. "I ain't lost in Dodge yet."

"Your horse is big and slow."

"My h–horse can cut on a dime and g–give you back a nickel's change."

Billy frowned. He had no idea what that meant.

"A–and he don't get dis–distracted."

Distracted? A sliver of concern rose up in Billy's gut. The rules were simple. Race the course. Come back to this spot. Was he missing something?

Prince Valiant shook his head and blew, eager for the run. Restless under a high noon sun, horses and riders waited in an alley at the edge of Dodge, near the train yard. Gerald, the rotund gentleman up ahead wearing a too-small tan suit with bulging buttons, stood where the alley met the road. Moving his head back and forth, he studied the intersection the two animals would cross. A crowd of twenty or so men had gathered in bunches on each side of the alley and up on the boardwalk. All of them watched eagerly for a signal from the man in the shabby suit.

As Billy understood it, they would shoot straight across Front Street, continue down the opposite alley, do a horseshoe around Boot Hill Cemetery, cross the railroad tracks, and follow them back to this spot. The marshal, a fella by the name of Wyatt Earp, didn't agree with racing horses in town. He'd thrown more than a few cowboys in jail for the deed. Gerald, the man who coordinated such events, had a handful of boys who would be distracting Earp and his deputies anytime now. A fast, clean race meant they would all be in and out in no time, and the town's law enforcement officers would be left sifting through the dust.

Prince Valiant was ready. His muscles quivered with the desire to cut loose. Gerald stepped deeper into the street, arms outstretched, a smoldering cigar in his mouth. Shifting stiffly in the saddle, Billy wondered why no one was *stopping* the traffic. As the answer struck him, Gerald slapped his sides and lunged for the boardwalk like hounds from Hell were coming for him. Billy and Seth kicked their horses and the animals bolted forward like lightning streaking across the sky.

The moment the horses burst onto Front Street, Billy knew this was a different kind of race. Prince Valiant reared and whinnied at the confusion—a flowing menagerie of horses, wagons, and men. Meanwhile, Seth and his mount zigged and zagged with such speed and precision, Billy would have sworn the horse was on rails.

He didn't need to be shown twice. He leaned into Prince Valiant and let the horse have his head, slapping him with the quirt to re-focus the animal.

As they lunged through the traffic, a horse and rider burst out from behind a freight wagon. Billy jerked the reins hard to the left, missed a collision, then he and his horse bounded forward. Cheers, jeers, and ungentlemanly gestures greeted the racers as they cut around wagons, pedestrians, and other horses. Billy understood now the advantage a cutting horse could have. The boy could actually win this thing if he took too much of a lead now. The thought burned like acid. Prince Valiant wasn't used to running a gauntlet. He was made for long, uninterrupted stretches. Still, he could dig his hooves in and cut with the best of them.

Seth and his horse made it the other side of the intersection. Billy lost sight of them because of the traffic. Desperation buzzed in his brain. He thought of Hannah, and how she used to stand at the finish line, cheering wildly for him. He thought of his father who'd told him that horse racing was a colossal waste of time. Steering with his good hand, Billy tightened his grip on the reins. He couldn't lose this race, *wouldn't* lose. He quirted his horse again. "Let's go, boy. Show 'em what you can do."

Within seconds he was nose-to-tail with Seth's horse. The traffic disappeared as they cleared Front Street and raced down the alley toward Boot Hill. Billy knew he needed to pull up on the inside of the other horse as they made their turn around the cemetery. After that, they would be on the home stretch where Prince Valiant could win it.

Dust and the sound of pounding hooves filled his brain. The Quarter Horse in front was stretched out, long and lean. But there was a price to pay for all that muscle. Billy hunkered down in the saddle, keeping his head close to Valiant's neck. He and his mount kept their attention trained on the animal in front of them.

They broke free of the buildings, and the wood rail fence around the cemetery came into view. The place was small, insignificant, and dotted with weathered wooden markers, a fitting tribute to men who had led small lives. He was determined not to be one of them.

Prince Valiant picked up speed as if he knew he had to put the other horse behind him, and this was the place to make the move. The urge to win was in his blood, if not in his brain. Billy's pulse trip-hammered in his chest. He was close enough to touch the other horse's flank.

Prince Valiant nosed in between his opponent and the fence. The red-haired boy raised his quirt to hit the approaching horse, but before he could bring his arm down, Prince Valiant shot past, picking up even more speed. Billy didn't look back. He and his horse came out of the turn, spotted the railroad tracks two hundred yards out, and lunged for them. He could hear Seth screaming at his horse, cursing him, trying to get every ounce of effort from him. Funny, Billy didn't hear any stuttering coming from the boy.

The lightning pace of Prince Valiant's pounding hooves felt like Billy's pulse. *Almost there.* They leapt the railroad tracks, turned hard to the left in a spray of dust and gravel, and headed hell-bent-for-leather for the back of the buildings where this had all started. In the distance he saw Gerald gesticulating wildly, arms flailing madly, then he disappeared into the alley.

Billy didn't take it for granted that he couldn't hear Seth's screams or his horse's hoofbeats. He and Prince Valiant aimed for the alley, charging for it like they were under cannon-fire. They leapt another set of tracks and pounded toward the alley where Gerald had been standing. They slowed and turned the corner, expecting to see Gerald and a crowd—

Billy pulled Prince Valiant up hard, practically putting the horse down on his haunches as they skidded to a stop. In the settling dust, a tall man, dressed in a black hat and long black duster, stood alone, calmly loading bullets into his revolver. Billy scanned the *empty* alley. The man raised his head, the Stetson slowly revealing cold blue eyes and a bushy handlebar mustache. He slid his gun into his holster and pushed aside his left lapel to reveal a silver star.

Gerald was waving me away.

The absence of pounding hoofbeats from behind could only mean that Seth had understood the signal. Air escaped Billy's lungs as he sagged in the saddle, regretting his arrogance.

"My name is Wyatt Earp, Dodge City marshal." The man's deep voice resonated with confidence. "That is one fine-looking piece of horseflesh, son. But racing it on busy streets is frowned upon." And, in case Billy had any questions about his immediate future, Earp added somberly, "You are under arrest, and your horse is hereby impounded."

---

*B*illy stepped into the eight-by-ten cell and winced as the door clanged shut behind him. He could feel Earp watching him but didn't turn. He needed to take all this in. He appraised the filthy, stained cot to his left and swore he saw something on it move. Or slither. Fighting a feeling of failure that threatened to swamp him like a flood, he trudged to the far wall, turned his back to it, snatched off his hat, and slid to the ground.

He'd started out with a good plan. Go west. Find Hannah. Get off the train in Dodge City for one or two horse races. Same as all his other choices, this one had been just about as smart as kicking a hornet's nest.

Let's see, just what have my stellar decisions cost me? The love of a good woman. A relationship with my son. Ever seeing my mother again.

A few bones in my right hand. The family fortune. My dignity. My horse.

I am on a roll.

Earp rested a boot on the iron crossbar at the bottom of the cell door and shook his head. Gripping the bars, he chuckled. "I have brought in some sorry sights, but I think you're about the sorriest. This is the last place a boy like you should find himself."

Billy rolled his head back against the wall and shut his eyes. "Most of the men you bring in here are, what, drunk and belligerent? Broken and defeated?" Billy's voice faded, softened to a tone that was merely thinking out loud as he raised his head to stare through Earp. "Is that what a man becomes when he loses everything?"

Earp scratched his nose. "Listen, son, I'm not your priest—"

"And I'm not your son."

"True enough. But you are in my cell. And that means you'll listen when I talk." Apparently taking Billy's silence as agreement, he went on talking. "For what it's worth, you may be dead broke— stripped of everything 'cept your long johns, and I'd still say you've got more going for you than ninety percent of the mongrels I haul in here."

Billy dragged his knees up and rested his hands on them. "You don't know anything about me. Everything I had going for me is gone."

Earp fell silent. His hard, empty eyes studied Billy for a few seconds. In the next instant, his stare drifted. Absently, he stroked the long bushy mustache that all but hid his mouth. "I know that what you think is going to kill you today will make you stronger tomorrow," he blinked and returned to the moment, "if you let it. That's the ticket, son. You have to *choose* to get back up and keep swingin'. You're the kind who will. That's what separates you from the hapless drunks."

Long after Earp left to make his rounds, Billy pondered the lawman's words. *Get back up and keep swingin'.*

His gaze traveled round the cell. Bricks, bars, and cobwebs. No exit, no hope.

Hannah would have told him to pray, to trust that God had a plan.

Disgusted, he snorted aloud at that thought. *Some plan.*

It had seemed so right and easy a month ago to take this path and thumb his nose at his father's threats. Billy could still hear the fury in the voice, warning him to calculate the losses.

"I told you before," Frank Page had said from the settee in their lavishly appointed parlor, "try to find her, contact her in any way, and I will cut you off—stop your tuition payments and cease paying your gambling debts. All of it will end. You'll be out on the street with nothing."

Billy hadn't doubted it for a second, but he'd prepared. Those gambling debts were a farce. He'd been saving money. Finding the Pinkerton report had only confirmed that his next step was the right one.

"She hates you," his father hammered. "I made sure she knew you abandoned her because you were afraid of losing your inheritance. She will not take you back. She has settled nicely into that *bawdy* mining town. Seems it suits her."

Billy didn't miss the implication, but then again, his father simply didn't know Hannah. Perhaps if she'd been abandoned in that town, alone with a child to take care of, that might have put a different light on things. But Hannah wasn't alone.

"Hannah may not love me anymore," Billy said rising to his feet to stare down at his father, "but she would never hate me. Not even me."

Did he still believe that? What if she were cold to his arrival? Or worse, indifferent? Hope was not in abundant supply at the moment. He didn't know how he was going to get out of jail, much less get to Hannah. He wanted to ask God for a miracle, but as Billy surveyed the cell again, he knew he couldn't ask for such an extravagant gift from Someone he didn't know. The

36

thought filled him with an ice-cold emptiness that struck deep at his soul.

---

*A*t dusk, the office door opened and Earp walked in, stepping aside for Eleanor. Surprised to see her, Billy stood up and met them at his cell door. "Eleanor, I'm so sorry about your deposit. I'll pay you back, I promise." He had no earthly idea how, but he wouldn't let another woman down.

"Eleanor here has called in a favor," Earp said, a scowl expressing his opinion of this development.

Billy didn't understand. His gaze ricocheted back and forth between the two.

"It is within my capacity as marshal," Earp continued, "to drop the charges and return to you your fine horse." A pair of keys materialized in his hand and he unlocked the cell door. He looked at Eleanor. "We're square?"

Eleanor slapped him on the arm. "We're square."

Earp cast an irritated glance back at Billy. "Your horse is out back. Now, get out of Dodge." He didn't wait for a response. Earp turned and let himself out into the orange glow of sunset.

Eleanor shifted away from the cell door. "Earp confiscated the bets. They're in your saddle bag—minus my winnings. Seems that since you *finished* the race, you won it."

Billy shook his head in amazement and pushed open the door. His freedom and his money had been given back to him through the kindness of a woman he'd met only hours before. "Why are you helping me?"

Eleanor shrugged, dropped her gaze to her feet. "It's what needed to be done."

"But why?"

He waited, needing to hear her explanation. She pursed her lips, thinking. "I was a Hannah." She raised her head as the confession left her lips, her eyes swimming with memories. "But no one ever came for me."

Billy felt as if he'd been punched again by Earl H. Goode. For the first time, he noticed the sadness in the lines of her face, and it cut him deep.

What kind of man left a trail like that?

A man like me.

Holy God, had he done that to Hannah? The thought horrified him. He'd never contemplated for one second the ashes he might have left her in. Oh, sure, she would have cried, but he'd figured she'd go on with her life. What if he'd left Hannah empty and used up like Eleanor? Had the sparkle left *her* shimmering ocean-blue eyes? Did the smile on the sweetest lips he'd ever tasted mask a broken heart now? If he found Hannah to be a shell of a girl like this, he'd spend the rest of his life trying to make it up to her.

But what if there was no coming back from this? What if Hannah was in Defiance, wasting away? Hell or high water, he had to make this right and give her a measure of peace.

Deeply troubled, he took Eleanor's hand in his. "Thank you, Eleanor. Thank you for giving me a second chance. And tell Earp I'll keep swinging."

CHAPTER 5

*H*annah Frink snapped a red-checked tablecloth into the air and let it drift like a snowflake onto the table. As it floated down, it revealed Emilio stacking firewood in the dining room's fireplace. The spring day was warm, but here in the Rockies the temperature plummeted after sunset. One of Emilio's duties as the hotel handyman was to keep the fireplaces and stoves always ready for a fire. Felling trees and chopping them into firewood not only made the girls' lives easier, the job had turned a scrawny, teenage boy into a young man with broad shoulders.

Surprised by her thoughts, Hannah blinked, flung her long blonde ponytail over her shoulder, and commenced smoothing out the wrinkles in the tablecloth. Lately, her friendship with Emilio, the boy she and her sisters had rescued from a life in Mr. McIntyre's saloon, had changed. Or at least in *her* mind it had. She would find herself admiring those shoulders or that warm, sweet smile he always had ready for her and her son, Little Billy. Emilio had one dimple on his left cheek that only showed when he grinned a certain way. And being so fair herself, she was captivated by his tawny skin and straight, shoulder-length black hair, evidence of his Mexican heritage.

Emilio cleared his throat, drawing Hannah's attention. He had emptied his arms and stood before her, crushing his dusty hat in his hands. "I was wondering, Miss Hannah, if you and Billy would like to go with me to pick yarrow?"

At first Hannah heard only his voice, not his words. She loved the deep velvety sound of it and the way his accent touched every syllable. Rather soft spoken, his voice fell like a gentle spring rain.

She was taken aback by the request, though, because of the subtle hope in his penetrating, dark eyes. "Yes, of course . . . wait. What?" Why did this request feel different from the dozens of times he'd asked her to help fetch firewood or supplies before? She was babbling but couldn't help it. "I'm sorry . . . help you pick what?"

His smile broadened, and Hannah's heart fluttered. A good two inches taller now than this time last year, Emilio had turned into a handsome young man right in front of her. He filled out that red plaid shirt nicely too. She rather liked the way his muscles strained against the fabric as he shook his coal-black hair out of the way and placed his hat back on his head. "Yarrow. Tomorrow, after the lunch rush." He dipped his head to pardon his exit, and rushed from the room like a little boy with a secret.

Perplexed by the emotions dancing around inside her, Hannah plucked another tablecloth from the stack on the table beside her. She hadn't even thought about another man since Billy had run off. Goodness, she was sixteen, not sixty. Maybe it was time to be a young girl again with a handsome beau on her arm. Well, two beaus, if she counted the seven-month-old boy upstairs in his crib. She giggled at the thought and decided to go check on the little cherub. These tablecloths weren't going anywhere.

As promised, after lunch the next day, Hannah met Emilio out back of the hotel, and he did indeed have a surprise. A small, but well-muscled, black-and-white pinto nibbled greedily at an apple in his hand.

"Oh my, Emilio, where did you get him?" She approached the horse slowly, hand extended to stroke his nose.

Emilio wiped his hand on his trousers and grinned proudly. "I saved all winter for him. He is good for riding, and he can pull a small wagon." She rubbed the animal's nose gently and wondered about the wisdom of putting such a small horse in hitch. "I was going to lead him, but if you are not bringing Billy, do you want to ride?"

Hannah moved her hand to the horse's halter and hooked her fingers round it. She hadn't been in a saddle in over a year. Did she dare?

"He is very gentle," Emilio added. "That's one reason I got him. In case you or your sisters need to fetch the doctor. If Billy gets hurt, we don't need to go for help on foot."

Hannah glanced up, impressed that Emilio had thought of that. Her admiration must have shown, for he cleared his throat and moved away to check the stirrups and cinch. "I call him Cochise," he said, tugging on the right stirrup and, she thought, fastidiously avoiding eye contact. "I met him once, the great Apache chief. He told me his name means 'strong like oak.'" Emilio moved around to the other side of the small horse, trusting that Hannah still held the halter. "I thought that was a good name for this boy."

Warmed by Emilio's thoughtfulness, Hannah waited content-edly as he yanked and tugged on the saddle. Moving on, he lifted the horse's feet one by one to check the shoes. She had a strong suspicion that he had already done this and was going through the steps again to appear busy. Compliments and admiration of any kind made Emilio uncomfortable.

"You have to tell me two things, Emilio."

He dropped Cochise's rear hoof and rested his arms on the horse's rump, waiting expectantly.

"You have to tell me what yarrow is, and you have to tell me how you met Cochise."

"*I* told you once that banditos raided my parents' ranch when I was five."

Hannah tried to listen to Emilio, but contentment distracted her. Riding behind him on Cochise, she closed her eyes and listened. As they crossed a high mountain meadow, the soft buzz of bees and the musical whistle of spring birds filled her mind. A few strands of hair had come loose from her pony tail and danced in the light spring breeze, tickling her nose.

"They took Rose and me with them. I don't remember much, just traveling around with them, tending to their horses."

With her arms wrapped around Emilio's waist, she couldn't help noticing how lean and strong he felt. And he'd bought Cochise in case they needed to fetch a doctor for her son. Emilio's concern for Billy cast him in a more grown-up light, a more attractive light.

"Cochise came into our camp one day to trade for horses."

The mild day and the horse's rhythm relaxed her, and she smiled to herself as her cheek came to rest on Emilio's back. Almost dreaming, Hannah could see him as a small boy, feeding the animals and fetching and toting for the bandits. She doubted it was a good life, especially with his sister, that witch Rose, shouting orders at him. She was so glad he had come to live with her and her sisters.

"I like that," he said rather huskily. "It makes me feel strong."

She jolted away from him but didn't relinquish her grip around his waist. "What? Oh, I'm sorry, I almost drifted off." She replayed his words and the gentle tone he'd used. Unsure of what he meant, she said simply, "You *are* strong, Emilio."

They rode in silence. After several minutes, she heard him sigh. "I know. I am like a brother." He sounded . . . disappointed?

Hannah's head was spinning. If this was anyone else but Emilio, she would swear he was trying to drop a hint.

"Emilio," she began. *Do you think I'm pretty? Emilio, do you like me?* But she muttered instead, "Sometimes I don't know what you are." She hadn't really meant to let that out, and her fingers clenched with embarrassment. His tan sweat-stained cowboy hat bobbed as his gaze went to her hands. She wondered if she should pull them away, but didn't.

"I think . . ." he spoke barely above a whisper, "that may be a good thing."

Hannah could hear the smile in his voice and leaned around his shoulder to peek up at him. Sure enough, he was grinning.

She settled back in the saddle and pondered him, hiding her own smile. "Emilio, you wouldn't by any chance be thinking about —oh!" He had kicked Cochise into a trot, and she had to tighten her grip around him to keep from back-flipping right off the horse.

Courting me, she had started to ask, but her *courage* had back-flipped off the saddle. They trotted on for a good half hour. When they emerged from the trees, the horse slowed to an easy walk.

"I dig the yarrow here."

He tugged on the reins and Cochise stopped. Emilio threw his leg over the saddle horn and slid to the ground in a fluid, natural move. Hannah scanned the sun-washed alpine pasture splashed with a vibrant palette of wildflowers. What did yarrow even look like? "So now will you tell me what it is?"

"Medicine." He helped her dismount and then handed her Cochise's reins. Spotting a plant, he bent down and plucked a long green weed with lacey blossoms in a bunch on top. He held it up for her to see, displaying it with pride as if it were a trophy. "Now is the time to collect yarrow if you want to stop bleeding. You can also use the leaves to make medicine for a cold and upset stomach. If you plant it in the garden, it will also make your soil better."

Impressed with his knowledge of the herb, Hannah took the plant and studied it. The leaves were spindly, the flowers small and delicate. She'd been doing a little nursing for Doc and told herself she should ask him about this plant. It sounded like it had several uses.

"In late spring we can use it to make potions that will help heal skin rashes and make swelling go down. You can even make snuff out of it."

Hannah realized her mouth was hanging open and snapped it shut. "How in the world do you know all this?"

He hesitated. "Rose knows more than I do."

The mere mention of his sister gave Hannah a chill. Rose knew about herbs because she used them in her witchcraft. Sitting in the state prison in Denver for shooting Mr. McIntyre, she wasn't doing much conjuring right now, much to Hannah's satisfaction.

Emilio's chin dipped a little, as if apologizing. "Rose always collected the plants that made her customers see things or go to sleep. But I found the herbs that could help people."

Hannah smiled. Emilio had to be about the nicest boy she'd ever met. Billy Page was a fading watercolor of a memory compared with him. Emilio's stare shot past her and his face clouded.

"Get on the horse, Hannah."

She didn't miss the unease in his voice and swiveled to see what had alarmed him. She sucked in a breath at the shape of a man sitting above them on a ridge. Silhouetted by the sun, she could make out the long lance he carried and the movement of feathers in his hair.

"Get on the horse *now*."

Hannah obeyed and hoisted herself astride Cochise.

Emilio followed immediately, sitting behind her this time, and kicked his mount into a gallop before Hannah could blink. She squeezed the saddle horn with a death grip, amazed at the animal's speed.

"Emilio, what's the matter? Who is that?"

They entered the woods and, from the safety of the shadows, he turned Cochise to take another look. The Indian still sat motionless on the ridge. "His name is One-Who-Cries. He won't live on the reservation, and he has killed many white people." He tugged on the reins and turned Cochise back toward the shadowy woods. "We have to let Mr. McIntyre know."

---

*S*omething about manual labor spoke to McIntyre's soul. Or maybe it was just the thought of building his own home on his own land. He lodged the ax in the peeled log he was notching and stepped back. He wanted a moment to appreciate the beauty of his valley, surrounded by the towering San Juan Mountains. Ponderosa pines as tall as mythical giants ringed him on three sides, and the smell of evergreens and damp ground wafted to him. The Animas River, miles of it, wound through his land. The longest and calmest stretch rolled right past this spot—his home site. He watched the sun dance off the moving water and listened to the gentle gurgling as it headed off into the valley. Not so loud as to drown out approaching visitors, but a soft sound to accompany one's outdoor activities. This was a perfect spot for fishing or splashing in the water with children.

He smiled. *Children.* He could almost see them, his and Naomi's offspring wading carefully with their arms outstretched, slipping and squealing with shock as they hit the ice-cold water. Before Naomi, before God, he'd never dared think his life might take such a path. He'd thought he was too far gone, not fit to be a husband, much less a father.

The thud of hoofbeats intruded, snatching him away from the pleasant imaginings. He eyed the tree line and listened. An easy lope by the sound of it, nothing that should alarm him. Still, he moved to where his gun belt was draped over a tree stump, slid the belt around his waist, and faced the woods where the rider would emerge.

Moments later, Emilio, his pinto's white mane and tail dancing in the breeze, shot out from the trees, and he waved at McIntyre. The boy slowed his horse and trotted over to him, the sound of squeaking leather rising over the gurgling of the stream. "Your telegrams came," he said, pulling two folded notes from his pocket.

McIntyre all but snatched the messages from Emilio's hand and read them quickly. He held one in each hand, contemplating the answers. One told him the circuit preacher was over in Mineral Point. Reverend Potter would be more than happy to perform the wedding anytime in the next three weeks. After that, he was headed to Pagosa Springs and wouldn't be back this way for another six weeks.

The other confirmed his worst fears. After Emilio reported seeing One-Who-Cries in the vicinity, McIntyre had sent a telegram to his old friend, Chief Ouray, to determine the state of affairs at the White River Reservation. But Ouray knew that McIntyre was really asking about the state of mind of the renegade. The chief's response burned like a volcano in McIntyre's blood: *Seven braves have left reservation. Now ride with One-Who-Cries. More death coming.*

McIntyre lifted his gaze to the valley around them, struck by the different paths each telegram represented. One foretold of a peaceful life full of the things most men desire—a good wife, beautiful children, a fine home. The other drew him back to a hard life, one rife with violence and justice meted out without mercy.

The hate that he held for One-Who-Cries boiled close to the surface, and this disturbed him. But the screams still echoed in his head. The loss still lingered in his heart. He wanted justice from the renegade, to see the life drain out of him. Even more, he wanted to be the one to pull the trigger. He shouldn't want those things, he knew, not as a man of faith who left vengeance and justice to God.

But maybe some things, a man had to handle himself.

———

*H*annah sniffed the yarrow Emilio held out to her. The flower had a sweet, spicy scent. "Mmm. It smells nice."

He took the plant and laid it on the kitchen table in front of them. A week after their unfinished hunt, he had gone on his own and returned with several bunches of the aromatic herb. He said he hadn't seen any further sign of the Indian. Not that Hannah was worried, but she was glad to hear it, just the same.

"There are different ways to prepare it." He grabbed a plant and started tearing the fern-like leaves from the stem. "Depends on the time of year."

His hands worked with skill. After watching him for a moment, Hannah reached out and grabbed a flower of her own to strip. He flashed a fleeting smile but concentrated hard on the flower. They worked in silence for a bit, but Hannah's mind whirled. She was enjoying sitting in the quiet kitchen alone with Emilio, but something had definitely shifted in their friendship. Usually, they could chat up a storm. Now, though, she thought there were volumes of things being said without either one of them uttering a word. She found it maddening.

"Did you enjoy your ride out to the meadow?"

Emilio nodded. "*Si*, the weather was very nice."

Again, more silence.

"Emilio, how old are you?" she asked, wondering how much more small talk she could manage.

He shrugged as he took a knife and cut the blossom off the

stem he had just stripped. "I don't know, seventeen, maybe eighteen."

With his unstable home life, if one could use such a gentle term, she wasn't surprised that he didn't know his exact age. A lot of people out West had lost track of such things. "Do you know when your birthday is?"

Emilio paused and stared off into space. "No, not really." But then he smiled broadly, remembering a clue. "It is in the spring, though. I know that much."

"Well, we'll just have to pick a date and throw a party." She laid her hand over his as excitement bubbled up in her like a fountain. The idea had just leapt to mind, and she was glad of it. "We're way overdue for a party. What about the end of the month, before the Flowers take the stage out?"

He glanced at her hand and then back to her face. He was so close she could smell the scent of leather and pine on him, mixed with the tangy yarrow. She put her hand over her heart, afraid Emilio could hear it racing.

Confused by her own reaction, she quickly grabbed another piece of the herb. "We could put up lanterns out back," she said, wishing the nervous wiggle in her voice would subside. "We could ask Shorty Johnson to come and play his banjo. It would be a wonderful party, with dancing and food."

Emilio didn't say anything, but she could sense him still watching her as she plucked the tiny leaves. Finally, he said, "Hannah, how is it that . . . I mean—" He broke off, hesitated, and started over. "I mean, you seem so nice. You're not like the girls at the Iron Horse. So how did you . . .?"

Oh. She figured out what he was trying to ask and decided to help him along. "So how did I wind up with a baby and no husband?" She turned to him, and he flinched a little at her brusque tone.

"*Si.*"

It was her turn to shrug. "Billy Page was the most handsome

boy in town. He was wealthy, and all the girls were after him." She twirled the flower in her hands, ashamed of herself. *Was I really that empty-headed?* All those reasons for caring about someone seemed so ridiculously trite now after everything she'd been through in the last year. "But he picked me. He lavished me with attention, made me feel so special." She shook her head, embarrassed she'd ever been so gullible. But she was at least grateful for Little Billy. "I bought it all, hook-line-and-sinker. I thought he was so in love with me and that we had something special."

Perhaps Emilio heard the shame and regret. This time, he covered her hand with his, and regarded her with tenderness. *"You* are special. Very special. He just wasn't smart enough to realize it."

Emilio leaned toward her and she closed her eyes, waiting for a kiss that seemed as natural as breathing. But the movement took him to his feet instead. She blinked, surprised that she was both embarrassed and disappointed.

"I—I have to go run errands for Mr. McIntyre," he said, practically tripping over his chair. "I'll be back to finish this up."

Hannah opened her mouth to speak, but no words escaped.

It didn't matter. Emilio was gone.

CHAPTER 6

*M*cIntyre tapped the engagement ring on his desk. The sound ricocheted like a rifle shot in the silence of the Iron Horse. The ring with a modest emerald once belonged to his mother and had made its way to him in a box of her things, shortly after her death. He wished she could have met Naomi, seen the direction his life was headed now. Part of him suspected that his mother had always known. Her faith had been rock solid.

She would have approved of Naomi.

McIntyre had known the moment he'd heard about the party that this was the night to ask her. The question he wrangled with now was *how*. Should he make it a quiet, private request? Or should he do the bended knee in front of everyone? Showmanship wasn't part of his personality, but asking her that way struck him as noble and honorable. It would hold him publicly accountable to be a decent man and good husband.

The snort of derision from his condemning past was almost audible. It sat in the room with him like a lurking shadow. After all, his audacity was astounding. Who was he to think he could

HEARTS IN DEFIANCE

make Naomi happy? What if he wound up bored by the sedate, responsible lifestyle? What if he decided he wasn't really meant for monogamy? What if his past was too much for her?

For him?

Frustrated by these questions, he nearly flung the ring across the room. But something stopped him. He waited and after a moment, heard, or rather felt the words: *Therefore if any man be in Christ, he is a new creature. Old things are passed away, behold, all things are become new.* Naomi had urged him repeatedly in the past few weeks to hold on to that Scripture. And he would try, because in that direction laid hope.

He didn't relish the alternative.

---

*M*cIntyre stood on the back stoop for a moment, enjoying the sight of his prospective bride laughing with her sisters, and Ian and Emilio. He was pleased to see that Naomi had again passed on her usual braid and left her hair free and flowing. Captivated by the joy shining in her eyes, not to mention the perfect fit of her pink paisley dress, he watched her with a hunger far more than physical. He'd never be able to make her understand how much he loved her. How could he? He didn't understand it himself.

Grudgingly, he dropped his perusal of her and admired the decorations. A string of glowing paper lanterns ran from the stoop over to one corner of the chicken coop, to a makeshift log support, and back, framing the backyard in a large, glowing square. Fried chicken, venison, mouth-watering fixings, and a birthday cake covered the kitchen table now sitting at the edge of the party. Shorty and Bud, staged in the back of a wagon with their fiddle and banjo, filled the air with a sprightly version of "Dixie." A small bonfire burned at the center of the activities for

51

light and warmth. McIntyre's former Flowers—Lily, Iris, Jasmine, and Daisy—stood near the musicians, smiling and tapping their toes.

He eyed the younger, paler Flower and corrected himself. *Daisy* went by her real name now. *Mollie* was no longer a Flower blooming in his brothel. Instead, she lived here at the hotel, blossoming in her new-found faith. His other girls, retired by him, had been spending hours here with Mollie and the sisters getting new clothes made to hide their past. Tonight, they wore simple cotton dresses with high necklines. They could now pass for any respectable women, with no telltale signs of their former vocation visible.

While he was pleased the girls were getting out of the business, he hated the part he'd played getting them into it. He hoped when they took the stage out of here, they'd leave Defiance and everything it had done to them in the dust. Maybe someday he could as well.

That reminded him, the stage was a good four hours late. Not unusual for the first one of the season. The roads, in places, were still covered in deep, melting slush. He hated dreading the arrival of each and every stagecoach. He truly hoped Naomi was up to facing the inevitable passengers.

Shaking off the thought, he reminded himself that this was a party. McIntyre descended the steps and strode over to the group. He appreciated the warm greetings from Ian and the sisters, but it was that glow in Naomi's eyes that made him hope he *was* becoming a better man. Bowing, he took her hand. "May I have this dance, your ladyship?"

Naomi clutched his fingers without hesitation. McIntyre led her around to the other side of the fire, closer to the musicians, and winked at Shorty. "I need a slow waltz, boys. And make it last a few minutes."

The musicians started a haunting rendition of "Annie Laurie," as McIntyre tilted his hat back. Smiling at Naomi with his best roguish grin, he pulled her close and watched the color rush to her cheeks. He couldn't help but remember the first time he'd ever seen her. Dirty and weary from the trail, that long braid tumbling down her back like Rapunzel's, she was still spirited enough even after months of travel to be offended by a nude painting.

"The day you walked into my saloon, you blushed." Smirking, he added, "over the painting of Eve."

Naomi shook her head and donned a stern expression as they danced near the fire. "Yes, I remember that lewd thing. I'm glad she's gone."

"Oh, but Eve was the perfect woman."

One of Naomi's brows rose, expressing her doubt.

"She wasn't any trouble," he teased. "She never sassed me, never acted as if she were better than me—"

"Never took a shot at you."

He flinched dramatically to keep the mood light. "Well, there is that." The fresh bullet scar on his shoulder twinged with the memory. "I don't miss Eve *or* Rose. But you, well . . ." He stared over her head, pretending utter consternation. "I just don't understand it. What would possess me to settle on the most stubborn, prideful woman God ever made?"

Naomi frowned and stepped on a polished boot tip, lingering long enough to let him know it was an intentional misstep. "Oh, I am so sorry," she deadpanned. "I suppose I'm out of practice."

His roguish grin reappearing, he lowered his lips to her cheek. In no hurry, he slowly traced her jaw back to her ear, enjoying with great satisfaction the instant hitch in her breath and the way she yielded to his touch. "I told you I can remedy that, princess," he whispered huskily, nuzzling her ear, "with eagerness."

For an instant, she felt almost limp in his arms, as if she were melting. Surprising him, though, she abruptly pushed him away as far as her arms would reach, creating a space between them wide enough for a plow horse to step through. "Why, I think we should start lessons right now, Mr. McIntyre." She followed his steps, but kept her arms stiff and straight as they danced, fighting a smile all the while. Ian and Rebecca joined the dance and waltzed pass them with quizzical expressions.

"I assume this means, Your Worship, you plan to keep me at arm's length?" He obligingly respected the space between them as he took two steps back and spun her.

Naomi raised her chin haughtily and peered off into the darkness. "Until you learn to appreciate me."

He thought that over for a second, then snatched her up and held her close with a grip so firm a gasp escaped her. He studied her face intently, determined to memorize every line. "I don't believe I am interested, Mrs. Miller, in ever letting anything come between us. Not now, not ever."

The starch evaporated from her, and she relaxed in his arms. "I'm going to hold you to that."

"I expect you will."

And with that, he knew the moment was right. He had rehearsed the words, run the scene through his head, and imagined her speechless, euphoric nod. He had two weeks to get the Reverend here. Sooner, if Naomi was agreeable. And they would be wed.

The fiddle began fading as the song neared its end, and McIntyre swatted down unexpected butterflies, irritated that they'd taken flight at all. He stopped dancing, released one of Naomi's hands, and motioned to Shorty to hold off on the next song. He touched the pocket of his green silk vest to make sure the ring was still there. Necessities in place, he dipped his chin at Ian. Reading the signal, his friend pulled Rebecca to a stop and motioned toward McIntyre and Naomi. The former Flowers, Hannah, and Emilio all turned to them as well, sensing something.

Silence descended, interrupted only by the crackling fire.

McIntyre squeezed Naomi's hand and stepped back. A deep *V* formed in her brow and an amused, but perplexed, smile played on her lips. As his muscles flexed to take him to one knee, beginning to lower him, Naomi's gaze unexpectedly shot past him to something over his shoulder. The color drained from her face.

McIntyre froze. Before he could react to her shock, a huge grin returned the glow to her cheeks. She clapped her hands excitedly and bounced past him, squealing, "Matthew!"

* * *

*M*atthew Miller stood in the shadows watching the party.

Party.

Anger squeezed his big hands into fists. He'd gone to so much trouble to get things ready, building a house, hiring a maid, leaving a questionable man in charge of his mill. The trip here hadn't exactly been a cake walk, either. He'd breathed coal smoke for days on the train, then high-tailed it like a mad dog to catch the first stagecoach in—a stagecoach he'd been obliged to help dig out of a snowdrift. Through it all, he'd scrambled to Defiance like a man on fire, and here they were having a *party.*

Jealousy coiled around Matthew's heart as he watched Naomi dancing with some fancy-dressed tinhorn. There was no mistaking the fire in his eyes. Or hers. So what now?

As he pondered the situation, the man holding Naomi motioned for the fiddle player to stop. He then waved to the older gentleman dancing with Rebecca and they stopped as well. Sensing something, the other guests halted their conversations.

Matthew realized the possibility unfolding before him and panic shocked his nerves.

No! He hadn't come all this way just to get here in time to kiss the bride, *again.* He forced himself to calm his breathing, to settle his mind. Whoever this dude was, Matthew still had one ace up his sleeve that no man on the earth could compete with, at least not anymore. He straightened up to his full six-foot-six-inch stature, rolled his head once to loosen his neck muscles, and eased out of the shadows.

CHAPTER 7

*M*ovement and a glimmer of blond hair pulled Naomi's gaze away from Charles just as he seemed on the verge of making an announcement. A tall, broad-shouldered man emerged from the shadows at the back stoop and her heart stopped. Wide, haunting hazel eyes, a round face in a halo of sandy-colored hair, a big, awkward smile . . .

She sucked in a breath as astonishment shot through her like an arrow.

John?

Her heart leapt at the sight of him, but in the breath of an instant, her emotions tumbled from hope, to grief, to a wistful joy.

Matthew!

How many years had it been since they'd seen John's twin brother? Shouts and squeals erupted from her and her sisters as they rushed up the steps to greet him. Hannah reached him first, throwing herself into his big, beefy arms. "Uncle Matt!" she gushed, using her pet name for him.

He swung her around, his booming laughter thundering across the backyard. "Is this little Hannah?" he teased, setting her down and pushing her to arm's length. "Why, she's grown into a beautiful woman."

The sisters laughed, and Rebecca hugged him next. "Oh, Matthew, it's wonderful to see you again."

"And you, Rebecca," but Matthew's attention streaked straight to Naomi.

She took her turn and stepped into hug him as well. Matthew swept her up and spun her around, laughing. "And the one my brother stole from me."

Matthew squeezed her tighter and kissed her on the cheek. Holding the smile, Naomi wiggled out of his arms and backed away, struggling to keep her expression pleasant and ignore how familiar he felt. "It's good to see you, Matthew. You haven't changed a bit."

His eyes flashed at her double-meaning. "Nope, not one iota."

In the pause, Naomi remembered their guests and couldn't imagine how awkward they must feel, especially Charles. "You've arrived in time for a party, Matthew. Isn't that always the case with you?"

"I don't miss many on purpose."

"Well, let me introduce you to our guests." She turned and waved for their company to join them. The men climbed the steps to the back stoop, but the Flowers hung back. "These are our friends. Emilio," The young man nodded. "Ian Donoghue . . ."

"'Tis a pleasure, Matthew." The two shook hands.

"Charles McIntyre." She had the urge to hang on his arm, but didn't. Charles' smile was as warm and welcoming as thin ice. She realized with a punch that he had been about to ask her something or make an announcement when she'd launched herself toward Matthew like a Chinese rocket. Her inadvertent rebuff was rude, but seeing the man who is the identical twin of your dead husband would rattle anyone.

Charles relaxed his smile and shook Matthew's hand, but then his brow furrowed. "I had no idea he had a twin," he said, his drawl rich with astonishment and something else, something not at all happy.

Matthew blinked. "Charles McIntyre? You knew my brother?"

Charles withdrew his hand and straightened. "I met him during the war."

"Don't be so modest," Naomi interjected, trying to heal what was most likely a seriously bruised ego. She clutched his arm, thinking the action would make him feel better and perhaps only leave Matthew a little confused. "Charles saved John's life at Chickamauga."

Matthew sagged. "John told me about that battle." He took Charles' hand and shook it again. "I thank you for what you did. Wish you could have done it again."

"Yes, me too." Clearing his throat, he shifted to Naomi. "Well, I think I'll be going. Seems you have a family reunion."

"Must you?" Naomi pressed, hoping he could read her eyes. She didn't want him to go.

"I think it would be best."

"Aye," Ian said, his Scottish burr distinct in the awkward pause. "I think we'll let the family get reacquainted."

Rebecca's countenance fell a little, but she didn't argue.

Matthew dipped his head apologetically. "I'm sorry if my arrival has put a damper on things."

"No, of course not," Naomi said with more enthusiasm than she felt.

"Good night," Charles said, slipping on his hat. He untangled himself from Naomi and touched her shoulder lightly. "I'll stop by tomorrow."

He filtered past her, followed by Ian, and then Emilio. "Oh, no, Emilio," Hannah snagged his sleeve. "You can't go. We didn't touch your cake."

"It's all right. Maybe we can have some in the kitchen later, *si*? You need to see your family."

Hannah brightened at that and nodded. Naomi respected the

boy's decency, but a wave of disappointment washed over her as the group filed through the hotel's back door. As the former Flowers shuffled by, Matthew clutched his heart melodramatically. "I truly am sorry to see you lovely ladies leave. We'll have to try this again."

"Oh, forgive my manners." Naomi gestured to the women. "This is Lily," the tall, curvaceous black girl nodded. "Jasmine," the delicate Asian Flower tilted her head. "Iris," the big-boned, boisterous redhead raised her chin. "And Mollie. They're all leaving Defiance." Naomi grasped Mollie's shoulder, "Oh, except for Mollie. She works here at the hotel."

"Well, ladies, I'm sorry I have missed the chance to pass the evening with you."

"Don't worry, there's plenty of dance partners over in Tent Town," Iris responded, tagging Matthew in the ribs. "But we're not on the menu." The other girls, all smiles, nodded. *They* were free and Naomi couldn't be happier for them. Wearing not a hint of makeup and new, modest dresses they'd assisted in making, she believed the outward transition was complete. The rest was between them and God, but she had hope for them. A lot of it.

Out of quips, Matthew held the door for them as they slipped into the hotel. He didn't, however, close it. He watched the ladies for a second more, and then turned back to the sisters, pressing his hat to his chest as if for protection.

"Maybe it's better that they left." He shifted his gaze to Hannah, an apology in his eyes. "I've got someone with me."

A sinking feeling hit Naomi. It couldn't be. Not on the same night. She moved closer to Hannah and crossed her arms.

"The train doesn't come any closer than Pagosa Springs," Matthew shifted on his feet and licked his lips. "There was a boy down there trying to figure out how to get the rest of the way to Defiance. He recognized me right off. *I* had a little trouble. He was about eleven the last time I saw him."

Hannah's expression froze. Naomi thought it a safe bet that she'd stopped breathing, as well. Matthew stepped away from the door. The floor inside squeaked and a figure stepped into the lanterns' light. Naomi's stomach dropped. The young, handsome Mr. Billy Page emerged from the dark. He looked at Naomi and Rebecca in turn without really greeting them, but his eyes quickly settled on Hannah and stayed there.

A palpable tension enveloped the group, like the breeze that hints at an approaching tornado. No one spoke and the stunned silence dragged on till Matthew couldn't stand it any longer. "Really, ladies, no one has anything to say to this boy?"

Fleetingly, Naomi had the desire to slap her brother-in-law. This was none of his affair, but she realized he was right— someone had to say something, otherwise they might stare at each other all night.

"What are you doing here, Billy?" she asked, failing to mask her dislike of the boy.

He studied Hannah a second more, as if hoping he might find guidance in her expression. Met with only stoic silence, he raised his chin. "I came for Hannah and my son."

The answer did nothing to break the tension. Naomi glanced at Rebecca over Hannah's head. They both peered down at their younger sister.

Wearing an inscrutable expression, she took a small step toward Billy. "I should let you see him then," she said, her voice thin and delicate.

Billy nodded, almost imperceptibly. Hannah drifted past him and Billy dutifully followed, clutching his bowler to his chest. Naomi, Matthew, and Rebecca stood in complete silence until their footsteps faded.

Finally, Matthew let out a long, slow whistle. "If that reception had been any chillier, I believe I'd have frostbite."

Neither Naomi nor Rebecca laughed. Naomi, for her part, was

stunned to see the boy. Certainly, love could have driven him the fifteen hundred miles to Defiance, but so could the desire to rebel against his father. And every time Billy had done that, fear had driven him right *back* to his domineering daddy.

CHAPTER 8

*H*annah walked slowly, calmly through the dim hotel lobby, holding her head high and her shoulders back, but inwardly, she wanted to curl up in a ball and cry. She wasn't sure if they would be tears of joy or misery, though. From behind her, she could hear the soft rustle of the bowler hat twirling in Billy's hands. A nervous habit he hadn't shed.

How could he show up now?

"You wouldn't believe how I've missed you, Hannah," he said as they climbed the steps.

Her first response to his lament was a spark of anger. Anger over the abandonment and betrayal.

. . . over the cowardice.

So many good things had come out of the situation, though, she couldn't hate him. It wouldn't be right. She'd told Mollie once that if Billy ever showed up, she'd forgive him because she loved him. Well, one out of two.

"Billy is a beautiful child," she said, ignoring his comment. "He looks the most like you, but I can see a little of your mother around his mouth."

She thought she heard a quiet, perhaps defeated, sigh from the man in tow behind her. "I can't wait to see him."

Hannah plucked a lamp off the wall and led them into her room. Silently, they padded up to the crib to gaze at her angel. Little Billy slept contentedly, his knees drawn up to his chest, his diaper-covered bottom shoved heavenward, and a thumb stashed securely in his mouth. Billy gasped and Hannah stepped away. She hung the lamp on the hook near the crib as he reached out and stroked the child's soft golden tuft of hair.

He raised a fist to his mouth as if holding back a sound. His eyes glistened and Hannah couldn't deny that the father of her baby was moved by the sight of his son. "He's beautiful, Hannah. And I only see you in those angelic little features."

She laced her fingers in front of her and bowed her head. A maelstrom of confusing emotions swirled in her heart. She wanted to run away from Billy, but knew he would take that as rejection. She needed desperately to be alone so she could sort out how she was feeling, because she had no idea.

Tall and muscular, Billy still wore his ash hair trimmed short and swept to the side. His smooth, handsome face, that deep, throaty laugh, and those sky-blue eyes used to set her heart a-fluttering. But now he seemed a bit, well, too much like a green-horn. His clothes were cut for city life. He hung his bowler on the crib's post, and while it looked well-worn, it was a *bowler*. Fashionable back east, in Defiance only the meanest of men wore one, presumably because they were spoiling for a fight. She didn't get that impression from Billy. Out here, he was just a dude.

Although, judging by her racing heart, she couldn't deny that she still liked that handsome face and sky-blue eyes. But there was something different about him. He carried himself more seriously and less arrogantly. He didn't have that boyish swagger she'd been so enamored of.

"I meant it, Hannah. I came for you." He tore his focus away from Little Billy and sought her out in the flickering lamplight. "How do you feel about me? Do we still have a chance?"

"I don't know." She didn't think that was what either one of them wanted to hear, but it was the truth. "You lied to me. You abandoned me. You let your father smear me, and you ran away." Billy flinched at the accusations she fired like a Gatling gun. Hannah immediately regretted her tone, the venom in it surprising her. "I'm sorry. I don't normally say things like that. It's just that I honestly thought I'd never see you again and . . ." She didn't finish the sentence. He got the gist of things.

"Don't apologize for the truth." Billy rested his elbows on the crib and shook his head. "I was sitting in a hotel in Paris three months after you left, thinking about you. It hit me then that there wasn't enough liquor and there weren't enough women in the world to make me forget you, but I was still too scared of my father to do anything about it." He smiled tenderly at Little Billy. "Then one day at Harvard, I saw a professor of mine in the park with his family. They were having a picnic. His son couldn't have been more than two years old." Billy's gaze misted over. "He was flying him around like a bird, dipping and spinning. The little boy was laughing hysterically." He swallowed, as if forcing down tears. "The sound drifted over to me and I realized . . ." he shifted his gaze back to Hannah, "I realized I was never going to hear my son laugh, unless I quit being a child myself."

Unexpectedly, a traitorous tear rolled down Hannah's cheek. Billy must have seen the gleam in the dim light. He walked over to her and gently wiped it away with his thumb. He rubbed the moisture between his fingers and sighed. "I am so sorry for the pain I've caused you, Hannah. Do you believe that?"

"Yes."

"Do you think you might give an old flame a second chance, maybe?" Billy flashed a rakish grin, the kind that used to launch butterflies in her stomach.

Now, she found herself thinking of Emilio. His smile, the way he doted on Little Billy, their changing friendship and the furtive glances of late. She admired his knowledge of plants and the way he worked so hard all the time. He was steady and, so far, trustworthy. And she knew for a fact that *he* had pushed back more than once against his domineering sister.

She swallowed, but didn't answer Billy's question. She didn't know what to say. Part of her wanted to hug him and kiss him and tell him how thrilled she was that he had come for her.

Part of her wanted to shoot him. She was still angry with him, and the revelation surprised her.

The silence stretched on too long. Billy shoved his hands into his pockets and lowered his head. He hunched his shoulders, bit his lip, rocked on his feet—the actions of a man planning his next words. "Well, I didn't come all this way expecting you to throw yourself into my arms." He peered up at her through long brown lashes, that grin making another appearance. "That is, however, something to work toward. I've got nothing but time now."

Resigned that this was going to be a long night, Naomi and Rebecca sat by the fire, watching Matthew devour about half the party's vittles. This giant of a man ate just like his twin. Naomi nodded politely as he continued a disjointed story of his early years in California, but her mind wasn't on his words.

Looking at him only made her think of John, how she used to love to hold those wide cheeks in her hands, or push his hat back and move strands of straw-colored hair out of his eyes. She remembered how he could pick her up with those tree-sized arms and carry her about as if she weighed no more than an empty dress. Big and wide, with hands the size of bear paws, yet he could hold her like she was as delicate as a china tea cup. Having John's mirror image sitting right in front of her made those memories too real.

But Matthew wasn't John. John was *not* sitting right in front of her. *God, please help me not to fall into confusion. He looks so much like him.*

"You two haven't heard a word I've said." Matthew stopped the biscuit about halfway to his mouth and bounced his gaze back and forth between the sisters. "Tell me. What am I missing?" When neither Naomi nor Rebecca responded immediately, he set the biscuit back on his plate, set the meal on the ground and addressed Naomi. "The last I heard from you, you despised this place and its debauched citizenry, and all you wanted was to get out. I moved heaven and hell to get here with the intention of relocating all of y'all to California, sure I would be doing you a favor. I have a house waiting for you with a maid. Now, I show up tonight and you're having a pretty cozy little party here. Pardon me for saying so, but you don't exactly appear to be in distress."

Relocating them? A house with a maid? Naomi made a miserable connection. "You didn't get my second letter?"

"Nope. Wanna fill me in?"

"Matthew, I never expected you to come after us." A growing sense of guilt blossomed in her. "I didn't ask you to."

He snorted indignantly. "My sisters-in-law get stranded in one of the roughest mining towns in the West and you didn't think I'd come after you?" He muttered a curse. "What do you take me for?"

Naomi flinched and stared into the fire. She'd been so angry with God when she'd written that first letter. She had hated everything about Defiance back then. Oh, how things had changed. She had told him everything in the second letter. She'd even hinted at her friendship with Charles. "Matthew, we've made a life here. It seemed the only choice we had."

"We had to do something," Rebecca interjected, defending their decision. "Naomi won the hotel so we jumped in with both feet. We had to support ourselves."

Matthew pinched the bridge of his nose and pursed his lips. He was never one to hold back and Naomi knew she and Rebecca were about to get both barrels. He didn't disappoint. "I'd say you've adapted pretty well here." He raked Naomi with an accusing stare. "My brother's been dead less than a year and you've got new *friends*. I saw the way that McIntyre looked at you, and you him. Want to explain that to me? And you *won* the hotel? Just what kind of a place are you running here?"

Rebecca gasped. Naomi surged to her feet, fists clenched. "That's always the way of it, isn't it? In desperate straits, a woman's only got one vocation to fall back on? If you weren't John's brother, you'd be sleeping on the street tonight."

"Now hold on, Naomi," Matthew rose, towering over her like a mountain. "Maybe I didn't mean that exactly." Rebecca stood, too, her dark brown eyes flashing in the firelight. If she was mad, Matthew had truly overstepped. He gently patted the air with his hands. "Girls, I didn't mean that at all, I just would like to know what the Sam Hill is going on here."

Naomi huffed a deep breath and almost stomped her foot. Instead, she fixed her gaze on Rebecca, seeking her sister's calm. With a subtle dip in her brow, she urged Naomi to settle down.

Stifling a growl, she turned her back on Matthew and fought for composure. Anger in her voice would only make telling him the truth more painful, and, mad as she was, she didn't wish to hurt him. Control regained, she crossed her arms and faced him again. "Charles had a woman who worked for him. She tried to kill us." The memory of that night in the hotel's kitchen was still an open wound. Naomi's knees nearly buckled recalling it and she sat down. Matthew and Rebecca followed suit, but he leaned forward, as if eager to hear this story. "He tried to take the gun away from her and she shot him. He was nothing short of a hero. I'm—we," she corrected, "*we* are quite close to him." Naomi could see questions still burning in Matthew's eyes. "He nearly died for us, Matthew. I know I made unkind references to him in that first letter, but he's a changed man. He's closed his saloon, given his girls seed money to start over with, and even bought them tickets on the stage out tomorrow."

Matthew absorbed the news with an icy stare. He stood, trudged over to the fire and rubbed his neck, as if the muscles were tight as banjo strings. With his back to the girls, he said, "This Charles McIntyre. He owns the *Iron Horse* Saloon?"

Naomi didn't understand the relevance of the question or how Matthew knew the name of the saloon, but she nodded. "Yes."

He heaved a great sigh and plunged his hands into his pockets. His wide shoulders drooped. "What you're really saying is that the man who used to run one of the wildest cathouses in the West is the reason you're staying in Defiance."

Naomi tried again to stem her anger and understand what things must look like from Matthew's point of view. "I told you, he stepped away from all that. He's turned out to be a decent man and a good friend. He's even going to church—"

Matthew's snort of disgust cut off the rest of her defense. He spun on the girls, his features lined with anger and betrayal. "Men like him don't change, Naomi. Do you have any idea what kind of reputation he has? Either of you?" Before they could answer, he rushed on. "I know the name." He pounded his chest. "*I* know the name and I don't frequent saloons and wh—*cat*houses. Charles McIntyre is known far and wide as the best judge of—" he stopped, searching for a word. "Female companionship. Not to mention, the Iron Horse was," he swallowed, as though forcing down the urge to vomit, "well, a den of all types of iniquity."

Naomi concentrated on the shadows beyond the fire, trying hard not to let the words hit home. But they did.

Matthew softened his tone. "I'm sorry to be so blunt, Naomi, but John was my brother. If he knew you and someone like McIntyre were together . . . do you understand what people will think when they see you with him? What they'll think you've done?" He faded off, but she could feel his stare drilling into her.

Silence brimming with frustration enveloped them. Rebecca

rubbed her temple and stood. "Matthew, perhaps you'd like to see your room now?"

His brow deeply furrowed, he worked his jaw back and forth, and then nodded. "Yeah."

Rebecca touched Naomi's shoulder. "I'm sure with a good night's sleep we'll all be less emotional in the morning."

---

*B*ut Naomi couldn't sleep. With the intention of clearing the food, she instead found herself standing at the head of the table, her fingers drumming, her thoughts adrift. Over and over, she kept hearing Charles's warning about his past haunting them, and his desire for her to believe in him. She wanted to, badly.

. . . known far and wide as the best judge of female companionship.

. . . a den of all types of iniquity.

. . . what they'll think you've done.

The meanings pricked her heart, drawing blood. She could hear John spouting accusations, but it wasn't John, it was *Matthew*. And he didn't know Charles. John would have been kinder. For a moment, Naomi wondered what she would be doing right now if the man upstairs was John, not his brother. She felt certain she would run to him, but part of her heart had been lost now—lost to Charles.

She almost growled aloud at the ridiculous scenario. John was dead. He wasn't coming back. Matthew wasn't John and Charles held her heart now. Period.

Startling Naomi, Hannah hugged her from behind and rested her cheek on Naomi's shoulder. "Quite a night, huh?"

Naomi exhaled and patted her sister's hand. "Did you get Billy settled?"

"Yes . . ."

Naomi sensed a question coming and waited for it.

"Why do you think he's here?"

She debated her answer and decided to state it flatly. "I think he's here because he either can't live without you or he's still intent on doing the opposite of what his father tells him."

She felt Hannah's nod on her shoulder. "So how do I find out which one it is?"

Naomi raised her eyebrows and blinked. "Darned if I know. I guess you just have to wait and see."

"I'm scared he'll break my heart again."

Naomi squeezed her little sister's hand tightly. "You are too smart for that now."

CHAPTER 9

cIntyre, a shot glass of whiskey in his hand, stood at his bedroom window and studied Defiance's main street. Soft circles of amber light from the street lanterns intermittently revealed one lone rider trotting down the shadowy avenue. The gentle thud of the hoofbeats echoed soothingly over McIntyre's mind.

He let his gaze drift over the rooftops to the points of light glowing off in the distance. Tent Town, the side of Defiance where vice still held sway. The faint sound of men laughing mixed with the siren call of girlish giggles. A piano started up and drunken voices chimed in for the chorus of 'Oh, My Darling Clementine,' the song fading in and out with the breeze. All the debauched entertainment he'd spent so much effort propagating now limited itself to Tent Town. But even over there, the crowds were smaller. Three decent women in Defiance had caused more than a few men to re-examine their paths.

He shifted his view again and looked down the street at the dark Trinity Inn, which stood in the elbow of the street, as the town followed the bend of the river. Like all the buildings on Main Street, it was constructed of pine lap siding, its golden hue now silver in the moonlight. Four large windows on both floors faced the street, and a balcony, supported by large logs, hid the entrance in its shadow. The slats in the balcony's rail were made of crooked, though skillfully placed, peeled branches. The sisters had repainted the trim, once a gaudy red, to a more respectable white. The hotel reflected the transition of Defiance from wild mining town to civilized settlement. He could see the future there, see his plans coming to fruition.

Or so he had thought.

Not a jealous or insecure man, McIntyre honestly didn't know what to think about Matthew showing up. No, that wasn't exactly true. He *did* know what he thought about the big man's arrival.

He didn't like it.

He raised his arm and leaned on the window frame, drumming his fingers on the glass. He'd never been much given to fretting over things he couldn't control and wasn't going to start now. He had to admit, though, this was a turn of events he could do without. Near as he could recall, Matthew was the mirror image of his brother. The resemblance was uncanny. That had to have some effect on Naomi.

Annoyed that he was dwelling on this, he slapped the glass and turned away from the window. Determined to put Naomi and her brother-in-law out of his mind, he strode to his desk and snatched up the telegram from Chief Ouray.

More death coming.

When it came to One-Who-Cries, death never left. The savage's name filled McIntyre's nostrils with the stench of burning flesh . . . and the sweet, coppery scent of blood, gallons of it. More than he'd ever seen on a battlefield. In the early years of Defiance, McIntyre had ridden with Federal troops hunting One-Who-Cries. Too often, they'd arrived a day late and a dollar short. The savage reveled in splattering evidence of his hate everywhere.

McIntyre's mind grudgingly drifted back to his first steps into this valley. The war was over. Georgia was in ashes. He'd come to

Colorado with a desperate need to distance himself from the brutality of the conflict. He had seen so many good men die, shot through with musket balls, ripped apart by cannons, hacked by swords and bayonets.

But nothing he saw in the war compared with the gleeful butchery committed by one insane Indian.

The Utes had attacked his camp as the sky started transforming from black to steel. Like lightning from a storming sky, dozens of arrows suddenly streaked into the light of a dying campfire. Unearthly shrieks shattered the quiet, raising the hair on his neck even now. The raiders had come without warning, like thieves in the night, and left as abruptly, taking three of his friends with them. The screams and images of what happened next would never leave him.

McIntyre grimaced as he tried to turn away from the picture of a friend—bloody, twitching, hanging from a pole . . . skinned alive.

Reliving the deaths of his friends served only to resurrect the hate he thought he'd buried. Apparently, the grave was shallow.

---

*B*illy rolled over on his side. A moment later he rolled over to the other. Frustrated, he flopped on to his back and stared at a ceiling hidden in darkness. Off in the distance he could make out the sounds of saloons—several of them. The crystal tittering of feminine laughter, the thundering voices of angry men, and the peppering of gunfire. The discordant chaos of pianos and banjos filled in the gaps. Had it not been for the other cow towns he'd stopped in on his way here, he would have been shocked at the level of noise. What did surprise him was how quiet *this* side of Defiance was.

He laced his hands over his stomach and shook his foot. He couldn't sleep, but it wasn't because of the noise outside. He couldn't get over how beautiful Hannah was. Oh, he had no trouble recalling the girl whose favorite spring dress brought out the cornflower blue of her eyes, or how she blushed a beautiful rose color when he kissed her. He remembered perfectly the pattern of freckles across her cheeks and the way she was forever tucking a loose strand of corn silk behind her ear.

The difference was she had grown into a stunning *woman*. She moved with a grace and confidence that impressed him. Motherhood, her journey out here, this town, they had infused her with a strength Billy had seen instantly. What if she had changed too much? Moved beyond him?

Muffled sounds coming from the kitchen interrupted his reverie and he assumed the sisters were cleaning up. His stomach rumbled for attention. True, he hadn't eaten since breakfast and that had only been one skinny biscuit with a piece of dry country ham. Hunger would be an honest excuse for dropping in.

He sat up and reached for his boots. If Hannah were there, perhaps they could talk a little more. If not, maybe Billy could get a sense of things from Naomi or Rebecca. Preferably Rebecca, who hid her disdain for him much better than the outspoken Naomi. His father had always said she was too hot-tempered for her own good, but according to the Pinkerton report, Naomi's fiery streak had served the girls well here in Defiance.

He tiptoed down the stairs, trying to soften the thud of his boots on the hardwood. As he approached the kitchen, he heard Hannah giggle . . . and a man's voice. The sound stopped Billy cold.

He listened, but couldn't make out the words. Swatting his fingers nervously against his thigh, he decided he had to know who was in there with her. Slowly he approached the batwings and peered over them.

Hannah and the Mexican boy from the party sat at a corner of the kitchen table, the simple, yellow birthday cake between them.

Fork in hand, they each nibbled at the pastry in a clearly intimate way.

"Well, anyway," Hannah said, twirling her fork on her plate, "at least now you don't have to share the cake with anybody but me."

Emilio leaned in a little closer and smiled at her. The hopeful expression on his face twisted Billy's guts. "There ees no one I would rather share it with."

Hannah's twirling stopped. The two stared at each other. Billy panicked. He burst through the doors with a loud greeting. "Hey, you two gonna keep that cake all to yourselves?" He felt like a fool, but he hadn't come fifteen hundred miles to lose Hannah to a greaser.

Hannah's expression remained inscrutable, but Emilio was clearly not pleased to see him. To his credit, he quickly wiped away the scowl and rose to his feet. "No, *señor*, please join us. There is plenty."

A little guilt panged Billy, but only a little. "Thank you." He took a seat and eyed the cake, and a plate of roast venison that hadn't been stored away for the night yet.

Sensing Emilio's awkwardness—and enjoying it—Billy stuck out his hand as the young man sank back into his seat. "By the way, we haven't been properly introduced. I'm Billy Page, the father of Hannah's baby. Maybe you've heard of me."

Daggers flew at him from Hannah's eyes, but Emilio didn't even hesitate. He shook Billy's hand and nodded. "*Si*. Hannah has told me all about you." His voice was deep, steady, revealing nothing of his emotions. "It is nice to meet you."

Billy nodded as well, sure of the undertones in the polite response. He assumed he knew where they each stood in regards to Hannah. He wondered if Hannah knew where she stood with each of them.

Fidgeting, she stood up. "You need a plate, Billy. Help yourself to the venison. Would you like coffee or water?"

She slid the meat over to him. Billy picked up a slice and

popped it into his mouth. Cold, but still tasty. "Thank you. Water will be fine."

As she shuffled about in the kitchen, Billy nibbled on another piece of the meat and stared at Emilio. "So, what do you do around here, Emilio? Are you the custodian?"

The boy frowned. "Custodian? I do not know this word."

Emilio sought out Hannah for an explanation. She slid the plate, fork, and a cup of water in front of Billy and tossed him a thinly-veiled look of displeasure. "It means someone who takes care of a building." She retook her seat on the other side of the table. Billy saw the firm set to her jaw and realized his jabs at the boy could backfire if he wasn't careful. "In that case," she continued, "we're all custodians. We all take care of the hotel. Emilio just does the heavier work. The more *manly* work."

The challenge in her raised chin was clear and Billy decided to tread more lightly. Still, a *greaser*? Surely she wasn't thinking about getting involved with him . . . if she hadn't already.

Emilio took one last bite of his cake then licked the yellow icing off the fork. "This was the best birthday cake I ever had, Miss Hannah. You should do more desserts."

"She always did have a sweet tooth," Billy interjected, trying to keep the two from talking directly to each other.

Hannah raised a skeptical brow at Emilio's comment, ignoring Billy's. "Is it the best because it's the *only* birthday cake you've ever had?"

Emilio laughed and Billy was left sitting out in the cold. Agitated, he tapped his foot. An undercurrent of emotions definitely swirled here, but he was relatively confident the friendship between the two hadn't gone any further yet. So what to do? If Emilio would just do the gentlemanly thing and *leave*.

Popping the last bite of venison into his mouth, Billy reached over with his unused fork and carved out a piece of this bewitching birthday cake. "How old are you today, Emilio?"

"Eighteen, I think."

Billy raised his eyebrows. "You think? Don't you know?"

"Not for certain. I—"

"Emilio is an orphan," Hannah offered too quickly. "He's moved around quite a bit." She locked her eyes on Billy. "But that's the way it is with a lot of people here in the West. Who you were in one place isn't who you have to be in the next."

Billy didn't really understand her point. Was she saying she'd reinvented herself? Or that he could? Maybe both.

Delighting Billy, Emilio rose and stepped behind his chair. "I have logging to do tomorrow. I should get to bed." He paused over Billy as if he wanted to ask a question but thought better of it. He nodded instead and turned his attention to Hannah. "Thank you for the party. Maybe you can finish teaching me this Virginia Reel another time."

Billy almost slammed his fork down. He knew a jab when one hit him. Hannah bid her friend good night and watched him drift through the batwings. As his footsteps faded, she settled back in her seat. Billy felt her stare, but decided to savor the cake for a moment. When the silence dragged on, he raised his head. She sat with her arms folded tightly across her chest, legs crossed, her foot bouncing, eyes boring into him. This didn't bode well.

"*Custodian,*" she repeated, clearly unhappy with his choice of the word. "You know who you sounded like when you said that? Your father."

"I didn't really mean anything by it. I was just trying to . . ." *To what? Make him look bad in front of Hannah.* That had certainly blown back on him. "What is he to you exactly?"

"A good friend . . . and a good man."

Jab two. Billy found himself wishing for the bell.

CHAPTER 10

One-Who-Cries shifted on his horse's back and stared through the pines at a group of settlers. A young girl, dark hair braided around the top of her head, stood beside the creek. Unaware of the Indians watching her, she tossed a stick for a yellow mongrel into the rushing water. The dog leaped excitedly into the foam like a bear cub hunting a fish.

A rock's throw beyond her, a white woman with loose hair the color of the sun stirred a steaming pot. One-Who-Cries caught a whiff of rabbit stew and his belly grumbled. Near her, an old couple rested against the wagon's rear wheel, empty tin plates in their hands. The old woman had her hair done up in the same strange braid as the young girl, like a vine around her head. The old man's rifle leaned on the wagon bed beside him.

One-Who-Cries thought there should be one more among them. The woman with yellow hair would have a husband. He scanned the camp, the woods behind the wagon, and the boulders opposite them.

Nothing.

Troubled, he caressed the rifle lying across his lap. Perhaps her man was dead. Perhaps she was alone, with only an old man for protection.

Like Two Moons had been.

The memory of his mother's mutilated body smoldered in his heart. Recalling her death made the killing easy.

Beside him, Black Elk tightened his legs around his horse and silently slid an arrow into his bow. Four other braves sat astride their horses, side-by-side with him and One-Who-Cries, watching and waiting.

The sun inched lower and lower behind them, lengthening their shadows as they waited. Restless, the mare beneath One-Who-Cries took a cautious step forward. He agreed. The time had come. With a whoop and a scream, he raised his rifle and kicked his horse. The Indians exploded from the woods like rampaging grizzlies. The young girl saw them first and screamed. The dog turned and barked a warning. Black Elk pulled and released his arrow in one silent, fluid move. The animal disappeared beneath the white foam without even so much as a yelp.

One-Who-Cries thundered past the girl, shot the old man as he reached for his rifle, and swung down from the saddle. Like an angry god come down to earth, he struck the old woman with the butt of his rifle before she could rise to her feet. He fed on the sound of shattering bone. She slumped on her husband, dead. The woman with yellow hair raised her spoon over her head and held it like a knife. Her terror-filled gaze leaped back and forth between the brave storming toward her and the one headed for the girl. She chose her target and hurled the spoon at One-Who-Cries' chest. "Get away from us!"

One-Who-Cries did not slow his charge as Black Elk raced over to the young girl at the creek and snatched her up into his saddle. She squealed in terror and commenced writhing like an angry snake. "Eva, help me!"

Eva tried to dodge One-Who-Cries and run toward Black Elk. "Let her go!" She raised her fist at him. "Let my sister go, you savage!" But One-Who-Cries caught her and spun her around. The fury in her eyes turned to the fear of a rabbit staring into the fangs of a mountain lion.

Behind him, the young girl screamed again, the shrill sound grating on his nerves. A sharp, resounding *smack* ended the screech. *Black Elk*. Smiling, One-Who-Cries dug his fingers into Eva's arms and pulled her closer. "You call us savages. You have no idea . . ."

Or perhaps she did. Eva jerked and pulled wildly and tried to wriggle free from his grasp. Impatient with her squirming, One-Who-Cries cuffed the woman across the face, the crisp sound rising over the water. "Be still and we will not hurt you."

Eva seemed not to hear or feel the pain. Acting like a wild animal with the scent of fire in its nostrils, she kicked and clawed and growled desperately. She thought to rake her nails down One-Who-Cries' face, but he grabbed her wrists. Twisting and writhing, she brought her knee up hard. A blinding pain blossomed like a fire in One-Who-Cries' loins. Flinching, he loosened his grip just enough to give Eva a brief opening. She wrenched free and sprinted away from him.

Beside them, the other braves had leaped into the wagon and were flinging blankets, trunks, bags of flour, and any loose items, out the back. They paused in their raiding to laugh at the blow the white woman had struck One-Who-Cries. Only Black Elk did not laugh.

One-Who-Cries straightened up. Black fury crashed over him like a rushing waterfall. It roared in his ears, sucked the air from his lungs. With that move, the woman had sung her death song, no matter how many rifles she was worth.

She sprinted toward a large boulder, her drab brown skirt billowing around her. "Jed! Jed! Help us!" One-Who-Cries was on her, bellowing with rage. He tackled the woman and the two of them tumbled to the ground and rolled behind a boulder. He raised a fist and brought it down with every ounce of hate his body held coiled in his lean muscles. Her screams changed, from anger and fear to the panicked screeching of a dying bird in an eagle's claws. He thought his head would come apart. Her shrieking felt like knives stabbing his brain and made his forehead throb. Scrambling to stop the noise, he grasped a rock and swung it hard into the side of her head again and again. Her skull shattered. Blood and brains splattered across the orange pine needles beneath them.

Winded, the burn of his hate fading, One-Who-Cries climbed to his feet and staggered out from behind the rock. He pushed long tendrils of black hair and feathers out of his face and met Black Elk's unexpected glare. The brave had draped the younger girl over his saddle like a dead deer. His stare said One-Who-Cries should have done the same thing with the yellow-haired girl.

But One-Who-Cries would not be scolded like a child and he raised his chin. Black Elk understood this and decided not to fight. Instead, he slid out of the saddle, snatched a tin plate from the dead white man and heaped stew onto it. One-Who-Cries could not eat, not while the anger still raged within him.

The braves ransacking the wagon returned to their task with excited whoops and yelps. One of them dumped a jar of peaches down his throat then tossed the empty glass aside. He grabbed a burning stick from the fire and threw it inside the wagon. The canvas caught quickly and smoke billowed toward the circle of blue sky above them. Two other braves, still digging through a box of dried goods, shouted curses at him and dragged their treasure out of range of the heat.

One-Who-Cries let the smoke lift his anger. He watched the ashes float away and wished he could be that free. Thinking more clearly, he could see what the girl's resistance had cost. She had been worth three rifles because she had yellow hair. She was worth nothing dead. If only she hadn't fought. He shook his head, refusing to think about the loss.

As Black Elk wolfed downed the serving of stew, movement in the bushes brought One-Who-Cries' mind back down to the earth. The missing white man staggered into the open. Black Elk dropped his plate and pulled his bow from his shoulder. The white man raised his Colt, but with an arm that shook like an old woman's. Black Elk swiftly loaded the arrow and drew back on the string. Before he could release it, One-Who-Cries lobbed the bloodied rock in his hand at the settler's arm. The gun flew loose from his fingers. Swaying, the man turned his empty palm up as if wondering how his weapon had disappeared.

Instinctively, One-Who-Cries took a step back. Something was wrong. The man's skin was almost yellow, a dull light filled his eyes, and his face sagged strangely. His confused gaze drifted over to the water and he took a few unsteady steps toward the creek.

Sickness.

Black Elk fired multiple arrows, as did two other braves. The white man managed two more steps then fell into the water, his body pinned like a porcupine.

One-Who-Cries walked up beside Black Elk, folded his arms across his chest and studied the dead white man. When he didn't speak, Black Elk did. "He was sick." He jerked his chin toward the girl draped over his saddle. "She might be, too. We should kill her and move on."

One-Who-Cries dropped his hands on his hips and stared down at his moccasins. "We promised Sanchez two women," he said more to himself than Black Elk. *The white woman should not have fought. And now we are too near the meeting place to turn back.* He wanted to bash her head in again.

There was one other place they could get women quickly. One-Who-Cries pondered Black Elk, the big brave towering over him like a hulking shadow, and an idea came to him. Black Elk had been to Defiance. And now he would go back.

CHAPTER 11

*W*rapped in an old, tattered quilt, Naomi sat down on a log by the river, her favorite place to pray. The radiance from a brilliant full moon washed the last hour before sunrise in shades of silver and gray. Above the pewter mountains, diamonds shimmered and blinked in the sky. As always, this view filled up her soul. If she couldn't sleep, at least she could marvel at God's handiwork.

How many times had she retreated to this spot over the last year? Initially she had come to fuss and fume. The ache of John's absence and her anger over God's *betrayal* had consumed her. Slowly, though, her loving Father had healed her and she had come to accept Defiance as a town in need of witnesses. Even more slowly, she had accepted her feelings for Charles.

"Why is Matthew here now, Lord?" she wondered aloud. "He makes my life with John so fresh and the grief so raw." She swallowed, surprised by the tightness in her throat. "I thought I'd laid him to rest."

Overwhelmed with emotions she couldn't make heads or tails of, she sagged on the log and watched the moon beams dance on the rippling water. She shouldn't be confused. John was dead.

Matthew was John's twin on the surface only. Charles had turned out to be a good man who loved her enough to take a bullet for her and her family. Yet, she was struggling—

"Couldn't sleep? May I be so bold as to assume that's because you were thinking of me?"

Charles' tease, wrapped in a silky, Southern drawl released a torrent of butterflies in her. He stood near the water's edge with his frockcoat pulled back on one side, his hand resting on the holstered .44. The other hand hung at his side and his fingers fidgeted, playing piano on his leg. He started toward her, hesitated, then ambled over and sat down. Lacing his fingers, he rested his elbows on his knees and stared out over the glimmering water. Naomi stared at him, taken aback by the uncertainty she sensed in him.

"Were you? Thinking about me?"

"Yes." She bit her lip, feeling guilty, even unfaithful somehow, that she hadn't been thinking about him *only*. Several seconds passed and he continued to stare at the water. Hugging herself against the chill, she waited, giving him time to find his words.

"It must be unimaginably difficult to see the ghost, so to speak, of John." He tapped his fingertips against one another. "And confusing."

"The grief feels fresh all over again." A muscle ticked in his cheek, as if he'd guessed that already and the thought wasn't welcome. She knew she needed to say something reassuring, for both their sakes. "Time. I just need time to deal with it."

"Is it just me, or is he the *spitting* image of John?"

"They are identical . . . *were* identical, in looks. That's where the similarities end. Matthew was quite a handful. He was always in trouble and John was forever getting him out of it."

Charles sighed, a sad sound that surprised her. She'd never seen him this unsure. He turned abruptly and straddled the log, moving closer to her. Pushing his hat back, he searched Naomi's face, his own gaze determined in the steely light of dawn. "I don't know what to think. I don't know if I should be worried or not. I told myself I wasn't, yet here I am at five o'clock in the morning hoping you'd be out here."

"You're worried about us?"

His taciturn expression hid his answer.

Drowning in confusion, she turned her head. "I won't lie. It's hard. He even almost smells like him." *Stupid!* She flinched at her insensitive words. He had come here to find assurance. She faced him and tried to feign a confidence she didn't actually possess. "I'm sure, after the shock wears off, I'll be fine." Charles pursed his lips as he mulled that over. Slowly, he reached out and touched her cheek. Naomi closed her eyes and tilted her face into his palm. "I'm sorry, Charles, I don't know why I'm being so . . ."

"Female." He said it as if he was resigned to the curse and dropped the hand.

Her eyes flew open and her hackles rose. "Well, pardon me for being a bit stunned by Matthew's arrival. You said it yourself. He's the spitting image of John. I think I'm entitled to be a little muddled. What I'm *not* is some weak-willed, water-kneed child around him just because of the resemblance. I'll have you know—"

Charles captured her cheeks with both his hands and kissed her with a vengeance. Furious, she pushed against him, but her resistance burned away as fast as summer grass hit by lightning. Eagerly, she slid into his arms and lost herself to the hunger of his lips and the tickle of his beard. A heady desire swept over her, but a breathless peace accompanied it, because she was meant for his embrace. He tightened his hold and kissed her ravenously, till she felt lightheaded. She floated on dreams of him, wishing she never had to wake up, never had to let him go.

And just as suddenly as he'd grabbed her, he released her, rose to his feet and took a step back. She would have been embarrassed at her reaction to him, except for the satisfied smirk on his lips. "If the matter of your affection takes a different direction, princess, I would appreciate being apprised of the change."

Infuriated by his arrogance, she also found it comforting. Trying to slow her galloping heart and hold a stern expression, she stood as well, albeit on wobbly legs. "Garnered quite a bit of information out of one kiss, did you, Mr. McIntyre?"

Nonchalantly, he pulled a cheroot out of his breast pocket and raised it to his lips, where the smirk still resided. "Why, yes, I believe I did, Mrs. Miller." He reached inside his coat for a match and lit it with a flick of his thumbnail. Puffing on the cheroot, he explained, "You are a woman of few words, Naomi. Your actions have always betrayed your heart. If you ever kiss another man like that, I hope I'm lying dead somewhere."

She smiled at the way he could take the bluntest statements and make them sound like romantic poetry. She stepped up to him and laced her fingers through his. "I'm not sleepy." Indeed, left to think about that kiss she might not sleep for days. She wondered if he knew how his touch melted her. "Would you mind escorting me on a walk?"

Perhaps remembering the Southern gentleman he was raised to be, he immediately offered her his arm. A mischievous smile lifted the corner of his mouth. "A walk? Yes, I suppose that will have to do for now."

Minutes later, they strolled down the quiet main street of Defiance. In the east, behind the jagged mountains, the sky had started its march past blue dawn to the reds and yellows of sunrise. Naomi clung to Charles' arm. Still reeling from the heat of that kiss, holding him dampened her memories of John. She wanted to remember him, of course, but not feel as if she could reach out and touch his cheek or hold his hand. That was too disorienting.

Oh, why did Matthew have to come to Defiance now?

"How did your family reunion go, by the way?"

"Fine, I suppose." She frowned, wondering why she felt the need to lie. "No. Not fine at all. He thought he was coming to rescue us, to take us back with him to California. He said he has a house for us with a maid." She hugged his arm tighter, concentrating on the feel of taut muscle beneath her fingers. "I feel so badly. I wrote him a second letter. I told him we were fine. He said he never got it."

"A house and a maid?" She thought Charles sounded less than pleased with that bit of news. He puffed on the slender cigar, pondering things, the soft thud of their shoes the only sound in the early light. "It sounds like he has a vested interest in this trip. Did you tell him about us?"

Naomi's step faltered slightly. "No. Not really." Aware that her answer sounded evasive, she pulled away and locked her hands behind her back. "Our conversation didn't really go that well. It was rather heated. For one thing, he knows who you are and heartily disapproves of you."

"A Miller who thinks I'm a scoundrel? How novel."

Naomi chuckled. "Yes, but maybe he'll come around like I did." Although, after the things he'd said last night, she figured the odds were pretty steep.

"Just how does he know about me?" His eyes narrowed. "Personal experience?"

"He said not." What he did say proved Charles' point about his scandalous reputation and her mood sank a bit. "He said everyone knows you."

Charles didn't react to that, not that she could tell. Instead, he puffed on his cheroot.

Naomi couldn't help but wonder about life inside a brothel. What did it mean Charles was the best judge of female companionship, *exactly*? The implications disturbed her, but she couldn't ask him. Based on his confession a few weeks back, Naomi had the impression he didn't really want to talk about his past. Truth be told, neither did she.

It would only remind her what a good, godly man John had been. She didn't want to see his mirror image, so tempting and real, staring back at her, recalling in perfect detail the one man she'd been with, the one man who had loved and honored her, been her best friend from the time they were children.

Old things are passed away; behold all things are become new.

The Scripture brought her comfort. The past was in the past. It had to stay there. "I will tell him about us, Charles. I just haven't had the right moment."

*W*ould there ever be a *right* moment? It grieved McIntyre to watch Naomi wrestle with things, things he might not want to know about. He'd almost popped the question when he'd found her down by the stream this morning, but something had held him back. The ring was burning a hole in his pocket, but Matthew's presence and Naomi's confusion over a ghost troubled him. McIntyre could understand it. He didn't necessarily have to feel that Naomi would choose him over John if the man was still alive, but he needed to be sure she had let go. He had every reason to believe she had. Didn't he?

He supposed the doubts came from the way *Matthew* had looked at Naomi.

Lost in the thought as he was, he didn't see Henry Thatcher in time, though he should have smelled the stench of whiskey. The man staggered around the corner and bumped into Naomi. Owl-eyed and swaying on his feet, he stepped back, but as he did, he laid one eager hand on her shoulder and gave her an appreciative once-over. A lecherous grin revealed his lack of teeth and obvious thoughts. McIntyre moved to intervene, but Naomi's temper ignited like a firecracker before he could speak.

"Get your hands off me!" She shoved the scrawny, stringy-haired Thatcher away from her. "Honestly, the men in this town."

Swaying on his feet, Thatcher's expression darkened. "Now, easy, love," he slurred, the liquor thickening his Cockney speech. "No need to be so unfriendly." His hand flopped back to Naomi's shoulder as his gaze roamed over her again.

Not sure if he was angrier with the men in Defiance or Naomi, McIntyre quickly inserted himself between her and Thatcher. Moving his fiery princess out of the way, he shoved Thatcher up against the wall of the drug store.

Thatcher's eyes rounded comically with surprise followed immediately by stark fear. "McIntyre?"

"Why, Henry Thatcher. One of the snakes come crawling back to Defiance." Thatcher was a cohort of Tom Hawthorn, the man who had nearly beaten Mollie to death last November. "And where is your partner in crime? Certainly not back in Defiance as well?"

His fear shined brighter. "I-I ain't seen the bloke in months."

Probably true.

Now what to do about his disrespecting Naomi? McIntyre chewed on his lip, forcing down the anger that made him want to shove his burning cheroot into Thatcher's eye. Such methods of justice seemed at odds with his faith. This gutless scoundrel standing before them, however, didn't know anything about that.

McIntyre leaned in and lowered his voice. "You're lucky I'm on my way somewhere, Thatcher." The man gulped, understanding the message. "Remove your hat and apologize to this lady for your unacceptable manners."

Thatcher licked his lips and snatched the dirty kepi off his head. It irritated McIntyre that the Cockney dog was even wearing the Confederate cap, but he stepped aside so Thatcher could offer the apology. "I am sorry. I thought she was one a your —" he bit that off and turned his attention to Naomi. "I am sorry, madam, for my unacceptable be'avior. I hope you'll be forgivin' me."

He didn't wait for her response. He smashed the cap on his head and hurried clumsily down the boardwalk. McIntyre and Naomi watched him stagger off to his tent—or rock. McIntyre shook his head. Thatcher was a small-time crook, but he'd been known to man-handle women. If Naomi had been alone . . .

He put his hand on her back and sighed as they resumed their walk. With a great effort, he controlled the frustration in his voice. "Naomi, would it be within the realm of possibility that occasionally you could meet a confrontation without throwing kerosene on it?"

"He was drunk." She crossed her arms across her chest, which was the same thing as a mule settling its back hooves.

McIntyre had to stop himself from rolling his eyes. "Yes, he was in a fair state, to be sure. But a soft answer turneth away wrath." He raised an eyebrow at her, pleased he could pull out a verse of Scripture to use on her. "It wouldn't hurt you to learn to keep your head down every now and again."

Surprising him, she loosened her arms a little. "Turn the other cheek?" She deflated, dropping her arms to her side, and he felt a bit like a cad for scolding her. "He thought I was one of your Flowers."

McIntyre absorbed the comment that felt like a punch to the gut. He had hoped she hadn't caught that. He tossed the half-smoked cheroot into the dirt, determined not to run from the situation. "He won't be the last either, Naomi. Should I say I'm sorry? I am."

She didn't respond to the question. Instead, after a thoughtful moment of silence, she said, "He was terrified of you."

A thousand illustrations as to *why* leaped to his mind, but he remained quiet. He had no wish to explain the dog-eat-dog world a man had to conquer in order to build a mining town in the wilderness. Show no weakness. Give no quarter.

"And, he hates you," she added.

The observation surprised him because it sounded vaguely like an accusation. "Most likely." He shrugged, wishing he could as easily shrug off his past. "Men out here only understand one thing, Naomi—strength." He'd been arguably merciless when building the town because that was the way it had to be. "His fear will keep him out of trouble . . . and away from what is mine."

CHAPTER 12

*C*Intyre **held the hotel door for Naomi.** The place was as quiet as a church on Saturday night, a sign that their guests were still asleep. The dining room was closed on Sundays, allowing the girls one leisurely day to call their own. McIntyre wanted to spend it with Naomi. It felt to him as if he had some ground to smooth over.

She let her shawl slide into his hands. As she hung it and his hat on the tree just inside the door, she touched his elbow. "I'll get the coffee and meet you in the dining room."

McIntyre nodded, and watched her go. Her completely natural gesture, a light brushing of her fingers across his arm, coupled with their walk arm-in-arm, warmed him all over and he chose for the moment to ignore his concerns over his sordid past.

"How do you feel about pancakes this morning, Mr. McIntyre?" From the stair landing, Rebecca followed the trail of his gaze, her lips twitching with amusement.

He bent his head, embarrassed that he'd been caught staring after Naomi with stars in his eyes. He couldn't begin to fathom what this woman had done to him. Nevertheless, he returned

Rebecca's smile with a devilish one of his own. "You're trying to put as much weight on me as you have on Ian."

She finished twining the braid in her chestnut hair as she descended the steps and winked at him. "Yes, it's an insidious plot. Fat men can't outrun us."

Chuckling from the banter, McIntyre stepped into the dining room, separated from the front of the hotel by a false wall. The laughter died on his lips when he discovered Matthew stoking the fire. Feeling like someone had just shoved a burr under his saddle, McIntyre pulled another cheroot and match from his breast pocket. A good smoke helped him relax. After the run-in with Thatcher, his patience was edgy at best and he didn't want to show any agitation around Matthew. A desire based on his gambler's instinct. That instinct told him not to turn his back on this man. "Good morning, Mr. Miller."

Matthew glanced over his shoulder and smiled, but not before McIntyre saw a flash of irritation. "Mr. Miller was my pa. Please, call me Matthew."

"All right, *Matthew*." The two shook hands then McIntyre struck the match on the mantle's river rock. He puffed on his cigar, bringing it to life. Exhaling, he asked, "So what is it you do in California?"

Matthew rested a boot on the hearth and watched the flames build. As if to hide fidgety fingers, he shoved his hands into his pockets. "Timber. Tell me, Mr. McIntyre, are you the same Charles McIntyre who owns the Iron Horse Saloon?"

McIntyre stopped in mid-puff, but resumed quickly. Wary, he exhaled. "I am, although, it's closed now, of course." Matthew's fingers drummed inside the pockets. He rocked on his heels and ran a hand through his chopped, blond hair. McIntyre knew the signs of someone spoiling for a fight. Wisely or not, he decided to oblige. "Is there something you want to say, Matthew?"

"What do two men who want the same woman say to each other?"

Masterfully hiding his surprise at the blunt question, McIntyre rolled the cheroot between his thumb and index finger for a moment. A year ago he would have started with *No woman in the world is worth fighting for.* Perhaps even added *besides, there's plenty more where she came from.* Now, he couldn't imagine those words coming out of his mouth, especially regarding Naomi. Instead, he had the burning desire to say something chivalrous like *why don't we step outside and settle this?* Of course, that approach yet again seemed at odds with his new-found faith. Falling back on his honed skill of bluffing, he waved the cheroot. "If memory serves, I believe *Victori exuviae* would do."

Matthew straightened and turned his mass on McIntyre. Not a small man himself, McIntyre was taken aback by the towering wall of flannel that masqueraded as the man's chest and shoulders.

"I don't know Latin, but I get the meaning." Matthew's lip curled as he sized up McIntyre. "A fancy education doesn't clean up somebody like you, though. The kind of man you are."

That sneer rankled McIntyre, challenging his patience. He ran his tongue over his teeth, and fought to keep the bluff.

"Why, I bet there isn't a man in the West who doesn't know your name," Matthew mocked. "'Charles McIntyre hires sportin' gals with all kinds of talents.'"

McIntyre inhaled on the cheroot, pondering how best to deal with this swaggering giant. Seemed his faith was getting tested every which way as of late. He almost longed for a time when he would have ruined the man at a game of poker merely for the insult. Now, however, something restrained him. He heard the echo of *vengeance is Mine* and tried to listen.

Matthew cocked his head to one side. "We've got two of your girls in Red Pine. My men speak very highly of them."

"That is no longer my vocation. It's true I have a reputation, but it'll die down in time." Which might be true, eventually. "I'm a legitimate businessman now and I plan on bringing industry into Defiance."

"But not before you drag Naomi and maybe her sisters through your muck?"

McIntyre had to remind himself not to bite through the cheroot, but the muscles in his jaws turned to iron. "I'm not dragging Naomi through anything. And I don't see how my relationship with her is any of your business."

"Hmmm. Seems you haven't had any compunctions about dragging *other* women into your quagmire. All those gals you've corrupted. How do you sleep at night?" Matthew clutched McIntyre's shoulder and raised his voice. "Sure, we'll have to talk about some potential logging business. You've got pretty timber in these mountains."

A hard smile tipped his mouth and McIntyre understood Naomi was coming up behind him.

Matthew's gaze shot past him. "Good morning, little sister." Matthew left McIntyre and hurried to meet Naomi.

Her eyes widened with surprise. "Oh, good morning, Matthew." McIntyre hoped she was disappointed as well. "I didn't expect you to be up. I'll have to get another cup from the kitchen."

"That would be greatly appreciated. Here—" Matthew took the tray of coffee from her. "Let me help you with that."

The pleasantries fell apart abruptly as the front door burst open and deputy marshal Wade Hayes, all six-feet-four of him, lurched into the lobby. Sliding to a stop in the center of the entrance, the long and lean deputy scanned the room. Chest heaving, he found McIntyre and rushed toward him.

"We got a problem over at the Lucky Deuce, Mr. McIntyre, and Sheriff Beckwith is out serving a warrant." He pushed unruly strands of copper hair off his forehead as he resituated his hat. "I could use some help."

"What seems to be the matter, Wade?" McIntyre wasn't sure if he should welcome or curse the intrusion.

"Joseph Black Elk woke up in a surly mood. He's got one of Jude's gals by the arm and is threatening to cut her."

Naomi gasped. McIntyre sighed. Life in Defiance. Tossing the cheroot into the fire, he motioned toward the door. "All right, let's go."

"Hold on a second." Matthew set the tray down. "Maybe I should go along. I could probably be a little help."

McIntyre barely stopped a sneer before it surfaced. "Those muscles won't stop a bullet or a blade."

"No, but it's been my experience that my size can have a *calming* effect on people."

Tension like a tight-wire hung between the two men, but McIntyre realized quickly they were wasting time for no good reason. "Fine."

*F*rom a hundred feet away, the Lucky Deuce sounded as if a randy buffalo had gotten loose inside. McIntyre could hear furniture crashing, glass shattering, and the booming voice of a man bellowing what sounded like gibberish. The terrified scream of a woman split the morning air, sending a chill skittering up his spine. He and Wade, guns drawn, pushed through the gawking crowd at the door and burst into the saloon, with Matthew on their heels.

The place was indeed a mess. Not one table or chair sat upright in the ramshackle tent saloon. Dozens of shattered bottles and the dangling shards of a large mirror lined the one real wall behind the slab bar. The stench of cheap whiskey alone was enough to cause inebriation. Black Elk, a tall, broad-chested Ute Indian, had Dolores by the wrist and was whipping her around like a rag doll. Waving his eight-inch blade about and hollering at the top of his lungs in Ute, he froze at the sight of the men at the door.

Black Elk's eyes narrowed and he pulled Dolores to him,

hooking his arm around her throat. Pointing the knife tip at her jugular, he warned the men, "Come near me and I'll kill her!"

"Joseph," McIntyre spoke calmly, "you don't want to hurt Dolores. Let her go and we'll all have a drink together."

"Ha!" the Indian yelled, his nostrils flaring with rage. Shaking his head, black tendrils snaking around his face, he snarled and pricked the girl's throat, drawing blood and a whimper from her. "I will kill her graveyard dead. Stay away from me!"

Slowly, one careful step at a time, the three men started fanning out. Matthew inched his way to Black Elk's left, Wade to the right, and McIntyre stayed in the center, trying to draw the man's attention. "Joseph, what's this all about? You haven't caused this kind of trouble before."

The Indian blinked and then flinched when the action poured sweat into his eyes. "Put that gun away, McIntyre, or you're going to have *another* dead white woman on your hands!"

Another? McIntyre squinted at Black Elk. He saw the man flinch again and almost bend over, as if he'd been hit with a cramp. "You're not looking well, Joseph." Something about the man's face struck McIntyre as odd, sort of drawn. His skin appeared thin and he was flushed. "You don't look well at all, as a matter of fact."

Black Elk waved the knife at him. "I'll kill her!"

McIntyre tilted his head. Black Elk's gaze was confused and wandering, as if he couldn't focus. "Black Elk, you're sick."

The Indian tightened his grip on Dolores. "Put your guns down and I'll walk out of here." He jabbed the girl in the ribs with the knife. "Otherwise, she's dead—" His features contorted into a hideous grimace and Black Elk staggered. Dolores whimpered and kept him on his feet, clearly afraid he might accidentally stab her if he fell.

Knowing this could go bad in the blink of an eye, McIntyre dropped his gun back into his holster and motioned for Wade to do the same. All three of the men raised their hands. "All right,

Joseph." McIntyre took a small step forward. "We want this to end on a high note for everyone. Now put your knife away before you cut her by accident."

McIntyre messaged Matthew with a subtle nod. Someone strong needed to subdue this man. Put him down with one punch, if possible. It was Matthew's lucky day.

Matthew returned the nod, almost imperceptibly, and inched a bit closer to Black Elk.

"Black Elk, where have you been the last few days?" McIntyre asked. If the crazy Indian was carrying something contagious, they'd have to try to retrace his footsteps.

The question set Black Elk to yelling. "I have been off killing white men and their women!" He shook his head and blinked again, as if trying to clear his vision. "One-Who-Cries is riding! War is coming with him!"

"What are you doing with One-Who—" Before McIntyre could finish the question, Matthew leaped on the man. Instantly McIntyre dove into the fray as well, followed by Wade. Black Elk's blade slashed crazily and McIntyre snatched a screaming Dolores out of the fracas. In a blur of blows, he and Matthew both landed punches to Black Elk's ribs as all three scrambled to grab the knife. The Indian howled and roared, the men grunted as fists pounded flesh, and boots scraped across the floor. In the tangled scuffle, the steel of Black Elk's knife flashed mere inches from McIntyre's nose. McIntyre swiped at the man's wrist but missed. The nauseating, muffled sound of a blade plunging into flesh brought a pained growl from Matthew. Like a crazed grizzly, he brought down a crashing blow from his huge right hand and Black Elk's eyes rolled to the back of his head. As limp as a rag doll, he slid to the floor.

Unfortunately, he then vomited violently at their feet. As the men jumped back, McIntyre caught sight of the blood seeping from between Matthew's fingers.

CHAPTER 13

*H*annah lifted her hand for one final wave at the departing stage. Iris, her fiery red hair a beacon you could see from the moon, blew a kiss. With one last wiggle of her fingers, she disappeared into the coach. Hannah swallowed to loosen the knot in her throat.

Please, Lord, she prayed, *let Iris, Lily, and Jasmine have a future that's brighter and more blessed than anything they can imagine.*

She sniffed back tears and told herself to accept the inevitability of change, of the way friends drift into your life, sometimes for only a season. Perhaps she would see those girls again one day. After all, Billy had come back into her life. Resisting the urge to think too much about him, she set her sights on the Boot & Co. Mercantile, a few buildings down the street.

"I have to go check Mr. Boot's ankle."

Beside her, watching the stage disappear into the dust, Naomi nodded. "Do you remember when they put gum in my hair?"

Hannah stopped and smiled. The first several months in Defiance hadn't been a cakewalk, to say the least. Now, here they were, nearly in tears over saying goodbye to women who had once mocked and teased them mercilessly.

"Charles asked me the other day if I could forgive any offense. When I think about those girls, how angry they made me, and how I feel about them now, I can say yes with a lot more confidence."

"What about Rose?" Hannah asked with a smirk, knowing the woman gave them both nightmares.

A stony expression settled on Naomi's face. "Don't you have some nursing to do?"

$\mathcal{H}$annah kneeled beside Luke Boot's outstretched leg, which rested on a stool, and proceeded to unwrap the bandage from his ankle. Her pale hair slid down across her shoulder, getting in her way, and she regretted not having braided it this morning.

"I need to get this thing off me, Miss Hannah," Mr. Boot whined, glancing around his mercantile and scratching his thick beard. "I can't run my store from the flat of my back."

"You won't be running your store at all if you don't stay off old, rickety ladders." She glanced over at Mr. Boot's helper, Freeman, a small Negro man who was setting out canned fruit on a shelf. "But it looks like Freeman's handling things."

She set the wrap aside and studied Mr. Boot's leg as she tied her hair up into a quick knot. His skin was as pale as the belly of a dead fish, except for a bluish tint down around his ankle. The swelling had decreased noticeably. "All right, Doc said if the swelling was going down, we could stop the cold compresses after today. I'd say you're almost there. Maybe you can stand for a while tomorrow. You should get a cane or a crutch."

Mr. Boot wagged his head, unhappy with the news. "I need to be up and around *today*."

"Well, too much moving around and you might re-injure that

ankle." Hannah picked up the gauze and started wrapping the injured joint. "But suit yourself. It's your leg."

Out of the corner of her eye, she saw his other leg bouncing and knew he was weighing her instructions.

"You're awful young to be giving such firm medical advice." The bouncing leg slowed, eventually stopped. "Well, fine, one more day of sitting won't kill me. 'Least I don't have to have Freeman help me soak it in any more spring water." He shivered. "That was cold."

"Yes, but that did more good for the swelling than anything, though snow would have been better."

Suddenly, Mr. Boot leaned forward, capturing Hannah's full attention with his flickering, eager eyes. "Is it really true, Little Miss Hannah, what they say?" His voice dropped to a conspiratorial whisper. "That *none* of you gals is in the business? That even Mollie got Jesus?" He gaped longingly at the top Hannah's head. "I sure miss her golden hair."

He reached out as if to touch the crown of Hannah's head, but she abruptly rose to her feet. Mollie had warned Hannah about Mr. Boot. He had been a regular customer of hers at the Iron Horse and said he had no problem *squeezing the produce* anytime or any place he wanted. Hannah had better watch out and be prepared to move quickly.

A patient who was all hands was a hazard of the job, but she wouldn't let it discourage her. Trying to turn the tables, she donned a grim expression and touched Mr. Boot's hand. "Yes, sir, the awful rumors are true. In fact, if you come by the hotel about ten, you can join us for church."

*R*ebecca poured the perfect amount of pancake batter into the frying pan and set the bowl down. Spatula in hand, she waited for the proper number of bubbles to rise before flipping the flapjack. Beside her, Ian scraped bacon slices into his pan, using a long fork to lay the sizzling meat flat.

Rebecca had become so accustomed to cooking beside him, sometimes she felt they were an old married couple. Most of the time, she just wondered if this friendship was ever going to move forward. He'd asked once to court her, but at nearly forty, the very idea had sent her into a panic, and she had rejected him. Ian had understood and asked if they could be *dear* friends.

"I have just finished *Around the World in Eighty Days*, Miss Rebecca. Another fine suggestion. Mr. Fogg was quite resourceful."

And that was their way. She and Ian could talk about books, religion, politics. Anything and everything. Still, there was so much more between them. She positively thrilled at his touch, and had danced on air in his arms the other night. Oh, but Rebecca wasn't getting any younger. Her fortieth birthday was only a few months away and Ian's presence brought home the realization that she still had a lot of living, a lot of loving, to do.

So what to do about this rut that she and Ian had fallen into? Was there no way to prompt a change? He'd been nothing but a friend, at her very own suggestion, since her initial rejection. A measured, deliberate man, perhaps he was waiting for a signal. *Maybe this delay is all my fault?*

"Ouch!" The bacon grease popped, hitting the back of Rebecca's hand. She rubbed the spot vigorously, but Ian dropped his fork and took her hand in his. He bent his head to examine the spot and she studied the gray hair curling around his face. She lived for moments like this, to have him so near her, touching her. Ian made her feel safe. He'd even fought for her honor once. He respected her intelligence and always treated her with the utmost gentlemanly behavior.

But she wondered if, maybe, he didn't find her desirable after all. Maybe when they were together, he saw the lines above her lip or the crow's feet at the corners of her eyes. Maybe she was too plain and dark against her fair, beautiful sisters. Or maybe he thought they were both just too old for a silly romance.

He looked up at her, through his rugged brow and a spark of mischief glinted in his deep blue eyes. "It occurs to me, Miss Rebecca, that I have been remiss in telling ye something." His thumb moved slowly over her hand, caressing the skin. She held her breath and waited to hear more of his lovely Scottish burr. "Yer pancake is burning."

Flustered, Rebecca snatched her hand away and clumsily flipped the pancake. Black on one side, she huffed in dismay and busily set about tossing it aside and pouring a new pancake. She tried to focus on the cooking but her mind reeled with disappointment.

Your pancake is burning? Is that all he could think to say? All these months of talking about books, and Scotland, and recipes, and family histories, and *that's* it?

Several minutes passed in silence as they worked on breakfast together. Part of Rebecca wanted to scream at Ian, beg him to notice her disappointment. Another part desperately wanted this chore over, so she could go upstairs and be alone to scold herself that forty-year-old women do not cry over ill-fated relationships.

Ian made a few light comments about his Jules Verne book, to which Rebecca responded rather half-heartedly. Eventually, he noticed. "Miss Rebecca, is something the matter?"

She wanted to tell him, but at the same time, she didn't want to discuss her crushing disappointment. What was she supposed to say? *Well, Ian, I've come to the fairly obvious conclusion that you and I are friends. Great friends. Life-long friends. You might even love me. But you are not in love with me. I'll accept that and pack away my silly little school-girl dreams.*

She could only manage, "I'm fine."

They continued on with their preparations, but Rebecca could feel Ian watching her. She swung her braid out of the way as she bent down to check the biscuits, and when she stood back up, he was standing in front of her, waiting. Tall, a bit barrel-chested now because of her cooking, Ian was a very handsome man at fifty, even in a white apron. The lines in his face just added character and his salt-and-pepper beard a sense of security. She'd been dreaming of kissing those lines for months now. Could the man not see it every time they were together?

He cleared his throat and Rebecca was surprised by his uncertain, nervous glances. "Rebecca, what I said a few minutes ago. I didnae think it came out right." He cleared his throat again and shifted his feet. "I mean to say—that is, I *need* to say I've grown quite tired of being friends and hope ye feel the same way. It would make this much easier." Rebecca blinked, but didn't know what to say. She was afraid to even hope. Sighing, Ian shook his head. "Aye, I'm making a bumbling mess of this. And it's not going to get any better." He grabbed her shoulders. "Now ye've set your dress on fire."

CHAPTER 14

*c*Intyre **thought Matthew might live, but wouldn't swear to it.** Blood streamed from the man's side, right at his ribs. Holding Black Elk's bloody knife, Matthew tried to twist enough to see the slash in his flesh but couldn't do it. Frustrated, he swore and eyed McIntyre. "Is it bad?"

McIntyre peeled off his frock coat. "Doesn't look too deep. I think you'll live. Here, press this on it."

Matthew took the jacket, raising a skeptical brow. "Bit fancy, isn't it?" Without waiting for an answer, he crushed it to his side.

McIntyre thought he did so with a little too much relish. To hide a disdainful curl in his lip, he squatted down and inspected Joseph Black Elk, careful to avoid the vomit. Too bad he couldn't avoid the smell. The Indian had messed his pants as well.

This just kept getting better and better.

With the back of his hand, he touched Black Elk's forehead. No fever, but his breathing was shallow and uneven. "Wade, run and get a wagon. We need to get these two to Doc." Wade didn't need to be told twice. The deputy bolted from the saloon. "And tell everyone to stay out of here!" McIntyre yelled after him.

Still squatting, he rubbed his chin and pondered the Indian's last words. *One-Who-Cries is riding. War is coming with him.* So he's been riding with the savage? And what did he mean about *another* white woman? Had One-Who-Cries attacked somewhere near Defiance, or was the Indian delirious from whatever sickness he was carrying?

The clink of glass drew his attention and he stood up. One-handed, Matthew poured himself a drink and raised it up. "One bottle survived." He tipped the glass in a toast and tossed it back. McIntyre flinched. The Lucky Deuce had the worst whiskey he'd ever tasted in his life. Matthew hissed and whistled as the shot went down. "That's poison if I've ever had any." He shivered dramatically as the liquid hit its mark. Undeterred, he grabbed the bottle again and offered it to McIntyre.

He waved it away.

Matthew inclined his head, but shook off the rejection with a bored shrug. He changed his focus to Black Elk. "You don't think he's got typhoid or cholera or anything, do you?"

"I don't know. No fever, could be anything." McIntyre studied the big man at the bar, drinking bad whiskey and acting as if the cut in his side was a scratch. If nothing else, he was tough. "Thank you for your assistance."

"Not necessary." Matthew refilled the shot glass. "You know, family men and preachers don't settle towns like this." He tossed down the drink. "Men like us do. We're up for it. It's how we fit into this world." He cut a mischievous sideways glance at McIntyre. "In other words, trouble becomes us."

In other words, men like Matthew—and McIntyre—were suited for towns like Defiance. Rabble. Scum. The thinly-veiled insult irritated McIntyre. Just because the town still needed law and order didn't mean it wouldn't shape up, he along with it. If he'd learned anything about God from the sisters, changing his ways was exactly what was supposed to happen as he grew in his faith.

He almost argued with Matthew about this supposed fraternity of lawless men. He almost shared with him the timber and ranching businesses he was courting, the potential for change in the town when the railroad finalized the agreement.

Almost.

Because they were now rivals, he decided not to share anything more than necessary with Matthew, and that definitely included Naomi.

Dolores stepped between the two and took hold of Matthew's impromptu dressing. A pretty little thing with auburn curls, she offered the big man a sincere but shaky smile. "Thank you." Over her shoulder, she added, "both of you." Carefully, she peeled the coat away from Matthew's side. "Why don't you let me redo this for you? You can't just smash it on there and expect it to stop the bleeding."

He obediently raised his arm to give her better access. "Thank you, ma'am." His gaze boldly climbed every inch of Dolores. "Maybe it was worth it."

McIntyre's jaw tightened. Watching Matthew watch Dolores set his blood to boiling. He surely acted like a man who had been in a cathouse or two. And *he* had dared lecture McIntyre about Naomi? McIntyre would be old, bent, and toothless before he let that happen again.

As Dolores tended her patient, McIntyre tried to turn his attention back to the mess they may well have all gotten themselves into. *Any* amount of quarantine with Matthew, Wade and Dolores would be hell on earth. "Did Black Elk come in here alone last night?" he asked the girl. "Did he look all right?"

Dolores nodded as she neatly folded the jacket and pressed it against her patient's side. "He seemed a little foggy and grabbed his gut a time or two. He had coins, though. That's the only reason Jude let him in the place."

So where did Black Elk get coins? They had to find out where he'd been, if there was *any* possibility the Indian was walking about spreading disease . . .

CHAPTER 15

"*W*ell, I don't think he's contagious." Doc Cooke came out of a back room, wiping his hands on a towel and reeking of rubbing alcohol. "My best guess is Beaver Fever. He could have gotten it drinking from a tainted creek or from an infected person who prepared his food."

He tossed the towel over his shoulder and joined a shirtless Matthew sitting atop a metal examination table. McIntyre had never seen a man with that much muscle. Matthew's arms were the size of McIntyre's legs and a woman could wash clothes on his rippled abdomen. Tall and somewhat well-muscled himself, he felt like a scrawny coyote next to this man.

"Well, let's see what we have here," Doc mumbled, sliding his spectacles farther up his nose. Matthew turned so the doctor could see his side better and removed the jacket. He grunted and jerked when the doctor probed the wound.

A little tender? McIntyre noted with satisfaction. While he had no sympathy for Matthew, he did feel bad for the girl caught in the middle. "Dolores can go then, I assume, Doc?"

She raised her head up at the question. Once the possibility of infectious disease had hit her, her shaky smile had fled altogether.

Pulling herself into a tight ball, she had claimed a seat by the window and not uttered a sound in the last hour.

"Yes, I think that will be fine." Doc glanced at the girl over the top of his round spectacles. "You and Black Elk didn't share any food or drink, correct?" She shook her head enthusiastically. "All right, just let me know immediately if you get to feeling poorly."

"Sure, Doc." The girl scrambled for the door.

"Dolores." McIntyre stopped her as she grabbed hold of the door knob. "One last time, you're sure Black Elk didn't say anything that would tell us where he's been the last few days?"

"Nothing I can recall. If I think of something, I'll let you know."

He believed her, and the girl skedaddled like wolves were nipping at her skirt. McIntyre sighed and leaned against the wall, fanning himself with his hat. Beaver Fever. Indians were usually fairly skilled at avoiding that. "How long before symptoms show up, Doc?"

The physician pressed a gauze pad soaked in alcohol to Matthew's side and the man hissed. "Onset of symptoms is anywhere from one to two weeks."

The wheels in McIntyre's head spun. Beaver Fever usually came from tainted water, more than from food. But Doc mentioned an infected person could have prepared something. And Black Elk, who had *coins*, had said a *white* woman was dead. Was there a connection? McIntyre stared at the patient's closed door, anxious for answers.

Where had this Indian been and what did One-Who-Cries have to do with it? "Is he conscious?"

Doc Cooke commenced sewing up Matthew's side with a very long, hooked needle, evoking a sharp hiss from the man. "He's in and out, thanks to the hammer blow to the head," he lifted an accusing glance to Matthew, "but he'll come around."

McIntyre twirled his hat on his index finger. At least Black Elk wasn't contagious. That was a blessing. The office door rattled and, without knocking, Marshal Pender Beckwith stomped in, taking over the room with a flurry of his canvas duster. "McIntyre, I could use another rider. I need to serve a warrant on a George Betts. He's hiding out with friends over in Carson."

Alert with purpose, the man's beady eyes and chiseled, bony face held no warmth and only added to the Marshal's no-nonsense reputation. A tough and cunning lawman, the rabble of Defiance was in the process of learning their new marshal didn't play. McIntyre would hate to be hunted by him . . . and he surely didn't want to go hunting with him. "I thought you'd left already."

"Did. Then I got word he's not alone and might know I'm coming. Not something I want to walk into with no back-up."

Implying Wade was no back-up at all. McIntyre's eyes skipped over to the deputy, who had dropped down into a seat near the cold pot-bellied stove and also not uttered a word since they got here. Pale as grass covered by a spring snow, he had confessed he didn't do well with blood and needles.

McIntyre sighed.

Admittedly, he was a better choice than the skittish deputy, but he was frustrated by these constant interruptions to his plans. The spineless men in town needed to do their part and take on deputy duties. He slapped his hat against his leg for finality and pushed off the wall. "Fine."

Carson was several hours from here. He'd have plenty of time to bring Beckwith up to speed on Black Elk, including a possible connection to One-Who-Cries. He studied Matthew, trying not to relish the pained wince as Doc pulled the second stitch tight. He'd better find a smidgen of sympathy for him, he needed a favor and loathed asking the brute, but he had no other choice. "Would you mind letting Naomi know? I'll be back as soon as I can."

All of the color drained from Matthew as he clamped his jaws shut. Still, he managed a nod. McIntyre hid a smile as he followed Beckwith and Wade out the door.

CHAPTER 16

*H*uffing in dismay, Rebecca stripped off her now soaking wet skirt and threw it across her room. Her petticoat hadn't been spared the scorching, either. Mortified, she untied it and kicked it off.

She plopped down on her bed and cradled her cheeks in her hands, wagging her head back and forth. The images of Ian patting at her rear end like a mad man wouldn't leave her. That humiliation was followed by the dousing pitcher of water, courtesy of Naomi. Though her aim had been awful, practically drowning Rebecca, enough of the water had hit the small flames to extinguish them. Rebecca couldn't recall ever being so humiliated in her life. These things didn't happen to her. Naomi was the only disaster in the kitchen. She desperately needed to get her focus back before she burnt the place down to the ground.

Still, there was a silver lining here. Clasping her hands over her heart, Rebecca fell back on her bed and grinned like a little girl with a huge secret. Ian had been about to say something clearly more interesting than anything he'd said in the last year.

He's tired of being friends.

A giggle much beneath her advanced years bubbled up.

"Rebecca," Naomi called through the door, "are you all right?"

Ridiculously giddy for a woman of forty, Rebecca fought for control of the effervescent laughter and sat up. "I'm absolutely fine. You can come in."

Naomi entered slowly, a suspicious dip in her brow. "You don't sound fine."

Her eyes bugged when Rebecca put a hand over her mouth, muffling another giggle. "Oh, I can't help it." She rose from the bed and reached for Naomi's hand. "I think Ian was finally about to say something *relevant*."

Naomi laughed and covered her sister's hand with hers, squeezing hard. "Oh, I hope so. It's so good to see you happy . . . and *living*." The reference to Rebecca's all-too-lengthy mourning period sobered them both. "Ben and Gracie wouldn't have wanted you to mourn for them the way you have . . . for as long as you have."

Rebecca dropped her gaze. "I know." Years of visiting her husband's and daughter's graves, remembering birthdays in solitude, wallowing in guilt for surviving the fire. They were dark years. Defiance had at least helped her find a divine spark again and Ian, bless his heart, had fanned it to life.

Naomi clutched her sister's shoulders. "So tell me what he said."

Rebecca's fine mood returned. "He said he'd grown tired of being friends and hoped I felt the same way."

Naomi inclined her head, as if asking for more.

"Oh, that's when my skirt, which I'd closed in the oven door, caught on fire."

Naomi laughed again, but the sound died quickly under a puckered brow. "You don't think he meant something else, do you?" Rebecca did not want to hear anything pessimistic, but her scowl did not stop Naomi from proceeding with the dark thought. "I mean, could he have meant he's giving up? I'm sorry, I don't mean to spoil anything. I just . . . well, you've been waiting on him for so long. What if he's lost his nerve?"

Rebecca was disheartened by the possibility and turned away from Naomi. What if Ian hadn't read the longing she'd telegraphed him daily and was admitting defeat?

Naomi laid a hand on her shoulder. "Maybe the man needs a hint."

Rebecca sighed, overwhelmed by the seeming fruitlessness of all this. "I don't remember how to drop one."

"Then, sister, hit him over the head with it."

---

*B*illy kicked himself again as he watched Hannah out of the corner of his eye. Bouncing Little Billy on her lap, she listened and nodded as the Scottish fellow delivered a simple sermon to the small group in the dining room. Their Sunday service. Unfortunately, Billy couldn't hear anything but the marshal's order repeating over and over in his head. The lawman had stopped in just as their hymns were beginning, pointed a boney finger at Emilio and told him to get his mount. His gaze had barely touched on Billy as he scanned the rest of the group. A group comprised of women, an infant, an older gentleman in an argyle sweater, and a dude with a bowler on his knee.

He should have ignored the dismissal in the marshal's eyes and leapt to his feet. Emilio hadn't hesitated for even a split second. But doubts had instantly assailed Billy. He wasn't sure if it was his place to join something like that, being new in town. It had sounded dangerous. Not that he was afraid, necessarily, but he was no lawman.

He sucked on his cheek, pondering the town. Defiance was pretty wide open. First, a crazy Indian brawling at a saloon required McIntyre's assistance, followed by the call to bring in a gunman. Add to that the gunshots peppering the air last night and

Billy could just hear his father lambasting him for his decision to come to the lawless, bawdy mining town.

"My son," Ian read and Billy jerked his head up as if called, "forget not My law, but let thine heart keep My commandments."

He sighed and Hannah tossed him a disapproving look, mistakenly thinking him bored. Great. Billy needed to do something to get a hand up on ol' Emilio or his son there was going to grow up speaking Spanish. He stopped his knee from bouncing and attempted to pay attention to Ian's sermon.

" . . . Trust in the Lord with all thine heart and lean not unto thine own understanding."

Guilt tweaked Billy. His own understanding sure had done a bang-up job for him so far.

"In all thy ways acknowledge Him, and He shall direct thy paths."

Ian spoke for a few minutes about trusting God with big details and little ones. They all mattered to God because His children mattered to Him. Billy tried to see the Lord as a loving father, but a fat, cigar-smoking man in an expensive suit came to mind instead. One who didn't care about his children, only that they obey and serve him. Love didn't enter into the equation.

After the closing prayer, he floundered for a moment as the sisters, Mollie, and Ian started putting chairs back around the dining tables. Eager to recoup a few points with Hannah, he jumped up to help. He was amazed at how she functioned with Little Billy on her hip. Single-handed, literally, the girl was a furniture-moving maestro, shoving tables and chairs back in place with ease, but she didn't turn Billy's way once. And moving furniture sure wasn't as manly as chasing bandits.

If there was any silver lining here, it was Hannah's avoidance of him. If she didn't care, why wouldn't she look at him? Focusing on that, he followed her to the kitchen and blurted out, "May I hold my son?" He didn't know where the request had come from and immediately regretted it. He didn't know how to hold a baby. What if he dropped him or broke him somehow?

Hannah paused at the batwings, considering the request. "All right." She handed Little Billy over. "We're going to get Sunday dinner on the table. Why don't you take him out back in the sunshine? But keep an eye on him, especially near the stream. He's starting to crawl."

Smiling inwardly at her motherly directions, Billy folded his son in his arms, but with a stiff, awkward grip.

Hannah grinned. "No, like this." She grabbed his hands and rearranged Billy's hold so the baby sat on the inside of his forearm, with his other hand on the child's back.

More at ease, he searched his son's face and met a pair of innocent angel eyes. Unexpectedly, Billy's heart did a kind of funny flutter. The infant babbled something nonsensical and touched his father's nose. Billy grinned. Giggling, the child flailed, landing a pretty good right hook on Billy's cheek. "Whoa, hold on there, son," he said, grabbing the wild hand. "It's a little too early for boxing lessons."

Hannah laughed, a magical sound like a breeze through wind chimes, and Billy hungered to hear it again. She tickled Little Billy's back. "We'll call you when it's on the table."

Holding him as if he were as fragile as a snowflake, Billy wandered out into the sunshine with his son. "Hey, you wanna go over here and see the horses?" Stopping near the small corral, he whistled for his horse. Prince Valiant trotted up, blowing and shaking his head, curious about the pint-sized human. Little Billy put his hand out and the horse allowed the stubby fingers to caress his nose. Apparently tickled with the animal, Little Billy kicked and giggled and turned a disarming grin on his father.

Joy and amazement broke loose in Billy's soul and his heart did that fluttery thing again. "Hey, buddy," he whispered, "I'm your . . . dada."

The meaning of the statement wafted over him like a welcome

summer breeze and he kissed his son on the forehead, savoring the sweet smell of talcum powder and maybe a hint of vanilla. His throat constricted on him and he squeezed his eyes shut. Hugging his son as tightly as he dared, he fought back against the guilt clinging like a dead vine to his soul.

"Oh, I am so sorry, little man . . ." His voice broke and he swallowed against the emotions tying him up in knots. "I am so sorry for letting you go. I won't leave you ever again, no matter what."

CHAPTER 17

*H*annah stood at the window over the dry sink and smiled at the interaction between father and son. How could she be so moved by the sight of them playing together, and yet seriously contemplate sending Billy away? She wished she could just yank out her heart and lock it and all her memories up in a box.

Oh, especially the memories. Watching the two together, she couldn't stop herself from going back to the night that had started all these changes, inflicted all these heart breaks. She could still feel the hay poking through the quilt as she lay down in the wagon. Billy beside her, they stared up at a midnight blue sky littered with glittering stars and a shimmering, magical Milky Way. On a cold, still, January evening, the clear sky seemed to reveal everything but the very gate of Heaven.

"I love you, Hannah." Not the first time he'd said it, she giggled with ecstasy. This time, though, his voice held a husky, emotional edge to it. "Pa isn't thrilled I'm seeing you, and I'm sorry for that. Sorry for him." Billy rolled up to an elbow, laid his gloved hand over Hannah's resting on her stomach. "I can't eat. I can't sleep. I can't stop thinking about you, what you mean to me."

Tears backing up on her, Hannah reached up to move a lock of hair out of his eyes. She knew all too well what Frank Page thought about any woman, much less Hannah, who might derail the grand plans he had for his son, the future senator from North Carolina. "Must be the moonlight. I've been warned about your sweet talk under a starry sky."

"Hannah, I've never felt this way about a girl. I want to spend my life with you. I want to marry you."

"You want to give up all that Page money?" She tried to keep her voice light, her hope tamped down. "You know your father would disown you if you married me."

He stroked her cheek with leather-clad fingers. "I don't care. He can keep it all. I don't need it. I *need* you."

Billy leaned down and kissed her, a soft, gentle nuzzling at first that grew to a breath-stealing embrace. An embrace that went on and on till she couldn't think, couldn't draw a breath without feeling him in her soul. Her heart raced at breakneck speed, pulsing in her ears.

And somehow, almost magically, Hannah found herself with Billy in his farm foreman's cabin. Mr. Tulley was nowhere to be seen but a warm fire burned in the brick fireplace as if he'd left only moments before. She and Billy were alone.

Slowly he slipped the buttons loose on Hannah's coat, all the while kissing her, telling her he loved her more than his own life, begging her to be his wife. Overcome with passion, Hannah clawed at the buttons on Billy's jacket. Not one single rational thought resided in her head. She just wanted to be with him, every inch of him, in every way possible. He loved her. The passion would always be like this. They'd be together forever.

Hannah swallowed and jerked herself out of the reverie. Her wide-eyed naiveté embarrassed her, her sin shamed her. It had seemed so romantic, so grown up. Until Page Sr. found out about the baby, at which point Billy ran like a scalded dog. Praise God she had found forgiveness and He had worked her foolishness for good. Exactly as promised in Romans 8:28. She would be eternally humbled by her heavenly Father's grace.

Rebecca came up beside her and sighed. "It would appear he likes him."

"Little Billy likes everybody." She felt her sister's surprised stare and realized the statement had sounded bitter. Her turn to sigh. "I don't know what he's after. I can't sort through it all. I felt like I was just beginning to recover from him." She sniffed. "Listen to me. *Recover*. Like he's some sort of ailment."

Rebecca rubbed her sister's back. "Honey, he delivered a pretty crushing blow by running out on you. You've been healing. So don't rush things."

Hannah tried a little teasing to lighten her mood. "Guess you know all about being patient, don't you?"

Rebecca's features, normally so refined and regal, scrunched in disapproval. She huffed and lightly yanked Hannah's braid. "I don't need you reminding me."

Naomi wandered in and, following their gazes, joined them at the window. Billy sat in the grass gesturing with silly, exaggerated motions as he chattered away at his son. "No denying who the father of that child is," she said, wagging her head. Hannah had seen the similarities early on, but with Billy side-by-side with his son, well, Naomi was right. The bloodlines were inarguable. Not that there'd ever been any doubt. "Has he asked you to go for a walk?"

Hannah raised her brow. "No."

"He will," Naomi turned to her, "and when he does, I'll watch Little Billy, if you want to go."

"You're so sure?"

"No one in this hotel is blind, Hannah. We all, including Billy, can see how Emilio looks at you. Now Emilio's gone off with the marshal. Billy will want time alone with you while he can get it."

Hannah dropped her gaze to the dishes in the sink. She wasn't sure she wanted to be alone with Billy.

"I wish I knew if Charles and Matthew went with the marshal as well." Naomi rubbed her arms, as if warding off a chill. "I'm worried about them."

"Well, I can tell you *I* didn't go."

Uncle Matt's voice from the door spun them around. Holding on to the batwings, his unbuttoned shirt revealed his broad chest and a wide band of gauze running around his midsection, just below the ribs. Sweat beaded on his forehead and he swayed slightly on his feet, moving the café doors.

"Uncle Matt!" Hannah rushed to him, tossing aside a dish towel to come under one arm. "Let's get you a seat."

Naomi edged up beneath him on the other side and they led him back to the dining room, Rebecca lending support to his back and shoulders. Although Hannah knew if Uncle Matt went down, the three of them wouldn't be able to stop him.

Rebecca slid a chair into position for him at a table near the fireplace. "What happened to you, Matthew?"

The girls eased him down into the seat as an assortment of grimaces cascaded across his face. "Nothing a few stitches didn't fix."

"Stitches?" Naomi pushed his shirt aside and surveyed the large bandage on his lower right side, a small spider web of blood already seeping through. Her gaze flicked across that wide chest. "Matthew, tell us what happened? Where's Charles?"

Hannah might not be able to discern her own heart so well, but she could read other people as easily as a church hymnal. She hadn't missed the way Naomi dragged her eyes away from Uncle Matt's muscles. Nor did she miss the flash of jealousy in *his* eyes when she asked about Mr. McIntyre.

"That fella Black Elk was a mite faster than I gave him credit for. We took him down, though. Turns out he's got Beaver Fever."

The girls gasped. "What in the world is that?" Naomi asked.

"The doc said you get it from bad water or from a person who carries the infection." Uncle Matt shifted on the seat, struggling to get comfortable. "As far as McIntyre, I'm not really sure what happened to him. I was busy getting twelve stitches. Your town doctor has the touch of a butcher."

"Uncle Matt, do you need anything?" Hannah patted his shoulder lovingly, as if he were an injured child. "Can I get you something? We might even have a little whiskey somewhere if you'd like some for the pain?"

He touched her cheek and smiled. "No, darlin', don't touch the stuff. I just need to rest a minute. That ride back in the wagon was a bit rougher than I expected. Although," he sniffed the air. "I could stand a bite. That wouldn't be Rebecca's fried chicken I smell?"

"Here, Hannah," Rebecca tagged her on the elbow. "Why don't we finish getting dinner on the table? We'll make Matthew a plate."

"Oh, thank you, Rebecca, honey. You always were an angel in the kitchen."

All three of the girls squashed giggles, or at least tried to. "Only now," Hannah grabbed her sister's arm and pulled her toward the kitchen, "we're thinking she's an angel of destruction."

---

*N*aomi bit her lip to thwart a grin.

Matthew cocked his head to one side. "What was that all about?"

"Rebecca had a very uncharacteristic accident in the kitchen this morning. She burned something."

"Oh," Matthew half-nodded, but the motion was derailed by a grimace. He grunted. "Naomi, would you be a dear," he raised his arms and sat up a bit, "and check this wrap? It feels too tight around me." Rebecca and Hannah had been subtly nudged into the kitchen and Naomi realized she'd been left alone with Matthew by design—his.

"Certainly." She bent over and tried to adjust the bandage but the angle was awkward and brought her face too close to his. Surprised by trembling, uncertain hands, she dropped to her knees just to the side of his legs. "I should be able to reach it better this way."

"I kind of liked that other way." His gaze was deep and so familiar. Naomi blinked and reached around him, staring into his broad, strong shoulder, just like the one that she had caressed and kissed so many times before. She felt him sniff her hair and she breathed in the scent of sweat and whiskey and . . . pipe tobacco? Something like the electricity from a thunderstorm danced all over her skin.

She wanted to look up and lose herself in John's deep, hypnotic gaze just once more. Maybe gently touch his cheek. Strange, she could almost feel Matthew's stare willing her to do exactly that.

He's not John! A voice screamed at her.

She took a breath, trying to focus. Rotating her shoulders as she worked the bandage, she asked, "If you don't drink, why do you smell like a whiskey barrel?"

"That Black Elk fella busted every bottle in the saloon. A man could get drunk just breathing the air."

She loosened the gauze, brought it back around the front, running her fingers a little too slowly over the steel-like muscles of his stomach. Her pulse picking up steam, she tied the bandage more securely. "There." Her fingers lingered on his warm skin, almost as if they had a will of their own. She looked up. Flashing azure eyes captivated her, bringing back a rush of memories and feelings. Same as John's, they went a shade greener when he was . . .

His skin flushed and Naomi swallowed. The heat from Matthew radiated through her like rays from an August sun. He licked his lips, stared at Naomi's mouth. "Naomi, I need . . ." He paused and started over. "I need to apologize for last night."

She twisted her head, tearing away from that seductive gaze. "There's no need. I should apologize to you." Shocked at her hammering pulse, she moved back and dropped herself into a chair opposite him. "But I guess there are a few things we should get straight."

She had to think for a moment to recall exactly what they were. "First off, I'm so sorry, Matthew, that you came all this way expecting us to leave with you. I gave you every reason to think we were in desperate straits. I had no idea we'd make friends the way we did. I didn't think it possible in the beginning." But they *had* made friends, with some of the most lost sheep she'd ever known: prostitutes, drunkards, and reprobates.

"You can understand my concern, though, about leaving you here?" he said gently. "I'm in town five minutes and the first man I meet is Charles McIntyre, the most famous *pimp* in the West." He shook his head in disgust. "Now I'm stabbed, and the marshal's bringing in a gunman. This is no place for you girls—" he sucked in a breath through his teeth and grabbed his side. Naomi half-rose from her seat, but he waved her down. "I'm fine. Whatever Doc numbed it with is wearing off."

"Well," clutching her braid, Naomi surveyed the dining room, and then smiled at Matthew. "We don't have to solve any of this today." She took his hand and wished almost immediately she hadn't. It was like holding John's. If she closed her eyes, for one second, and just felt his warmth, it would be a perfect illusion.

Matthew covered her hand with his and waited. His stare held her spellbound. "I'm just glad you're all right, Matthew." The words seemed to have too much weight. "We . . . um, we . . . should eat and you should rest." She pulled away. "I'll go see what's taking so long."

She rushed to get away from him, but stopped just short of bursting into the kitchen. This confusing Matthew with John was treacherous. She wished Charles was back. She needed his touch to remind her she was living in the present before the ghosts from her past could drag her back.

———

*M*oving like his stitches had been sewn with tissue paper, Matthew hooked a foot around another chair and pulled it closer. Holding his breath, he hiked his feet up into it and leaned back a little more in his chair. His side was burning and throbbing, but leaning back helped.

Stupid Ute. If he saw that kid vertical again, he'd kill him. It hadn't escaped Matthew that if he'd been a hair slower, that Injun's Bowie knife could have put a quick end to his wild-and-woolly ways. He hadn't come to Defiance for this, not at all. 'Course it was his own fault for offering to help.

He settled a little deeper into the chair and let his thoughts roam back to Naomi. He could tell she was confused, and that pleased him no end. He'd heard the wobble in her voice, seen her hands shake when she worked on his bandage. He'd sniffed her hair and she hadn't pulled away. Yep, McIntyre didn't have this all sewn up just yet.

Too bad he hadn't been prepared for Mr. Fancy Pants to go riding off with the marshal. He might have been able to plan something with Naomi, like a stroll. As it was, maybe another opportunity would present itself. He could always complain about his side and maneuver her up to his room.

No, that would just scare her. He'd have to do this nice and easy—like John would.

Just like John . . .

CHAPTER 18

*H*ead low to the ground, the horse sniffed and navigated through the carnage with care. Chief Ouray held the reins loosely, sure of his mount's steady temperament. He was also sure who had killed these people. His eyes roamed over the burned bodies, the over-turned, charred wagon, the ransacked trunks. Dead three, maybe four days. Warily, his horse skirted a broken rifle and several shattered jars of peaches lying on the ground. Beside them, a pot sat overturned, its moldy stew spilled in the dirt.

The crease in his brow deepened. A ghostly quiet filled the forest around him. In the camp site, clothes, shoes, frying pans, and tin plates littered the ground. A brass casing glittered in the weeds. Strands of blood-soaked golden hair and a white, bloated hand, fingers frozen in death, beckoned to him from behind a boulder. He wondered why brother wolf or even the vultures had not ventured to this spot. Only evil spirits kept them away.

Or sickness.

So tired of death, he let the horse wander over to the little creek to drink, but jerked the animal's head up when he saw what lay in it. A swollen white man, eyes nearly popping out of his skull, lay chest-down in the water several feet upstream. Head twisted toward Ouray, he stared at the chief with blank, white orbs. Ouray wrinkled his nose in disgust. This settler had messed his pants badly and his body smelled particularly foul. Four arrows protruded from his back like the quills on a porcupine.

Ouray spun his horse away and again surveyed the slaughter. He assumed they had attacked the settlers with the intention of taking spoils. The discovery of the sick man, though, perhaps as he was trying to escape, changed their plans. In fear, had they left everything behind to run?

No, that was not right.

He peered closer at the tracks on the ground, pondered them, and then looked off into the shadowy woods.

They had taken a captive.

---

*H*annah wrapped gently on Doc's door, in case patients inside were sleeping. She waited and momentarily his grizzled face filled the entrance. "Hannah, come in, come in." He opened the door wider and waved her into his front room. "I'm delighted to see you again. You're not here by any chance to do a little more nursing?"

"If you need me." Hannah stepped inside and pointed at the closed bedroom door. "I hear you have a patient. Some kind of fever?"

Doc sighed and shut the door. He ran a tired hand through his shock of grayish blond hair. "A form of food poisoning. Something in the water, most often." His brow creased with puzzlement. "Indians don't get it too much. Usually it's some dumb miner who didn't see the dead elk rotting in the water upstream." He let the puzzle go with a shake of his head. "He's gonna be a sick rascal for a few days. That giant pummeling him in the noggin didn't help matters much either, but I understand they had to subdue him. For now, we just need to keep fluids in the boy. If you're up to nursing him, that is. As I said, he's an Indian." Hannah inclined her head, not sure of the connection. "Some folks might not want to treat one."

"I'm the last person in the world to think I'm better than somebody else."

"I had a notion you might say that. You'll make a good nurse, girl."

The compliment put wings on Hannah's feet. Last December, after the big avalanche, she had helped nurse men for several days. Amidst the suffering and death, a seed had been planted. After praying about it, she had grown even more certain this was something God wanted her to do. Now she was trying to find the path to this dream. She still worked at the hotel because Doc couldn't afford a nurse and she had obligations to her sisters, but she volunteered as much as she could.

Doc handed her a basin of cold water and a rag. "I was about to go in and spend some time with the boy. I bet he'd rather see your pretty, smiling face."

"He doesn't have anything catching that I could take back to Little Billy?"

"Just wash your hands when you leave and you'll be fine." Convinced, Hannah took the items and let herself into Black Elk's room.

"Hannah?" She paused halfway through the door. "If he does wake up, see if you can get any information on where he might have gotten into tainted food or water."

She nodded and entered the room. The Indian lay sleeping on the bed, shirtless, the sheet pulled up to his waist. She set the bowl on the nightstand next to a cup of water. Quietly, she dipped the rag. "Black Elk, can you hear me?" No response. His breathing remained steady, but it sounded shallow. Wringing out the water, she spoke again before touching him with it. "Black Elk, my name is Hannah. Can you hear me?" Carefully, she laid the rag on his forehead and waited a moment. When he didn't stir, she settled into the chair beside the bed.

At liberty to stare, she studied his profile. Strong and proud, skin the color of desert sand, she thought him majestic and rather imposing, even asleep. In a way, she couldn't blame the Indians for hating the white man, but both sides had committed horrific atrocities. Only Jesus could bring peace to such a mess. She closed her eyes and whispered a prayer. A prayer for healing, mercy, and salvation for Black Elk. Courage for her to talk of her faith if he awoke. He couldn't die lost. Perhaps that was why she was sitting in this chair right now.

"Please God," she whispered, "give me the right words to help this man."

Immediately, a still, small voice answered back, *Show him.*

She was startled to realize Black Elk was staring at her. In his brown, almost black, eyes she saw a mix of fear and sadness. "He killed you," the Indian whispered.

What? His voice was weak, his words slightly slurred. She assumed he was delirious. Ignoring the comment, Hannah smiled tenderly and took the rag off his forehead. Aware he was watching her, she dipped it again in the cold spring water. Though he didn't have a high fever, cooling a patient's brow was still a comfort. She replaced the rag, sat down on the edge of the bed and took Black Elk's hand in hers.

"He killed you," he repeated, this time sounding more emphatic.

"No, I'm fine, Black Elk. You must be dreaming."

He sighed and shut his eyes, weakly moving his head from side to side. "People near Horse Mesa."

Hannah bit her lip. Was Black Elk telling her something that had happened a long time ago or recently? She couldn't make sense of it. Tentatively, she asked, "Black Elk, can you tell me what happened?"

For a moment, she thought he hadn't heard or couldn't respond. Finally, he croaked out, "Water."

Hannah reached for the cup. Slipping her hand through his long, black hair to cradle his head, she lifted him up enough to take a sip. Black Elk clutched the cup and took two more weak gulps. His strength used up, he lay back down.

"You have something called Beaver Fever. Do you think you drank some bad water?"

"The stew," he whispered. "The man was sick."

She sat back, unable to pull this together. "A man at Horse Mesa?"

"One-Who-Cries had a vision . . ." Hannah leaned closer, straining to hear his weak voice. "Between here and White River, no whites will be safe."

One-Who-Cries. Emilio had given Hannah a few more details on the renegade. He was a brave known for killing whites any chance he had. He instigated a fight down at the White River Reservation last year reportedly for the sole reason of taking several, hot-blooded braves with him. He'd done it again just recently. She didn't see the connection between any of that and Black Elk. Emilio said the reservation was over one hundred miles away. What in the world was Black Elk talking about?

"We found them next to the creek at Horse Mesa," he continued. "Like you, she was pale, with hair the color of the sun." He sighed, as if resigned to his story's ending. "She shouldn't have fought . . . but we took her sister."

Took her sister? Goosebumps raced over Hannah's arms. "Black Elk, if you attacked some white folks, why are you in Defiance?" Realizing a life in addition to Black Elk's might be hanging in the balance, she leaned even closer and placed her hand lightly on his chest. Keeping the panic from her voice, she asked, "Were you with One-Who-Cries? Where is he? Where's the girl?"

Black Elk's eyes closed as he drifted off to sleep again.

CHAPTER 19

*B*y dusk, Billy finally managed to coax Hannah into a walk with him. They started out behind the hotel and ambled up a path along the stream. He shoved his hands into his pockets and marveled over the scenery here. He'd seen the Swiss Alps as a kid, but the Rocky Mountains were grander, more colorful. He paused to take in the ring of craggy mountains that surrounded the town, the snow on top of the peaks turning various shades of purple and pink as the sun set. The mountains were covered in patchwork forests, but the lower portions, and much of the valley, had been timbered heavily for buildings and firewood. Trees sprouted here and there on the valley floor, and, oddly, the ones that remained were all twenty and thirty feet high. He wondered randomly if, perhaps, they'd been left for shade.

A gunshot from somewhere on the other side of Defiance echoed through the valley and made the question irrelevant.

Hannah stopped a few paces ahead of him and waited, staring off at the mountains in the opposite direction. She had her pink wool shawl pulled around so tightly, Billy thought she might manage to cut herself in two with it.

"So, when did you get the idea to become a nurse?" he asked, making small talk, biding his time.

"We had an avalanche here last winter. It was horrible. They brought men to the hotel broken to bits." She hunched her shoulders as if the memory made her shiver. "I don't know. It planted a seed, I guess. I want to help, and sometimes Doc gets overwhelmed. Just the fights in Tent Town can send him three or four patients at once."

"You'd be a good nurse." Billy meant it. Hannah had a tender side. She cared for people, and now she struck him as strong enough to deal with the blood and guts without fainting. He was amazed how much she'd grown up and she hadn't even turned seventeen yet.

The compliment failed to turn her around. Billy exhaled, ruffling the hair over his eyes. This was like trying to break through granite. "Hannah." She turned only slightly and met his gaze through her long, dark lashes. The sunset washed her in a magic orange hue. A loose strand of hair shimmered next to her face like a flame. He would have given the world to walk up and kiss her senseless. In danger of losing his self-control, he stared at his boots and scratched the back of his head. Maybe the best thing to do here was just get it all said. "Hannah, I've decided I'm not going anywhere."

She spun around to face him with a defiant, maybe suspicious, tilt to her chin. "And that should mean what to me?"

"Ah, shoot, Hannah." Billy kicked a small rock and wandered over to the stream. She was cold and distant, but he knew, just *knew*, there was still a spark there. "Why do you have to make this so hard?"

"Me?" she practically yelped.

Billy flinched. In his mind, he could see her stance change. Her hand was lodged on her hip, a sure sign she was as mad as a wet hen.

"You have no idea what *hard* is. I stood before our entire

congregation with your daddy staring daggers at me from the back pew." His head jerked up. "Do you know what they said to me? Did you ever hear?"

Heat raced up his neck, flushed his cheeks. He was ashamed to admit he'd never even asked.

"They called me a floozy and a trollop."

Her voice broke over the last word and he wanted to kill himself for having brought that on her.

"Even the people who defended me," he heard her sniff, "they sounded so disappointed in me."

What had he done to this girl? Shocked over the scorched remains that used to be the most beautiful soul in his world, Billy slowly turned to her. He drank in the shining blue eyes pooling with tears, loose golden braid running down her shoulder, soft pink lips that used to say his name with breathlessness.

"You *should* hate me," he said, realizing for the first time how bad it had been for her. Her chin trembled and she looked down. "I am so sorry, Hannah. I want you to know, I would die before I would ever hurt you like that again." But he knew, to her, these were just words—more words from Billy the Coward. She lowered her head and stared at the ground.

He walked over to her, clutched her shoulders, but she kept her eyes averted. "Look at me, Hannah." He wanted to shake her when she didn't budge, but held back. "*Look* at me." Hesitantly, she lifted her gaze to his. "You don't want to give me a second chance? Fine. I'll *earn* it. No matter how long it takes, no matter what I have to do, I'm not giving up on you and my son."

Every muscle in her face quivered like it was fighting for control. He'd betrayed her and destroyed her trust. Billy wished he could heal her, would do or give anything to try. His voice softened as he loosened his grip. "Even if you marry that greaser, I'm never running out on you again."

Hannah's eyes bugged and her mouth worked soundlessly for a second until she found her voice. "*Greaser?*" She blinked. "You mean Emilio?" She stepped back, wrenching free of his grip, and raised her fists at him. "Oh, if I was a man . . . I would beat some sense into you." Practically growling, she dropped her arms to her sides as if forcibly restraining the temptation. "Haven't your prejudices done enough damage? Money, education, and now skin color. There sure are a lot of requirements for your club."

Billy reached out to her, well aware he'd messed up again. "Hannah—"

"Don't *Hannah* me." She waved an agitated finger at him. "And don't ever call Emilio that again." She turned, took two quick steps, but something drew her up short. She spun back around on him, eyes storming like the North Atlantic in November. "Maybe that's exactly what you need. Maybe you do need to stay here for a while." She started to add something, but shook her head in disgust, whirled around and stomped back to the hotel.

Billy slapped his hand to his forehead. Was he never going to get this right? He'd caused her more hurt than he could ever imagine. Now she was as skittish of him as a scalded dog. Add to that all the aristocratic—no, be honest—*arrogant* attitudes of the Page family and he would be lucky if Hannah ever even prayed for him. Was there any coming back from this?

Keep swinging.

Lean not unto your own understanding.

Uninvited, Earp's words nagged at him not to give up. And the Scripture urged him to relinquish control. Unable to reconcile the contrasts, he picked up a smooth, round rock and lobbed it hard into the water.

---

*H*annah shut the door behind her and leaned back on it. A sob threatened to tear loose, but she wrestled it back into the shadows of her heart. Billy made her so mad and terrified her at the same time. She hated feeling this way, like trees tangled and broken after a storm. Heart aching, she hugged herself and let a few insistent tears escape.

Oh, God, can I believe anything he says? Has he changed? The vicious insults from her church family tore at her brain, keeping the betrayal raw. She knew it was wrong to hang on to it, but her disappointment in Billy ran soul-deep. *Help me to forgive him for putting me through that, Lord. I thought I had, but I haven't, God, and that's wrong.*

Like a soothing balm, the Lord brought to mind the face of her beloved son, the peace in Mollie's soul, and the warmth of her friendship with Emilio. Rebecca had finally stored away her grief over Ben and Gracie's death and shone like a new penny around Ian. Naomi had gone through a remarkable change, letting go of so much anger and rebellion, and Mr. McIntyre was working his way down the straight and narrow. God had worked many, many things for good. Things that, without her sin and Billy's betrayal, would most likely have never happened.

"I trust You, Father," she whispered with determination. "I trust You." *Please help me to forgive him, and, please, may he find out how much You love him.*

CHAPTER 20

*M*cIntyre leaned forward in the saddle and watched with admiration as Emilio studied the ground. He couldn't see beneath the ragged tan hat, but McIntyre could tell he was concentrating. Turned out, the boy was a fine tracker. He hadn't lost Betts's trail once in two days. He was leading them right to the outlaw's front door, wherever that was.

"They're still together," Emilio said, squatting to better study the ground. He tucked a strand of black hair behind his ear and nodded. "One of their horses threw a shoe."

Beckwith nodded in approval of the boy's skill. "They'll have to stop and fix that." He studied the forest of aspens around them. "Any kind of homestead or settlement nearby?"

McIntyre pointed with his chin. "Less than a mile. An abandoned miner's cabin. The trail forks in about half a mile." He resituated the reins in his hand, ready to ride. "If they went to the cabin, their tracks will turn right. Either way, we're about to catch up with them."

It didn't take long.

Long, eerie shadows stretched silently through the woods like the fingers of dead men. Gun drawn, McIntyre peered through the underbrush and pines at the small, dilapidated cabin. He heard no sounds except for the trickle of a nearby creek and the soft song of evening crickets. No voices. No clattering dishes. He noted, too, that no smoke puffed from the chimney and there weren't any horses in the corral. Frustrated, he studied the dark windows for movement inside.

Nothing. Still as a graveyard.

After several minutes of waiting, he heard Beckwith shift positions. McIntyre tried to smother his irritation. Here he was, sitting in the woods, apparently on a wild goose chase, while Matthew was probably enjoying the sisters' gushing ministrations. He could see the man, sitting by the fire, feet propped up on a chair and a pillow, Naomi handing him a cup of coffee.

He bit back a growl.

Emilio said the tracks went straight to the cabin, but maybe the men rode out the other side, aware that the determined posse was gaining on them. Finding out could be downright dicey. Huffing softly, McIntyre glanced quickly at the men on either side of him. One hard-scrabble marshal, two brave—but untested— boys. He couldn't keep doing this. The men in Defiance were going to have to step up, despite being nothing but a bunch of tough-talking blowhards. Always ready for a good lynching, their blustery chatter died to a whisper if there was the possibility a real fight might be involved—

All at once, glass shattered, the earsplitting explosions of rifle fire and a .44 reverberated over them, and a dull thump hit his hat. Reacting to the shrapnel, McIntyre ducked behind a slender pine and aimed his gun at the cabin. More glass shattered in the dwelling and guns blazed simultaneously from both groups in rapid, thundering succession. Bullets and smoke filled the air. Lead hit the pine next to McIntyre, showering him with bark. He changed his position again, taking cover more to the right and behind a larger tree.

A white puff of smoke wafted away from the outhouse and he

realized that was the location of the .44. He yelled at Beckwith over the gunfire, "There's one in the outhouse!" Beckwith, revolver in one hand, rifle in the other, nodded and charged for a group of aspens closer to the lone building. McIntyre alternated shots at the cabin and the outhouse to give the lawman cover.

A flutter of movement behind a bedraggled curtain tipped McIntyre off. He fired and heard a scream.

First blood. A psychological victory for the posse.

"George Betts, this is Marshal Beckwith!"

McIntyre looked over. The marshal, standing behind a fat aspen, holstered the revolver and shoved bullets into the rifle with smooth, unhurried moves. "I've got a warrant for your arrest for horse stealing." Emilio and Wade stopped firing and tucked in tighter behind their trees. The return fire petered out and an eerie hush fell over the group. The outlaws were listening. "And now I've got cause to bring in your friends." Beckwith lifted his hat and used his forearm to wipe away sweat. The determined set of his jaw as he replaced the Stetson told McIntyre the marshal was through wasting time. "Surrender now and I won't press charges for attempting to kill an officer of the law and his deputies!" Not even the crickets risked an answer. "I will not make the offer twice!" Beckwith reached for his Colt, but a thoughtful expression crossed his stern face. Changing his tact, he leveled the Sharps Carbine on the outhouse.

In the pristine silence, McIntyre thought he heard, from behind the outhouse's plank door, the click-click of a rotating cylinder as an unseen hand pulled back on a hammer. Beckwith reacted to the sound and fired the Sharps. A deafening explosion like cannon fire rumbled through the woods, rattling the windows in the cabin. The bullet ripped through the outhouse door and shards of wood exploded out the back. McIntyre was sure he had seen a spray of blood mixed with the shrapnel.

Silence followed on the heels of the fading shot. "That was George," Beckwith hollered at the cabin, "you boys next?"

The Sharps shortened the outlaws' decision-making process considerably. "We're coming out, Marshal." A rifle flew out the window, thudding on the pine straw. "We ain't wanted for anything and we don't want to make this worse than it already is."

*A*s Beckwith and Wade handcuffed the two men, Emilio and McIntyre draped George Betts over the outlaw's horse. A grim duty. The Sharps had left a mangled, bloody mess of the man's head. McIntyre needed to find a feed sack or something to cover him. It was the decent thing to do.

"Mr. McIntyre . . . your hat."

McIntyre glanced across the saddle at Emilio, puzzled by his breathless voice and the shock reflected in his face. He realized the boy was staring wide-eyed at his Stetson. He snatched the hat off his head. He turned the Stetson around and poked his finger clean through a bullet hole, a perfect circle not an inch above his scalp. A tremor shot through his gut.

The thump he'd felt.

Close calls had never bothered him before. But now, staring at the empty space where black felt should have been, all he could think about was Naomi. If things had played out differently, it could well be him decorating this saddle and he'd kissed the woman a grand total of three times. Worse, he had never even said *I love you*. Three words that, when spoken in earnest, meant a man was willing to accept a permanent change in his life.

A fancy education doesn't clean somebody like you up, though. The kind of man you are.

McIntyre tried to ignore Matthew's words as he placed the hat back on his head and finished tending to Betts. Holding his expression still and his reaction hidden, he passed Emilio the end of a rope. "Tie his feet. Pass the rope back to me underneath."

Why, I bet there isn't a man in the West who doesn't know your name.

But not before you drag Naomi and maybe her sisters through your mud?

As McIntyre secured Betts to the saddle, Matthew's accusations and his own self-doubt nagged at him. He hated wondering if he was really good enough for her.

The bullet hole in his hat meant something. He had told Naomi once that God had gone to a lot of trouble to bring her to Defiance, to him. And now God had saved him from a bullet that had very nearly parted his skull. The only reason he could think of was Naomi. To love her. Honor her. Share his life with her.

He pondered Betts, dead as driftwood, and decided. Matthew notwithstanding, it was time to propose.

———

*T*he young woman marched with such purpose toward the doors of the Iron Horse Saloon that Naomi drew up. Curious, she peered through moving, bobbing shoulders on the boardwalk and watched. The girl grabbed the doorknob, shoved against it. It didn't open and she stepped back, dropping a hand on her hip in obvious frustration. A pretty thing with strawberry-blonde hair piled atop her head, she wore a faded but stylish red dress, tailored too tightly and cut too low. In her left hand, she clutched a fraying carpet valise.

Naomi swallowed. A summer dove?

Jealousy turned her arms and legs to rubber, and made her stomach churn. Feeling nauseous, she forced her feet to move her body toward the girl, rather than across the street to the mercantile.

Dreading the conversation, Naomi slowly approached her. "Are you looking for—?"

"Charles McIntyre." The woman turned, her stance screaming

her irritation. "They told me he'd closed this place, but I didn't believe it." She spoke with a heavy accent. French, Naomi guessed, and laced with displeasure. "That doesn't leave me no place but Tent Town now."

"So, you're a . . .?"

"Flower? *Oui*. Summers only. The rest of the year I prefer to bloom in New Orleans." The woman switched the valise to her other hand and assessed Naomi top to bottom. Her expression, initially reserved like a bored housecat, changed to disapproval. "You his current?"

"I'm sorry?"

The woman frowned, as if Naomi was stupid, and spoke more slowly. "Are you keeping him company or is the position open? Anything would be better than Tent Town."

Naomi struggled to sort through her feelings about this woman and her question. Stumbling about mentally, she said, "I am his special friend." The absurd answer made her want to crawl under a rock. "I mean, we are—"

"Whatever, honey," the woman dismissed her with an impatient wave. Turning to the street, she studied the traffic and tapped her fingers restlessly on her leg. "I don't care. I need to get settled for a few days so it's not a wasted trip. Broken Spoke still open?"

Jealousy and insecurities scrambled Naomi's brain, but love nudged her, insistently . . . *annoyingly*. She took a deep breath and raised her chin. "You don't have to do that." The words nearly choked her. The woman swung her head around, narrow eyes showing surprise and suspicion.

Oh, God, give me the strength to do the right thing, though it's as bitter as gall. "I own a hotel. You could stay there . . . for free. You wouldn't have to do . . . that kind of work."

The woman twirled slowly to Naomi and once again appraised her, but with deliberation this time. Momentarily, her face lit up. "You're one of them Hallelujah Army people aren't you? God, and

Jesus, and all that? Well, no thanks, *ma chèrie*, I'll stick with the sinners." She winked, "they have more fun."

Finished with Naomi, the girl picked up her skirt and stepped into the street.

Right and wrong, love and hate warred in Naomi. She didn't want to see this woman go, but at the same time, she was relieved she was going. The guilt of such a selfish thought stung. What if she'd rushed Lily, Jasmine or Iris out of town? Truth was, this gal had no idea what she was walking away from. Why *wouldn't* she want a chance to change her life? What made these soiled doves so resentful of the gospel?

And how many times would Naomi have to go through this? Standing up to the women who would reject her and her God, but not her man?

Would living as a believer in Defiance ever get easier? And if she called herself that, then she had to put feet on her faith. If she couldn't stop the woman, she could at least pray for her. Frustrated enough to kick something, Naomi called, "What's your name?"

Throwing her arms out to the side, the woman whirled gaily between horses passing in opposite directions. "Amaryllis!" Without missing a step, she continued her march across the busy street.

* * *

aomi tried not to stare as Matthew devoured his fifth piece of fried chicken. An empty platter on her hip, she scanned the dining room. One lone gentleman, a well-dressed representative from a mining conglomerate, and a few scruffy miners, finished off the dinner rush. Slow enough for her to rest a moment.

Smiling, she sat down opposite her clearly starving brother-in-law. "I take it today's menu meets with your approval?" The Miller boys had always been able to pack in stunning amounts of food. Matthew had slept away one whole day recovering from his wound, and now polished off his meal like a bear coming out of hibernation.

"You have no idea," he said, licking his fingers with enthusiasm, "how I have missed Rebecca's cooking."

Naomi recalled more than a few church picnics where men were almost willing to fight over her sister's chicken. Here, they were willing to fight over women like Amaryllis.

The cheerfulness of the thought must have shown. "What's wrong, Naomi," Matthew asked gently. "Or is that a stupid question?"

She shifted anxiously in the seat. The last thing she wanted was to tell Matthew that women had started coming into town to see Charles. She didn't think she could stand another sermon on the evils of pimps and brothels. Forcing down her somber mood, she pasted on a weak smile. "We're just a little behind on the cooking is all. Seems we have some hearty appetites in the hotel."

Matthew chuckled but Naomi had the sense he was merely being polite. Absently tracing the pattern engraved in the butter knife, he asked, "Do you remember the time John and I tried to blow that stump out of Pa's pasture?"

Relieved to have a new subject, she giggled, remembering well the colossal amount of dynamite the brothers had used. "When you shoved an *entire* box of TNT underneath the roots?"

They both started laughing, drawing surprised glances from the customers. "Lord, Naomi, that explosion rattled windows all the way into Raleigh." He grabbed his side, laughing and flinching at the same time. "I thought Pa was gonna kill us. And we were deaf for a week."

"And do you remember," Naomi slapped her leg, her voice rolling with laughter, "the stump blew straight up about forty feet—"

"—And came back down in the exact same spot," he finished.

By now, Matthew was wiping tears out of his eyes and the guests were staring openly. "Took a team of six horses to drag the monster out of the ground. Pa didn't let us near dynamite for a year."

"And the paper reported it as an earthquake." They both guffawed over that, holding their sides and gasping for breath. After a several more seconds, the laughter faded grudgingly and Naomi shook her head, trying to regain her composure. "How old were we?"

"Thirteen." A half-smile played around his lips. "Just about the time we started getting into all kinds of trouble." He wiggled his eyebrows. "Remember your first kiss?"

Naomi felt the blush spread like a wildfire. Embarrassed, she rose and started clearing a table. "We don't need to remember those particular moments, Matthew." Yes, she had started out on a trail leading to him, but thankfully, John had changed her direction. "Especially since nothing came of them."

"I always wondered if you just got confused somehow, seeing as how we looked so much alike."

Scraping and stacking plates, she kept her back to him. "Exactly, Matthew. You two *looked* alike. I had to look deeper to see the differences."

She heard his fingers tapping on the table. "Explain it to me again, Naomi. Why John? Why did you pick him over me?"

That was almost like asking someone to explain the differences between Cain and Abel. She didn't wish to be ugly, though. "He loved me and always put me first. As I recall, with you I was about, what, fourth down the line? Behind Virginia Clark, Jim Beam and a game of Faro."

"That's a little unfair, don't you think?"

"No." Listing the differences between the two brothers brought focus back into her heart, made her stronger. She turned to Matthew, pointing at him with a dirty fork. "John loved me. You just wanted a prize on your arm."

"Only at first, Naomi. True, everything *was* a competition between him and me—"

"You hated losing."

"But I grew out of that."

"Not until it was too late." The afternoon was waning fast and she noticed a chill creeping into the room. Buying time to sort her thoughts, Naomi walked over and tossed a few pieces of wood into the fireplace. "Or I suppose it would be fair to say *almost* too late. You and John reconciled. We were all eager to see you and start over." Trying not to ignore the customers, she grabbed a pitcher of buttermilk from the kitchen's serving counter and offered to refill their drinks. They thanked her but waved her off.

"I'd bet dollars to dumplings you made him write that first letter."

"You'd be right." Naomi set the pitcher back on the shelf, but stayed there for a moment, watching Ian and Rebecca starting the clean-up work in the kitchen. She wondered where Charles and Emilio were, but tried not to worry. She strode back over to the table where she'd left her platter, piled high with dishes "I told John you were probably too ashamed to ask for forgiveness, but either way, he had to give it."

"I don't know if *I* would be inclined to forgive a man who pawed at my wife on our wedding night."

"You were drunk."

"A drunk man's tongue speaks a sober man's mind," he said, his voice filled with regret.

Naomi didn't respond. The things Matthew said that night, that he loved her and hated John, that he would kill him for stealing Naomi, they were all too dark to dwell on. Matthew reached out and wrapped his big, masculine fingers around her wrist. "I don't drink anymore, Naomi." His voice was low and husky. "I got a handle on my temper. I'm not my brother, but I'm a better man than I was."

"We were all so young then, ruled by our passions." She tried to ignore the warmth of his hand. "I'm just glad those weren't the last words he ever heard from you." She tugged away from him and turned toward the kitchen.

"But I ripped your gown. I've always been sorry for that."

Naomi stopped. Matthew's apology released a flood of memories. One, in particular, leapt from its grave.

On her wedding night, as the last of the guests filtered out of the parsonage, Naomi snuck around back to her family's wagon. Careful not to snag her gown, she reached over the wagon side for her valise. While her parents had moved some of her things to John's farm, this bag held clothes appropriate for a *special* night.

Smiling to herself, she turned and discovered the looming silhouette of John watching her. A slight spring breeze, though, carried the smell of liquor, correcting her guess. "Matthew." She was vaguely uneasy at being alone with him. All through the wedding and the reception she'd caught him watching her with an angry flame in his eyes. She suspected the cause, but wouldn't deal with it now.

She clutched the valise in front of her. "Did you enjoy the ceremony and the reception?"

"It was a sight to behold, that's for sure. Kind of funny, I was the best man but you married my brother." His tone was sharp and mean. Matthew only got snide like this when shored up by a little alcohol. Refusing to let him spoil her mood, she moved to step past him. His big hand snaked out and caught her arm. "We didn't have a dance yet, Naomi."

She huffed, wishing he'd learn to handle his liquor. Still, there was something different in his meanness tonight, something . . . dangerous. "Fine. Let's go inside and take one last spin around the floor."

"What's the matter with right here?"

With the grace and strength of a drunken bull, Matthew knocked the valise out of the way and snatched Naomi up against him. Furious, she pushed at his chest, but his arms held her in place like a vice. "Let me go right now, Matthew."

Roaring with laughter, he threw his head back and spun Naomi like she was a rag doll in his arms. Then he staggered to a stop. Swaying on his feet, he stared down at her. The weak crescent moon couldn't veil the desire in his face, and it made her uneasy.

"Matthew, I said, let me go!"

"No . . ." One arm tightened around her like a band of iron. He wagged his finger at her. "No, I think I should get one good kiss before you ride off with my brother."

I'd rather kiss a rattlesnake.

She was too close to get in a good strike, but she slapped Matthew with everything she had in her. Stunned, he dropped her and Naomi lunged for the parsonage, fighting her voluminous silk skirt. Matthew snatched at her shoulder, his fingers digging into the material. She heard the ripping, screeching sound of silk tearing and he pulled her again into his beefy arms. She fought harder, praying she wouldn't have to scream, but when his lips came down on hers, smothering her, she knew she had no choice.

As she turned her head away to find that scream, the huge, hulking figure of John sailed through the night, slamming her and Matthew to the ground. A hand clutched futilely at Naomi's bodice, but she scrambled away, leaving tattered lace in Matthew's hands.

Tangled in her billowing skirt, arms pin-wheeling, she clambered to her feet. Behind her, fists pounded on flesh and bone. Thuds and grunts filled the night. Matthew and John writhed, rolled, and spun madly on the ground, growling and swiping at each other like wolves fighting to the death. Gasping for breath, Naomi sought safety behind the horse harnessed to their wagon. Stuck watching the brawl, she wondered desperately where she could a get a gun to stop it.

"I'll kill you! I'll kill you!" Matthew bellowed. "You stole her from me!"

They rolled, and John sat atop Matthew, banging his head into the ground with each word he growled. "Touch her again and I *will* kill *you!*"

Matthew bucked, managing to pull his legs up between them and then pushed with the force of an ornery mule. John went flying backwards, crashing into the wagon. The side rail creaked and groaned with the impact as a loud grunt escaped him. He bounced off the wagon and landed in the grass face down. Both men, wearily, staggered to their feet. Chests heaving, coats hanging in shreds, they squared off and raised their fists again.

"No!" Naomi burst out from behind the horse in a cloud of white silk and positioned herself between the two men. "You have to stop this!" The moonlight revealed their sorry state. Torn frocks, disheveled hair, bloodied noses, all because of her. Livid, she squeezed her hands into tight fists and raised them in front of her. "Just. Stop. It."

The three stood there, pain and rage circulating around them like the dust from a stampede. She had more to say but the cool night breeze kissed her naked shoulder. Embarrassed, Naomi tried to pull the ripped sleeve and bodice back up over her exposed flesh, but the dress wouldn't stay. The torn satin was beyond repair. Her throat squeezed tightly with unexpected emotion. John stepped over to her and gently folded her in his arms. She collapsed against him, shocked by the tears that gushed forth.

"He tore my dress," she whispered in a choked voice, but what she meant was that Matthew had truly frightened her. Naomi felt John's body tighten into cold steel.

"I'm sorry, Naomi," Matthew said, sounding horrified. "I'm so sorry. I can't believe I'm losing you—"

"Lost." John straightened. "You've lost her. Now you should leave, Matthew. Go someplace very far away." John had an edge in his voice Naomi had never heard before. It was cold like the grave. "Go someplace I can't find you."

The last words John ever spoke to his brother.

The memory chilled Naomi. She swallowed, surprised by how dry her mouth had become. No wonder she hadn't thought about that night in years. Matthew had left her feeling violated, and, oddly, ashamed, as if his behavior had been her fault. For a while, she'd hated him for causing the twisted emotions. But John had loved her and supported her, helped her let go of feelings that hurt only her. That was why she had eventually encouraged him to reconcile with his brother. Both of them had needed the freedom of forgiveness.

She shook off the memory and turned to Matthew. "I forgave you a long time ago."

"I've thought about you every day, Naomi. Every single day." A veil dropped and his eyes revealed everything in his heart. "I've never stopped loving you, not for one single second."

CHAPTER 21

*N*aomi yawned and stretched and enjoyed the church-like quiet of the main street at 6:00 am. A shroud of fog lay over the tops of the buildings, muffling the sounds of people stirring and horses neighing. She'd spent a miserable, sleepless night tossing and turning. Midnight thoughts of Matthew's declaration intertwined with hazy dreams of John and Charles. She'd floated in and out of memories and teetered on the edge of consciousness all night long, sometimes not knowing where the dreams ended and reality began.

In the light of day, things weren't much clearer. John felt too near with Matthew around. The more she saw of him, the more she *needed* to see Charles. Where was he? What had he and Emilio gotten themselves into with the marshal?

Taking a sip of her coffee, she nodded as Sarah and Silas Madden rolled up in their wagon, punctual as usual. The short, rotund Sarah made the best pastries Naomi had ever tasted. Meeting her at the bakery had been a true Godsend. The girls had all just about reached the level of cooking they could handle and were feeling overwhelmed. Sarah came by twice a week now and dropped off pies, bread, cakes, and a few dozen cinnamon rolls.

"Good morning, Sarah. Good morning, Silas."

Sarah's husband, as skinny as his wife was plump, nodded and removed his hat. "Good morning, Miss Naomi."

Naomi smiled, always amused by Silas's bald head. So smooth it shined. He set the brake and leaped down from the wagon with the agility of a much younger man. "Come on, dumplin'." He raised a hand to help his wife down. Naomi sauntered around to the back of the wagon. Cloth-covered trays and baskets filled the space. She sighed as the scent of fresh sourdough bread and apple turnovers wafted through the air, warm and fresh and mouth-watering.

"I've brought you some extra things, Miss Naomi," Sarah waddled up beside her. "Silas and I have to go work on our place in the valley. Our son and his family are coming in from Missouri. I have to clean up for them, so I won't be back again until *next* week."

"Oh? I thought you lived here in town."

"Part-time." Silas came up on the other side of Naomi and reached for a box of something that smelled like cinnamon and apples. "We've got us a small spread about halfway between here and Silverton. Being part owners in the bakery in town was sort of an afterthought. Sarah has always enjoyed making her pastries."

Sarah took the box of pies from her husband. "I like the farm but it's isolated, so we split our time. We have a boy out there who takes care of things. In return, we let him pan our creeks."

Naomi hefted a small tray up on her arm, careful not to spill her precious coffee. "Well, we're very grateful for your baked goods, Sarah." She swung her tray around. "I hope you hurry back."

*A*t McIntyre's insistence, Beckwith's posse rode all night under a three-quarter moon to get back to Defiance by daybreak. Only a few early risers were on the street as the lawmen, outlaws tied and in tow, trotted toward the marshal's office. McIntyre yawned as daylight lightened his grogginess but did nothing for his body. Every muscle and bone ached.

He had to admire the marshal. A good twenty years older, the man never stopped, never even slowed down, and rode his horse like he'd been born to the saddle. Almost three days riding and McIntyre didn't think the lawman was any the worse for wear.

He, on the other hand, wanted coffee, a bath, his bed, and Naomi. Not in that order, either, but with the ghost-of-husband-past lurking around the hotel, he felt compelled to clean himself up. He touched the brim of his hat to Beckwith, and he and Emilio trotted on down the street.

Tired of posting, he pulled his horse back to a walk and rested in the saddle. The livery stable was on the other end of town, past the hotel. He desperately wanted to stop in and see Naomi, but he wasn't presentable. To confirm this, he rubbed his jaw and the stubble grazed his hand like sandpaper. Ahead of him about a hundred yards, he saw her and the Maddens unloading the baked goods. Arms full, they disappeared inside.

Something hit Charles at that moment. There weren't any words to describe it. Just a *knowing*—he had to ask her to marry him.

Now. Because I might not ever have another chance. He rode up to the wagon to wait and was surprised that in spite of his resolve, those infernal butterflies surfaced again.

"One of Mees Sarah's turnovers sure sounds good about now."

McIntyre nodded absently at Emilio's comment, as his attention was focused on the front door. He realized he had a death grip on his reins and flexed his fingers.

"Can I put your horse away for you, Mr. McIntyre?"

"No, thank you, Emilio." McIntyre dismounted, frustrated by the stiffness in his body. He felt more like fifty-six than thirty-six. Rubbing his right leg, the pain there a reminder of Chickamauga, he jerked his thumb toward the livery. "I'll be along directly."

Emilio nodded and he and Cochise trotted off. After a few minutes, Silas, Sarah and Naomi stepped back outside. Naomi counted out some cash as she walked. "Two, three, four . . ." The group stopped on the boardwalk. As she handed Sarah the money, she saw him. Dusty, wrinkled, and stubbly, he knew he could pass for something the cat had dragged in, but Naomi's face lit up.

The morning sun glinted off stray strands of her hair, threads of spun gold wafting in the morning breeze. Her eyes, the green of a spring pasture, sparkled at him. Her soft lips, curved into a brilliant smile, inviting his kisses. She was, without a doubt, the most beautiful woman he'd ever seen. He forced down a grin and tried to maintain the proper air of manly stoicism, but the grin persisted. He'd done it. She was looking at him with the same glow she'd had for John once before.

Silas and Sarah shared a knowing glance and chuckled. "Well, Sarah," Silas scratched his ear, "I reckon we should be going."

"Oh," Naomi shifted her attention back to the couple. "I'm sorry. Thank you again. I'll see you next week."

As Naomi took a step down off the boardwalk toward McIntyre, he wrapped the reins around the hitching post and waited for her. The way she radiated joy and love did him in. He could have stood there and basked in the warmth of her gaze forever.

He wanted to kiss her in the worst way, in a most ungentlemanly way, but he would stand down. Still, he couldn't help half-yearning for the days when carnal thoughts of Naomi were as guilt-free as breathing. But for now, even if it killed him, he would treat her like a princess. He would prove to her, Matthew, and himself, that he was a changed man, a better man who could finally value purity.

"Where have you been? I've been worried."

The tenderness in her voice startled him. The only other time she'd spoken to him like that, they'd both thought he was dying. "Beckwith needed riders. I asked Matthew to tell you."

McIntyre would have interpreted the V in her brow as an expression of unease, except she smoothed it away with a brush of her hand before he could be sure. "He couldn't recall what had happened to you. He said he was busy getting stitches."

Eyes locked, they drifted toward each other, as if pulled by a magnetic force. Only the hitching post separated them but McIntyre found the distance maddening. She gripped the post and he placed his hands on the wood right beside hers, not touching her. He breathed in the aroma of fresh, warm bread and lilac soap, truly intoxicating scents. "Naomi, the other night, I was going to ask you something."

"Yes." She looked coyly up at him through long, sultry lashes.

He charted the blue flecks amidst the jade, committing them to memory. But he wasn't going to live on memory anymore. He cleared his throat and sought divine guidance for the words about to come out of his mouth. *Lord, make me eloquent.* "I've always been a man who knew his own mind. I know what I want and I endeavor to go after it."

"I wouldn't argue with that."

"Yes, well," he cleared his throat again. He touched her cheek and blurted out, "Will you marry me, Naomi?"

She smirked at the question. "Charles, you told me once that I'm as tough as some men you know. Still, I can be as prissy as any woman. I don't think a marriage proposal should be a joke."

While she had a point, he was somewhat surprised at her cavalier attitude about this and dropped his hand. "You think I'm joking? Believe it or not, your highness, I have a good reason for asking now, at this very moment." He took off his hat and poked his index finger through the bullet hole.

She gasped. "What in the world?" She touched the hat, then his head, as if to make sure his scalp was still intact. "Are you all right?"

"I'm fine. More than fine." He replaced the hat and tilted it back, wondering how to go about this without sounding like a drunk, lovesick cowboy, yet get her to take him seriously. "I was going to get down on one knee in front of everyone, and that was still my plan, until this." He glanced up at his hat and shook his head in disgust. "I could have died yesterday chasing a worthless horse thief and you would have never known how I feel." Her raised brow wasn't the reaction he wanted, either, so he softened his voice. "And I'm not taking another step away from you until you do know."

Judging by the shine in her eyes, McIntyre thought he was on the right track. He brought her hands to his lips and kissed her fingers. "God still has a lot of work to do in me, Naomi. I think we've established that. But without you, I don't see the point. I can't waste any more time. Do me the honor of becoming my wife . . . please."

She wove her fingers in with his. "Say you love me. You realize you've said everything *but* that."

"Don't you realize that's *all* I've been saying? Nevertheless . . ." He bowed slightly in agreement and enunciated the words. "I. Love. You."

She closed her eyes, as if absorbing the words. "I love you, too, Charles, and I will marry you. Even though you are still a work in progress."

Naomi rose up on her tiptoes expecting a kiss but McIntyre pulled his head back. "Are you sure? You're ready to move on? If there are reservations about me or ghosts from our pasts . . ."

He thought perhaps a fleeting shadow of something darker passed over her expression, but she nodded. "I love you. We'll be all right."

Dog-tired, he still found the strength to reach down and sweep her over the hitching post, drawing a gasp and a giggle from her.

He held her in his arms and grinned. All kinds of ideas and images, mixed with an amazing sense of contentment, rocketed through him as he leaned in to seal the bargain. They both eagerly deepened the kiss, but he jerked back and dropped her to her feet when plodding hoofbeats intruded. Hands still on Naomi's waist, he glanced at the passing rider. A ragged, dirty miner tipped his hat and slowed down to watch the show.

McIntyre met the man's gaze and showed his disapproval with one raised brow. The man kicked his horse back to a faster clip. But not fast enough. McIntyre wanted to kick himself for putting Naomi in such a compromising situation right there on the street.

"This won't do for your reputation, Mrs. Miller." He stepped a respectable distance back and swept off his hat. "With your permission, I can have the Reverend here in a few days."

"A few days?"

The dismay in her voice dragged his soaring mood back to earth. "Three at the most. It's that or we have to wait at least six weeks. He's the circuit preacher, remember? He'll be moving out of the area."

Naomi crossed her arms and chewed nervously on a thumbnail. Her gaze flitted around the street. "But a few days. Matthew will still be here."

She hadn't actually aimed the comment at him, he thought, but McIntyre wasn't of a mind to ignore it, either. "Why is that a problem?"

Never since he had met Naomi had he seen her act evasively as she was now. She shifted, backed up to the hitching post. Her eyes darted everywhere on the street and he thought she might bite off that thumbnail. Momentarily, his drilling, impatient stare brought her back to him.

She rolled a shoulder. "Matthew expressed . . . some affection for me—that I don't return—but I don't wish for him to leave on bad terms. This could certainly cause some hard feelings."

Rising irritation stoked a fire in McIntyre. Matthew's

hypocrisy was along the lines of epic. McIntyre wasn't good enough for Naomi, but a whiskey-swilling, lying lumberjack was? He found Naomi's concern for Matthew's feelings more than a little annoying as well.

"I see." He knew a wise man would retreat at this moment. Get a bath and some sleep. He was tired and not feeling very wise. "What did he say exactly?"

Naomi straightened up. "You have to believe me when I tell you it's all one-sided. It almost always has been."

"*Almost* always?" Obviously there was more here than he'd suspected.

"You haven't been here for me to tell you anything, Charles, so don't look at me like that. I just hate for Matthew to leave angry and hurt again." Naomi huffed an exasperated breath, ruffling her bangs. "Matthew and John had a . . . falling out on our wedding night. They had a horrible fight and that's why Matthew left for California. It was years before he and John reconciled. I just hate to see him go under such sad circumstances again."

McIntyre took a step back and rested his hand on his gun. She had hesitated over the phrase *falling out*. Knowing he shouldn't ask, he did anyway. "And the cause of their fight?"

Her face clouded and she found something to stare at over his shoulder. "He . . ." As if taking on a character from a play, she lightened her expression and tone, pasted a shaky smile across her mouth, and turned to her audience. "He had a little too much to drink and, well, pawed at me. It was nothing, really."

The false cheer in her voice wouldn't have fooled a child. Naomi was a terrible liar. Having a fair sense of the type of man John was, McIntyre could make a good guess as to what had happened. "Naomi, for John to get riled enough—"

"Charles, it was a long time ago. Matthew was a loose cannon in his younger days. And he was so drunk that night. He's quit drinking. He's made something of himself. I believe he's a changed man. I don't want any trouble between you two." She raised her chin in challenge. "You do believe a man can change, don't you?"

He hated the triumph in her stance. Besides, what could he tell her? Matthew had ogled a saloon girl and tossed back a few shots of whiskey after being stabbed? Hardly evidence he hadn't been rehabilitated. But Matthew wasn't the saint Naomi wanted him to be. He had laid hands on her, what, seven, eight years ago? McIntyre had to assume he was capable of repeating the action. It would be the last mistake Matthew ever made.

"Oh, this has gone so badly. Please," she grabbed his lapel and tugged him close. "Why don't you go get cleaned up? Shower, shave, rest for a bit. Perhaps we could go for a buggy ride this afternoon?" She rose up on her tip-toes so her lips were a breath from his. "We could celebrate our engagement." She brushed his lips with hers, with a pressure lighter than butterfly wings.

His irritation over Matthew dissipated like fog yielding to a summer day.

"I said 'yes.' Get the preacher on the next stage." Their breath mingled and he forgot everything but this moment, this woman who would be his wife.

Fighting the spell she cast over him, he kissed the corner of her mouth, all that he would allow, and sighed. "I think the next few days will be the longest I have ever endured."

---

*S*miling over Charles' proposal, Naomi stopped at the batwings and watched her sisters and Mollie bustling around the kitchen. Admiration mixed with her joy. They'd suffered through their share of heartache in the last year—Hannah's scandal, John's death, Mollie's brutal beating—yet, here they were in a wild mining town—happy as larks.

Naomi truly did enjoy living and working with these girls. As far as her sisters went, they were closer now than they'd ever been, but she was ready to share her life with Charles. She believed that was the reason she was here, or at least one of the reasons.

She pushed through the doors, clasped her hands at her waist and waited for the girls to notice her. Scraping scrambled eggs from a frying pan into a bowl, Rebecca saw her first. She set the pan back down on the stove and turned to her sister, a knowing smile dancing on her lips. Her pause pulled Hannah's eyes up from a sliced tomato she was about to dice. Mollie followed their gazes and stilled the biscuit cutter in the dough.

Their attention captured, Naomi took a deep breath. "Charles asked me to marry him."

Stunned silence transformed into hoots and giggles. The girls hurled themselves at Naomi to hug and congratulate her. After the warm wishes and kisses on the cheek, she took a step back from the group. "I said yes—"

"Well, of course you did," Hannah interrupted.

"But what about you?" Naomi asked pointedly. She scanned the three beaming women before her. "What happens to us? The hotel?" One by one, their smiles melted away. "Charles has land outside of town. It's over an hour away."

Head bowed, Rebecca sat down on the bench at the table and drummed her fingers. After a moment, she shrugged. "You love him. It will be all right." She rapped on the table, as if to emphasize her words. "It'll be like it was at home in Cary. We'll still be close to each other, Naomi."

Hannah bit her bottom lip and shook her head slowly. Naomi eased a few steps closer to her. "What is it, Hannah?"

She twitched her lips uncertainly for a moment. Finally, she looked up, her brow crinkled with worry. "What *are* we going to do? Are we going to run this hotel forever?"

Naomi realized with a jolt that Hannah didn't want to. How could she have not seen that coming? Her desire to be a nurse was sincere, and growing. "Hannah, I'm sure Rebecca would agree with me when I tell you, don't *put off* nursing because of us or this hotel. Especially if you think it's what God wants for you."

"I don't know what God wants for me."

"You will, in time," Rebecca said. "I've been toying lately with the idea of a newspaper. Maybe we *won't* run the hotel forever."

"And I still want to go home to Kansas," Mollie said taking a small step forward. "As soon as I hear back from my family."

"Whoa, whoa, whoa," Naomi said waving her hand, stunned at what she was hearing. "What are you all saying? Are you all sick of the hotel?"

For a moment the three girls stared back at Naomi with startled looks. Then they exchanged guilty glances with each other. Rebecca licked her lips and slowly rose to her feet again. "Not sick of it, Naomi, merely entertaining possibilities."

Naomi studied one face after the other, feeling a little bushwhacked. But it was her own fault. Head over heels for Charles, she hadn't been thinking about anything but him. Not what a future with him might look like. Not what her sisters might want out of life too. The hotel had been born of necessity. A logical business decision that kept a roof over their heads and a steady income flowing. Now, with a little time and planning, other possibilities could be open to them all.

"Well, nobody said we had to make this place our life's work," Naomi conceded.

Rebecca smiled and took Naomi's hand. "And nobody said we have to make these decisions today. Why don't we plan a wedding first?"

CHAPTER 22

*M*cIntyre was gratified that each new morning brought with it a desire to read God's Word. If he kept it up, would the guilt eventually stop slithering around his soul? Would this sense of being unworthy cease hunting him from the shadows? Could he change into a man who willingly bowed his knee to a loving God?

He slipped out of bed and into black trousers and a white silk shirt, left unbuttoned. Knowing Brannagh would be up shortly with his breakfast, he sat down at his desk. The Bible greeted him with a sense of peace. He laid his hand atop the leather-covered book and prayed. *Help me find the answers, Lord.* Still feeling inadequate about his right to come before God, McIntyre ran a hand through his hair. Diving in, he randomly flipped to Acts chapter 9.

And Saul, yet breathing out threatenings and slaughter against the disciples of the Lord, went unto the high priest,

And desired of him letters to Damascus to the synagogues, that if he found any of this Way, whether they were men or women, he might bring them bound unto Jerusalem.

Intrigued by this evil, brutal man, McIntyre backed up to Chapter 8 and read. Paul had kidnapped, beaten, brutalized, tortured, and imprisoned believers. He had separated families, killed men and women, and left behind a trail of orphans. His name had been a synonym for terror. Yet, one encounter with Christ had changed Paul, thoroughly and completely, from the inside out.

McIntyre was particularly struck by Chapter 9, verse 26:

And when Saul was come to Jerusalem, he assayed to join himself to the disciples: but they were all afraid of him, and believed not that he was a disciple.

They didn't believe he was a changed man. McIntyre found comfort in the commonality.

He leaned back from the book and pondered the similarities between himself and Paul. He thought about his early days in Defiance and the brutal ways in which he had established *his* town. The souls he had willingly beaten or buried just so he could keep his throne. The girls he'd so casually hired as prostitutes. And the men he'd enticed into his saloons to lose their souls to liquor, gambling, and sirens.

He had breathed out his own *threatenings* on the citizens of Defiance, and the past sat heavy on his shoulders. Paul, though, after one amazing encounter with Christ, had turned his life into a force for good, for God. The tenacious, determined apostle traveled, witnessed, healed, spread the gospel, and lived a completely different life. He hadn't done it to prove himself a better man. He simply *was* a better man because of his relationship with Christ.

McIntyre shut the Bible, envious that Paul had not only found forgiveness, but *lived* like he was forgiven, moving beyond his past, surrendering everything to God. He hungered to know his trick.

I have done so many things, God, for which You shouldn't forgive me. I don't even have the right to ask—

"Helloooo, anyone here?"

The silky, feminine voice sounded familiar, but he couldn't quite place it. Dreading what a woman in his saloon probably meant, he walked out into the hallway. Below him, a young, petite Negro girl in a painfully low-cut dress glanced around the quiet room.

From his vantage point, McIntyre had a sudden, clear, and unintended view of her generous bosom. His stare lingered for an instant. Ashamed of the instinctive reaction, he shook himself free and started down the stairs. "What can I do for you?"

Startled, she clutched her throat and tracked the voice. Circles under her eyes, the cheap dress and faded feathers in her hair told her story. "I'm lookin' for a job, but," she motioned to the empty saloon, "you don't appear to be hiring."

"What's your name?" he asked as he approached her.

"Amanda." She stared at McIntyre as if waiting for a reaction. He didn't have one for her. "I worked here a few years ago. You called me Poppy."

He nodded, the name returning her to his memory. She hadn't stayed long. Left with a miner, as he recalled. He couldn't recall having slept with her, but knew that didn't mean anything. Some women were memorable. Some were not. "I thought you got married."

"That didn't work out."

So she was back in the business. He jerked a thumb toward the door "Well, the Iron Horse is closed. But there are five other—" he cut off the suggestion. Troubled by his willingness to toss her back to the cesspool, he walked past her to the bar and stared at himself in the mirror. Handsome, well-dressed, a rogue with dark hair, slightly long and curly, and perfectly trimmed beard. He *looked* like the old McIntyre. The old McIntyre would have sent her to the other side of town.

Back to Jerusalem in chains.

He thought of Amaryllis. Naomi had said the woman had refused the offer of a free room, a chance to choose a different path. McIntyre knew making such an offer hadn't come easy to her. God love her, she'd made it anyway. He wondered if she would have though, had she'd known about his relationship with Amaryllis.

Yes, she most likely would have.

And he couldn't do any less.

He studied Amanda in the mirror. Christ had died for this girl, just as he had for McIntyre. They both had to try to start over.

Brannagh, his bartender and now personal assistant, had left a pitcher of water on the counter, along with a few bottles of liquor. He poured a glass of water and asked, "Can I get you something to drink, Amanda?"

"Sure, yeah. Whiskey'd be fine."

"How 'bout water?"

Brow creasing, she shrugged a shoulder. "OK, that's good too."

He walked the drink over to her. "Tell me, Amanda, do you want out?"

Glass at her lips, she paused before taking the sip. "Sure. Don't we all?"

"If you could do something different, what would it be?"

Suspicion played on her face. "I'd be a duchess, I reckon."

"Is that what you would want? A house and servants?"

Realizing he was serious, she sniffed and shook her head. "No, I'd like to be a teacher, especially for little ones just learnin' to read."

A glimmer of a notion formed in his mind. "If you had the money and the opportunity, would you go back to school to learn to be a proper teacher?"

She stared straight through him for a moment, pondering the crazy idea. "In a magical world filled with unicorns and fairies, I'd go to Wellesley." She blinked. "My teacher at the freedmen's school went there. But I believe I left my magic wand back in Denver."

McIntyre reached up and scratched his beard. "Maybe *you* did..."

CHAPTER 23

annah hated having a soft heart. Why couldn't she be tough and a little low on compassion like Naomi? She flinched at the rather unkind thought, but her sister had floated by Billy in the dining room the past several mornings as he ate his breakfast alone, and hadn't shown him an ounce of concern. She'd poured his coffee, checked on him occasionally, but kept right on moving, ignoring the hunched shoulders, drumming fingers, and the way he pushed his food around the plate instead of eating it.

This morning Hannah couldn't take it anymore. Family ate in the kitchen. Besides, Billy could feed Little Billy and she wouldn't have to juggle his care with caring for the customers.

So far, the idea was paying off. Billy and son wore only modest amounts of porridge on their faces and clothes. Coming in from the dining room, she stopped, raised an eyebrow at the pair, and used her apron to wipe cereal off the father's cheek. Billy's eyes warmed at her touch and he smiled. A little alarmed at the flip her stomach did, Hannah jerked her hand away. She hurried over to the stove where Rebecca loaded her with several plates, each full of hash browns, bacon, eggs, and pancakes. Hannah was quite proud she could carry four meals this way. Head high, she sashayed past the two boys and backed through the swinging doors.

When she returned to the kitchen several minutes later, Emilio had stationed himself at the opposite end of the table and was wolfing down his breakfast. "Good morning, Emilio." She greeted him with a sing-song voice as she deposited a ton of dirty dishes into the sink. His mouth full, he nodded and waved a fork.

Hannah assumed Billy had barely spoken to him. Furthermore, he probably supposed Emilio was just getting his day started. She decided to correct that assumption.

"Emilio, how's the hen house? Did you get the fence fixed?"

"*Si*, I fixed the hole first thing this morning."

"And the woodbox?"

"It's filled."

"Milk?"

"In the spring house." He took a sip of coffee. "And I'm fixing that loose step right after breakfast."

Hannah skimmed her glance over Billy, whose lips were a tight line. "That's wonderful, Emilio. Now, I was wondering . . ." She plopped cinnamon rolls onto saucers as she prepared to put in motion another idea. "We've got a piece of furniture down at the stagecoach office. Came in yesterday. I thought you and Billy could go get it today." Both men jerked their heads up as if Hannah had just used profanity. Forks froze in midair. She bit down on her lip to stop the grin from escaping and picked up the pastry-laden tray. "I didn't think either of you would mind. Besides, Billy needs something to do."

Without waiting for a response, she slipped gracefully through the batwings.

*B*illy hadn't missed Hannah's impish grin twitching around the corners of her beautiful, inviting lips. Pulling an empty spoon from Little Billy's mouth, he turned a not-so-friendly gaze on Emilio. Their eyes battled. For a second, the tension was palpable.

Unexpectedly, Emilio shrugged a shoulder. "Ees fine with me."

"Well, me too," Billy added defensively. He scooped up a little more porridge and waved it in front of the child. "Sure, we can move some furniture for Mama." Like a little bird, the boy opened his mouth, waiting for his breakfast. "Let me finish feeding my son, and I'll be right with you."

---

*T*he morning sunshine warming his shoulders, Billy assessed Defiance as he and Emilio strode down the crowded sidewalk. Most of the buildings were new, having not yet lost the slight golden hue that pine holds onto for a few years. Main Street itself was a busy flow of mud-encrusted miners, mules, horses, and freight wagons coming and going at an almost fevered clip. Above the creak of leather and buzzing, male voices, he noticed the constant clanging sound of metal. Reverberating in the air like church bells, gold pans hung from every saddle and backpack on the street, swaying, ringing, and glinting in the sun.

Defiance could be described as chaotic, but it was not *in* chaos, Billy realized. These men had places to go, things to accomplish, and gold to find.

A wall of plaid and leather pushed its way roughly past Billy, nearly knocking him off the boardwalk. Without thinking, he spun. "Hey, why don't you watch where you're going?"

The man stopped and Billy's mind immediately leaped back to Earl H. Goode. The miner, as broad as a plow horse and carrying a pick ax on his shoulder, slowly turned. A hairy, barrel-chested gentleman, he scowled as he appraised Billy. Billy fought the temptation to swallow or glance at Emilio, who had stopped beside him. The miner spit tobacco juice at his feet. "Git home, pup," he said, sneering. "I hear your mama callin' ya."

He turned and continued his trek down the boardwalk. Billy had never felt like such a flea in his life.

Beside him, Emilio chuckled. "Come on, *pup*. We need to get that furniture."

Pup? Billy clamped his jaws shut, forcing himself to take a breath before he responded. He turned and his eyes followed Emilio as the boy walked a few steps ahead. "Call me *pup* again, *greaser*, and I'll knock your teeth down your throat."

Emilio stopped as if he'd run into a wall. He dropped his hands on his hips and shook his head. Billy couldn't tell if he was laughing or arguing with himself. Maybe both. A few passersby seemed to sense the tension and slowed their progress, necks craning.

Emilio backed up a step and pivoted to Billy. "I don't want to fight you. Hannah wouldn't like it."

Billy snorted. *"Hannah wouldn't like it?"* he mocked. "Well aren't you the considerate gentleman."

The shadow of a storm darkened Emilio's face. Billy imagined he could hear the rumble of thunder. Teeth clenched, Emilio took two more steps and came nose-to-nose with Billy, bowler and cowboy hat colliding. "At least *I* respect her."

No conscious thought led Billy to hit Emilio with a sledge-hammer of a punch, he just did it. The boy's head snapped back, he staggered a step or two, growled and came back to throw a clumsy hook. Billy dodged it and hit Emilio with a combination right jab and left uppercut. The tan cowboy hat went flying as Emilio again staggered back. This time, he took a moment longer to recover. A sizable crowd of laughing, jostling men formed—amazingly fast, Billy thought—and encircled the boys.

Billy raised his hands and shuffled skillfully back and forth in front of Emilio. He watched his opponent but stole wary glances at the crowd as well, in case someone else decided to join the fracas. Black hair hanging in his eyes, Emilio touched his lip and looked at his fingers. Blood. Billy's confidence soared. He could beat the hound out of this greaser. He'd be shouting orders at him in a few minutes instead of working alongside him.

Emilio shook his hair back and raised his fists. Determination burned in his dark eyes. Billy grinned. The two boys moved in and circled each other like animals in a cage. The fast-growing crowd shouted, but Billy ignored the noise. He saw flashes of gold as money changed hands.

Emilio stepped in and swung a wild haymaker. Billy ducked and lunged with another uppercut. Emilio's head snapped back. This time, blood spattered. Billy felt the spray hit his face. The boy cupped his bleeding nose briefly and straightened up. Shaking off the pain, he once again put up his dukes, but Billy saw him sway before regaining his balance.

"More, greaser?" Although he felt like a rooster ready to crow, Billy grudgingly admired the boy's tenacity. Some of the men around him cheered or roared with laughter. The crowd had grown, now running three and four bodies deep. Hairy, smelly miners watched eagerly, hungry for blood.

"Come on, Emilio," someone else yelled. "The tin horn with the bowler ain't no match for you."

"Shoot, city boy, you can take that, *greaser!*" Billy didn't know where the shouts came from, but they sounded ugly and eager for someone's misery.

Unexpectedly, Emilio lowered his head and charged like a bull. Caught at the waist, Billy, arms pin-wheeling, could only tumble back into the crowd, which parted like water. The two toppled into the street, sending up a dust cloud and spooking a horse tied in front of the Land Office. Emilio punched ferociously, landing three stunning blows to Billy's head and ribs. Unsettled that the tables had turned, Billy flailed, kicked and squirmed. The punches kept raining down. He heard his nose crack and the pain made his eyes water.

Emilio couldn't fight, but he could brawl. *Well, if there aren't any rules* . . . Billy grabbed a handful of dirt and threw it. As Emilio blinked and wiped, Billy tried to scramble out from under him.

Still wiping at his eyes with one hand, Emilio clawed for Billy with the other. The two rolled around on the ground, kicking, gouging, grunting, fists thudding on flesh. Like snakes fighting to the death, they rolled and grappled. The crowd roared and Billy sucked wind like a dying fish, his arms growing heavier and heavier. Growling with Herculean effort, he shoved Emilio off.

Gasping for breath, the boy rolled a few feet away and struggled to all fours. Billy copied him. Like panting dogs, they stared at each other from their hands and knees. Billy wondered if he looked as bad as Emilio. Face smeared with blood, the boy's eye was swelling shut, something wasn't quite right with the angle of his nose, his cheek sported a nice gash, his bottom lip was purple and already twice its normal size. His hair shot in every direction and his shirt hung in rags.

A sudden wave of blackness threatened to fog Billy's brain and he collapsed on his hip. Stars danced in his head and he tasted the copper of his own blood. He glanced down at his knuckles. Skinned and bleeding. The hand that had barely recovered from his last fight was swelling fast. His ribs ached like he'd been kicked by a mule. His head hurt too, but he couldn't pinpoint whether his nose, jaw, forehead or mouth was the center of the pain.

Chest heaving, Emilio fell back on his bum and wiped his mouth with the back of his hand. "We forgot the wagon."

CHAPTER 24

*D*escending the steps, Naomi was surprised to see Matthew hobbling through the front door, a new cane in his hand. Her stomach dropped at the prospect of telling him about Charles's proposal. She really didn't want to hurt him, but perhaps the sooner they got this out of the way, the easier it would be for both of them to move on.

He shut the front door and, holding his side, limped his way across the entry toward the dining room. Dreading this, but resolved, she wiped sweaty palms on her apron and licked her lips. "You missed lunch, Matthew." He sagged a bit at the sound of her voice. "But I could fix you a sandwich or perhaps some country ham and a biscuit."

"No, thank you, Naomi."

The awkwardness between them stamped every word they spoke. She bit her lip, knowing it was about to get worse. He waited for her at the entrance of the dining room, but she could only offer him quick, guilty glances. "I see you picked up a cane. From the general store?"

"Yeah, I had to get some fresh air before I started climbing the walls, but by the time I'd walked that far, my side was hurting pretty good." He twirled the dark brown cane. "I missed a good street fight. Would have liked to watch it, but that chair in the dining room was calling my name."

"That's the first fight in a while." She clasped her hands in front of her and rocked on her heels. But it wouldn't be the last. And it didn't matter at the moment. "Matthew, I need to tell you something."

"Uh-oh." He hobbled on into the dining room and took his favorite seat next to the fireplace. Naomi quietly followed him but didn't sit down. Resting his cane's tip between his feet, he drummed his fingers along the handle and waited. "What is it?"

"Charles asked me to marry him this morning. I said yes. The preacher will be here in a few days."

Before the announcement could even register with him, a loud commotion drew their attention to the front door. Billy and Emilio, resembling the bloody survivors of an Indian attack and carrying a large wooden crate between them, bounced and slammed their way into the center of the front room. They set the crate down with an unceremonious thud. Like troops returning from a lost battle, they slowly removed their hats and waited. Their expressions, what she could see beneath the blood, seemed to dare her to scold them.

Naomi couldn't scold them. Their condition left her speechless.

Matthew hobbled up beside her and whistled. "You two have been busy." The young men traded uneasy glances and Matthew laughed. "Sorry I missed it."

Snapping out of her shock, Naomi stomped forward to examine them. "Good grief, what happened?" She touched Emilio's jaw, lowering it so she could get a better view of his swollen eye and various abrasions. Shaking her head in disapproval, she moved her attention to Billy. Pushing his forehead back, she eyed his cuts and rapidly swelling, bloody nose. She caught him flexing his fingers and gently lifted his abused hand to eye level. It was already twice its normal size.

"Oh my goodness!" Hannah cried from the top of the stairs. Jaw clenched, she stormed down the staircase like Stonewall Jackson chasing Yankees. The two boys shifted uncomfortably. Pleasantly shocked at her little sister's flaring temper, Naomi stepped aside.

Hannah planted herself between Emilio and Billy and jammed her hands onto her hips, her chest heaving. "You two did this to each other, didn't you?"

Immediately the boys started talking over each other and pointing like angry toddlers.

"He started it—"

"I told him you wouldn't—"

"He called me a—"

"Enough!" Hannah bellowed. The boys clammed up like someone had slapped them. Naomi crossed her arms and grinned with enormous pride as Hannah's temper sizzled like the fuse on a stick of dynamite. She was hopping mad and the fireworks were promising indeed.

"You can't walk two blocks without coming to blows?"

"I tried not to," Emilio argued, but pride got the better of him and he straightened up. "Sometimes, a man must fight for his honor."

Hannah raised her brow then nailed Billy with a sideways glare.

Apparently trying to wring the life out of his bowler, he raised it to his chest. "He called me a pup."

Naomi heard a snort from Matthew.

"A pup?" Hannah's eyebrows arched. "So how did *you* offend *his honor?*"

The boys squirmed as if they would prefer to be anywhere but here. Hannah started tapping her toe. Billy buckled and stepped toward her, slicing the air with that ridiculous hat.

"Darn it, Hannah, we had words, but I didn't hit him until he said I don't respect you."

Hannah's jaw dropped and she backed up a step. After a moment, her expression transformed from shock to something harder and inscrutable. Naomi wondered if she was trying not to give too much away.

"Who won?" Hannah asked softly. The boys answered with stoic silence.

"Fine." Her scorching gaze raked the bloodied pulps standing before her. "You two go out to the back porch. I don't want blood in my kitchen. I'll be there shortly to clean you up."

Head held high, Hannah marched off to the kitchen. Naomi had only been this proud of her little sister one other time, during her confession to the whole church, which she had done alone when Billy wasn't even in the state.

"Well, boys . . ." Naomi laughed, absolutely delighted with her little sister's display of temper. "You have lit a fire under Hannah Frink. I like her this way, don't you—?" she turned to include Matthew in the comment, but he was gone. Relieved, she turned back to Emilio and Billy. They were a pitiful sight. Beaten, swollen, covered head to toe in dirt and blood, and yet neither of them had claimed victory. Puzzled, she let the question pass and motioned toward the back. "Get on out to the back stoop." They shuffled off, heads lowered, shoulders bent, both holding their hats over their hearts as if they were heading off to an execution . . . theirs. "And don't get blood on anything."

CHAPTER 25

*B*illy took a seat on the back steps, one beyond the shadow cast by the building, and leaned against the handrail. He hurt. Not as badly as after the beating from Earl H. Goode, but darn near it. Emilio had a sledge hammer for a punch, but he was sloppy and let his guard down too much. The sun felt good, though. It eased some of the aching.

He opened one eye and watched Emilio. He had plunked down on the top step and was carefully pressing his shirt tail to his bloody knuckles. Billy was confident he could have beaten Emilio if they'd both been using Queensbury Rules. As it was, street brawling had proven a bit more effective. In all honesty, he would have given the match to the greaser.

"You won the fight, *si?*"

Surprised by Emilio's observation, Billy's other eye flew open. "No, I don't think so." Not that he wanted to give Emilio any kind of slap on the back, but truth was truth. "If you knew how to fight, I *would* have beaten you."

Emilio frowned. Gently, he touched his swollen jaw and worked it back and forth. "I do know how to fight."

"No, no you don't." Beginning to stiffen up like an old man, Billy shifted. "You know how to brawl. There's a difference." Emilio's perplexed look deepened, and Billy sighed.

"Boxing. It has rules. It makes you and your opponent more equal so the outcome is determined by skill, not by how much sand you can throw. There's strategy and you try to find weaknesses—"

"That's what I thought I was doing."

Well, Billy couldn't really argue with that. Emilio had tackled him, knowing he had to stop Billy from throwing punches. He could respect that move.

He heard the quick thump-thump-thump of boot heels and shifted on the step as Hannah emerged on the porch. Her cheeks were still flushed and little golden wisps of hair drifted around her face. Eyeing the boys disapprovingly, she stood with her arms wrapped around a basin of water and a brown canvas bag hanging from her shoulder. "You go on a short, simple errand and come back looking like this?" Shaking her head, she sat down beside Emilio and placed the basin on the floor between them. "How did the buffet table fare?"

Neither of the boys responded. She gave up with an indignant huff and dug through her bag. She pulled out a roll of cotton gauze, cut and folded it into roughly a four by four square, doused it with witch hazel and handed it down to Billy. "Here, put this on that nose. Yours looks worse than his."

Billy did as he was instructed and was surprised at the relief, though the smell made his eyes water. "Got anything for my hand or my eye?"

"Yes, in a just minute." Her voice had softened a bit. More gentle and low, it reminded him of good things, peaceful things. He could use a little peace. So far, his trip to Defiance had been a train wreck.

Hannah went to work on Emilio, gently clutching his face and cleaning up the mess. He was all wide-eyed and gawking like a school boy as she fussed over him. Billy forced himself to watch and not say a word.

"Hmmm," she murmured as the blood wiped away, revealing a good cut intersecting his fat upper lip, as well as the one on his cheek. "I don't think you need stitches, but that's going to be pretty tender." With a light touch, she rubbed a horrid-smelling salve into the wound and the cut on his cheek. The boy wrinkled his nose at the odor.

She held Emilio's hands one at a time, and gingerly wiped witch hazel over his bruised and bloodied knuckles, lingering, in Billy's opinion, a bit too long over each finger.

"Wiggle your fingers." Emilio did as ordered. Hannah nodded. She worked on with confidence and efficiency, seemingly unaware of Emilio's puppy dog eyes. Billy wished *he* was. "Nothing is broken. Wash your hands a lot, though, and use soap so these cuts don't get infected."

Billy couldn't help but see how much Hannah had grown up. He recalled one of the last times he'd seen her back in Cary. Billy had followed her crazy trail of sock puppets from the church sanctuary to the basement, picking them up as he went along. He had six in his hands when he caught up with her at her Sunday school class—a class for which she was always harried. The children never seemed to mind. They adored her, with or without her puppets.

So did Billy.

And now here she was up to her elbows in blood, tending to the aftermath of a stupid brawl.

Emilio took off his hat and placed it humbly across his chest. "Thank you, Hannah. You're a good nurse."

Hannah beamed. Blushing as bright as a June rose, she smacked him playfully on the shoulder. "Git on inside." Hopelessness as heavy as a wet wool blanket fell over Billy. Would he ever make her blush like that again?

She took a deep breath as Emilio disappeared inside the hotel. Straightening her shoulders, she turned her attention to Billy. "Come here."

Her firm, deep gaze made him long desperately for better days. "Yes, ma'am." He moved as fast as his aching body would allow and settled into Emilio's seat.

By now, the floor of the porch was covered with bloody rags, ointment jars and bottles of tinctures. She touched his nose lightly and he flinched, but mostly because he thought her touch *might* hurt. "Can you breathe through it?" He sniffed a breath. "All right. Good." She used water and witch hazel to clean his face, assessing the damage with a skilled eye. "Could be worse." She unwrapped a thin, rectangular strip of meat, so cold ice crystals still clung to it, and draped it over his nose.

"I thought you were supposed to put meat on a shiner," he questioned, his voice nasally.

"This is special meat. It was soaked in . . . well, things you don't want to know about."

Billy twitched an eyebrow, but held the steak in place, feeling like an idiot. He watched her closely as she examined his right hand, touching lightly, pressing on his digits. She moved with grace and confidence, and like a surprise punch to the gut, the awareness that he was losing—maybe had already lost her—sucked the wind out of him. "You don't need me. You don't need anybody."

He caught the slightest hitch in her breath. She pressed his thumb and rotated it slowly back and forth. Finished, she sat back and released his hand. "Maybe that's the best way to be."

Billy thought of Eleanor, back in Dodge City. Life was hard out west for a woman. He admired any of them who could make it here. He saw now that Hannah would have made it, with or without her sisters, and without turning to anything like prostitution. He had to hand it to her.

"Here, Hannah, I thought you might need this." They pulled

away from each other as Mollie stepped on to the stoop, toting a pitcher of fresh water.

"Oh, yes. Thank you."

The girl set it down and tossed the basin of red-tinged water over the rail. "How are the boys?" she asked, handing Hannah the empty bowl.

Billy bristled at being called a boy. Maybe *Emilio* was a boy . . .

Hannah poured the fresh water into the basin and shrugged. "Somehow they managed not to break anything."

"All right, well, I'll go ahead and get the green beans simmering. Holler if you need anything."

Hannah thanked her and turned back to the patient. Mollie excused herself and Billy stared after her retreating figure till she closed the door. She reminded him a lot of Hannah. Close in age, their coloring and shapes were so similar. But Mollie had age behind her eyes, as if she'd done a hard round or two in life. "So what's the story with Mollie?"

Hannah fastidiously studied his purple lip as she dabbed witch hazel on it. "I don't think she'd mind me telling you. She used to work for Mr. McIntyre."

"*She* was a Flower?" He pulled back, leaving Hannah's hand in mid-air. Mollie carried herself so primly and properly in her buttoned-up calico dress. *That explains the age in her eyes.*

"The day she accepted Jesus, a customer had nearly beaten her to death." Hannah winced and Billy could see she still ached for her friend. She dabbed at his lip again. "I've never seen a human so abused. But everything worked out. She's happy now and is so full of the Lord. She has a beautiful spirit."

"She's definitely beautiful," he agreed absently. Hannah's jaw tightened and her lips thinned into a tense line. Billy didn't miss the change in her expression. Was she jealous? Did he dare to hope? He focused on her, willing her to look at him, or at least notice how close they were. Her hand grew warm on his cheek but she kept an emotional distance between them.

"I doubt Emilio started the fight," Hannah said as she carefully dabbed the smelly ointment on to his lip. "He's a gentle sort. What sort are you?"

What sort am I? The sort who wants to keep swinging.

"I don't know. I want to do the right thing." He thought about the courage it had taken to get to this point and how he had nothing to show for it, except more cuts and bruises. "I just keep making mistakes, though."

Her hand paused and she offered him a sympathetic smile. Shaking her head, she laughed softly. "I can't take you seriously with this on your nose." She peeled up the steak, laid it over his right eye, and pressed his hand to it. "That's so much better. Keep it there for a while," she said, dipping a cloth in the fresh water. "You know, I'm very fond of Emilio." Billy's jaw clenched, but he didn't make a sound. After what he'd said about Mollie, maybe this was just a little revenge. "But I don't think I love him. Yet."

She wrung the rag with small hands not afraid of work. Determined, she finished wiping away the stubborn spots of blood around his nose. "He'd be easy to love. He's a good man."

"So I hear. Repeatedly." Hannah chuckled at his sullen tone. But Billy was a little tired of everyone defending the gre—he stopped the word. Emilio deserved at least some respect. He could fight like a man.

"You're probably a good man too, Billy." Hannah switched to working on his hands, her head bent over them as she talked. "I'm having trouble seeing it . . . seeing past the hurt." She painted more of Emilio's concoction on his knuckles, still stubbornly avoiding his gaze.

What he wouldn't give if they could just go back and start over. "You don't know how many times, Hannah, I've wished I would have handled things differently." He clutched her hand, the desperation to get through to her almost strangling his voice. "I've come fifteen hundred miles for you. I left my home, my family's fortune, my mother. I'm all out of ideas. I don't know what else to do."

"Good." Her expression softened and transformed into something downright angelic. "*Now* God can help you."

CHAPTER 26

"*Y*ou want her to stay *here?*" Naomi hated the angry tone in her voice. It made Amanda's gaze hit the floor like a dog about to take a beating. *But really, here?*

Charles gave the girl an apologetic nod and took Naomi's arm, pulling her several feet away from the hotel's registration desk. "I realize I didn't think this out very well, but you needn't be so rude."

"I didn't expect you to parade these women in front of me, Charles." He frowned and stole embarrassed glances around the room. Naomi bit her lip, but wasn't really sorry the handful of customers in the dining room had heard her.

Taking a breath, he spoke more calmly. "I would not do that to you, Naomi. You don't understand. I don't believe I ever . . ."

"You're not sure?"

Naomi knew her knee jerk reaction wasn't going to be kind. She clamped her jaws shut, forcing herself to take a moment. She knew this about Charles. He'd admitted his past. He hadn't gilded the lily in any way. To be fair, she'd told him she could take it.

And so she would. If it took every ounce of humility and self-control she had.

Naomi avoided Charles' drilling stare and glanced over at the girl. She was hugging herself and tapping her toes frantically. Naomi assumed the girl would be more comfortable sitting in a dentist's chair, especially after that welcome.

"Amanda only worked for me for a short time, Naomi. She married a miner, but, apparently, that relationship has come to an end. "

Naomi sighed. She had humiliated Amanda out of jealousy . . . irrational, immature jealousy.

"She wants out." Charles gentled his voice. "I want to help her. Like I did Lily and Iris and Jasmine."

Like I tried to do with Amaryllis.

The thought shamed Naomi for the lie it was. She hadn't tried to help Amaryllis. At least not because she loved her or had compassion for her. She had made the girl an offer out of a sense of obligation. Because it was the right thing to do.

Naomi, her shoulders bent with humility, marched back over to Amanda. She touched the girl on the elbow. "Amanda, my apologies. I didn't understand. You are more than welcome here."

The girl smiled, but it trembled. "No, I'm the one who doesn't understand. Mr. McIntyre, what is it you want me to do?"

"For one thing, quit the business."

"And do what for money?"

"About that . . ." Charles gazed at Naomi. His earnest expression said he was waiting for forgiveness and permission. Knowing she was the one who needed forgiveness, she nodded. McIntyre placed a hand lightly on Amanda's shoulder. "We're going to figure a way to send you to Wellesley. To become a teacher. And maybe you won't be the only one."

Amanda's mouth fell open. Naomi's heart burst with pride. "Charles." She slid her arms around his elbow. "That is won—"

"Forgive my manners, Amanda," he interrupted Naomi, stopping her praise. He grasped her hands with a surprising firmness, as if her touch was praise enough. "This is my fiancée, Naomi Miller. We're getting married in a few days."

Amanda blinked and her mouth formed a startled *o*. Finally, she managed, "I don't know what to say. Mr. McIntyre," she thrust out her hand, "thank you." The two shook. Her smile widening, Amanda reached out to Naomi. "Thank you, Mrs. Miller. I hope the two of you will be very happy."

"I'm sure it will be interesting." She grinned at Charles, but held on to Amanda's hand. "But let's talk about you."

Naomi led the way over to a corner table and motioned for them to take a seat. Their table was at the front of the dining room and Naomi stole a moment to gaze longingly out the window at the beautiful azure sky full of wispy clouds. There were times, thankfully few and far between, when she wished she and her sisters had bought a farm instead of a six-day-a-week restaurant. She missed being outdoors.

"I'm no St. Francis of Assisi," Charles tossed Naomi a wink, pulling her back to the moment, "but I can take a stab at righting a few wrongs. Amanda, if you're serious about becoming a teacher, I'll set up a scholarship for you."

The girl smiled cautiously. "A scholarship? You mean it?"

"I will pay your tuition to Wellesley or wherever you'd like to go, and provide you with expense money as long as you're in school."

She tilted her head. "Do I have to pay it back?"

"Only by becoming the best teacher you can."

Amanda studied the salt and pepper shakers on the table and pushed a stiff tawny curl behind her ear. "That would be such an amazing life . . . so different. I don't know what to say. Or do." She looked up at Charles and Naomi to explain. "I mean, in the meantime. I mean, thank you very much, Mr. McIntyre, but I imagine it will take time to get things set up. What do I do in the meantime, if not . . .?"

Naomi reached across the table and touched the girl's hand, noting her skin was such a pretty shade of chocolate. "Amanda, is there any chance you can cook? We could use an extra person badly. None of us are getting any time off. Your room is free and so are your meals. Oh, and we'll pay you, of course."

"Before you answer that," Charles leaned forward and spoke in a somber tone, "you should understand my terms for the scholarship. As of this moment, you are done working in saloons. Period. If you go back on your word, I'll cancel the scholarship. What you do with your education after school will be your business."

Amanda pondered the offer for several seconds. Naomi couldn't imagine what in the world could stand in the way of grabbing a brighter future. Finally, the girl stuck out her hand to Charles. "Mr. McIntyre, thank you. I can do this. I will make this work, for both our sakes."

---

*B*illy didn't go back inside after Hannah was done with him. He knew he should. After all, Mr. Perfect was in there probably building some Louis XIV furniture or installing a newfangled *ice* box.

But I don't think I love him. Yet.

He'd be easy to love. He's a good man.

He didn't understand what Hannah meant. Did she love Emilio or didn't she? Was there still a chance for her and Billy? And what was that about *now God can help you?*

Disgusted with the cryptic hints, Billy drifted to the corral and waited for Prince Valiant to approach.

Huffing and snorting, the horse trotted up to him. He shook his head and pawed the ground with his hoof, communicating a familiar desire. Billy grinned as the message sank in. He draped the steak over the fence. "Yeah, let's go for a ride."

Minutes later, horse and rider loped across a high mountain

meadow bathed in late afternoon sun. Riding bareback and using nothing but Val's halter and lead line for control, Billy tried to lose himself in the experience. The rhythm of the ride, the horse's powerful muscles rippling under his legs, the exhilaration of controlling a thousand pound animal, it nearly always cleared his mind. He even forgot the ache in his nose and hand.

Wind rushing past his ears, he breathed in the scent of pines and horse sweat and lolled with the nice, easy canter. Prince Valiant, though, wanted more. They entered the woods, a grove of widely spaced aspens, and Billy held the pace. Sun flickered through the budding spring leaves, peppering them with light. The two followed a ridge for a good half hour. When the trees opened up, they found themselves on the edge of wide, steep pasture covered in thick grass.

They had the feel of the ride. Their rhythm had melded into one.

Billy smiled. "Yah! Git up!"

He kicked the horse with his heels, tightened his legs, and grabbed a handful of mane with his sore hand. Billy hunkered down and Prince Valiant lunged forward, reaching a full gallop in three beats. Billy's heart thundered in his chest as he watched the ground race by. Exhilarated, he shut his eyes for a moment and listened to the rhythm of pounding hoofbeats and the wind of freedom rushing over him. Faster and faster. The horse stretched out long and lean, hooves striking the green grass below like lightning bolts.

The hill sloped down and Billy aimed Prince Valiant for a shadowy opening in the trees about two hundred or so yards ahead. As he picked a point at which to begin reining him in, the horse stumbled. In a flash, the world turned upside down. Dirt and grass flew. Prince Valiant screamed. Billy's head smacked the ground and his breath whooshed out of him. Before he knew what happened, he was staring at up at a blue sky, dust swirling over him.

CHAPTER 27

cIntyre shut the saloon's door behind him as he stepped out into the sweet, warm May sunshine. Fall was his favorite time of year, but this spring felt unusually good, full of hope and promise. Despite his concerns over Matthew's arrival, or One-Who-Cries' possible proximity, he'd never carried as much optimism for the future as he had at this very moment. He kept coming back to the word *hope*. For the first time in a long time, he felt as though his future held something more valuable than material gain.

"It seems congratulations are in order," Matthew called from somewhere behind him.

McIntyre's good mood dissipated like smoke. Swallowing his irritation, he turned. A few yards up the boardwalk, Matthew hobbled toward him, wearing a strained smile. "Or should I say *victori exuviae?*"

McIntyre paused and decided to be the bigger man. He met Matthew halfway and stuck out his hand. Matthew shifted his cane and the two shook hands. McIntyre sensed cold disdain simmered within the man but chose to ignore it. "Thank you, but it was never a competition and I shouldn't have implied that."

The two moseyed down the street together. Matthew shook his head. "No, Naomi certainly is not a prize bull."

"A prize *fighter*, maybe," McIntyre only half-joked and the two men chuckled. "You are heading to the telegraph office?" A logical question, as it was one of the last businesses before the main route over to Tent Town.

"Uh . . . yes."

McIntyre had asked only in an effort to make conversation but the pause in Matthew's answer betrayed the lie.

Matthew switched the cane back to his right hand. "Checking on things at my mill. I think another few days and I'll be heading home."

"Yes, I'm sure your business needs you back." McIntyre had to wonder why the man would lie about where he'd been . . . or was *going*? The conversation lagged awkwardly and he was glad for a reason to end the pleasantries. "Well, I've someone waiting on me. Good day."

He touched the brim of his hat and jumped off the boardwalk to cross the street. As he weaved through the traffic, he could feel the man's stare burning into his back. Momentarily stuck waiting for a lumbering freight wagon to pass, he wondered just who might turn out to be more dangerous, a murderous renegade Indian or a manipulative, lying white man. He realized it didn't matter. Neither should be ignored.

Laughter floated to him over the jangle of the wagon, bringing him back to the moment. He'd heard that laugh before. Curious, he turned back to the telegraph office. Matthew, not surprisingly, hobbled past it, falling in behind a boisterous group of miners. Carrying on loudly, the men disappeared around the corner of the next building, headed toward Tent Town. The familiar cackle had been faint, possibly even imagined.

McIntyre stayed a moment longer, listening, but a group of riders forced him to continue to the other side of the street. He climbed up on the boardwalk and turned back again. Surely Tom Hawthorn wouldn't be stupid enough to come back to Defiance.

Resting his hand on his gun, he paused over the memory of a bloody and abused Flower. Hawthorn had nearly beaten Mollie to death last November. The wretch had served his thirty-day sentence in the jail, paid his fine, and accepted his banishment from Defiance. McIntyre had watched him ride out of town, knowing that justice hadn't been done for Mollie. To his disgrace, he hadn't cared.

Only one man had ever defied McIntyre and re-entered town after a similar ruling. That man was dead. The gunfight had been the stuff of legends, cementing McIntyre's reputation as the soulless lord and master of Defiance. His town. His rules. No questions.

Now, such a stone-cold approach to running things was clearly at odds with the man he was trying to become. He struggled with how to reconcile the two. How did he keep respect and control if he wasn't willing to take a life without a second thought? Worse, what if he *was* still willing to play things that way? What would he do if push came to shove and he had an instant to choose?

McIntyre surveyed the street for another few seconds.

He knew eventually he'd find out.

---

*M*atthew's dislike for McIntyre was growing like a tumor. What did Naomi see in that pompous peacock? That she'd agreed to marry him just about took the wind out of Matthew's sails. He was getting pretty tired of the runner-up ribbon, and it had taken a strong dose of self-control not to pound McIntyre into the dirt.

But that wouldn't win Naomi back. Somehow, he had to show

her McIntyre's true colors. Men like him didn't change. There had to be a way to prove it.

His side throbbing, he inched over a step to allow a group of boisterous, swaggering miners room to pass him. He knew the signs. These fellas were on their way to getting liquored up good.

At least, that was Matthew's plan. Anything to ease this ache in his side and his heart.

The Lucky Deuce should have just the medicine he needed. Maybe that pretty little brunette would be there too. In his present condition, he didn't think he should do much with her, unless he wanted to risk tearing a stitch or two.

He grinned. Maybe she was worth it.

The possibility motivating his steps, he gimped along the boardwalk. Shortly, he cut down an alley. Once off Main Street, Defiance took a decided turn for the shabby. No stick buildings here. Mud from the laundry sucked at his boots and squished around his cane as he hobbled past the graying, tattered tent. On multiple clothes lines, holey long johns, dingy sheets and permanently stained canvas breeches kicked and whipped in the spring breeze.

One group of men sitting out in front of their neighborhood of tents was just as worn and frayed as their laundry. Pipe smoke swirled around their heads as they watched Matthew with tired, suspicious eyes. Several of them had tin lunch pails sitting at their feet. He wondered in passing if they were getting ready to head off to the mine or had just returned.

As he shuffled by a larger, newer tent, a young man ducked outside and tied the massive flap out of the way. A crowd of at least a dozen men spilled out, laughing and joking about the picture show. Obscene comments regarding the *ladies* in the images and the size of their assets drifted to Matthew. He knew a lot of men who enjoyed such shows, but he didn't see the point. Matthew Miller preferred the real deal, and pursued it at will.

A few steps further and he caught a whiff of something sweet. Opium. He shook his head. *This town doesn't miss a trick.*

He hobbled on and eventually the Lucky Deuce rose up from behind a row of yellowing, scraggly tents. The saloon was a step up from many of the other structures around it, since it wasn't all cloth. It had a stick-built back wall, and sides and a front that were about four feet tall. From that point, the canvas took over. He heard glass clinking as he approached but not much in the way of conversation.

He pushed the sagging canvas door open and surveyed the room. All the furniture had been righted, but spaces at the tables pointed to several chairs missing. The liquor shelves on the back wall were also only about a third full. A couple of seedy miners eyed him when he entered, but Matthew saw a shapely straw-berry-blonde behind the bar and marched straight for her. Her back to him, she was unloading a box of glasses, stacking them on a warped shelf near the tapped keg.

She turned at the sound of his thumping cane and gave him a knowing smile. "My, aren't you a big bear of a man." She set the glass down and leaned forward, resting her elbows on the bar. The luscious contents of her frayed bodice on display, she smiled seductively.

Yes, indeed, Matthew thought, ogling the girl. Why settle for a picture when you could get the real thing. And the Frenchie accent loaded his mind with all kinds of heady thoughts. "Howdy . . .?" He waited for her name.

"Call me Amaryllis." Her inviting smile grudgingly drew Matthew's eyes up to her mouth. "Get you something, *monsieur?*"

"In a minute." He wanted to work this, make sure the girl was properly pliable. Draw things out a bit with a few frilly words and a man could dredge up the sweeter side of a gal. "You are the pret-tiest thing I've seen in this town. Mind if I just kind of drink you in?" Amaryllis's bored expression said she had heard that one a time or two and she went back to stacking.

"Hey, I'm not some randy miner that ain't had any in months." The boredom stayed in place as she worked. "No, ma'am, I take the time to appreciate beauty. Like that pert nose of yours, and those milky shoulders . . ." Her stacking slowed as he talked. "Emerald green eyes, curves like Venus."

"Too bad golden tongues aren't worth as much as gold nuggets, *oui?* You would be rich."

Matthew fished a ten dollar gold piece out of his pocket and laid it on the rough-sawed bar. "Who says I'm not? Give me a bottle, two glasses, and keep the change."

At the sound of the money hitting the bar, Amaryllis swung around. She smiled like Midas about to touch a stone and reached for the coin. Matthew knew he had won some ground. He winked at her and moved to a table in the corner, near the cold buck stove. A moment later Amaryllis brought him his bottle. He motioned to the empty seat near him. "That second glass is for you. I'd like to toast my health."

Amaryllis hesitated, and then brought a reddish curl around to the front of her shoulder. A hungry smile tipped her lips and heat smoldered in her eyes. "That's mighty sweet of you, *mon chérie.* Don't mind if I do." She sat down and poured both drinks.

Matthew touched his side, the pounding downright distracting. He could stand to lie down, some place he could throw back a few and not have to worry about his language or keeping up the gentlemanly demeanor. He let his eyes roam over Amaryllis' pretty strawberry hair, piled attractively atop her head. He took another gander, too, at the tight, revealing red dress that pushed her bosom nice and high.

"Too bad I won't be hanging around Defiance all that long."

She stuck out her lip in a seductive pout. "Oh, but you can't leave until we have a nice party."

That made him chuckle. "Well, plans can change." He picked up his glass. "Let's toast to my weakness and say good-bye to her."

Amaryllis sighed deeply. "I used to be a man's weakness. Now I come to town and everything has changed. The Iron Horse is closed. The Garden is closed—"

"McIntyre? You know Charles McIntyre?"

Amaryllis grinned like the devil with a dark, decadent secret. "I know every inch of him." The air around Matthew warmed twenty degrees and he tugged at his collar. She licked her upper lip, slowly, provocatively, and Matthew swallowed. The woman knew exactly how to play this game. "I was his—how do you say— summer dove." Amaryllis rested her elbows on the table, shoving her creamy white breasts to the edge of bursting from her dress. "He told me himself I was his one weakness."

His one *weakness?*

Matthew slammed back the whiskey in an effort to cool his desire and clear an idea from his head. But as the liquor burned down his throat he heard a voice taunting *all's fair in love and war.*

CHAPTER 28

*B*illy gasped and struggled to suck in a breath but his chest wouldn't cooperate.

What the. . .

He heard Prince Valiant's terrified squeal and realized they'd taken a bad fall. Squeezing his eyes shut, Billy forced his lungs to function. Air cleared his head some and he clawed up to a sitting position. A black headache thundered through his brain. Beside him, Prince Valiant flailed and kicked his way back to his feet. He wouldn't put down his left front leg, but held it up, curled in.

"Oh, God, what have I done?" Billy moaned and climbed to his feet. The headache intensified, temporarily blacking out his vision. Gritting his teeth, he fought off the vertigo and staggered to his horse. Prince Valiant nickered, lowered his head, and pointed his ears straight out to the sides. "Boy, oh, Val, I'm so sorry." Billy rubbed his horse's nose lovingly. Slowly, he worked his way down until he squatted beside Val's leg. "What have I done? What have I done?" he muttered over and over as he gently ran his hand up and down the horse's cannon bone to his ankle.

He felt the heat in Val's pastern but the horse shied away from Billy's touch. After several attempts to assess the damage, he gave up. Heartsick over this new development, he grabbed the dangling rope and plunked down on the ground. He studied the vast empty pasture, cringed at the silence, and wondered just how far they were from town.

He eyed Prince Valiant's leg again.

Too far.

He cursed and raised his gaze to heaven. "Is this your idea of helping me? Well, thanks a heap!"

The horse jerked at the outburst and Billy almost let the lead line slide through his hand. "Whoa, boy, whoa, it's all right."

Shaking his head, Billy wiped sweat and dirt from his forehead. The aches and pains from the fight, now compounded by the fall, battered him with a vengeance. Even his little toe hurt. He cursed again and wondered what the heck had happened to his hat.

He spotted it a few feet away, flat and crumpled. Stiffly, moving like his joints were greased with sand, he struggled to a standing position. Dizziness skewed his vision again. He pinched the bridge of his nose and waited for it to pass.

"Yeah, this is just lovely, God." He sniffed, angry that his throat had tightened up. Feeling very small and alone in this big, green pasture, he wondered what he needed to do to stop being so stupid. Stupid for dallying with Hannah. Stupid for letting his father push him into abandoning her. Stupid for racing his horse across a pasture full of gopher holes and stumps.

Stupid for being angry with God.

He turned around so he could rub Prince Valiant's nose. Seemed his stupid choices only hurt the ones he cared about. "Maybe I *could* use a little help, God," he whispered, embarrassed he was even asking. After all, who was he to God? He leaned his head back to take in the wide azure sky, strung with thin strands of clouds. "Are you even there?"

"Hey, down there!"

Startled nearly out of his skin, Billy jumped back from Prince

Valiant and scanned the pasture above them. His mouth fell open in shock. Emilio stood in the saddle of his little pinto, waving his dirty, tan cowboy hat.

"Billy, are you all right?"

"No," he snapped, seething that God's idea of help was Emilio.

"You need help?"

He tried to ignore the question, but realized, grudgingly, that God *had* sent help. Time to stop being stupid. "Yeah, I think I broke Valiant's leg." The admission hurt like a mule's kick.

Emilio loped down the pasture and reined in skillfully along-side them. Nervous, Prince Valiant nickered, gingerly dropped his leg to shift positions, but raised it immediately. Emilio slid effort-lessly out of the saddle, passed Billy one rein, and touched the horse's nose. "Shhh, ees all right, boy." He ran his hands over Valiant's face, then his neck and shoulder, and worked his way slowly to the injured leg. Again, Valiant shied away at a touch there, but before Billy knew it, Emilio was gently rubbing and massaging the spot. "It's not broken."

Relief gushed through Billy. "Just a strain, right?"

"I think it may be the tendon," he said, stepping over to his own horse.

That wasn't great, but it was better than broken. Recovery would be longer, though.

Emilio unbuckled his saddle bag and flipped it. Rummaging through it quickly, he pulled out a dirty piece of gauze about four inches wide and three or so feet long. "This is all I have, but it will get him back to town."

Frowning, Billy watched as Emilio knelt down and expertly wrapped the injured leg. The timing of his arrival could only have been more perfect if he'd stopped the accident altogether. Which led him to ask, "What are you doing here, anyway?"

"Hannah asked me to come find you." He glanced up. "She saw you ride off and was worried."

Billy had to absorb that. She had sent Emilio after him. Did she care he might get hurt or did she *care*?

"She said that when you are upset, you don't ride wisely." Emilio stood up and pushed his sweat-stained hat back off his forehead. With the one good eye that wasn't nearly swollen shut, he searched Billy's face, sizing him up. "You should quit being so stupid."

Anger flared, but died almost instantly. Hadn't he just thought that very thing moments ago? Besides, he hurt too much for another fight. "Yeah, well, I'm working on it."

CHAPTER 29

*A*midst the squeak of leather and wood, McIntyre
leaned back in the chair in the marshal's office. His
telegram requesting the Reverend's presence for the wedding had
been sent and now he was committed. Sometime in the next few
days, Charles McIntyre would be a married man.

*Married. Committed to one woman for the rest of my life. The right
woman.*

Beckwith's eyes narrowed to slits. "You come to tell me something or just warm that chair?"

McIntyre blinked away images of a future he once had never
believed possible. Reaching into his breast pocket for a cheroot,
he dipped his head. "I'm a little distracted. I'm getting married."

"That is definitely the sort of thing that can distract a man,"
Beckwith deadpanned.

McIntyre couldn't be sure but the marshal's mouth almost
twitched, as if he'd thought about cracking a smile. He doubted
he'd ever know.

The lawman picked up the cold, half-smoked stogie sitting on
his desk. "And it does call for a smoke." McIntyre lit his own then
obliged the lawman with the same match. As smoke swirled above

them, Beckwith leaned back as well and crossed a boot over his knee. "Mrs. Miller?" McIntyre nodded. "Well, it's good to see a man like you trying to become respectable."

McIntyre's jaw clenched. *A man like you.* Lately, he'd come to despise that phrase. As, perhaps, Paul had? But that wasn't why he was here now. "Have you learned anything else about One-Who-Cries?"

"I've done a little homework." Beckwith took a long drag on his cigar and exhaled. "Mostly he's been a lone renegade, hitting isolated claims and folk who are foolish enough to let their guard down. Seems to pick his targets carefully. No more than three or four victims at a time."

McIntyre knew all that. One-Who-Cries was of the Uncompaghre tribe, but had branched off on his own several years ago. His targets were smaller because he wanted to kill white people in the most brutal ways he could imagine. Men, women, children—it didn't matter. He lived to rape, burn, dismember. The warrior was determined to instill fear in the heart of every white man in Colorado. One horribly tortured and dismembered body was better than three with simple bullet holes.

Beckwith shuffled through the papers on his desk and settled on one with several notes scrawled on it. He skimmed it, set it back down, tapped it with his index finger. "The band he's leading suffers from infighting. The young men he managed to get off the reservation last year have mostly scattered in recent weeks, but he picked up several more by rabble-rousing. The Indian agent down there, a blockhead by the name of Meeker, couldn't catch him. He dispatched troops, but they lost the trail after two days."

McIntyre realized that was the situation Chief Ouray had referred to in his telegram. "Meeker is a disaster as an Indian agent," he said. "He has this turn-the-ponies-into-plow-horses idea and the Utes hate it. White River is a breeding ground for angry, hot-tempered braves."

"The Red Man will not assimilate." Beckwith sounded

supremely confident in his assessment. "I agree that this Meeker is driving the Utes into a corner. He's pushing them into a fight. Only good thing to come out of it is he'll be the first to die."

"I'm surprised One-Who-Cries hasn't killed him already. The Indian is . . ." McIntyre pushed away the stomach-churning images his nemesis evoked and crushed his cheroot in the ash tray. ". . . unusually violent, to put it mildly."

Beckwith shrugged, as if unimpressed. "Indians are a blood-thirsty lot, in general. What you don't know is that Black Elk gave Hannah some information" Intrigued, McIntyre leaned in. "I'm trying to track down the facts. She said he and One-Who-Cries attacked some folks at Horse Mesa. That's where he got his food poisoning and apparently One-Who-Cries abducted a girl. Black Elk further stated that One-Who-Cries is going to spread death and destruction between here and White River. Seems the savage has had a vision or some such."

McIntyre rubbed his neck and shifted in the chair. "One-Who-Cries is not known for the accuracy of his visions, merely the bloodiness of them." The lawman grunted. McIntyre thought Beckwith sounded almost bored with the situation and that worried him. Fighting Indians was not the same thing as fighting outlaws. The difference was like night and day. Again, the image of a dearly-beloved friend being skinned like a deer—a *live* deer—streaked through his mind. McIntyre pinched the bridge of his nose in a futile attempt to block the memory. "I would urge you, Marshal, not to underestimate One-Who-Cries. He's been running wild for nearly ten years and we haven't caught him yet. We came close once . . . the last time, we got the jump on him." McIntyre flexed his fingers as the picture of One-Who-Cries' hawkish face rose in his mind. "I wasn't any farther from him than I am from you. I raised my rifle . . . and got clubbed from behind." The Indian's escape was still a bitter disappointment, especially since they'd carried back three dead soldiers. *How many had died since then?* "He's a rabid dog, Marshal, in need of killing."

"Just a matter of time. His range is getting smaller and smaller."

"What about the girl? Is that true?" God, for her sake, he prayed it wasn't.

Beckwith fingered a thin stack of yellow papers with Western Union printed at the top. "I sent out telegrams requesting information. The sheriff in Ruby said a peddler and his family came through about a week ago. They sold tainted food to a couple of miners and if Indians got 'em, good riddance."

"Black Elk's food poisoning?" McIntyre said more to himself than Beckwith.

"Most likely. The sheriff said the family was headed to Gunnison. They haven't been seen around there yet."

"Maybe they've camped somewhere." Entirely possible. There were dozens of places to wash off trail dust and rest. Unfortunately, Horse Mesa was one of them.

"Maybe." Beckwith sounded doubtful . . . or bored. "The sheriff in Gunnison is going to look for them. Said he'd let us know if he found anything. What I can't figure is if everything Black Elk says is true, why is he here in town? You'd think he'd still be with One-Who-Cries."

McIntyre ran his hands through his hair. Taking a deep breath, he laced his fingers behind his head and wished he had the answer. "He's a nomad and mostly a loner. Maybe he decided he didn't have the stomach for slaughter. I know he hasn't been in Defiance for over three years."

The marshal crushed his cigar in a coffee mug, the creases in his forehead smoothing out. "Well, either way, One-Who-Cries should be out of the area by now. From what I've learned, he's rarely seen in the same place twice."

Troubled by Beckwith's nonchalant attitude, McIntyre stood up and grabbed his hat off the marshal's desk. "That all the information Hannah got out of him?"

"So far. Doc says he went through a bad spell, but seems to

have turned a corner. We'll see. Maybe he'll feel more like talking this evening."

McIntyre slipped his Stetson on, dissatisfied with the lack of solid information. If One-Who-Cries had any designs on Defiance or its outlying settlements, they needed to know. Maybe it meant nothing at all that Black Elk was here, but McIntyre didn't like One-Who-Cries within a hundred miles of Defiance. A thousand miles would be too close.

---

*S*tartled by a yelp from behind her, Hannah nearly dropped the heavy Dutch oven full of baked beans. Quickly setting it on the stove, she turned as Mollie and a young Negro girl hugged and gushed noisily in the kitchen.

"Amanda! Oh, my goodness," Mollie squealed. "What are you doing here?"

As the two friends embraced, Hannah raised a brow at Rebecca, who had paused peeling eggs at the table to watch the reunion. She shrugged, at a loss as well. Mollie quickly remembered her manners, though, and stepped back to introduce her friend. "I'm sorry. This is Amanda. I worked with her for a short time down at—I mean, we were both—that is to say, Flowers. We were both Flowers." Amanda dropped her gaze, but Mollie laughed and elbowed her friend lightly. "It's all right. They're friends." The girl raised her chin, buoyed by the comment.

"So, if you're here, I take it you're not working at a saloon." Mollie wondered, sounding hopeful. "Am I right?"

"I'm *working* here." She glanced at Rebecca and Hannah. "Naomi hired me, and Mr. McIntyre says he is going to help me go to school."

The girls' mouths dropped open. Mr. McIntyre was going to send Amanda to school? Hannah thought that was a much better idea than merely giving his former Flowers cash.

"Amanda, you'll have to catch me up—*us*—catch *us* up on that." Mollie grabbed the girl's arm and the four settled at the kitchen table.

"You could have knocked me over with a feather, I'll tell you that," Amanda said, shaking her head in disbelief. "I went in, hoping to get a nice, cushy job at the cleanest saloon in town, but he asked me, straight up, did I want out?" She splayed out her hands on the table and tapped it nervously. "What was I supposed to say, especially when I realized he was serious?"

"You mean you didn't mean it?" Hannah asked.

"No, no. I meant it. I just didn't think he'd do anything about it. Now he's working on setting up a scholarship for me, living expenses, and Naomi put me on here as a cook. It all happened . . ." she snapped her fingers, "just like that."

"Hallelujah," Rebecca said, raising her hands to heaven. "I am so tired of working six days a week."

"So what's changed in Defiance?" Amanda asked Mollie. "Is Rose still around?"

Mollie sighed. "How much time do you have? She's in the new state prison, but the marshal is still taking depositions—"

"Marshal? Wade's gone?"

Mollie let slip a knowing smile. "That's right, Wade was sweet on you."

"And I was a big fool. I ran off with Toby Johnson. He couldn't stay sober for more than two days at a stretch. It didn't last a year." The regret thick in her voice, Amanda looked down at her hands.

"Amanda . . ." Hannah waited for the girl to look up. "*You* are in the right place. We make mistakes. But they don't make us. Mollie and I can tell you all about that."

"And we will." Mollie winked at Hannah. "In due time."

After a few minutes of friendly conversation, the urgency of getting food ready for paying customers prompted them all to get to work, including Amanda. Hannah liked the way the girl jumped right in and took over the stew, but something nagged at her. She figured it was the way Amanda had said *What was I supposed to say.* Maybe it didn't mean anything. Most likely it didn't. Who wouldn't want out of that life? But the girl cooked and moved about the kitchen with almost grim determination. As if she was fighting an internal struggle.

Troubled, Hannah sat down beside Rebecca and commenced helping her peel a dozen hard-boiled eggs. Mollie and Amanda chatted about their home states and future plans. The kitchen bubbled over with the sound of sizzling steaks, friendly conversation, and light-hearted laughs. The smiles, though, didn't quite reach Amanda's eyes. Unable to put her finger on what was wrong, Hannah gave up and turned the conversation toward wedding preparations.

CHAPTER 30

*B*illy talked in hushed, gentle tones to Prince Valiant while Emilio scoured the lean-to for his medicine bag. The walk back to the hotel had taken them much longer than they'd expected, but they'd made it by sunset. Now, before he lost all the light, Emilio said he had a treatment he wanted to get on the horse. He had draped Cochise's reins over the fence and jogged over to the lean-to.

Billy tied Prince Valiant to the fence and unsaddled Emilio's horse for him. It was the least he could do. The kid had been exceptionally patient on the walk back, never rushing, and he'd checked the injured leg at least a dozen times. Under different circumstances, Billy was willing to admit he and Emilio might have actually been friends.

Though they hadn't talked much on the way back, Billy had learned that Emilio had hung with some pretty tough characters, his sister being the worst of them all, apparently. Emilio had told Billy the story of what Rose had done and his stomach rolled at the thought of a crazy woman threatening Hannah and Little Billy.

Carrying a bottle filled with a golden liquid that had the same tint as beer, Emilio quick-stepped back over to Prince Valiant. "We need to put this on him a couple of times a day, for about a week." He squatted down and pulled a long, cotton dabber out of the bottle. It reeked with an odor like camphor, menthol and a week-old corpse. Grimacing, Billy threw Cochise's saddle over the fence and watched Emilio for a moment. He removed the wrap and slathered the liquid all over the horse's leg, dipping the stick repeatedly.

Billy blinked, the stench so heavy in the air it brought tears to his eyes. "What is in that concoction?"

In the fading light, Emilio grinned and his teeth gleamed. Apparently he got this question a lot. "Peppermint oil, peppers, camphor, herbs, a few other things. It works well."

"Bet it keeps bugs away, too."

"*Si*, it does." Emilio capped the bottle, handed it to Billy, and rewrapped Prince Valiant's leg with great care. Billy swirled the pungent brew around and chuckled. One minute, they were trying to kill each other, and the next, Emilio was saving his horse.

"Thanks." No, that sounded stiff and proud . . . like his father. Billy knew he could be a better man than that and touched Emilio on the shoulder. "I mean it. Thank you."

---

irelight flickered in the white girl's eyes. They were wide with fear. One-Who-Cries knew that look. He had seen it enough in his own people. He enjoyed being the cause of it for her. His smile growing, he pulled his knife out of his sheath and watched her expression as the light glinted off his blade. With a soft whimper, the girl drew her bound hands up in front of her and cowered deeper into the shadows.

"You'd better put that back, *amigo*," an impatient voice warned from the darkness. A man in a ragged sombrero and poncho stepped out of the shadows and approached their fire. "Your temper has cost you three rifles already." Squatting, he pulled out his own knife and used the light of the flames to inspect the blade. His hawkish features set like stone, he flipped one edge of his frayed poncho over his shoulder and carved a piece of rabbit loose from the spit. He snatched the steaming meat with the tips of his fingers and quickly dropped it to the plate at his feet. Blowing on the burned flesh, he warned One-Who-Cries, "You can't keep killing the merchandise. If you don't hold up your end of the bargain, Sanchez will not trade with you again. *Comprende?*"

One-Who-Cries sneered at the man, wondering if he should kill him or not. "This girl's sister is dead only because *she* fought. Her death is on her head."

"You lost your temper. You should learn to control it."

"She was a stupid white woman . . . and you should learn to keep your mouth shut."

The Mexican's jaw tightened. "A stupid white woman worth *three* rifles."

One-Who-Cries considered this. A full belly made it easier to put the knife back. He had done enough killing for one day. "True, it would have been easier if I had not killed her. But I already know where to go to get another woman with yellow hair." He ripped a piece of meat off the spit with his bare hands. "I will have another woman before we make the trade. Maybe more than one."

Taking a bite of his rabbit, the man glanced at the girl in the shadows. Tangled strands of molasses-colored hair hung in her face. "Good and healthy like her, he will give you one rifle. But you don't get the three unless—"

"Unless she has yellow hair." One-Who-Cries stared into the flames and wondered if a roasting Mexican smelled like a burning white man. He would have to find out another time. "Tell Sanchez to have extra rifles. I will have extra women."

*M*cIntyre tied a blue silk cravat at his neck as he stood in front of his mirror appraising his appearance. Neatly trimmed beard and mustache, precisely tailored vest and pants, a new gray frock coat, glossed black boots. His wavy, dark hair, still damp, grazed his collar. He laughed inwardly at how he used to dress to impress everyone, and now he only cared to impress Naomi.

The answer to his telegram resided in his breast pocket. The preacher would be here on Friday's noon stage. *Please set the wedding for some time Saturday.* McIntyre was sure the wheels were in motion for an enchanting event. He wanted to believe he could make the wedding *night* magical, but there was a finger of concern that poked at him.

Would she think of John? It was only natural if she did. But would she compare the two—?

Perhaps she would wonder if McIntyre was comparing her.

Frustrated, he snatched the cravat out and tied it again. Ridiculous thoughts. It didn't matter. In time, both their pasts would fade.

He heard the door downstairs squeak, followed by the tromp of boots. Brannagh's husky voice floated up to him as his right-hand man greeted someone, and then the boots, more than one pair, headed up the stairs.

A sharp tap on his door and Ian's lively Scottish accent. "Are ye presentable, mon?"

"Not until I get this cravat tied."

His friend ignored the comment and entered, followed by two young men who had clearly had a rough day. Cuts and bruises marred their faces, blood and dirt spattered their clothes. "I've come to ask ye a favor," Ian tapped the floor with his cane and swept off his Balmoral bonnet, swinging it toward Emilio and Billy, "for the boys here."

"For what? A surgeon?" McIntyre assumed this had been the

fight he'd heard about earlier today. Fat lips, swollen noses, and black eyes. Bruised and cut cheeks. Seemed it was a respectable fight. Emilio fared a little better, but only a little. "You win?"

The boy shifted uncomfortably and strangled the hat in his hands. "No, sir, I just cleaned up a little better."

"Which is why we're here," Ian interrupted. "I should think these boys could avail themselves of yer bath facilities, seeing as how Maude's Bathhouse could tempt them into trouble."

McIntyre heard the humor bubbling in Ian's voice, but didn't get the joke. Maude's was fit for a preacher on *Wednesday* nights. It was Saturday nights you needed to keep your pistol in the tub with you. Still, it was a stone's throw from the Lucky Deuce and they could definitely find trouble *there*. Emilio had proven himself a steady, focused lad. The other boy, who must be Billy, was the big question mark. "Fine, boys. You're more than welcome. Emilio, you know where everything is and Brannagh should still have water heated." He checked with Ian to see if the instructions met with his approval. The Scotsman nodded. "By the way," McIntyre crossed the room to Billy and offered his hand. "We haven't met formally. I'm Charles McIntyre."

"Billy Page. And thank you for the bath." Billy took his hand gingerly, and McIntyre saw the war wounds.

"You're welcome." McIntyre nodded, pondering the banker's son. He'd spent a few thousand dollars determining the boy's whereabouts last year, only to have Hannah reject the information. She'd never contacted him, yet here he was.

Naomi might kill him for this, but these two looked like they could use a drink, solely for medicinal purposes, of course. "Help yourselves to a gentlemanly amount of whiskey, if you are so inclined. And the emphasis is on *gentlemanly*. But I think you two could use it. And, Billy, when you're done, could I have a word with you?"

Nodding and mumbling their thanks, the two boys shuffled out the door. McIntyre stepped back in front of his mirror, determined to tie the cravat to perfection. "Now, what was that all about, Ian? Why are you here and not back at the hotel with an apron tied around your waist?"

"The restaurant's a wee bit slow tonight." He settled into an armchair near the window and gazed out over the mostly empty street, his fingers dancing atop the wolf's head on his cane. "I'm taking a much needed break, as is Rebecca. The new lass— Amanda is it?—is cooking."

McIntyre followed Ian's gaze out the window. Prior to the Iron Horse closing down, the avenue had flowed with scores of men, on foot and on horse, going back and forth, spending their evenings in debauchery. From his saloon to the ones in Tent Town they'd traveled, all night long. Drinking. Gambling. Carousing. How had he ever been proud of his association with that? At least now the activities were restricted to Tent Town.

"Do ye remember Defiance on a Wednesday night a year ago?" Ian asked.

"A particular Wednesday night?"

"Nay, just the crowd and the traffic and the caliber of men?"

McIntyre fluffed his tie, finally pleased. "I'm not sorry things have changed. Surely you're not." He snatched his hat off the corner of his mirror and faced his friend. "So why did you bring those boys here? They could have gone to the bathhouse without any trouble."

"Perhaps 'tis true, but ye've got this building right down the walk from the hotel. Besides, I hadn't been by in a while."

This is where McIntyre would normally pour them each a snifter of brandy or a shot of good whiskey. He didn't need it or want it now, though. He just wanted to get to Naomi and tell her the preacher was coming. "Well, you almost missed me. I heard back from Reverend Potter. He'll be on Friday's stage. He's asked that we have the wedding Saturday." The slightest hint of his self-doubts laced the last sentence.

"Aye, that is good news." Ian inclined his head. "But . . .?"

"I still struggle with . . ." He shook off the lost sentence and marched to the window. "It seems I'm trying to change everything about my life, Ian, and sometimes I wonder if I've bit off more than I can chew. Reaching too high, as it were." He hated that thought. He'd never doubted himself like this. But he'd also never seen his sinfulness with such lucidity. "Am I right for her? Will I be good to her? What if I wake up one morning and I don't want to read the Bible?"

Ian pursed his lips and stared down at the Oriental rug on McIntyre's floor. "Scripture calls it a race, lad. Not a casual stroll. Furthermore, we are admonished to fight the good fight." He looked up then. "If following Jesus was easy, we would not be told to put on the full armor of God. I've no advice for ye, other than *persevere*. God has brought ye this far. He'll finish what He's started."

Good advice. Sound advice. And it did bring McIntyre a measure of peace.

A little stiffly, Ian rose to his feet. McIntyre saw the troubled contemplation his friend still wore and kicked himself for not being more attentive. "What is it? Something else?"

Ian scratched the back of his head, causing a few strands of his silver hair to point in various directions. "Rebecca. I'd like to ask the woman to marry me, but now I'm thinking I should wait a bit."

"What for?"

"Till ye and Naomi are married. I'm not sure how a woman would feel about having such an event *shared*, so to speak."

McIntyre sucked on his cheek. He was not willing in any way, shape, or form to try guessing how Naomi might feel about this. In his very limited experience with brides, McIntyre had noticed they tended to get a bit *irrational* about the smallest things.

He stuck his finger through the bullet hole in his hat and decided Naomi wasn't the irrational kind. She was quite pragmatic. "Ian, we're not guaranteed our next breath. *I'm* through waiting."

Ian nodded slowly as if mulling over the advice, then he took his friend's hand. "I didnae tell ye congratulations. I hope ye'll be very happy."

"I've no doubt it will be interesting."

"Aye, Rebecca and I, should she accept my proposal, will be like an old, comfortable pair of shoes together. Ye and Naomi, I suspect, will live a life of thunder and lightning."

McIntyre was fascinated by Ian's prediction. Slipping his hat on his head, he asked, "Which is better, do you think?"

"While Rebecca and I will live longer," he winked, "Ye and Naomi will live more passionately." Grinning, he strode to the door. "I'll see ye back at the hotel."

Smiling over Ian's reference to thunder and lightning, McIntyre stepped to his dresser and pulled two new shirts from the top drawer. Momentarily, he heard a soft knock on the door. "Come in."

Billy popped his head in, hair wet and slicked back. "You wanted to see me?"

McIntyre nodded. "Yes, I wanted to give you and Emilio new shirts. I would prefer that you two not show up at my wedding poorly attired and unwashed." He handed him the items.

Billy read the labels and raised his eyebrows. "These are very nice shirts. Thank you."

McIntyre plucked a cheroot from his breast pocket and waved the comment away with it. "My pleasure. Regarding the other matter," he strode to his desk and dropped the smoke into the ash tray. "I thought it the decent thing to let you know—last year I hired Beckwith to track you down." He turned to Billy and leaned on the desk. "I don't normally spy on folks, but I suppose you could say I had a moment of chivalrous weakness."

Billy ran his hand through his hair and brought it to rest on his neck. "I don't understand. Once you found me, what did you do with that information?"

McIntyre shrugged and reached for the cheroot again. "It made its way back to Hannah. I understand she chose not to contact you. How did you find her, if you don't mind me asking?"

Billy frowned as if he was digesting this information. Apparently he had not been aware that Hannah could have reached out to him, if she had been so inclined. The girl had pride.

"I—I found a Pinkerton report in my father's desk. I had already made up my mind to find Hannah. The report made it easier."

Silence fell between them as McIntyre pondered what kind of man Billy Page might turn out to be. He'd come a long way to see Hannah, although Naomi wasn't yet sold on his reasons. McIntyre, on the other hand, had no doubt. "Naomi told me a little about your father. Was the price high to come after Hannah?"

"It cost me everything my father thinks matters in life."

"And what do you think?'

"Everything that matters to me is right here in Defiance."

One-Who-Cries did not like to wait. And he did not like being this close to Defiance knowing he couldn't kill McIntyre . . . yet. First, he needed guns. To get guns, he needed the girl with yellow hair.

His horse stamped her feet, the sound swallowed quickly by the thick forest of aspens. Where was Black Elk? If he found out the worthless Indian was lying drunk in a saloon somewhere . . .

He clenched his jaw, angry that the brave was late . . . or not coming at all. Perhaps this was part of the Great Spirit's plan, to teach One-Who-Cries patience. How long had he prayed for a vision telling him when he could finally skin McIntyre alive? Eight winters? He avenged the murder of his mother and little brother every day. But still he waited to kill the white man who had fouled Hopping Bird and left her with a half-breed child.

Memories, dark and bitter, rained down on him like falling leaves, pulling him back to a blazing council fire.

"Hopping Bird is my daughter and I will do with her as I see fit." Ouray crossed his arms over his chest, his face hard and unrelenting in the flickering light.

One-Who-Cries clenched his hands into tight fists. He felt the eyes of the council on him, urging restraint. But a boy of seventeen winters would not be held back by foolish old men afraid of the Blue Coats.

He stepped back so he could see Ouray and the council members seated behind him. Their dead stares enraged him, made him feel small. Seething, he pounded a fist into his chest. "She was promised to me. Me!" His eyes darted to McIntyre, standing quietly in the shadows. "I will kill that white man before he can touch her."

McIntyre took a step forward. Chief Ouray raised his hand, signaling him to stay put. "You disgrace yourself before the council, One-Who-Cries. Speaking against your chief is not the Ute way."

"First Two Moons and then Fat Buffalo!" Spittle flew from One-Who-Cries' mouth. He raised a fist at his chief, wishing he could pound the old man's skull into pulp. The fibers in his body grew as tight as drying rawhide and he shook with his anger. "Their bones are still smoldering and you would give her to this—"

"Leave, One-Who-Cries," Ouray said softly. "Leave your tribe freely and in peace. If you stay, there will be no peace between us." The old man's solemn warning haunted him, echoing in his heart.

One-Who-Cries had left . . . and there had been no peace on that path either. Tired, often covered in white man's blood, the emptiness in his heart still burned, emptiness only Hopping Bird could fill.

Before two summers had passed, his tribe was moved to White Mountain Reservation.

He exhaled quietly and recalled his first scouting trip there to find her. Riding among the people, he looked into their soulless eyes and shivered. They were skeletons wrapped in filthy blankets, shuffling about as if they were lost in the spirit world. He sniffed and smelled dung and wood fires, but not the scent of roasting meat. He heard no laughter from the children. The teepees, ragged and hastily built, moved with the breeze.

Once such a proud people, these Utes had been broken. Fuming, he wondered how a chief could condemn his people to this.

Hugging a rolled up blanket, Hopping Bird shuffled up to his horse. One-Who-Cries wanted to weep and rage when he saw her. She was a fragile shell of the girl he had left. She smiled at him as he dismounted, but the greeting was as thin as a morning mist. Her dress of blue checkered cloth hung from her thin body. Her dark hair that once glimmered like a black snake in spring, dangled in dingy braids down her shoulders. She was dying in this place and One-Who-Cries could not stand it.

"I have come for you, Hopping Bird. I will kill McIntyre for you, if need be. But I will not leave without you."

She loosened her grip on the blanket in her arms and shook her head. "He is not here. He left me before the Utes were moved to the reservation."

One-Who-Cries was only a little relieved. He had wanted the chance to see McIntyre without Ouray watching like a mother bear. "Then come with me now."

He saw a light of hope flicker in her eyes, but she looked away quickly. "Two Spears?" She spoke over her shoulder. When no one replied, she said it again. "Two Spears, come here."

A small child slowly peeked out from behind a barrel. He was chubby, covered in dirt, and nibbling on a piece of fry bread. One-

Who-Cries' little brother Fat Buffalo had lived with a piece clutched in his hands. The memory stung.

This child toddled up behind his mother and hid in the folds of her skirt. Hopping Bird reached around and touched him on the shoulder. "He is my son. I cannot leave him. I cannot leave my people."

The frightened, curious eyes risked a broader peek out from behind his mother. One-Who-Cries took a small step back. For all the hate in his heart, One-Who-Cries loved Hopping Bird and she loved this child. Why else would she starve herself so that he would grow fat and live?

"Where is his father?"

"Once the treaty was signed, he traded my father many horses and cattle . . . for land. And he said he did not want a wife. He said he would work to keep the peace between us and the Blue Coats. And he promised supplies."

Supplies? One-Who-Cries looked around again and saw only hunger and death. He almost choked on his hate. It burned in his blood turning his spirit to ashes. His fingers itched to slice McIntyre open like an elk and watch his intestines spill out on the ground.

One-Who-Cries pulled himself free of this painful memory and scrounged for one more pleasant. Though Hopping Bird had refused to leave the reservation, she had become his wife. He went often to see her and bring her food, blankets, what supplies he could sneak to her and Two Spears. The boy, ten winters now, was good with a sling. He would be a great warrior one day. Hopping Bird had visions and she had seen this.

One-Who-Cries exhaled, frustrated with the pace of things. Most of Hopping Bird's visions had been very clear—that One-Who-Cries would kill many white men, take their women, burn their homes. Yet she had not seen when to attack Defiance or Charles McIntyre. One-Who-Cries had come so close once he could have reached out and struck the white man down with his fist. But Yankee soldiers had saved him.

Many winters had passed since that battle. One day, the waiting would be over. One-Who-Cries would meet McIntyre again and the murders of Two Moons and Fat Buffalo, the slow death of the Ute people, the broken spirit in Hopping Bird, it would all be avenged.

He peered into the shadows and listened to the woods around him. The horse swished her tail back and forth, shifted her hooves. Birds whistled and called in peace.

Black Elk was not coming.

One-Who-Cries raised his chin. He would have to get the woman himself. And perhaps, this would be his chance to kill Charles McIntyre.

CHAPTER 31

"All right, Amanda, that's the last table." Hannah deposited a heap of dishes on the counter next to the sink and turned to the new girl. Amanda scrubbed a cast iron pan with a vengeance, her concentration practically scalding the grime off it. Hannah cocked her head to one side and pondered the girl. She'd cooked like this, too, as if a burnt steak or under-cooked potatoes might result in the collision of heaven and earth. Hannah had never seen anyone concentrate so hard, as if she was trying to avoid thinking about something else altogether.

Maybe, she thought, a few encouraging words would make them both feel better. "You did a really fine job tonight. Thank you for jumping in to help like you did."

"It was nothing." Amanda wiped a sleeve across her forehead to fight back a few stray wiry curls and changed scrubbing hands. "I have to stay busy."

"Well, how was your first night, Amanda?"

She and Hannah turned as Naomi floated through the café doors. Floated was the right word too, Hannah thought. Her sister had stars in her eyes, a glow about her, and moved like she had clouds beneath her feet. Amanda didn't seem to notice.

"Oh, fine," the new girl said, turning back to her work. She turned the pot upside down and placed it in the dish rack to dry. "This wasn't a hard evening at all."

"Well, it's going to get easier. I have some news." Naomi laced her fingers together in front of her and shrugged her shoulders as if she was nervous. "The preacher is coming on the Friday stage and Charles would like us all to concentrate on the wedding. He's buying us out for the next three days. Maybe even a day or two more."

Hannah's mouth fell open. They'd worked so hard, from the moment they'd set foot in Defiance last July. Now, finally, a holiday of sorts. She grabbed Naomi's hands and laughed. "Oh, praise the Lord. A break!" Hannah hugged her sister, squeezing the breath out of her. "We'll have time to make all kinds of decorations for the wedding!" Naomi hugged her back, stiff as a board at first, but shortly Hannah felt her relax.

"You're all right with this then? You think I'm doing the right thing?"

Hannah stepped back to arm's length, but kept a hold on Naomi's shoulders. "I already said so. He loves you and you love him. And John would want you to be happy. What else do you need?"

"I need to tell Rebecca." She started to turn, stopped, and smiled at Hannah. "I would never have seen any of this coming. Not in a million years."

"Doesn't it simply amaze you the things God's love can accomplish? I mean, he's really a changed man. Don't you think?"

For an instant, a shadow clouded Naomi's face, but she lifted her chin and it fled. "Yes. Yes, I believe he is a changed man. And speaking of changed men, at least concerning clothes, Emilio and Billy are out front."

Unbidden, something stirred in Hannah. It felt a little bittersweet. She wanted to see Billy. She wanted to see Emilio. And, yet, now she found herself a little afraid of both of them. With regards to Billy, she could understand it. But Emilio?

Naomi pulled her hand away from Hannah and hurried toward the café doors. "Let me tell Rebecca we're closed." Over her shoulder, "Thank you again, Amanda."

Almost the moment she was gone, Billy and Emilio pushed through the doors. Their transformation was, indeed, startling. In spite of swollen noses, puffy lips and gouged cheeks, their faces were freshly washed and shaven. She knew that must have been quite a delicate procedure. Plus, they both wore clean clothes, including crisp white cotton shirts with pleated bibs—tailored shirts, expensive shirts. They were sure putting on the dog.

She was struck for the first time by the differences in their coloring, what wasn't black-and-blue. Billy's short, dirty blonde hair was still wet and combed smartly to the side. Emilio's jet black hair was also still wet and he'd run a comb through it. Straight and tucked behind his ears, it curled up a good inch past his collar. She realized their contradictory appearances hinted at broader differences as well. Billy, clean-cut, educated and civilized. Emilio, as long-haired as an Indian, but gentle and wise beyond his years.

Hannah bit her lip, a little unnerved by the handsome gentlemen before her. She studied them carefully while trying to ignore Billy's unwavering stare. Intent and direct, he almost seemed to be trying to tell her something. Uncomfortable with the determined gaze, she shifted her focus to Emilio.

He tapped his hat against his tan pants and lowered his chin. "We're sorry we're late, but Mr. McIntyre wanted us to have these shirts."

Hannah didn't know where to start with that. "You mean, Mr. McIntyre *gave* you those?" *How oddly generous.*

"*Si.* He said we should wear them to the wedding if they fit."

"Well, they fit nicely. You're both very handsome." The compliment had snuck out and Hannah wished immediately she could take it back. Complimenting them both, but specifically Billy, felt dangerous somehow. Eager to get past it, she remembered her manners. "Oh, I'm sorry. Amanda, let me introduce Billy and Emilio to you. Gentlemen, this is Amanda Hines. She's our new cook, until she goes off to teaching college."

Amanda nodded at the boys as she slipped off her apron. The three exchanged greetings, but she quickly returned to Hannah. "Unless you need me, I'll head on to bed?"

"Yes, please do. And thank you again for your help. These two scoundrels have plates in the warmer. I'll get them."

Amanda hesitated. She bit her lip as she laid the apron on the counter. "About tomorrow . . . if we're closed, what should I do? I really do nee—*like* to keep busy."

Hannah grabbed the apron and turned to the warmer. "We can talk about it at breakfast. You can either help us with wedding food or decorations, or do hotel chores. We'll figure it out." Using the apron as a mitt, she pulled two dinner plates from the oven and set them on the kitchen table. "Go on now and get some rest."

"All right."

Amanda nodded good evening as Billy and Emilio settled down at the kitchen table. Hannah could tell right away there was far less tension between the two and that irked her, she realized. She handed them both forks, halting almost imperceptibly when Billy's steely gaze hit her. Swallowing, she sat down across from them and whispered a blessing as both boys dug into the warmed-over roast and mashed potatoes.

Hannah watched them eat for a moment, but the chewing noises in the quiet kitchen only made the silence more awkward. "You want to tell me how Prince Valiant is? Really?"

Billy and Emilio froze. *Guilty as charged*, Hannah thought.

Billy finished his bite of potatoes. "It's his tendon. I won't be riding or racing him for a while. How did you know?"

"I know what liniment smells like." She scrunched up her nose at Emilio. "Especially your version. The whole back yard smelled to high heaven."

"*Si*, it smells bad, but it works good."

The silence returned and Hannah wanted to scream. Why couldn't they just talk and be friendly? It seemed Billy and Emilio had made progress toward that end, but what about her? Where did she fit in with these two? Why wouldn't they talk to her tonight?

"So, how is it that Mr. McIntyre came to give you two of his shirts?"

"Emilio here was going to show me where the bathhouse was and that Donohue fella overheard. He took us down to Mr. McIntyre's place and he let us use his bathroom."

"Really?" Hannah leaned forward, her curiosity getting the best of her. She'd heard so many stories about the rooms in the Iron Horse Saloon. "What was it like? Was there gold and marble everywhere?"

At first, she thought neither boy was going to answer, then, as if by mutual consent, they nodded.

"Pretty much, that's true." Billy sliced off a piece of roast and shoveled it into his mouth. "There were four tubs and they all had gold trim."

"And the counter is marble and the floor, too." Emilio shrugged. "I've seen it before, though. I used to lug the water up for the customers. It was nice to use it for a change. I know it cost a lot of money to get the marble to Defiance."

"It is fairly swanky, especially for the likes of this town." Billy didn't sound particularly impressed, though, as if he'd seen better. "But it was nice of him to let us use it. I think he wanted to make sure we'll clean up for the wedding."

"Well, obviously you will." Hannah bit her lip. She needed to stop paying them compliments. She felt like her words carried too much weight. She rested her elbows on the table and traced a knothole in the wood, puzzled that she was dawdling. "Well, it's getting late . . . Oh, Mr. McIntyre bought the hotel for a few days so we can close and get ready for the wedding. We'll need your help, if you're both willing."

"*Si*, that should be fun."

"Oh, yeah, nothing I'd rather do." Billy muttered the statement under his breath as he used a biscuit to sop up a little broth. As he raised the dripping mess to his mouth, Hannah's glare stopped him in his tracks.

"We wouldn't want to keep you from anything more important, Billy." She sat up and folded her arms across her chest. "I mean, it is only my sister's wedding. I'm sure anything a Page had to do would be more important." Guilt pinged Hannah. She was developing quite the gift for sassy comebacks. But they didn't make her feel any better.

"That's not what I meant. I don't know what I meant." Next to Billy, Emilio studied the ceiling, almost as if he was embarrassed for him. "I just wish I knew what to do."

"We could build them an arbor to stand under." Billy and Hannah swung startled gazes to Emilio. He tugged at his collar, apparently intimidated by the gawking. "I thought that it would make the ceremony . . . pretty."

Hannah would have sworn there was a pink tinge rising in Emilio's cheeks. The suggestion was a beautiful idea and she appreciated his sensitivity, though she wasn't sure Billy had been referring to the wedding with that statement. He was gawking at Emilio like he'd just suggested they *shoot* the happy couple.

Hannah reached across the table and clutched Emilio's hand. "Emilio, that's a beautiful idea." She snatched a quick sideways peek at Billy. "Very insightful."

Billy rose to his feet. "I think I'll step out back and get a little air." His shoulders sagged and his tone sounded weary. "Emilio, if you need any help with that . . . that arbor thing, just let me know."

"We could get the wood first thing in the morning."

"Sure."

Billy pushed his way through the batwings without any enthusiasm. His stance, his step, everything about him said defeat. Puzzling over what had just happened, Hannah stared at the door as it swung back and forth and finally stopped. She couldn't ignore Emilio's eyes on her, and wiped away the troubled crease in her forehead. She was still holding his hand and slowly pulled it away.

"This must be hard for you, *si?*"

She sighed, but didn't look at him. She didn't want to see him staring back at her with hope. What she wanted had just walked outside.

Would she never learn? Why couldn't she show strength when it came to him? Grow a backbone? Grow up?

Emilio was strong and steady, kind and loving, generous and honest. He was handsome in a dark, rugged way, too. He would be a much better catch than Billy. And clearly a better father. Finally, she gave in and met his gaze.

His eyes were soft and kind, but they shone with unexpected steel. "If you're still going down to Doc Cooke's tonight, I'll sleep in his front room." The firm tone in his voice intrigued her, left her with the feeling he was laying a claim. "You shouldn't be there alone."

"Well, all right, if you want to. I have to tend to Little Billy first."

Half an hour later, she went out back searching for Billy. Pulling her shawl close, Hannah took a moment to adjust to the half-moon light. Slowly, his shape emerged from the shadows. He stood down by the water, thumbs hooked in his back pockets, staring up at the moon. A twinge of melancholy hit her. He evoked such a kaleidoscope of emotions. She loved him. She hated him. She wanted to run to him. She wanted to run from him.

Emilio was so much safer.

Pulling strength from what felt like a dwindling reserve, she marched out to him. A few paces away, she stopped and cleared her throat. Slowly, he turned.

"Would you mind checking on Little Billy before you go to bed? I'm going to spend the night at Doc's office." Those blue eyes, silver in the moonlight, pierced her heart. Silently, they echoed all the desperate confessions he'd made since arriving in Defiance. That didn't mean she wanted to listen. If she did, she might believe them.

"You're going out after dark? May I accompany you?"

"I won't be alone. Emilio is going to stay . . ." Spoken aloud, the arrangement sounded inappropriate.

"Oh?"

"Doc has two patients who need watching."

"Oh. Would you mind if I came along, too?"

"Actually, I was hoping you would stay here with Little Billy." Hannah almost told him straight up *I don't want you along*. Truth was, she didn't want Emilio along either, not really. She wanted some time alone. "Of course, Rebecca, Naomi, even Mollie can help you if you need something. He is sleeping and generally sleeps through the night now. You should be fine." Pulling the shawl tighter against the cold and the emptiness, she turned and marched back toward the hotel.

She never heard Billy come up from behind. Suddenly, he was there, spinning her around, pressing his lips to hers. At first Hannah was too stunned to react, then she tried to pull away, but he held on tighter, moving a hand to the back of her head to keep his lips pinned to hers. "Please forgive me, Hannah. I love you."

She shoved against his chest but he held on to her as if his arms were forged from steel. Fury turned to defeat and she whimpered as the fight raging within her turned. She pushed against him one last time, but the battle was lost. Her hands came up around Billy's neck and she clung to him, and to the memory of their first kiss at the Christmas social. Her heart hammering wildly, she let herself forget the betrayal. For the moment, she pretended these were the strong arms of an honorable man. This was the deep, passionate kiss of a noble husband who would fight all odds to keep his family together.

Only none of that was true, and she'd fallen prey to his kiss again. Growling, she shoved Billy off her. A scream rose to her throat. "No!"

"Hannah, please . . ." Billy reached for her.

"No!" she screamed again, furious with herself. "I will not ever let you hurt me like that again."

She ran to the hotel, to a safe place. To Emilio.

CHAPTER 32

*H*annah stared hard at the shadowy boardwalk beneath her feet, intermittently illuminated by the street lamps. Emilio walked beside her, probably confused by her silence. Bawdy laughter and the sounds from a couple of different pianos wafted over to them from Tent Town, mixing the drinking songs into an unrecognizable, out-of-tune mess. This street used to sound like that, she remembered. Now, the traffic was light, and the few pedestrians on the boardwalk with them seemed sober, most likely on their way to Tent Town. Later on, sober might be debatable.

"I know Black Elk," Emilio said. "He doesn't shy away from trouble. You understand that's why I'm not leaving you alone with him?"

"Oh, the man's handcuffed to the bed." Hannah waved his concern away. "And Marshal Beckwith and Wade will stop by at least twice tonight. Not to mention, Doc's office isn't a hundred yards away from the Marshal's office. You really don't need to stay."

Besides, nursing someone helped her bring perspective to her own problems. She bit her lip, reliving Billy's kiss. The desperation in his voice when he'd asked for her forgiveness and said *I love you*. Had she overreacted? Why did he confuse her so badly? Maybe he did deserve a second chance, but she couldn't see herself giving it to him. The fear of getting hurt again was like a huge towering brick wall between them.

Oh, Lord, forgive me. Am I being haughty and proud? But I just can't stand the thought of more heartbreak.

She glanced up at Emilio for confirmation she was in the right place and was surprised to find him peering down at her. He moved a strand of black hair away from his forehead and smiled. "Would you rather I was someone else?"

She cared for him too much to lie. "Honestly, I don't know."

His countenance fell, only a little, and he nodded, as if respecting the truth.

A few minutes later they tromped up on the porch of Doc's office and Hannah knocked. Doc's muffled voice bid them enter and they found the physician working on Uncle Matt's side again.

Hannah gasped. "What happened?"

Doc looked up at his patient, a challenge in his raised brow. Uncle Matt smooshed a clumsy finger against his lips, hitting his nose in the process. "I haf been engaged thith efening." The slurred words and hint of whiskey in the air filled in the details. "Get it? *Engaged?*" He laughed drunkenly, wobbling on the table.

"Be still, son, 'less you want me sew up your liver instead of this wound." Doc straightened the man and made sure he was done teetering. Convinced of it, he hooked in another stitch.

Hannah still wasn't following the story. "But how did you tear your stitches?"

This time Doc didn't wait for Uncle Matt. "Mr. Miller here was involved in, well, let's say activities a *healthy* man would have shied away from."

Uncle Matt chuckled and hiccupped. "Amaryllith ith quite the energetic girl."

Hannah didn't have to think too hard to get the picture, and she wasn't happy about it. He had plainly said he didn't drink. And now, he'd not only ripped his stitches loose horsing around with some floozy, he was drunk as the proverbial skunk. Maybe because of Billy, Hannah was particularly sensitive to being lied to. She'd always adored Uncle Matt because of his quick wit and devil-may-care attitude. Life had certainly tainted her view of those traits.

"I guess we need to get you back to the hotel." She stepped closer to study Doc's progress. "Or is he staying here?"

Doc snipped a string and set the needle and scissors on the table. "No, I don't have a bed for him so he's all yours. Just walk him slowly."

Hannah pleaded silently with Emilio. He frowned, but nodded and wagged a finger at her. "Once he's settled, I'll come back."

Doc rolled out of the way as Emilio slipped his arms around Uncle Matt. "All right, *senor*, the party is over. Let's go."

"I'm done sewing you up, son. Lock him up if you have to, Emilio, but keep him away from Tent Town for at least two or three days."

"*Si*, we'll handle him, Doc."

*B*illy leaned on the crib and watched his son sleeping in the faint moonlight. As the minutes ticked by, the only sound in the room was the peaceful breathing of the innocent babe. If he'd ever seen perfection in the human form, he was looking at it now. His throat took on that painful tightness again and he tried to shake it off. When had he become so emotional?

When he realized all he stood to lose.

He hung his head and tried hard to imagine a future in Defiance without his son and Hannah. What if he actually lost them to Emilio? What would he do? Where would he live? And that was assuming he survived the loss. Right now, he didn't think it possible. His heart had never felt so crushed.

He'd had a split-second of confidence that she still cared about him when she'd returned his kiss. But that notion had gone up in flames when the growl had ripped loose from her throat. The sound and the despair in it had torn out his heart.

He lifted his head at a soft rustle behind him, but he didn't turn.

Several moments passed till, finally, he heard the muffled sound of a woman clearing her throat. "Billy, why are you here?" Naomi asked the question in a surprisingly gentle tone. "Really."

He half-turned to her, but kept his hands on the crib. The troubled crease in her forehead made him wonder if she was interested in more than just running him off.

Quietly, she drifted up beside him and smiled at the little angel before them. "You said you came for her. Because you're rebelling against Frank or because you love her?"

There were about a dozen answers to the question and Billy sighed. "I've never stopped missing her. Then I started wondering what kind of a man I was that I could be cowed by Pa just because I was afraid of him. Only a yellow coward would run like I did." He clutched the rail, the reasons sticking in his craw. "I wanted to stand up to him. I didn't care what it cost me. I wanted her back and I wanted to thumb my nose at Pa. He said she'd hate me. I didn't believe that, but now," he turned to Naomi, "I'm losing her and it scares the hell out of me, Naomi. I realize now that every decision I've made to get here was because I do love her. I was afraid of what that meant. What am I supposed to do if I can't win her back? What happens to my son?"

For the first time since he'd known this woman, he saw compassion in her eyes. The crease in her brow deepened and he thought maybe she finally had sympathy for him. She bit her bottom lip and shook her head. "Funny how sometimes we have to lose things we value to find out what's really important in our lives." She smiled at him and touched his elbow. "God loves you, Billy, every bit as much as He loves Hannah and this child. Find the truth in that and maybe you'll be able to let go if you have to. But I'll pray that you don't."

He turned back to Little Billy.

Let go? The thought twisted his insides. There was no conceivable way he'd ever do that. Just the *idea* threatened to stop his heart. He couldn't live without his son. He couldn't live without Hannah.

He laced his fingers together and sent up a prayer before he realized it. *Oh, God, no, please anything but that. They have to be with me. With me.*

CHAPTER 33

*H*annah sat quietly next to a softly snoring Black Elk and perused a three-year-old copy of Medicinal Quarterly. From the main room she could hear the Regulator wall clock ticking the wee hours away. In the silence, everything seemed too loud. The turning of the pages. The soft scrape of her cotton dress as she shifted in the ladder back chair. Her own breathing.

A change in Black Elk's breathing brought her head up. The Indian lay awake. His dark eyes, trained on her, sparkled with unnerving intensity. "I think I will live." His voice, though stronger, still held a raspy edge.

"Well, that *is* good news. And I'm sure you'll be back to your old self in no time." She set the periodical on the table next to her, embarrassed by the flippant words. What was his old self? Was she suggesting he go back to riding with One-Who-Cries and attacking settlers? Hannah decided the only way around the awkward silence was to plow right on through it. "Do you have any idea how you got sick?"

"The white man's food." Surprising Hannah with his quick answer, he shocked her further by sitting up and tossing his legs out of the bed. The sheet didn't move with him, and he sat there, nearly naked. He tossed long black hair over his shoulder and snatched violently at the handcuff. The clanking metal jolted Hannah and she rose to her feet, ready to run.

He smiled at her, as if he enjoyed frightening her. She wanted to bolt, but decided not to give this patient the satisfaction. Slowly, her chin up, she settled back into the chair. Black Elk's eyes widened slightly, in approval of her courage? "A white man at Horse Mesa was very sick. He smelled like death and rabbit stew. We filled his back with arrows."

Hannah held on to her stoic expression but felt the twinge in her jaw at the nonchalant declaration of murder. "If he was dying, why did you kill him?"

The Indian shrugged with a chilling indifference. "Because we could."

Hannah guessed that with Black Elk's returning health also came an unhealthy sense of bravado. Young men it seemed, no matter their race, enjoyed bragging. Perhaps she could use that. "You took a girl, didn't you? Where is she?"

"With One-Who-Cries."

"Why did he take her?" Black Elk didn't answer. He merely stared at Hannah, smirking. Sitting there, barely clothed, no doubt thinking he was quite the dangerous brave, Hannah wondered how he carried that big head atop his shoulders. She tapped her fingers on her knee as she tried to guess the questions that would keep him talking. "Why do you have a Christian name?"

Black Elk froze in the middle of a stretch to show off his rippled stomach and sizable arms. Regarding her coolly, as if she were a bug, he took a deep breath, puffing out his chest. "My mother was a Cheyenne converted to Christianity by missionaries. She believed whites and Indians could live together in peace."

"I take it you don't think that's possible."

For an instant so fleeting she could have imagined it, a shadow of sadness hastened across the young man's face. But it died in a curled lip. He yanked the handcuff that kept him shackled to the bed and flexed his fingers restlessly. "I believe you should all die for what you've done to my people."

Hannah gulped. The hatred in Black Elk's voice astounded her. *God, please reach this man before he gives himself completely over to darkness.*

"I had a woman," he said softly. "We lived with the Utes on the Yampa River. Four moons ago, a group of miners burned the village to the ground, her with it."

Touched by the tragedy, Hannah started to reach out to him, but caught herself. "Black Elk, I'm sorry for your loss but you can't repay murder with murder. Then the killing will never stop."

"Your own Holy Book says an 'eye for an eye.' "

"The 'eye for an eye' Scripture refers to a legal punishment. The rest of the Bible is the story of a Savior who wants to share your heartbreaks with you and help you overcome them. Hate will just burn you up from the inside out . . . And that means her murderers will win again."

He'd been staring off into space, but that brought his head around.

Several seconds passed as he stared at her. Hannah prayed for the words that would help him. Perhaps as repayment for her attempted counseling, he offered her another tantalizing piece of information. "One-Who-Cries met an outlaw who will trade us guns for women. The white people at Horse Mesa. They had pretty daughters. Like you."

Hannah leaned back, startled at the revelation. Mouth agape, she asked, "Did you come here to get captives?"

He worked his jaw back and forth, as if pondering how to answer. "I came here to drink."

Hannah frowned. The answer could be the truth, but she didn't trust it. "You said one girl fought?"

"She fought like a warrior." *Did he almost smile?* "I have never seen a woman fight like that. She made One-Who-Cries very angry and he bashed her head with a rock."

Hannah couldn't imagine the horror those girls had gone through. Had the older sister fought to protect her younger sibling? Naomi would do that. And wind up dead. Black Elk rubbed his temple with his free hand and slid back beneath the sheets. He struck Hannah as weary, not merely tired.

"The girl you took. What will happen to her?" Hannah asked as gently as she could. "Has she been traded already?"

Again, an indifferent shrug. "I do not know. After Horse Mesa," he shifted his gaze out the window to the mountains painted in moonlight, "I came here . . . to drink." Again, something about the statement sounded less than honest. It sounded rehearsed.

"So you don't know where One-Who-Cries is or the whereabouts of the girl?" When he didn't answer quickly, she dangled some bait. "Black Elk, you're in a lot of trouble for breaking up that saloon and trying to hurt Dolores. You also stabbed a man. If you tell me something helpful, or tell Marshal Beckwith something helpful, things may go easier for you."

Fire ignited in his eyes as he turned to glare at her. Moving like a streak of lightning, he reached out with his free hand and grabbed her wrist. Fear tasted like acid in Hannah's mouth. "The *justice* I get in Defiance will be of my own making."

Black Elk squeezed her wrist tighter and tighter and sneered at her as the pain increased. As she cried out, Emilio burst into the room and pulled her out of the man's grasp. The Indian resisted for only a moment. He let Hannah go and his sneer changed to a confident smile.

Emilio wrapped her in his arms and glared at the Black Elk. "You're done here, Hannah."

Black Elk laid his head on his pillow and laughed bitterly as the pair left Doc's.

CHAPTER 34

The morning sun was just sneaking over the high peaks around Defiance as Hannah and Emilio marched for the marshal's office. Black Elk's angry, dark eyes haunted her and her wrist still ached from his brutal grip. He frightened her now that she'd really seen the loathing he harbored for whites.

The jangle of an approaching wagon intruded on her thoughts, and a familiar voice made her turn. "Good morning, Miss Hannah. Emilio." Silas Madden tipped his hat and pulled his wagon to a halt. "Can I give you a ride to the hotel?"

"Good morning, Silas. My goodness, you're in town early. I thought Naomi said you and Sarah were working out at your place until next week."

"We are, but I had to come into town for lumber, nails, and a few other things. So I'm not going to the hotel, but I'm happy to drop you."

Hannah shook her head. "We appreciate the offer, Silas, but we're actually going to the marshal's."

"All righty, then." He tipped his hat again and slapped the reins, putting his team back to work. Seconds later, he drove across the street and around to the back of the mercantile.

As she and Emilio crossed the street, her thoughts went back to Black Elk. "I should have known he was going to do something like that. I caught him staring at me several times last night."

"I think you should stay away from him now," Emilio said. "If everything he said is true, maybe he came to town to scout for women to trade."

Hannah's steps faltered. The idea struck her as preposterous. On the other hand, towns had a concentration of women. "Would they do that?"

"*Si*, towns have been raided before, but only when there were many warriors. Black Elk may have come hunting to see if there were any easy targets."

"He said he came here to drink."

"Maybe."

"Either way, One-Who-Cries is going to try to trade the girl, and the marshal needs to know that."

Hannah couldn't help but think about the poor girl who had been kidnapped and her sister, dead now because she'd fought. The story haunted her. *But for the grace of God, there go I . . .* She prayed the girl would make it home alive.

----

*M*atthew opened his eyes but the bolt of pain that rocketed through his head slammed them shut again. His head felt like he'd been stepped on by an elephant and his side throbbed with a bone-jarring beat. He was sure his mouth had been stuffed with cotton, and his stomach was more than a little queasy.

I am getting too old for this. Scorpion stings would feel better.

Slowly, through a sludgy haze, memories came back. Cheap

whiskey. A very willing Amaryllis. He touched his side and wondered what had happened to her doing all the work.

The fresh clean bandage reminded him of the Doc's office, and Hannah. The Mexican kid had helped him back to the hotel. He didn't remember what he'd said and if Naomi had seen them stumbling in.

He rubbed his temples, wondering if she was a lost cause. If she caught him in too many lies, it wouldn't matter about the ace he had up his sleeve. Well, there was only one way to find out. Holding his breath, he forced himself to sit up. He flinched when the pain hit him from every direction.

A groan worked its way out of him and he sat perfectly still, waiting to either die or feel better. After a moment, things had improved minutely and he swung his feet over the bed as delicately as if they were newborn babes.

His head swimming, he inhaled the scent of bacon and eggs drifting up from the kitchen. For a second his stomach rebelled and he thought he might have to lunge for the chamber pot, but the sensation passed and he breathed a little easier. A soft rap at his door made him look up, his eyes rolling in their sockets like rusty ball bearings. What he wouldn't give for a cup of willow bark or peppermint tea.

"Matthew, I just wanted to check on you. Are you all right?"

Naomi. And she didn't sound as if she was addressing a liquor-swilling, skirt-chasing scoundrel. Matthew cleared the dust from his throat. "I'll live. Come on in."

The door opened an inch, stopped, and then Naomi pushed it all the way open and stepped in. He noticed she kept her hand on the door knob.

Standing tall and straight like a general, she assessed him with no emotion in her expression. "Hannah told me you busted your stitches open."

Without waiting for a reply, she marched over to the curtains and pulled them aside. Light exploded into the room and

Matthew decided firing a cannon next to his head would have been kinder. Groaning, he fell back on the bed and laid his arm over his eyes. "That all she told you?"

In the silence as he waited for her answer, the ticking hallway clock sounded like a giant Japanese gong. His head throbbed in time with it.

"Matthew, I wish . . ." she faded off, but he'd heard a twinge of compassion in her tone. "Things haven't worked out between us. You have to let it go. Drinking and carousing don't hurt me. That kind of behavior only hurts you. You're a business owner, a respectable man." He heard the rustle of her dress move back toward the door. "You're allowed, I suppose, to drown your sorrows, but you can't let your drinking spiral out of control again. I'm not worth it. No one is."

Matthew almost smiled. Almost. "The blow—your engagement —it caught me off guard. I fell off the wagon." He lowered his voice and tried to sound appropriately ashamed. "I'm sorry. I'm still not the man my brother was."

"You can't keep comparing yourself to him."

He moved his hand to his chest and drank in her image. She stood with her back to him, but he savored the curves of her waist and hips flattered by a red, flower-covered calico dress. That long, golden braid that he'd so often dreamed of undoing trailed down her back. What he wouldn't give to have all those soft waves rain down on him.

Holding his side, he forced himself to sit up, not making any attempt to hide his pain. "Would you pour me a glass of water, Naomi?"

"Certainly."

Naomi strode quickly to the pitcher beside his bed and poured him a mug full. Matthew took a sip, making sure his mouth would function. Drier than the desert, he finished the water in two gulps. The water settled his stomach and did a lot to clear his head. Feeling more human now, he rolled the mug back and forth in his hands as he wondered how to continue cultivating her sympathy. She sat down beside him and he grinned inwardly.

"I've never been able to think straight around you, Naomi. Never." He turned to her, wishing he could gently grasp her hands in his, but, instead, he tried to hold her gaze with a solemn expression. "I'll never get over you. You were my first love, woman."

He saw the slightest movement in her lips at the use of the old pet name. John used to call her that. Matthew had said it low and steely too, like his brother used to. She swallowed and he knew he was getting somewhere. Her eyes filled with unmistakable longing.

Slowly, like he was reaching out to a skittish pony, he raised his hand and touched her hair. Her chest rose and fell faster as her gaze drifted down to his mouth. He moved a hair closer, half-expecting her to pull away. She didn't move a muscle and he continued inching toward her.

"With you beside me, Naomi . . ." he spoke gently, reverently. Her soft, pink lips a breath away, he promised her, "I could be a man like John."

Naomi blinked and pulled away, leaving his hand floating in mid-air. Her mouth fell open but she didn't make a sound. Matthew saw the panic growing in her eyes and reached for her hand. "Naomi . . ."

She stood and backed away, raising her hand to stop him. "Matthew, no." Her panicked expression changed into sorrow. "You're not John. I'd give anything if you were, but you're not. We both have to move on."

She turned and fled from his room. If he'd been in better condition, he would have lunged for her, pressed her against the wall and kissed her until she forgot John Miller, and that scoundrel Charles McIntyre too.

He sighed. She'd almost let him kiss her.

Clearly, she was still vulnerable.

He figured he had one more shot at Naomi . . . if Amaryllis could be trusted.

---

*N*aomi raced to the end of the hallway at the back of the hotel, the closest, darkest corner she could find. Furious with herself, she leaned her head against the wall and tried to keep from pounding on the wood with her fists. Oh, she had come so close to doing something unforgivable. The temptation, the promise of just one kiss to remind her of John . . .

Oh, Lord, what was I thinking?

She splayed her hands on the wall trying to hold back the shame. Just as she felt Matthew's breath brushing her lips, Charles' face had flashed before her. Matthew said he could be a man like John. No. He could not. Neither could Charles. They should not be compared to John or ever asked to measure up. They were their own men. And that was precisely why she loved Charles McIntyre. He wasn't trying to be anyone but himself.

A liberating sense of resolve enveloped her soul. She would not fall prey to Matthew's charms *ever* again. Only one man mattered to her now. Nearly betraying Charles had brought that home like a lightning strike.

Raising her chin, she stepped out of the shadows and ran into Hannah coming out of her room, Little Billy on her hip. Her little sister jumped back, clutching her son.

"Good grief, Naomi. You startled me."

"I'm sorry." She reached over and tickled her nephew's ribs. "Good mornin', Dumplin'." Little Billy's eyes lit up with glee and he reached for her. Melting into a gooey lump of love, Naomi took her precious nephew from his mother and kissed his forehead. "How are you this morning? Is Mama done feeding you? Ready to get the day started?"

Hannah chuckled and ruffled her son's hair. "He was still asleep when I got back from Doc's, so I took a little nap, too."

"Good. You needed the rest." Naomi ran her fingers up and down Little Billy's chest. "Uh, oh, it's the tickle spider!" Little Billy laughed wildly and swatted at her hand but that spider just kept coming back for more.

"You're so good with children. I hope you and Charles can have a bunch." Like an arrow piercing her lungs, Naomi felt the deflating sting, no matter how unintentional, and apparently the pain showed. "I'm sorry, Naomi. I shouldn't have said that."

She bit her lip and handed Little Billy back to Hannah. "No, it's fine. I am not going to worry about it. The doctor said I was capable, so either we *will* have a bunch or we won't." She rubbed her nephew's back and smiled at her sister, trying to force the illusion she was not concerned about conceiving children. "So, what are we doing today to get ready for this wedding?"

"*You* have a fitting, right after breakfast." She put her fingers to her lips. "Shhh. It's supposed to be a surprise." Naomi dipped her head in agreement. "And Mollie and I are going to the mercantile to get a few things."

They walked down the hall toward the stairs as Hannah switched her son to the other hip. "By the way," Hannah stopped at the first door along the hallway and stared at it, frowning. "You haven't seen Amanda this morning, have you? I knocked earlier but didn't get an answer."

That was puzzling. Although, considering the way the girl had worked last night, Naomi wondered if she was still sleeping because she was exhausted. "Try again."

Hannah rapped on the door with the back of her hand. After several seconds, she repeated the action, but much louder. When they still received no response, Hannah questioned Naomi with a look. Naomi nodded and Hannah slowly opened the door. "Amanda?"

Hunching her shoulders in a prepared apology, Hannah

widened the door and stepped into the room. Naomi stayed in the hallway but she could tell from the darkness that Amanda hadn't opened the curtains. Hannah crossed the room and moved one aside to let in the light. Naomi stepped through the doorway and knew immediately Amanda was gone.

Hannah turned slowly, surveying the room. Sighing, she shook her head. The bed didn't even have a wrinkle in it. "I knew something was wrong. Last night, she seemed *agitated* that she might not have anything to do today."

Naomi folded her arms and stared down at the floor. "I don't understand this. Where would she go? *Why* would she go?"

CHAPTER 35

*N*aomi felt so badly for Mollie. Seated across the kitchen table, the girl sat beside Hannah and sipped her coffee without any enthusiasm. She stared down into the steaming cup, her expression forlorn, and sighed. "Sadly, I think I know where she might have gone."

"I don't understand, Mollie," Naomi said, frustrated by Amanda's unexpected departure. "Why would she leave? This was her chance for a whole new future."

"I've been in this town over two years now. I saw girls get proposed to all the time. And a few of the men doing the asking were really good men. But, sometimes . . ." She licked her lips as she tried to find the words. "Sometimes, the girls would bolt at the last second and go right back to working in the saloon. It didn't make any sense to me until one day a gal told me she was too far gone. That life beats you down. Makes you believe you're nothing. That you don't deserve anything better." Mollie's chin quivered, "I came too close to believing that lie."

Hannah reached over and took her friend's hand. She didn't say anything. She didn't need to. Mollie squeezed her hand in return and nodded. Naomi watched the interaction, pleased that these two had become friends. They needed each other, and each held the other accountable.

Mollie patted Hannah's hand and started to rise. "I'll meet you at the mercantile. Let me see if I can find her."

Hannah held on. "I'll go with you if you like."

"Uh, no, no, that's all right. You go on. I'll be along shortly."

The wiggle in Mollie's voice worried Naomi and she determined wherever the girl was headed, she wasn't going alone.

*uch to Naomi's dismay, she headed for Tent Town.

Holding the hem of her simple, beige homespun dress out of the dust, she dogged Mollie's path from a discreet distance. The girl wound her way through cribs—the one-room shacks reserved for prostitutes—and ragged tents to the dark heart of Defiance.

The tantalizing aroma of frying bacon and sizzling venison mingled with the stench of urine and unwashed bodies. Many of the working girls sat outside their abodes, half-dressed, faces gaunt, liquor bottles in their hands. Unlike the haughty Flowers formerly of the Iron Horse, these girls would not look at Naomi as she passed. The hopelessness here broke her heart. She couldn't imagine how it made Mollie feel.

She could have been any one of these girls.

But the reverse was also true, and that's why they were wading through this tide of broken spirits searching for Amanda.

The men here, some walking down the narrow, weedy street, some sitting in front of their bedraggled tents, watched Mollie with brazen stares, and then Naomi as she passed by moments later. To Mollie's credit, she strode with her head held high, eyes politely averted. Naomi attempted to do the same as she scurried past the men, but the deeper she wandered in to Tent Town, the more alone she felt. She didn't belong here and Charles would be furious with her for this expedition, one she regretted a little more with every wink and hungry grin cast her way.

Lord, I'm not sure this was the smartest thing to do. Please keep us safe . . . and help us find Amanda.

Mollie left the dusty main road, which was little more than a rutted path, and cut through a small neighborhood of weather-beaten tents built on flimsy, wooden foundations. An older man sat outside of one, shaving with a straight razor. His water bowl rested on a tree stump and his mirror hung from a stripped pine sapling. He watched her walk around the edge of his camp, but only as a reflex. Bored with her, he went back to the spot above his lip and ignored Naomi completely as she hurried through. Thankful for his inattention, she skirted around another dwelling and emerged onto a row of surprisingly new, crisp, white tents. Too close to Mollie, she stepped back and peered around the corner, peeking through the needles of a scraggly cedar.

Mollie had stopped. Naomi followed the path of her gaze and realized she had spotted Amanda sitting outside the next tent, rolling a stocking up one leg. Mollie's shoulders slumped and she walked slowly up to the girl. "Amanda, what are you doing here?" The disappointment in Mollie's voice tugged at Naomi's heart.

Startled, Amanda dropped her leg and stood up. The surprise quickly changed to disinterest. Waving her hand dismissively, the girl dropped back down to her log seat. Wearing nothing but a dingy camisole and simple petticoat, she hiked the undergarment up to her thigh to finish with her stockings. "I decided I don't like the idea of being beholden to Mr. McIntyre."

"That's an excuse and you know it." Amanda spun on the log, turning her back on her guest, and started working a stocking up her other leg. Mollie's hands clenched into fists. "You're afraid."

Amanda's hands slowed. "I ain't afraid." But there was no conviction in her voice.

"Yes, you are." Mollie softened her tone and walked around to face Amanda. "You're afraid you don't have what it takes to walk away from this. To take responsibility for yourself instead of letting men use you."

Amanda's head jerked up. "You shouldn't be so holier-than-thou. I've seen girls like you try to change."

"They always come back to it," a gruff voice taunted from inside the tent. The flap flicked up and a man stepped out. He was tall, with unkempt chestnut hair that flew in every direction. His shirt, half-tucked and wrinkled, hung open, and his suspenders lounged lazily on his hips. He rubbed Amanda's shoulders and stared at Mollie. Only able to see the man from the back, Naomi thought his rigid stance seemed defiant. "In a year, *you'll* give up and come right back to what you know." He squeezed Amanda's shoulders and handed her a tin flask. "Ain't that right, Amanda?"

Amanda didn't say anything. With shaky hands, she uncorked the flask and took a swig. She paused for a moment, as if the liquid sliding down her throat brought her peace. Mollie stared at the container. "What is that?"

The man took it out of Amanda's hand and raised it for Mollie to see. "Why, this is my special brew. Amanda said she had an affinity for laudanum and bourbon—"

"Laudanum?" Mollie growled through clenched teeth. She dropped to her knees in front of Amanda. "Is that why you left? Are you addicted?"

Naomi bit her lip to stifle a gasp. What a mess the girl had gotten herself into. She was tempted to step out of hiding, but Mollie spoke before she could.

"Amanda, please come back to the hotel with me. We can get you cleaned up, we can help you—"

The man shoved Mollie, knocking her on her bottom, and jerked Amanda to her feet. "Amanda and I have more business inside. Take your preachin' someplace else."

Naomi started forward, but thought better of interfering.

Something told her that Mollie had to handle this. Clenching her fists, she settled back and prayed she was doing the right thing by sitting this out . . . unless the man touched Mollie again.

"All right." Mollie climbed to her feet, her gaze locked on Amanda. "I just want to say one thing: You do not have to live like this. There's a way out. Find me when you're ready."

"Sure," the girl whispered dreamily.

The despair on Mollie's face said she'd hit a spiritual brick wall. Sad for Mollie as well as Amanda, Naomi lowered her head and turned away.

At a weedy, tramped down intersection a few yards off, she stopped to wait for Mollie. To her right, laundry and tents swayed in the breeze. On her left, the Broken Spoke Saloon loomed like a house of horror and she shuddered. The canvas had torn in several places, especially on top. Ripped sides flicked noisily in the breeze. The wood façade, warped and twisted, barely gave the front door anything to hang onto and it sagged as if a giant had tugged on it.

Rose had gone to work there after leaving the Iron Horse. She had attacked Diamond Lil in there, blinding the woman, and planned her attack on the sisters from there. She was rotting in the state prison now, and this saloon, closed for the last several weeks, was doing the same thing. Charles, the Broken Spoke's owner, had shut it down too.

Naomi shivered, glad she'd never had to see the inside of such a place.

"Did you follow me?"

Naomi flinched, unsure of whether Mollie sounded upset or pleased. She turned to her friend who was slowly walking toward her. The girl carried herself straight and tall, but her expression was tense. Naomi sighed and shoved her hands into her pockets. "I'm sorry, Mollie, but I didn't think it was safe for you to come over here by yourself."

After a moment, the tension left her and she smiled, though it was a sad one. "I guess you heard then?" Naomi nodded. Mollie wagged her head. "I don't know what to do. She's throwing away such an incredible opportunity."

The two girls ambled along, side by side, their heads bowed with defeat. "You can't help people who don't want to change— even God lets us make our own choices, Mollie. And He doesn't force Himself on us." Naomi thought the words sounded like platitudes and she wished God had made her more compassionate. "At least Amanda knows there is a place she can go. That we'll take her in—"

She heard Mollie gasp and wheeled around reflexively. A man had spun the girl to face him and was digging his fingers into her shoulder. "Lordy, Lordy," the mostly-toothless, bald miner sang. "If it ain't little Daisy, the Flower that spouts Bible speeches!"

Mollie snatched free from the man's grip and stepped back. Paling at the sight of him, she whispered, "Tom Hawthorn."

Naomi didn't know the man, but she recognized the name. Hawthorn had nearly killed Mollie last November. Naomi had unfortunately arrived for the aftermath of the brutal beating. Vicious bruises on the girl's face and ribs, the bloody, broken nose and swollen eyes all smacked of a man with some deadly demons.

Mollie took another step back and raised her chin. Naomi felt a surge of pride. Oh, she had been beaten, but this man had not broken her. Hawthorn had served thirty days in jail, followed by Charles banishing him from town. His return testified to either a mental disorder or a death wish.

Mollie echoed her thoughts. "You've taken leave of your senses, Hawthorn. Mr. McIntyre sent you packing. He won't like it that you're back without his permission."

The miner blinked and the unmistakable stink of alcohol hit Naomi. Dread wiggled in her gut as his lip curled into an ugly sneer. He cursed, taking the Lord's name in vain, and stepped toward Mollie. Naomi took a step toward Hawthorn.

Hawthorn ignored her and leaned down to within an inch of Mollie's face. "I don't care what McIntyre likes. I'm a free man and I'll go and come as I please. I got a stake in a claim here and ain't leaving it just because he says so."

"If you hurt me, he'll come after you. You're already in a lot of trouble."

Hawthorn laughed, an evil cackle that made the hairs rise up on Naomi's arms, and he grabbed hold of Mollie. "You and me got things to do, missy. And if you try that Jesus talk on me again, I'll snap your neck like a twig."

"Take your filthy hands off of her right now." Livid, Naomi tried to force herself between the two people. She could barely contain her rage. She absolutely *hated* this kind of man, the kind who got his courage from a bottle and preferred an easy target to batter. The thought of sinking her fingernails into his face almost made her smile.

"Well, if it ain't a mouse trying to roar like a lion." He snatched Mollie to his chest with one arm and shoved Naomi away with the other. Sniffing, he surveyed her, top to bottom and back again. Naomi knew she didn't intimidate the heavy, well-muscled Hawthorn, but she was still dangerous, if he had enough sense to see it. "Well," he said again, a lecherous grin spreading across his pockmarked face. "Why don't you make me? Better yet . . ." As if offering to assist a lady into a carriage, he shifted Mollie off to his side and extended a dirty, scarred hand to Naomi. "Why don't we all three go back to my tent for a little entertainment."

Smiling sweetly, Naomi softened her gaze and cocked her head ever so slightly. Unfortunately, she had underestimated the level of debauchery that still seethed on this side of town and now she and Mollie were in a fix. Near as she could tell, there was only one way to get out of it.

Hawthorn's lewd grin spread as he fell for Naomi's beguiling invitation. Holding her smile, she hiked her skirt and delivered a ferocious kick to the man's groin. As he doubled over with a groan, Naomi yelled, "Run, Mollie! Run!" Mollie easily wrenched loose from him, but as she and Naomi turned to dash for their freedom, Naomi's head snapped back and pain shot down her neck. "Run, Mollie!" she screamed again as the man used her braid like a leash to snatch her back. "Get Charles!"

CHAPTER 36

Before Naomi or Mollie could run or fight, gunfire exploded over their heads like a thunder clap. Hawthorn yanked Naomi against his broad chest and wrapped his arm around her as he spun toward the sound. Naomi nearly fainted with relief. Charles leaped down the steps of the Broken Spoke and strode toward them, eyes blazing, gun pointed precisely at the center of Tom Hawthorn's head.

The emptiness in Charles' eyes, the seething fury of it, shocked Naomi and her anger with Hawthorn evaporated. *He's going to kill this man.* "Charles, don't!" She felt Hawthorn stiffen.

Oh, God, she prayed, *please don't let him take this man's life. He's not that Charles McIntyre anymore. He'll regret it.*

Charles marched within about six feet of her and Hawthorn, the gun still leveled at the man's forehead. "Hawthorn, you are holding the woman I am about to marry." He sounded incredulous, as if he couldn't believe Hawthorn's audacity.

The man shifted his grip and brought his arm around Naomi's neck. "Good. You won't risk shooting her."

"Oh, there's no risk of that."

"Charles, just wound him." Naomi spoke quickly, but barely above a whisper. This was a critical moment for all of them. Hawthorn tightened his grip slightly around her neck and laughed. "Yes, *Charles*, just wound me."

The blood flowing to Naomi's brain slowed and she clawed at the arm around her throat. The fire that had energized her kick merged with a confusion that seeped through her consciousness like cold molasses. She blinked, but her thoughts were slowing, growing fuzzy.

"I told you when you got out of jail to leave Defiance." Charles cocked the pistol. "And I know you did. But you were actually foolish enough to come back." Charles shook his head. "And now you've laid hands upon my fiancée." His voice, low and calm, belonged to an angel of death. Even in this strange fog, the tone chilled Naomi. "You know I cannot let such an affront pass."

Hawthorn's arm constricted a bit tighter and a gray wave loomed before her. Her vision dimming, she could barely make out men coming to the scene, weaving through lines of laundry, popping out from tents, settling in around the edges of the inter-section. A few grinned, several tipped their hats back in antic-ipation.

She felt Hawthorn suck in a breath and tighten his arm even more. Her thoughts grew dark, like a dying flame, and she closed her eyes. Light sliced into her brain as he shoved her toward Charles. Disoriented, she staggered to him and he wrapped her in a welcoming arm, pulling her to his side.

Hawthorn raised his hands. "There's your woman. Holster that hog leg and we'll have a fair fight."

"What makes you think you deserve a fair fight?" Charles sounded appalled by the idea.

Naomi shook her head, clearing the mist. Panic and anger both hit her as she realized what had just happened. She looked back at Hawthorn and let the anger win. For an instant she imagined snatching Charles' gun from his hand and shooting the man herself, but her reason rushed back. This needed to end so they could all walk away. "Charles, you don't have to do this."

"I absolutely have to do this." He glanced down at her, but she didn't see any tenderness in his face. Something dark and forsaken, something without a conscience boiled in Charles, radiated from him in waves. The set of his jaw, the slight sneer in his lip. Here was the man who had settled Defiance. The man they were all afraid of. She didn't know this Charles and didn't want to. The gun in his hand didn't move, didn't even pulsate with his heartbeat. He stared over her head at Tom. "He's crossed too many lines now."

"Marshal Beckwith can handle the likes of him. This isn't your job." She laid a hand on his chest. "If you do this, I think you'll regret it."

"He's the man who beat Mollie." His stare never left Hawthorn, but she thought she detected the slightest waver in his conviction. "Because of me, my law, my *justice*, he served thirty days and then walked away."

"There's real law here now. Mollie and I can press charges."

"And how long do you think that would keep him in jail?"

"Come on, McIntyre," Hawthorn goaded, raising his fists. "Set the lady aside and let's dance."

Naomi ignored the man. "You can't kill him. You can't justify that before God. Think for a moment and you'll see that."

"I'll call it self-defense."

"He's unarmed." Naomi stole a glance at the gun in his hand, as still as if it was frozen in time. "You can't just shoot him."

"Naomi, if I don't deal with this man in the right way," he dropped his voice to a whisper, "every miner in this town will think *respectable* means *soft*. That could mean you're not safe, or your sisters, or Little Billy."

Naomi deflated over the argument. Maybe she didn't understand the way things worked out West, even after all this time. Praying she would see Christ reflected in Charles' eyes instead of that fearsome darkness, she nodded. "Fine," she pulled away, "But do you have to *kill* him?"

CHAPTER 37

"*I* never said I was going to kill him."

But the desire to kill Tom Hawthorn when he saw Naomi strangling in his arms had allowed McIntyre the purest sense of hate he'd tasted since watching One-Who-Cries skin his friends alive. He'd had a clean shot. He could have blown the man's head off with the twitch of his trigger finger and no woman —Naomi, Mollie, any woman at all—would have had to worry about him ever again. Naomi's pleading, though, had brought on an unexpected sense of uncertainty.

All right, God, if I shouldn't kill him, how do I get him to stay out of Defiance? How do I keep the respect of this town and not come across as weak?

Amazingly, a Scripture rose up in his mind. *My grace is sufficient for thee. For My strength is made perfect in weakness.*

Mercifully God dropped an idea into his head. *Thank You, Father.* Holding Hawthorn's gaze, McIntyre slid his gun into his holster, peeled off his gun belt and handed it to Naomi. "Pride goeth before a fall, Naomi. Maybe there is a way."

Eyes wide and full of hope, she took the gun, reacting to its weight with a small gasp. McIntyre stripped off his coat. Satisfaction swelled Hawthorn's chest and he quickly peeled out of his dirty miner's coat and shirt and threw them at the feet of the crowd. Naomi held Charles' coat and shirt draped over one arm, his gun hanging from her elbow.

Now bare-chested, he tried not to be distracted by the fleeting admiration on Naomi's face. He had kept in shape by boxing with Brannagh behind the saloon. Well-developed shoulders, muscular arms and a tight stomach would allow him to defend against and absorb blows, but he hoped that wouldn't be necessary. He had something else in mind.

He raised his fists, tossed a quick wink at Naomi and stepped toward Hawthorn. He hadn't done this in a long time, but he had lived for this game in college and had perfected his skills to an impressive degree. "One round, five minutes, Hawthorn. Tap me with a *fist* and you can have a free pass in Defiance."

The crowd reacted with a collective gasp. Hawthorn's brow rose, pleased as he was with the offer, but almost instantly suspicion followed. "What's the catch?"

McIntyre hunkered down another inch, brought his fists up a bit more. "No catch. I say you can't touch me . . . I'll give you five minutes to try." McIntyre scanned the crowd and found Sean O'Connell, the man known for arranging and judging fights in Defiance.

He already had his pocket watch in his hand and nodded at McIntyre. "Gentlemen, five minutes start in three . . . two . . . one. Go."

McIntyre shuffled his feet and moved toward Hawthorn. His opponent wasn't a big man, but he was muscular and had a long reach. Not a cake walk, but McIntyre thought he could take him.

Hawthorn raised his fists and charged towards McIntyre. He threw a right jab, straight on, no finesse. McIntyre ducked it, came up and tagged Hawthorn hard in the temple, then moved behind him. Clearly surprised, Hawthorn spun and threw a wild haymaker. McIntyre leaned back like a snake avoiding a big cat's swiping paw. Instantly, he reached back in and hit Hawthorn with a sharp left hook. Laughter rippled through the crowd. While Hawthorn was still blinking off the punch, McIntyre danced behind him, hitting him in the ribs with a fast right jab as he passed by. He heard the laughter again, saw a man elbow his buddy and point.

Hawthorn leaned into the no-doubt stinging ribs and stepped back, putting distance between him and McIntyre. The fleeting shadow of fear glimmered in the man's grizzled face because he'd figured it out. McIntyre wasn't going to beat the hound out of him.

He was going to utterly and completely humiliate him.

The two men circled each other, Hawthorn flat-footed as a camel. McIntyre bounced, shuffled, and held his expression still as death. Hawthorn watched him intently now, most likely looking for weaknesses. Growling, the man stepped in, and sliced at McIntyre with a fast right hook. McIntyre dodged it, countered with a vicious uppercut and again stepped out of range. He had heard Hawthorn's teeth clatter and knew that last punch had rattled him good.

Surprising McIntyre, Hawthorn came at him with a flurry of wild punches. McIntyre blocked, parried, punched. With a haughty flourish, he actually slipped past the man and smacked him on the rear end. The crowd erupted in laughter and cheers.

Hawthorn spun, already slicked with sweat.

"Two minutes, Gentlemen," O'Connell informed the fighters.

McIntyre knew he had to get a bit more grandiose if he was going to pull this off. Praying for wisdom and speed, he dropped his hands to his side and rested his feet. For a moment, Hawthorn was taken aback, dropping his guard slightly. Then McIntyre raised one hand and waved Hawthorn in, taunting him. The crowd collectively gasped over the audacious move.

Growling, the man obliged and dove at McIntyre with the intent of tackling him, but McIntyre side-stepped at the last possible moment and tripped Hawthorn. The man sprawled head-first into the dirt. The crowd started booing him and catcalling.

"Go home, laddy, we hear your Mum calling."

"Come back when you've learned to fight."

"Reckon yer getting yer schooling today, eh, Hawthorn?"

"No wonder you beat women. You can't beat a man."

Just a little more, Lord, and this man will never show himself in Defiance again.

Laughter and ridicule raining down on him, Hawthorn surveyed the crowd. McIntyre saw the warning in his eyes and readied himself for another volley of punches. Hawthorn came up out of the dirt swinging a bowie knife. He sliced and lashed at McIntyre's ribs and came so close, McIntyre felt the breeze on his skin. Naomi covered her mouth but didn't utter a sound, and the crowd turned ugly. Profanities flew at the man. McIntyre thought if he could survive this, he might well have accomplished his goal.

Hawthorn charged again. McIntyre grabbed the hand with the knife and jabbed twice, hard and lightning-fast, first into Hawthorn's face, breaking his nose, and then at his stomach, knocking out the man's wind. Hawthorn staggered and doubled over, blood streaming down his face. Finished dallying, McIntyre went on the offensive again, pummeling the man with powerful blows to his head and ribs. The crowd roared. Hawthorn collapsed on his knees, dazed. The knife fell through his fingers. Clapping, cheers, and jeers filled the air and a few onlookers spit at Hawthorn.

McIntyre aimed and delivered a vicious left hook to the man's right cheek, causing a spray of blood. Hawthorn leaned to the left, swaying like a tree in the wind. He fell forward slowly and crashed in the dust.

O'Connell ran out and grabbed McIntyre's right hand. Raising it above his head he yelled to the crowd, "We have our winner, gents!" More applause and cheers were accompanied by aston-ished whistles.

Exhausted, McIntyre sagged just as Naomi came up and wrapped her arms around him. She smiled, admiration glowing in her eyes. "You didn't kill him."

"All right, break it up, break it up!" Beckwith slashed through the crowd, parting it like a grizzly thrashing through the underbrush. The men scattered grudgingly, still laughing and shaking their heads in amazement. Beckwith assessed the scene. Lips pursed into a thin line, he reached down and claimed the Bowie knife. O'Connell dropped McIntyre's hand like it had turned white hot and donned an expression of angelic innocence.

Beckwith speared McIntyre with a suspicious, sidelong glare. "Mollie said you were going to shoot someone." He nudged Hawthorn with the toe of his boot. "I take it that plan changed?"

McIntyre nodded and draped an arm over Naomi's shoulders, astonished that the limb felt like it weighed a thousand pounds. "Merely a small disagreement, Marshal."

"No need to arrest anyone, I assume?"

"Not this time, but if you see Tom Hawthorn in town after this, arrest him for his own safety."

The marshal pondered the warning for all of about a half-second. Finished here, he spun and headed back the way he'd come.

Naomi wrangled McIntyre's shirt free from the items she was holding and offered it to him. Feeling as if his arms were encased in wet cement, he slowly shoved the nearly dead weights into the sleeves.

"I don't think I'll ever get used to the violence this place breeds," she said, trying to arrange the shirt on his sweat-slicked shoulders. "I was doing all right until the very end when you had to . . ." She trailed off.

"Finish it?"

"Yes, finish it. The *sound* of the beating . . ." She flinched and shook her head. "Between you, and Billy and Emilio, we need to open a hospital."

He smiled, surprised that even his face felt heavy.

Naomi shifted to face him more directly. "So, what were you doing over here? Why were you coming out of the Broken Spoke?"

The hint of suspicion didn't escape him, but he supposed he couldn't blame her. Why would a man like him be on this side of Defiance? *Then again* . . . "I believe I could ask you the same thing."

"*I* wasn't coming out of the Broken Spoke." He cut his eyes at her, not amused by the quip. She sighed. "I followed Mollie. She was trying to find Amanda. And you?"

"I sold the Broken—" he stopped buckling his gun belt and cocked his head. "Amanda?"

Naomi shook her head. "She wasn't in her room this morning. Mollie told Hannah she was going to look for her. I was afraid she might come to Tent Town. I didn't think she should be here alone."

"And you were going to make all the difference to her safety?" He made no attempt to hide his exasperation. "All one hundred and ten pounds of you?"

Naomi stiffened into a portrait of indignation. He'd spit the comment out with a little too much acid, admittedly, but still, would the woman never learn? The realization that he could have lost her today nearly buckled his knees and he leaned closer, lowering his voice. "You don't know what it did to me when I saw him choking you. It was all I could do *not* to pull that trigger. It might be a little helpful if you would stop acting like a cougar and realize you're just a kitten."

Her mouth fell open. "Don't talk to me like that, and don't treat me like a child."

"Then stop acting like one and think of someone other than yourself."

Oh, she wanted to argue. He could see the fire in her eyes. She looked away from him as her cheeks flamed. "I'm not the one riding with every posse Beckwith calls up." She reached up, grazed the bullet hole in his hat and shook her head. "I want *you* to be more careful." Her shoulders slumped, her breathing slowed and, finally, she sighed in defeat. "I should be, too. I should have asked Emilio or Billy or even Ian to follow her. I just didn't think it was still so lawless here."

He tilted her chin up, too exhausted to keep this fight going. "You *will* be more careful next time?"

"I will."

"I'm sorry, I feel like this is my fault." Mollie skirted a wide berth around Hawthorn and approached them. "I shouldn't have come over here. Amanda is . . ." She faded off and McIntyre nodded. This new man he sought to become wrestled for the first time with stinging disappointment, in himself for nearly giving in to a mindless rage, and in Amanda for throwing away a brighter future.

"You had to try," he said. "I'll speak to her again. Perhaps that will make the difference."

A few feet from them, his battered opponent stirred. McIntyre stepped in front of the girls, in case the man had any fight left in him. He prayed he didn't. McIntyre didn't think he had the strength to lift an arm, much less throw another punch.

Hawthorn rose to all fours, and stayed there for a moment. Getting a second wind, he staggered to his feet, his back to the group. He turned and met McIntyre's gaze. Hate flickered in his eyes but died out. Wiping the blood from his face, he saluted the victor with a cursory nod and turned away.

Hawthorn slapped a drying sheet out of his way, dipped behind the line and disappeared into a floating, drifting forest of laundry. The man hadn't retrieved his shirt or coat, which lay untouched in the dirt. Perhaps he would, but McIntyre suspected Hawthorn wanted to get out of Defiance as quickly and as quietly as possible.

So they had settled their differences God's way and it had

worked out. He stole a glance up at heaven and offered his appreciation again, still marveling at the wisdom of the answer.

———

*R*ebecca plucked six straight pins from the cushion on the bed and wedged them between her lips. Moving carefully, she knelt behind Naomi's wedding gown hanging on the dress form so she could finish pinning the bustle. This dress might just turn out to be the most ravishing creation she had ever sewn, or re-sewn, as it were.

Thank God they'd brought it with them. So far, she had cut both the underskirt and the peplum, pinned them into a more narrow style, and now only needed to shape and pin the bustle. The sewing itself would go quickly.

Surprised by an unexpected burst of melancholy, she settled back on her knees and studied the gown. For a moment, she caressed the white silk and thought about her own wedding. A little white church. Ben standing at the altar, his curly, dark hair grazing his collar, a huge grin lighting his face. Sweet, patient, soft-spoken Ben who had given her such a beautiful child in Gracie.

A lump formed in her throat like it always did when she thought about the missed birthdays and empty Christmases. Seven years without them. It felt like a hundred. Sometimes it felt like mere minutes.

"Miss Rebecca?"

Startled, she nearly swallowed the pins. Quickly, Rebecca wiped her eyes and peered around the dress.

Ian nodded. "Aye, I thought I would find ye here." He stepped into the room as she rose to her feet, plucking pins from her mouth. Flapping his Balmoral bonnet against his leg, he surveyed the dress. "Miss Naomi will be such a picture of loveliness in that, I'd best be prepared to catch Charles when his knees buckle."

Rebecca laughed and came around to join him. "Yes, I was just thinking it will be the prettiest dress I've ever made. You know, we've gotten quite a lot of use out of it. It was my dress before it was Naomi's."

"Was it now?" He nodded again, but something about his demeanor struck her as odd. Still flapping his hat, he also rocked slightly on his heels. "I'm sure you were a lovely bride as well." He reached up and scratched his silvery beard on the left side . . . and then on the right. Rebecca wondered if he could possibly be . . . nervous?

Oh, Lord, please let him be here to talk about something other than Phineas Fog. Trying to feign calm and polite disinterest, she fiddled with the pins in her palm and waited for him to speak.

Ian raised his hand to his mouth and cleared his throat. "So, I've come, Miss Rebecca, to see if ye would like to join me for dinner tonight?"

Rebecca wanted to keep her hope afloat, but she didn't understand the invitation. They ate dinner together almost every night. "You do remember that the restaurant is closed? Frankly, we weren't planning on cooking even for ourselves. We thought we might simply have biscuits and beans."

Uncertainty turned into resolve on Ian's face and he stepped closer to Rebecca, so close she almost stepped back. "Nay, I was inviting ye to dinner at my cabin. Ye've never been and I would like to cook us dinner."

She had to lock her jaw to keep her mouth from falling open. She looked into his eyes, the blue of an infinite ocean, and flicked a glance over the wrinkles that framed them. "I'd love to."

"I'll send Emilio for ye aboot six, if that's fine?"

"Yes it is. Fine indeed." An enormous grin threatened to break loose but she wrestled it into a precariously-controlled smile.

"Well, then," Ian bobbed his head. "Till six."

Rebecca stood stock still and breathless till she heard the front door close, before she dared believe.

Oh, Father, please let him say he loves me. Please let him tell me I'm beautiful.

The prayer sounded ridiculous, but Rebecca wanted to know, one last time, that she was still a desirable woman. That the wrinkles around her own eyes were alluring, that her girlish charms had matured into elegance.

I see love so often in his eyes, Lord, but he never reaches out. I am not getting any younger and the days are slipping by. Our life on this earth is a quick breath and then we're gone. Please encourage Ian to hear the ticking of the clock.

CHAPTER 38

*H*olding her breath because the wedding dress was as loaded with pins as a plump porcupine, Naomi carefully slid her arms through the pearl-covered sleeves and turned toward the mirror.

She sucked in an awed breath. Rebecca's skill with a needle was nothing short of miraculous.

Holding the back together, her sister smiled expectantly. "Well . . .?"

Naomi was stunned. She simply couldn't believe the work Rebecca had done in such a short amount of time. The biggest change, of course, was in the skirt. Once a huge, voluminous wave of pearls and silk, the overskirt had been cut and gathered in back, forming a beautiful and very stylish bustle. The underskirt, simple silk with a row of pearl clam shells at the hem, had also been cut, gathered, and pinned into a more slender style than the previous fashion.

The dress was gorgeous and nearly a perfect fit. Naomi touched the shoulder, remembering the tear. Rebecca had spent three days *after* the wedding repairing the dress so Naomi wouldn't have a reminder of the fight.

Embarrassed that her eyes had filled with tears, she blinked quickly to keep them from spilling over. "Oh, I swanny, you've missed your calling, Rebecca. You've outdone yourself." Naomi imagined stepping out the back door, slowly walking down the steps, past a small crowd of guests . . . to Charles. She knew he would be dressed to the nines. And now, Naomi had a dress to match. "Do you know what the best part is?" Rebecca raised her chin, waiting for the answer. "Charles has no idea I brought my wedding dress with me. I bet he thinks I'll wear my blue muslin."

"Well, honey, I would venture to guess we'll be picking his eyes up off the ground after he gets a gander at you in this." Rebecca laughed and then abruptly sighed. She fluffed the skirt once more and shook her head. "I may be sewing on it right up till three o'clock Saturday, but I'll make it." She dropped to her knees and double-checked the pins at the hem and the bustle. "All right, go ahead and change out of it. I think I've got everything the way I want it." She pulled away and eyed the dress skeptically. "Well, maybe I could tighten the bodice a bit." She scrutinized Naomi's midsection. Twisting her lips in deep thought, she gave the overall image another gander in the mirror. "Yes, I should definitely tighten that. You've lost weight in Defiance."

Naomi turned a tiny bit to each side for a better assessment. "I've gained more heart."

Working a pin into the bodice, Rebecca talked to their reflection. "Ian asked me to dinner tonight . . . at his cabin."

"Finally." Naomi moved to clap her hands, but stopped herself before a pin could prick her. "Oh, I am so glad."

"Well, I don't want to put the cart before the horse, but why else would he want me to join him at his cabin if not to speak his mind?"

"At the pace he moves, I wouldn't be surprised if he just wants to show you a new Jules Verne book." Pain pricked her ribs. "Ow!"

"Oh, I'm sorry. Did I stick you?"

Naomi saw the unhappy dip in Rebecca's brow and kicked

herself for the gloomy comment. "On the other hand, I'm sure it's more likely he'll declare that he's madly in love with you and we'll have to have a double ceremony Saturday."

Before Rebecca could reply, gunshots, much closer than Tent Town, thundered down on the hotel. The sisters froze, their fear reflected in each other's eyes. More gun fire erupted. Scores of shots ringing out in alarming, chaotic sequences. Several seconds later an unnatural silence enveloped Defiance.

"That was too close."

Naomi nodded, wondering how close. "It sounded like it was on Main Street, down near the mercantile or Iron Horse."

"Get changed, I'll go see what I can find out." Rebecca hurried out the door as Naomi started the frustrating and dangerous process of peeling out of her fitted pin cushion. She changed as quickly as she could, while trying not to feed the fear that nagged at her. Had Tom Hawthorn decided to get revenge for his humiliation? Where was Charles? Was he all right?

Several minutes behind Rebecca, she raced down the stairs, but skidded to a halt on the landing, a deep sense of dread filling her spirit. Mollie, Hannah and Rebecca stood together at the door, grief etched deeply in their expressions. Naomi grabbed the rail. *Oh, God, not . . .* "What is it?"

Slowly, Rebecca stepped forward. "Silas has been shot, Naomi. He's dead."

Shock and sadness engulfed her and she immediately thought of Sarah. She descended the stairs, each step deepening her heartbreak. Such dear, sweet friends. What horrible news. "What happened?"

"A group of men tried to rob the bank. Silas was in the mercantile near a window. It was a stray bullet." Rebecca shrugged. "The marshal doesn't even know who shot him."

Naomi wished for a chair. She wanted to sit down, put her head in her hands, and weep. She knew only too well how this news would devastate Sarah. An ache that would never really subside. An emptiness that would never be filled.

Hannah swallowed and took a small step forward. She spoke in a frail, quivering voice. "Doc asked if I would come down and clean up Silas. I would appreciate help. The marshal wants us to take him home first thing tomorrow."

CHAPTER 39

*B*illy stepped out of the marshal's office, followed by Emilio. He took a deep breath and tried to clear his head of the image of Silas Madden shot right between the eyes. He flinched, not sure if he was more disturbed by the image seared in his brain, or that he and Emilio had hunkered down behind a miner's loaded pack mule to avoid the same fate. Explaining themselves to the marshal wasn't the most enjoyable conversation he'd ever had, but what were two unarmed men supposed to do?

Beneath a gray sky spitting occasional rain drops, he scanned the street. Ragged miners, their eyes glittering with Gold Fever, flowed down it like a muddy, debris-filled creek. Packs on their backs and on their horses, they moved with selfish deliberation toward their goal of striking it rich. None of them seemed disturbed in the least by the gunfight that took place less than half an hour ago. Bodies had littered the street, blood still stained it, but now things were back to normal. He wondered irrationally if the coming rain would wash away the red dirt.

Queasy, he dragged his hand through his hair and placed his hat back on his head. "Do things ever settle down in Defiance?"

Emilio stepped up beside him. "It's better than it used to be."

"This is no place for Hannah and Little Billy."

"Speaking of . . ." Emilio pointed across the street. The two boys watched as Hannah, holding Little Billy, trudged with Mollie, Rebecca and Naomi up the boardwalk, moving as if they were in a funeral procession. "I bet they're going to Doc's. Silas was a friend."

Billy checked the traffic, stepped off the walk, and wove his way through it to get to the girls, Emilio trailing him. Somberly, Billy fell into step beside Hannah, who acknowledged him with a quick, sad glance. He didn't know how, but he wanted to help. "I'm sorry. I hear Silas was a friend."

"Yes, yes he was." As if weary of the weight, she shifted Little Billy to her other hip. "Sarah is a dear friend as well. This will devastate her. We're going to try to clean him up and take him to her." Hannah's lip trembled. "This is going to break her heart."

Billy wondered what in the world they could do to clean up a hole in a man's forehead.

The group walked a few more steps in silence. Needing the comfort of innocence and pure love, he reached for his son. "Here, I'd like to carry the rascal." Hannah didn't resist. Billy enfolded his son and made a silly face at him as he spoke. "This sure is one rough place you ladies chose to settle in."

"No, God chose it for us," Naomi said from behind them. "And robberies happen everywhere." Was she defending this place? Billy gawked at her over his shoulder, but snapped his mouth shut. "Beckwith has only been marshal since November," she added defiantly. "He'll clean it up."

Wishing he could say at least one right thing, Billy pinched the bridge of his nose as they turned down an alley and headed for a small house set off by itself. Doc's office. In the front yard, the group passed a freight wagon loaded with the bodies of the would-be bank robbers. The girls gasped at the sight of the four dead men stacked like cord wood. Trying to ignore the macabre scene, Billy shielded his son's eyes as he pounded up the porch's steps and grabbed the door. He held it open for the ladies as they hurried in.

Hannah went immediately to Doc who was fishing a bullet out of Mr. Boot's shoulder. "Can I help, Doc?"

"Nah, I've got this, barely a flesh wound." Boot, sitting on the edge of the table, grimaced as the doctor plucked the tip of the tweezers loose from his flesh and held up a piece of lead bathed in blood. "It wasn't deep at all."

The man squeezed his eyes shut and tossed his stringy hair. "Easy for you to say."

Hannah touched Boot on the shoulder. "Just be thankful, Mr. Boot, that it didn't strike anywhere more important."

He nodded. "I know. I saw them bring in Silas. Darn shame."

Reminded of the reason for their visit, Billy removed his hat. Emilio quickly copied him.

Boot hissed as Doc swabbed the wound down with alcohol, earning an impatient glare from the physician. "Boot, you could stand to toughen up some." He shifted his gaze to Hannah and gentled his voice. "Silas is in the other examination room. Do what you can to clean him up. Wrap him in the quilt on the bed."

She nodded and slipped into the room. The other girls quietly followed her. Restless, Billy glanced around the doc's office. Neat and clean, jars, vials, and bandages covered the counters. Cabinets of medicine and supplies lined one wall. As his eyes roamed, he caught movement behind a cracked door. Had he seen an eye? He watched the door for several more seconds. Finally, from behind the thin wood, he heard the high-pitched clank of metal on metal.

"Emilio?" Doc walked over to the dry sink with a tray of bloody instruments in his hands and set them in it.

The boy straightened a bit. "*Si?*"

"I think you've got some time. Beckwith was just here doin' the paperwork on those bodies outside. I forgot to tell him Black Elk needs to be taken off our hands." He poured a basin of water into the pan. "Ask him to come arrest him or release him, but I need that bed opened up." Scowling, he grabbed the bar of soap sitting on the shelf. "Wouldn't have had a place for Silas there if I hadn't discharged Jim Riley this morning."

"*Si.*" Emilio slapped his hat back on his head. "I will be right back. Do you want to come?" he asked Billy. Billy shook his head. He wanted to stay.

The patient, Mr. Boot, plucked a shirt from the table and carefully inched his way into the garment. "Doc, I have to tell ya, I've finally come around to your way of thinking. I'm through with Defiance. Besides, my mother needs me." Grunting, he rose to his feet. "Let me know if you hear of a buyer."

Scrubbing instruments, Doc nodded. "All right, but don't be thinkin' you'll leave town before this bill is paid."

Boot rolled his eyes, grabbed his cane from beside the table, and gimped to the door. "I ain't skipped out on one yet." He reached for the doorknob. "There's always a first time, though." Grunting again, he let himself out.

As Doc washed up, Billy's thoughts wandered to the Indian in the other room. "So, this Black Elk. Is he the savage who tore up the saloon?"

"Yep." There. The eye again. Billy was sure that time. Black Elk was watching . . . and listening. "Speakin' of which . . ." Doc dried his hands and strode toward the patient's room. Billy saw the eye disappear, heard the creak of springs and the clank of metal again. Doc opened the door. "You all right, Black Elk? Need anything?"

"I need out of here." The terse answer surprised Billy. Black Elk definitely didn't sound sick any more. Curious to take a gander at a real Indian, Billy leaned way over, straining to see around Doc. Black Elk's skin was the color of a new saddle and his eyes were as black as coal. Sniffing, he glared at Billy. "And I need that Pale Face to quit staring at me." He motioned towards Billy, the action clanking his handcuff attached to the bed's headboard.

Doc laughed. "You got bigger problems than him, son." He shut the door on Black Elk and grinned at Billy, shaking his head. "Hell is empty—"

"And all the devils are here." The doctor raised a brow. Billy shifted his son onto his other arm and shrugged. "My father believed in educating his oldest son so he could become a politician, though I can't figure why a politician needs to know any Shakespeare."

"Agreed. Machiavelli would serve you better."

"But it's true."

Doc inclined his head, not following.

"All the devils *are* here," Billy motioned toward the town. "I thought Dodge City was bad ."

"Ah," Doc waved him off as he went about straightening up things, resituating instruments and supplies. "Defiance is settling down. More God-fearin' folk are comin' in every day. Won't be long, I'm sure, before we have a church, a school, and a dress shop." He passed by and ruffled Little Billy's hair.

Billy smiled and took his son over to gaze out the window. Doc's office, on the edge of town, was situated behind the land office and near the entrance to the Sunny Side Mine. A group of six or so men meandered by, long, slender shadows trailing behind them. Billy assumed they worked at the mine.

What was he going to work at? He couldn't keep hanging around the hotel, following Hannah about and babysitting Billy— he kissed his son's forehead—though that wasn't so bad. He'd meant it when he'd said he was staying, even if he lost Hannah to Emilio. The thought sat in his gut like a stone and he hugged the baby in his arms.

"Doc, I need a job. You happen to know where I could look? Or maybe there's a business in town for sale."

Doc wandered up beside him, staring out the window in the same direction. "A business, eh?"

"My father is a banker and has several interests. I know a fair amount about running them."

"You good with numbers, are you?"

"Very."

"Well, that man hobblin' back into town," he motioned toward Boot walking at a snail's pace toward Main Street, "owns the mercantile now. He started out as the manager but bought it a few months ago. Anyway, I figured it'd be too much for him as Mr. Boot doesn't have a constitution suited for the West. After that wrenched ankle, getting' shot today was the icing on the cake." He ribbed Billy. "I'd bet he'll give ya a deal on it."

Billy could run a mercantile in his sleep and, in a boom town, sell it pretty quickly when he decided to depart, if the need arose. Pondering the possibility, he watched Boot until the man disappeared around the corner of the land office.

CHAPTER 40

"Silas was a good man. The kind Defiance needed. He will be missed."

Naomi nodded in agreement with Charles and reached for a fried chicken leg. He had brought her to a beautiful spot next to the Animas River for their dinner. Seated on a blanket nestled in ankle-high spring grass, she gazed up at the surrounding mountains, their peaks veiled in gray clouds. They thought the rain would hold off, maybe not come at all. Either way, the gloomy weather matched her mood.

She couldn't shake the feel of Silas's cold, lifeless flesh. She'd never assisted in the preparation of a dead body before. It made no sense, how a man could be alive and breathing one moment and gone the next.

The bullet hole in Charles' hat taunted her. He'd told her he wanted to keep the Stetson as a reminder of how fragile life is. She knew that already and didn't need any reminders. Now Sarah had her own. "I hate how the news will hit her. It's a devastating blow."

Charles reclined on one elbow and nodded his agreement. "She's a strong woman, like you. She'll be all right."

Then, as if his thoughts changed direction on a whim, he plucked an apple from the basket, rose to his feet and took it over to his horse. "Naomi, I understand every woman wants to have the perfect wedding," Charles sliced the apple in halves with his pen knife and offered one to the horse, "but this is Defiance. I hope you and your sisters won't put an unreasonable amount of work into the wedding. I suggest . . ." he flashed his devilish grin, "for purely selfish reasons of course, we keep this as simple as possible . . . so we can get on with . . . *things.*"

In love with his rogue's smile and eager to get on with *things* herself, Naomi wished her blushing cheeks didn't give away her every thought. But wouldn't he be taken aback when he saw that their *work* included a stunning remake of her wedding dress. "Mostly, it will be simple, Charles. We're not planning anything elaborate." Surprising herself, she dared a flirtatious remark of her own. "I'm looking forward to other *things* as well." Embarrassed, she lowered her gaze to the blanket.

Charles, however, did not come back right away with another saucy remark. He allowed the horse to finish the snack then rejoined her, reclining on his elbow again, but closer to her this time. Instead of more flirting, he studied her with pained eyes. "Are you sure you want a scallywag like me for a husband?"

His nearness made her heart race, and his melancholy tone drew her closer. What was it Mollie had said? *They'd all done things in the Iron Horse they wanted to forget.* She put the chicken leg back on her plate and looked him in the eye. "Charles, the past is in the past. You have to try to leave it there."

"Defiance is making that difficult."

"That's why His mercies are new every day."

He dropped a hand to her knee as his eyes clouded over with disappointment. "I could have killed Tom Hawthorn today, without a second thought. How I used to be . . . is closer to the surface than I wanted to admit. He'll never know it, but you saved his life."

"It wasn't me."

His gaze jerked back to her and he nodded, humbled. "Both of you."

Naomi absently traced the paisley pattern in her sleeve and wondered what it must be like to be Charles McIntyre, to be a man intent on living in the Light when so much darkness haunted him.

The emotion in his eyes changed. What smoldered there forced heat to her cheeks. "Lie beside me, princess."

She turned her head a bit and raised an eyebrow. "I don't know. Is that safe?"

"No." He took her hand and sighed. "I mean yes. Even if it kills me, yes."

Laughing, and so in love with him she was dizzy being near him, she obediently wiggled down beside him. Resting her head on his arm, she reached up and lightly traced his beard around his lips, along his jaw, the faint lines at the corner of his eyes. She would remember those stunning, devilish dark eyes for eternity, even when age had dulled the mischievous sparkle.

He slid his fingers down her cheek. Gently, he reached into her hair, resting his thumb on her jaw. "I've been thinking about the hotel and how helpful Amanda could have been. I want to hire more help for you. I want to free you up to enjoy life a little. You all work too much."

I want? She dropped her hand and tried not to get tangled up in his directness, but it rankled her. His predilection to fix things without consulting anyone made her feel insignificant. "It really isn't profitable enough yet. We figured one more summer, and then we can hire three or four more people."

"Naomi," his lips fought a smile, "do you realize how much money I have?"

She suspected he had quite a lot. She knew the Sunnyside Mine ran twenty-four hours a day, seven days a week. There was a lot of silver and gold in Charles' mountain, but she'd never sought to put a number to his assets. It simply didn't matter to her. What did matter was whether he was going to share her life or take it over—a habit he'd shown a propensity for doing since they'd met.

"Charles, the hotel is something my sisters and I built together." She proceeded cautiously, unsure of how to put this. "What we do with it . . ." She shook her head, deciding against saying *is our business.* Naomi was better at starting fights than avoiding them, but this had to be settled. "Well, I mean, hiring more help to free us up some might be something we could consider, I suppose. But this is the kind of thing I have to discuss with Rebecca and Hannah *first.*"

"I'm not trying to tell you what to do, Naomi," he smiled indulgently, as if he was talking to a petulant child, "but my fortune is yours. You have a vast ocean of opportunities before you now. What would you *like* to do? I could hope you'd want to be a doting wife, but somehow I don't think that's in the cards." He slid his hand down her arm to rest it on her waist. "You can run the hotel, but hire more help. You can sell the infernal thing and start an entirely new business with your sisters, or finance your own venture." He leaned down and brushed her lips with his, a touch as light as a butterfly "I want you, above all else, to be happy."

Naomi tore her gaze away from him and watched the swirling storm clouds racing overhead. Her thoughts were just as chaotic. What *did* she want to do? She hadn't thought about Charles' money and the life they could lead. She'd thought only of trying to stay near her sisters. But Hannah wanted to be a nurse and the closest school was back east somewhere. Rebecca, though a wonderful cook and seamstress, had mentioned the newspaper idea twice now. Apparently, she missed her old trade.

And while Naomi hadn't wanted to admit it, she was tired of the hotel. It made her feel so cooped up sometimes, slaving over a stove, hauling dirty dishes back to the kitchen, fending off the forward customers who thought the girls should be on the menu as well.

Once upon a time, she had been a farmer's wife and his business partner. She'd learned a thing or two about growing crops and raising livestock. She missed being outdoors. But how did any of that support Charles or give her a new direction? He had the mine under control, didn't dabble with saloons anymore, and was working with Ian on how to bring about a more respectable Defiance. Where did she fit in? Could she help him run his ranch?

Charles touched a spot between her eyes and tapped it lightly. "That troubled crease is going to leave a mark, princess. I didn't mean to give you so much to think about."

She touched her forehead, coming back to the more immediate problem. "Do you remember our first day in Defiance? How you walked around the hotel laying out our next steps in rapid-fire succession, like a Gatling gun?"

Charles chuckled, and Naomi felt a little insulted.

"I remember it well. You were livid with my suggestions. I did overwhelm you a bit, I suppose."

"It wasn't the *amount* of information, Charles. It was the *way* you presented it. You had this swaggering, lord-of-all attitude. You started issuing orders with the assumption that we wouldn't question them."

He pulled away from her. "I was merely offering my experienced advice."

"You were giving commands." In spite of trying to remain calm, Naomi could hear the frustration coloring her tone. "All I'm saying is that you don't get to run everything, even when it comes to me."

"Forgive me, Naomi, but I assumed as your husband, my input would be expected, welcomed, possibly even valued."

The edge in *his* voice made her pull away and sit up on her knees. "You're not my husband yet and I want some say in my own affairs."

Wetting his lips, Charles sat up slowly. He swiped a hand across his beard, and then rested it on his raised knee. "Naomi, you're foolish to turn down my help. As I recall, we've had nearly this same conversation and you wound up accepting my advice, my carpenters, my plans, and the end result was a successful hotel."

Naomi clenched her teeth to keep from saying something she'd regret. Charles shook his head and exhaled. "Fine. I've bought the restaurant out for the next few days. I think you should—" he scowled and rephrased. "I would *suggest* you talk to your sisters about taking another few days off . . .," he softened his voice and reached for her hand, "so that you and I can spend some time together after the wedding."

She didn't know if it was the longing in his voice, the love in his eyes, or the thought of spending time with Charles as his wife, but Naomi melted.

"Naomi, I am a man who makes things happen. Granted, most of the ventures I've run wouldn't get me sainthood, but I do know how to take care of business. I'll try not to run rough-shod over you if you will consider my advice." He lay back down and drummed antsy fingers on his stomach. "Ian observed the other day that he and Rebecca, should they get married, would be like an old, comfortable pair of shoes. You and I, on the other hand," he cut his eyes at her, and she saw the teasing that danced in them, "he said we will live a life of thunder and lightning."

As if God was in agreement, thunder rumbled through the valley.

CHAPTER 41

*R*ebecca pulled a brush through her long, dark locks **and savored the caress of the bristles on her scalp.** Sitting at her vanity, she tried to put Silas and Sarah out of her mind and focus on her dinner with Ian. She imagined an intimate, candlelit affair and smiled at the sudden thrumming of her pulse.

She felt alive.

But her heart drew her back to the life Sarah would be facing tomorrow. In a breath, her future with Silas was gone.

Someone knocked at the door and she paused with the brush in her hand. "Yes?"

"It's me, Emilio. I am supposed to drive you up to Mr. Donoghue's. Whenever you're ready, the wagon is waiting downstairs."

Butterflies flitted in her stomach and Rebecca eyed herself in the vanity mirror one last time. She had moments when she was shocked by the age creeping up on her, and the increasing number of gray hairs flowing amidst the black. But tonight, her brown eyes glittered with a youthful intensity. The deep burgundy of a simple muslin dress brought out a glow in her skin. Biting her lip, she tied a matching ribbon in her hair then pinched her cheeks for some color.

Seven years. Seven years since a man had kissed her. Seven years since Ben had made love to her. The thought sent a natural blush racing to her cheeks. Did Ian love her? Did he think about kissing her? Did he think about more?

Oh, God, please don't let him break my heart tonight. I just want to hear three words from him. After that, the rest will fall into place.

*J*an's cabin sat in the center of a steep pasture, surrounded by wildflowers and bathed in twilight. A coffeepot stuffed with bright yellow daisies brightened the front porch. As she climbed the steps and caught the scent of wild roses, she noted, too, that somehow he'd managed to trim the grass in the front yard. The door creaked and she looked up.

"Good evening, Miss Rebecca. Welcome to my humble abode."

Ian met her wearing a crisp, white shirt tucked into new dungarees. She'd never seen him wear those before. She thought he preferred the linen trousers. And she'd never seen him without his argyle sweater. The plain shirt downplayed that endearing middle-aged paunch of his. The dungarees were quite attractive as well, in a rugged sort of way. Embarrassed that she'd scanned him head to toe, she motioned to his yard as she stepped on to the porch.

"Your yard is lovely, Ian. How in the world did you mow it?"

Smiling, his eyes glowing with an energy Rebecca also hadn't seen before, Ian reached up and scratched his freshly-trimmed beard. "I borrowed a goot."

She cocked her head slightly. "A what?"

Ian gritted his teeth. "The farm animal. A gooooat," he enunciated.

"Oh," she laughed at the language barrier.

"Ye are quite lovely this evening, Miss Rebecca," he said, his voice bold and husky.

She could *feel* the compliment, the caress of his eyes, and almost sighed aloud. "You look very nice too—in those clothes." Knowing her face gave away too much of her adoration, she turned to admire the view. From his porch, Ian could see the whole town. Defiance rested on the floor of an expansive, flat valley amidst ranges of steep, snow-capped mountains. Thick, green pines and a lesser number of hardwoods covered their lower elevations as a wide, bustling stream snaked its way through the middle of the valley. This was the stream that flowed behind the hotel. Dozens of trails snaked out from the town into the higher elevations and, at the far end, Rebecca could see another road coming in from a pass between the mountains. "What a lovely view to see every night."

As she watched, the final rays of sun disappeared behind Redemption Pass off to her right. Roiling, menacing clouds tumbled over the mountains at the opposite end of the valley. A flash of lightning illuminated the dark clouds from within and she wondered if the storm would reach them.

"Dinner is ready, if ye're hungry."

Rebecca started at the nearness of his voice from behind her. Standing so close, she could feel the heat of him and wished she could lean back on him. She imagined him wrapping his arms around her as they stood watching the night fall. Intoxicated by the thought, slowly she turned and fell into his wide, welcoming eyes. They'd never been this close before, at least not without a steak frying nearby. "I'm starving." She wanted to scream the words.

Ian swallowed and moved toward her. His chest brushed her bosom and he stepped back. He cleared his throat. "Right this way." He motioned toward the cabin's open door. Rebecca didn't move. Her whole body felt like one big, hammering pulse. She held his gaze, willing him to touch her. He pursed his lips and took her hand. She swore a spark leaped between them. "I'll leave the door open for propriety's sake."

She nodded. "Thank you."

Still, neither of them moved toward the door. They were both waiting. For what, she didn't know. She could feel the debate raging in him. Finally, he tugged her toward the door and the moment ended.

Rebecca stepped into his cabin, wondering what had just happened. Clearly, Ian wanted to say something, do something, but he held back. Why? Trying to pay attention to her surroundings, she took in the simple, sparsely decorated cabin. He'd nailed fruit boxes to one wall for shelves. Nearby, a narrow plank desk sat covered with architectural sketches. His neatly made bed occupied the back wall. A pot-bellied stove stood a few feet over from it and warmed the room nicely. She smiled at the small table sitting in front of the stove. Candlelight illuminated two tin plates covered with baked pheasant, baked yams, and stewed apples. And she hadn't cooked one morsel of it. But how had he cooked it?

Ian motioned to a stool. "Isna Buckingham Palace—"

"Ian, please, it's lovely." Rebecca sat down on the stool and grabbed the sides to move it forward just as Ian did. His hands covered hers, his breath tickled her ear . . . and they both stilled. Chills rippled down her spine. It would be so simple to just turn her head and find his lips.

Ian shook his head, again breaking the spell, and helped her slide her seat forward. Linen napkins, real silverware, he'd outdone himself. It all seemed set up for a special evening. Finding hope in that, she decided she could wait on him to reveal his thoughts—and heart.

He sat down opposite her and blessed the meal. She cut into the pheasant and took a bite. "Ian, this is wonderful but how—where—did you cook it?"

"Out back. There's hardly room to change yer mind in here. Since I've been working at the hotel with ye, I've not had much time for cooking. And as ye can see," he patted his stomach, "I'm none the worse for it."

Rebecca savored another bite of pheasant as he spoke. She closed her eyes and experienced the smoky, nutty flavor and hint of rosemary. "You can cook. It's very good."

He exhaled. "It's been a while since I did pheasant."

"Not too long, apparently."

For a time, the sound of forks and knives scraping across the tin was the only sound in the small cabin. Rebecca didn't think it was a tense silence, just a patient kind. *Back to that*, she thought, glancing up at Ian. Yes, she'd learned a lot about patience thanks to Ian Donoghue.

"That was sad business today, what with Silas getting killed," he said between bites. "Defiance still has a way to go 'til it's civilized."

"The news will break Sarah's heart in two. I'm glad Hannah and Mollie will take him home."

"Aye, 'tis best that such news comes from a friend."

"It just goes to show how precious and fragile life is."

Ian halted his fork and seemed to think that over before finishing the bite of bird. "How long had ye been married when yer husband and child died?"

Thoughts about Ben and Gracie never failed to bring a stab of pain. "Ben and I were married nine years. He and Gracie have been gone seven years this summer." Oh, but she didn't wish to dwell on her loss. Finished with her meal, she laid the napkin on the table and smiled up at Ian, intent on staying in this moment. "You did yourself proud, Ian. You can cook for me every night."

She'd meant the compliment to be light-hearted, but once out, it hung in the air between them. The look in Ian's eyes changed again, heavy with emotion, and Rebecca's heart started that all too-familiar and, so far, pointless gallop. Determination settled in his jaw and he reached across the table for her hand.

"Rebecca, last year I asked for permission to court ye, and ye denied me." She opened her mouth to argue, to explain, but he pushed on. "Since then, I've waited. Waited to see if I thought yer feelings toward me would change and if ye felt strong enough to love again."

Gently, he moved his thumb back and forth across the back of her hand. Rebecca breathed in quick, shallow gasps. *'I love you, Rebecca.' Just say it, Ian. Please. I . . . love . . . you.*

"It pains me greatly to say I've seen no hint, nothing—"

"Oh, good grief, Ian," Rebecca blurted. Huffing, she slapped the table and rose. She marched to the door and stood there, not seeing the view of twinkling lights and glowing tents or the half-moon just rising over the mountains. Shaking her head in consternation, she folded her arms tightly across her chest. "How can you be so blind?" She hugged herself tighter, afraid that if she couldn't keep her self-control, she might turn around and kick him in the shin.

"Ye mean . . . I'm struck dumb."

She heard the shock in his voice and snorted. "Dumb as an ox." Her voice broke on the last word and she started blinking to stop the tears. "I can't do this." Mortified that she was on the verge of weeping like a silly girl, Rebecca pounded across the porch and rushed down the path toward town. It wasn't safe to walk alone, but she didn't care. Who would attempt to waylay an old woman anyway? Ian didn't want her. No one wanted her.

CHAPTER 42

*R*ebecca wanted to scream as she pounded down the path. She nearly did when gruff hands grabbed her and spun her around.

Ian.

Ashamed of her emotional reaction, she tried to pull out of his grasp, looking anywhere but at him. He clutched her tightly to him with one arm and tilted her chin up. "Ye didnae let me finish." He wiped a tear away with his thumb and she settled against him . . . a little. "I wanted a hundred times to just come right out and ask how ye felt. Then ye started burning things when I tried to speak of it and I started wondering if maybe ye thought I was too old. That I've nothing left to offer a wife."

Rebecca squeezed her eyes shut and twisted her head. Fear had held them back from so much.

"The fact is ye make me feel like a young man again, full of vim and vinegar." He pressed his lips to her forehead as he spoke. "I'm not meself without ye. I feel . . . undone. Ye're the first person I want to see every day . . . and I go to bed every night dreaming aboot ye. Aboot life with ye. Aboot . . . loving again."

HEATHER BLANTON

His words fell on Rebecca like rain on dry ground. She felt her
soul filling back up, running over. He dragged his lips down her
forehead and across her eye, to her nose, to her lips. "If ye'll have
this fat old man, I'd like to marry ye, my bonny Rebecca."

Rebecca laughed and threw her arms around him. She kissed
him firmly, giddy with joy, but after a moment, she pulled back,
shocked at herself. They hung on each other's gaze, drinking each
other in. Ian kissed her, possessively, hungrily. Rebecca nearly
wept as her senses jolted to life. Lightning flashed in her veins as
she inhaled his scent, felt the stubble of his beard on her cheek,
the heat from his arms as he enfolded her. He kissed her and
kissed her wildly, like a starving man snatching at bread, and she
kissed him the same way. Desperate, crazed, joyous.

"My bonny Rebecca," he whispered into her throat. "Say ye'll
marry me this night and wake beside me in the morning."

"Wh—what?" The touch of his lips against her skin seared her
brain. Thoughts wouldn't form.

With a groan, he pulled away from her, leaving her feeling lost
and abandoned. Dying for him, she tried to kiss him again, but he
clutched her hands between them. "I have learned this day,
Rebecca, that Marshal Beckwith is a Justice of the Peace."

"What?" Why did she keep saying that?

"I thought perhaps if we married quietly, it wouldna interfere
with Charles and Naomi. If ye'd like to have the preacher marry
us, though, we could repeat our vows." Rebecca blinked, trying to
take this in, to understand the ramifications. Ian squeezed her
hands tighter. "I've thought for many months now that we're
wasting too much time apart, Rebecca. I want my life with ye to
start right now."

"But the preacher will be here tomorrow."

"Aye . . . Aye." The second time he said it, Rebecca heard the
defeat in his voice.

"I'm not saying no, Ian." She backed away from him and
rubbed her forehead. "I just need to think a moment."

She didn't feel that she needed a preacher per se to make the marriage legal. She would, of course, prefer it, but she didn't want to interfere with Naomi's wedding, either. If she and Ian waited, it might be weeks, possibly months, before the preacher made his way back around to Defiance. On the other hand, she was trying to finish Naomi's wedding dress. She didn't really have time to be distracted by Ian right now. It felt strange, too, to make such a decision without her sisters.

Strange, maybe, but not wrong. Ian stood straight and tall, his hands hanging at his sides, clenching and unclenching as he waited. In the shadowy light of the rising moon, she could see the hope in his face, feel the love radiating from him. They'd wasted so much time already.

"I could have married you the day I met you, I think," she said, recalling Ian marching into the hotel, his arms full of architectural drawings.

He closed the distance between them and grasped her shoulders. "Aye, the moment I saw ye, ye took my breath away. Ye are the most beautiful, most stunning woman I've ever met. But ye know it's more than that?" She nodded, thrilled with his compliment. He did think she was beautiful, after all. "I love ye, Rebecca, and I always will. Come and grow old with me."

She touched his cheek, slid the back of her fingers across his beard. "The best is yet to be, the last of life for which the first was made."

Thank You, Father. Thank You.

---

*B*illy stood alone in the middle of the quiet, empty kitchen, lost. He raked his fingers through his hair and sighed, missing all the bustling activity that usually went on in here. McIntyre had taken Naomi off for a buggy ride. Rebecca was dining with Ian. Emilio was off escorting Mollie to Tent

Town for one last talk with Amanda. He admired the girl's compassion.

And he appreciated that he was alone in the hotel with Hannah.

Aside from the guests, of course. He wanted to knock on her door and ask if she and Little Billy would like to go for a walk. Although at this moment, he lacked any gumption to do so. Coming to Defiance felt like a two-steps-forward, three-steps-back sort of journey.

Why am I here, if I can't make any headway with her?

The question hadn't been directed at God, but Billy sensed He was listening.

The kitchen falling into twilight shadows, he sat down in the chair at the head of the table and hid in the growing darkness. Still trying to understand her, he ran that kiss through his head for the thousandth time. She'd given in for one second. For one fleeting instant, he'd held the old Hannah in his arms.

Then she had practically growled at him and flown into Emilio's arms.

Emilio. In spite of everything, Billy liked him. Emilio was his own man, confident in himself. A good, decent person, he treated Hannah—and all the ladies—with a tremendous amount of respect. He'd accused Billy of *not* respecting Hannah and he was right, which is why Billy had punched him. The truth hurt.

He respected her now, for sure. Hannah had grown into a strong, beautiful woman, a loving, capable mother, and she managed her duties, both in the hotel and for Doc, with alacrity and skill. While he'd never thought of her as dim-witted, Defiance had brought forth amazing maturity and wisdom in her.

So what if Billy bought the mercantile and Hannah never came back to him? What if she married Emilio? Would he be able to live with watching Emilio and Little Billy walk down the street together, father and son? Or Hannah sitting beside Emilio in church, her arm hooked around his? He rubbed his eyes, trying to erase the images. The whole scenario was a nightmare.

And his soul cried out. "God, please don't let me lose her," he whispered. "Just show me what to do and I'll do it . . . anything."

CHAPTER 43

*A*bout to push through the café door, Hannah froze. She'd almost barged in on Billy, but when she realized he was just sitting there, alone in the dark kitchen, she stopped. She knew a man in agony when she saw one. Feeling a little guilty, she watched him for a moment, wishing she could read his mind, discover a clue as to what he was thinking.

Part of her ached for him, part of her wanted to go in there, wrap him in a tight hug, stroke his dirty-blonde hair, and tell him everything would be all right. If he would simply trust in the Lord.

The coward in her wanted to back away silently, as if she'd never seen him there, slouching, with the weight of his world on his shoulders.

But she couldn't ignore the gently whispered prayer and her heart broke for him. She made a little warning sound with her boots. Billy started but didn't turn around as she entered the kitchen.

"Goodness, what are you doing sitting here in the dark?" She marched over to the table and plucked a match from the box in the center. She lit the lamp overhead, but kept it low. Unsure of her next words, she sat down in the chair closest to him.

He stared down at his hands, splayed out on the table in front of him. "How long were you standing there?"

She debated the answer and decided to go with the truth. "Long enough."

He sighed deeply and leaned back in the chair, dragging his hands to the edge of the table. "Well, if nothing else, at least you've got me praying."

Stray hairs had fallen across his eyes and she had to clench her fist to keep from reaching up and moving them. "That means a lot to me." Again she thought of that night in Mr. Tulley's cabin. Billy had been so patient and gentle. He hadn't rushed any part of it and he'd loved her, so slowly and easily.

She dragged a hand across her mouth, trying to wipe away the memory of his kiss. How many times had she asked God to forgive her for their sin? A thousand? And she had asked God to take away her feelings for Billy.

Broken, he turned to her and she realized *that* prayer had not been answered.

Or was the answer no?

"I was sitting here thinking what I would do if you married Emilio." The wounded look sliced clear down to her heart. "It would be hell, and what I deserve." He shook his head and shrugged a shoulder. "But I can't leave. I can't leave you and my son."

"Not even if your Pa demanded you come home or promised you the whole Page fortune?"

Billy snorted, as if the idea was ludicrous and irrelevant. "Not even."

She thought long and hard before she spoke again, trying to sort things out and say this just right. "I need time, Billy. I think I know in my heart that you do still love me and that you won't hurt me again like that." She wrangled with the next statement and said it slowly, gently. "But I need to see the proof. And I don't know exactly what proof looks like."

He pondered that for a moment, then straightened up and reached for her hand. A breath away from her, though, he curled his fingers in and didn't touch her. "Fair enough."

---

*H*er head still reeling from Rebecca's news, Naomi hung back as her sister and Ian stepped inside the marshal's office, followed by Hannah carrying her son, Mollie, Emilio, and Billy. The thud of their heels on the boardwalk gone, hers and Charles' footfalls sounded lonely on the deserted street.

She'd been thinking hard about everything Rebecca had told her, her reasons for marrying Ian now. The argument that she didn't want to intrude on Naomi's wedding was silly, but the other part, about not wanting to waste any more time, Naomi couldn't get that out of her head. Resolute, she stepped in front of Charles and turned to him, laying her hand on his chest to halt him. "I have something to say before we witness this wedding."

His brow arched and his mouth twitched. She knew he was amused. "I'm listening." She pulled him out of the street lamp's circle of light to the shadowy edge, lightly clutching his lapels. A cold rain drop sprinkled here and there on them, the storm apparently still uncertain of its timing. Like the rain, the crickets' song was hit-and-miss in the chilly air, their voices reminding her that spring would fade into summer before they knew it. Time was such a precious commodity.

Perhaps seeing her concern, Charles encircled her waist and asked, "What is it, Naomi?"

"Why don't we get married tonight?"

"Is that what you really want?" Her hesitation answered his question and he smiled at her. "I'm fine waiting for the preacher."

"That's just it." She looked again at that hole in his hat. "Maybe in Defiance you shouldn't wait. You almost got shot. Silas did get shot. Rebecca and Ian knew they were supposed to be together the moment they met. Maybe we should be living life while we can."

Biting the inside of his cheek, he seemed to ponder her offer for a moment. He slid his hands around to her ribs as the wheels turned. Finally, he shook his head. "I've been reading, Naomi, and I understand that the Church is the bride of Christ. That tells me that Jesus sets some stock in the wedding ritual. He likes a beautiful bride, a pure bride."

"I've been married before, remember."

"But the wedding is a symbol for a relationship, a deep, abiding one. It is also an outward symbol . . . one I want this town to see. So, no, Mrs. Miller," she could see the gleam of his teeth and hear the humor in his voice, "if you're asking me to marry you tonight, I'd have to reject your proposal."

"You're sure?"

"No, I am not," he answered instantly and they both laughed. "I realize I could walk into that office and walk out with you as my wife." He wrapped her in his arms again, pulling her snuggly up against his chest. "My conviction on this matter is shaky at best. So be warned. If you insist on this course, I will be forced to comply. Against my will, you understand." He leaned down and kissed her and Naomi's knees turned to water. "Please insist," he whispered huskily, nibbling on her lips.

The jangle of a wagon and the boisterous, inappropriate conversation of the two male passengers interrupted them. Grudgingly, Naomi and Charles stepped apart, still holding hands. He stared at her from the shadows, waiting. She huffed a great sigh. Oh, she didn't want to say this. "Fine. We'll wait."

"Fine. Besides, I'm not quite ready."

"You're *not* ready? Not ready for what?"

The mischievous grin reappeared as he walked by her, pulling her along. "Just a few more things to be done, don't worry, I'll be ready Saturday night."

To Naomi's amazement, Marshal Beckwith conducted a beautiful, thoughtful ceremony. He even offered a few inspired words of wisdom. The group had gathered around him and the couple in the center of the jail. Someone had hung up a blanket to shield them from a lone prisoner in the last cell.

Naomi was surprised that Ian had exchanged his normal dress of argyle sweater and trousers for a crisp white shirt and blue dungarees. Rebecca wore her burgundy dress and held a small bouquet of hastily picked wildflowers. A lovely couple, indeed, Naomi couldn't be happier for them.

Their pledges of love finished, Marshal Beckwith tucked the Bible underneath his arm and startled everyone by plucking two rings from his breast pocket. His chiseled face softened a bit as he explained that Mr. McIntyre had a collection of such things in his safe. Naomi didn't like knowing that miners had gambled away their wedding rings, but she also knew that the couple now using these would never take them off. Warmed by the thoughtful gift, Naomi hugged Charles' arm and gave him an approving smile. The man thought of everything.

Beckwith finished the ceremony by solemnly placing Rebecca's hands in Ian's. "May you always share with each other the gift of love and be one in heart and in mind. Therefore, what God hath joined together, let no man put asunder. By the power vested in me by the new State of Colorado and Almighty God, I now pronounce you man and wife." Beckwith winked at Ian. "You may kiss your bride."

---

*N*aomi searched the mountain where Ian's cabin sat, but couldn't see it from the steps of the hotel. Charles came up behind her and wrapped her in a warm embrace. He smelled of apple-flavored tobacco and something else manly. His scent, that devilish beard, his dark eyes, sometimes they were overwhelming. She settled back into him and tried for the millionth time to understand how he affected her. She could feel so at peace with him and yet so alive. In his touch, with every caress, every kiss, he brought her a soul-deep . . . *finality*. Like a story at its end.

"Ironic, isn't it," he said, resting his chin atop her head.

The temperature had started dropping to a more normal feel for a late spring night in the Rockies. Chilly, she snuggled deeper. "What is?"

"That *you* wanted to get married tonight and *I* said wait."

"Oh." She chuckled. "Are you sorry? After all, it could be us—" She bit that off, surprised at herself.

"Yes, it could be us enjoying our wedding night."

They fell silent and Naomi was fairly certain they were both imagining the same thing. Oh, how she longed to be with Charles like that, but at the same time, the thought terrified her. "Rebecca has been alone for so long. I wonder how it will be for them." She hadn't really meant to share that thought, yet Charles seemed to know exactly what she meant.

"I told Ian," he kissed the top of her head with a slow lingering caress, "to take it slowly . . ." He kissed the back of her head the same way and Naomi's pulse started pounding like war drums. "That they have all night." His lips slid around to her ear and he kissed her there, nibbling on her lobe. She swallowed, beginning to feel faint. "If he took it slow and easy . . ." Naomi tilted her head as he brushed his lips down to her neck. Charles' voice softened and filled with the thick, husky sound of desire. "She'd let him know . . ."

His hands moved back and forth from her ribs to her stomach. He kissed her temple. His hot breath fogged her rational mind and she raised a hand to his neck, twining her fingers through his black curls. His beard gently grazed her cheek. His lips went back to her neck. Naomi's heart thundered. " . . . when the timing was right." She'd completely lost track of what he was saying. She couldn't think and she felt like a living spark of electricity. He stopped kissing her and his hands on her waist stilled. "You have no idea, Naomi, what it takes to leave you every night." The passion in his voice, his battle to control himself, was intoxicating. He moved his hands to her shoulders. "Especially tonight . . . when I didn't have to."

He sighed and pulled her into his arms. She slid inside his coat and held him tightly, resting her cheek on the lapel of his satin vest. For a time, they stood there, holding each other and listening to the rowdy sounds emanating from Tent Town. When he spoke, the uncertainty she heard tore at her heart. "My mother was a godly woman and yet she couldn't turn my father . . ." He faded off and his chest rose with a deep breath. "He was a scoundrel of the worst sort. I want to be a better man than that. I want to be a better father."

"Oh, Charles," she squeezed him tighter, knowing he already was a better man, and would be a better father, if they could conceive. "You will be." She closed her eyes and finally shared her deepest fear. "But what if I can't give you children?" Her voice broke on the last word and she bit down, trying to keep tears at bay.

He hugged her tighter and kissed the top of her head. "It has not escaped my notice that you and John had no children after several years of marriage. Coupled with the fact that you can't cook, I don't know what I'm doing here."

She gasped and stepped back from him. The smirk on his face motivated her to deliver a healthy jab to his ribs. He flinched and she fumed. "I can't believe you made a joke about that."

He touched her cheek and grinned wryly. "Hannah mentioned that she hopes we have *a passel*, I believe were her words. I assumed from that, you're capable." He pulled her back into his embrace and kissed the top of her head again. "I look forward to many, many attempts at building a family with you, Naomi, whatever the outcome."

CHAPTER 44

One-Who-Cries tightened his grip on the hilt of his knife, squeezing until he felt his fingers would break.

Hopping Bird, dead?

He gritted his teeth and waited for the young brave before him, gasping for breath, to finish the story. He had run all the way from the White River Reservation with the news. "Two soldiers got drunk . . . they were pushing Two Spears around . . . Hopping Bird . . ." He leaned forward and rested his hands on his buckskin covered knees, his breaths slowing. "Hopping Bird tried to stop them and one of them cracked her skull with his gun."

The fire popped behind the boy. One-Who-Cries closed his eyes and listened to the snap of flames and the song of crickets. He could feel the hate rising. Like a flooding river after a spring storm, dangerous and unstoppable. "Where is the boy?"

"Chief Ouray came and took him away."

The darkness of his fury closed over him. Blackness swallowed his world and silence followed. He couldn't breathe. Suddenly, a thousand torches ignited all at once in his mind. He saw Blue Coats running and screaming, burning arrows protruding from their backs. He saw Charles McIntyre hanging from a pole, his skin peeled off and his blood glistening in the firelight. He saw the traitor, Chief Ouray, face down in the dirt, his head squashed like a melon.

The force of the vision, as real as a physical blow, dropped him to his knees. He clutched a handful of sand. Like a starving man, he feasted on the hate that poured into him, drawing strength from it.

Hopping Bird was gone . . . and One-Who-Cries tasted death on the night wind.

Billy and Emilio stared down at the carefully-wrapped body of Silas Madden resting on Doc's bed. The tattered pink-and-blue quilt and jute twine outlined his form perfectly. Billy rolled one shoulder and resigned himself to the task. "Well, let's get this done."

He slid his arms under Silas's knees and calves. Emilio did the same at the man's neck and shoulders. They lifted together. Billy was surprised by the substantial bulk and unnatural stiffness in the body. Together, they turned and headed through the door to Doc's front room. The physician stood at the head of the coffin, holding the lid. The scent of fresh pine mingled with the medicinal odors of alcohol and lye soap and Billy wondered if he'd ever think of pine the same way again. Carefully, as if Silas might complain if they mishandled him, they lowered him into the box.

With Billy's help, Doc dropped the lid into place and motioned with his head toward something behind Emilio. "There's four nails and a hammer right there behind you, son."

They secured the lid well enough to hold it until they reached Sarah's place. Finished, Doc straightened and wearily brushed some sawdust off his hands. "All right, boys. He's all yours. Tell Sarah I'll be out in a few days with the death certificate—no. Scratch that. Just tell her I'll be out in a few days." His tone changed unexpectedly from somber professionalism to simply aggravated. "And stop at the marshal's office on your way out. Tell him to come get that Indian in there or I'll deliver him myself and bill the town."

---

*E*milio snapped the reins and drove the wagon away from Doc's. Billy settled on the seat beside him, curious about how long this trip out to Sarah's would take. Long enough, he hoped, to spend some time with Hannah. After their talk in the kitchen, along with the wedding last night, he felt a little more hopeful about things. He thought that maybe a wedding could put a girl in a mind to forgive a man.

Emilio pulled up in front of the hotel and set the brake. Mollie and Hannah spilled out of the front door giggling, until they saw the coffin. Sobering, they approached the wagon and peered in.

"Where are we supposed to sit?" Hannah asked, pulling her thick blue shawl tighter. While the day was shaping up to be a warm one, Billy realized their freight sure put a chill on things.

Emilio removed his hat, tucked his glossy, black hair behind his ears, and shifted over on the wagon's seat. "Three can ride up here. We can put one on the tail gate, or we can ride two up and two in back."

Rebecca walked out of the hotel, holding the baby, and Billy saw his chance. "Hannah, I'll sit in back with you and help you with Little Billy." Had he heard a frustrated breath out of Emilio?

Regardless, he jumped down from the wagon and met Rebecca at the bottom of the steps. He started to take his son from her, but paused. Rebecca shined. Her cheeks were flushed, her dark hair was plaited in a loose, almost messy braid, fatigue showed in the shadows around her eyes . . . and yet, she *glowed*.

"Married life agrees with you, Rebecca." He couldn't resist a sly smile. "You look quite fetching this morning." Her cheeks flamed and Billy winked. She let him have his son but playfully smacked him on the arm as he turned. The street muddy from the evening's rain, he slogged past Hannah and talked over his shoulder. "I put some hay and a quilt back here. It won't be so terrible."

Out of the corner of his eye, he saw Hannah bite her lip, but Mollie grinned and nodded, encouraging her? Naomi strode out of the hotel at that moment with a picnic basket in one hand and a carpetbag in the other. She carried the items to the wagon and lifted the basket, grimacing as her boots sunk into the mud-clogged street. "Snacks. This will get you there and back. And, Hannah," she waved the other bag, "here's the satchel for your son. I doubt you would have gotten far without the extra diapers." She raised the carpetbag to drop it over the side of the wagon, but paused in midair at the sight of the coffin. Pursing her lips, she settled the bag and basket in the hay.

"All right, y'all," she stepped away from the wagon and climbed back up to the porch. "You've got to get out of here. It's almost noon. Get on to Sarah's. Hannah, tell her if there's anything she needs—"

"Anything at all," Rebecca interjected.

"—tell her to ask."

"And tell her we'll be praying for her," Rebecca finished.

"We have to stop at the marshal's first," Emilio said, offering Mollie a helping hand into the seat beside him. "It shouldn't take long."

Billy smiled down at his son. Holding his daddy's hand, the baby sat up with innocent, curious eyes, drinking in the world as Hannah settled in beside them. *Take as long as you need, Emilio. As long as you need.*

*B*illy climbed off the back of the wagon at the marshal's office and met Emilio at the door. The raised voices of Beckwith and McIntyre filtered out to them.

" . . . It's simply an abundance of caution, Marshal," McIntyre was saying as the two boys hesitantly let themselves in. The men acknowledged them with cursory glances but went immediately back to their heated discussion. Wade observed things from a few feet away, expression bland, arms crossed, keeping his opinions to himself. "Fact is, we don't know where he is and these boys don't have any experience with Indians," McIntyre said.

"McIntyre..." Beckwith, sounding both irritated and patronizing said firmly, "I'm not going anywhere till I hear something about that girl. Now, I'm going to load these two up for bear," he motioned to Billy and Emilio, "and send Wade with them, soon as he brings me Black Elk. Three men, six rifles. Even if they do have trouble, they'll out-shoot One-Who-Cries, but I'm telling you, he's not anywhere in this valley."

"Most likely you're right, Marshal, but I think you are being too casual about the danger. You should go with them."

"Why don't you go with them?"

"Wait a minute, wait a minute," Billy stepped forward, not sure he liked what he was hearing. "What's going on here? Is this trip out to the Madden's place not safe? We're taking Little Billy with us, not to mention Hannah and Mollie. Should they stay behind?"

Beckwith and McIntyre eyed each other defiantly. After a tense second, the marshal spit a stream of tobacco juice with uncanny accuracy at a spittoon near his desk and addressed the boys. "Because he's fought 'em, McIntyre here sees Indians behind every tree. One-Who-Cries has a posse out of Gunnison after him. There're soldiers from Fort Morgan on the prowl for him too. Even if he was in the area, he doesn't have time to attack the likes of you. He's running for his life."

McIntyre shoved his hat onto his head and turned to Billy and

Emilio. "Go straight to Sarah's, help her bury her dead, then come straight back. No picnics along the road, no sightseeing. Is that understood, boys?" They both nodded. McIntyre's shoulders dropped a bit. "Most likely, the marshal here is right. If I didn't think so, I *would* be riding with you."

McIntyre didn't exactly stomp out of the marshal's office, but it was pretty clear he was disturbed by this trip. Someone slapped a Sharp's rifle into Billy's hand, jerking his eyes away from the closing door. He studied the weapon as if it had magically appeared out of thin air.

Emilio tapped the gun, drawing Billy's attention. "Have you ever shot one of these?"

"Once or twice." He tugged the weapon away from his friend. In one semester and a half at Harvard, Billy had joined the boxing team *and* the rifle team, as he had natural gifts for both.

He'd used one gift here already. He hoped there would be no need for the other.

Billy stepped out into the high-noon glare and lowered his hat, surprised that so much of the day had slipped away from them. Carrying a rifle in each hand, courtesy of the marshal, he tucked them into the driver's side of the wagon.

"What are those for?"

He didn't really want to answer Hannah's question. "Just a precaution." He could feel Mollie staring at him too, from the wagon seat. "Two beautiful women," he glanced at Little Billy, bouncing on Hannah's knees. "Pretty, precious cargo."

Emilio stepped up behind him and slipped two more rifles into the hay. Billy took the four boxes of cartridges the boy was balancing in his left arm and settled them in the back as well. Everything in place, Emilio slapped the wagon rail. "That's it."

He sounded confident and relaxed, but Billy couldn't release his sense of disquiet. Maybe he was just paranoid, not being familiar with Indian threats. They weren't exactly a problem back

East. "What do you think?" He leaned into Emilio and lowered his voice. "Is this a good idea?"

"I think we'll be fine. When we get out of town, we'll carry the rifles so they can be seen. Silas's place is only about three hours out at an easy pace. It's not so far."

Emilio's assessment made him feel better. Young, but wise, and Billy respected him. "All right, just tell me when you want me to drive."

Billy strode to the back of the wagon and climbed up beside Hannah, his mood lightened by Emilio's confidence and the pretty gal now sitting next to him.

CHAPTER 45

*N*aomi leaned against her bedroom door and watched Rebecca pull the sewing supplies out of her sewing basket. Readying things to work on Naomi's wedding dress, she set the items out on the bed, one at a time, lining them up—pin cushion, scissors, a box of hooks and eyes, and a roll of ribbon.

Naomi knew her sister was stalling . . . and trying to hide a grin. She opened her hands in light-hearted frustration. "Well, aren't you going to tell me anything about your wedding night? Anything at all?"

Stepping behind the dress form, Rebecca dropped to her knees so she could reach the bustle and giggled. "It was perfect."

Before Naomi could reply, she heard the sound she herself had been dreaming about. The unmistakable pounding of a six-horse team thundered past their window. Naomi clutched her stomach as fear and excitement blossomed in her. "Hear that?"

"The noon stage." Rebecca grinned. "Now who's nervous?"

Nervous didn't begin to describe it. Heart pounding, palms sweating, Naomi was taken aback by her reaction. She exhaled deeply, trying to expel some of the butterflies. "I told Charles I'd meet the stage and get Reverend Potter settled. Now I'm not sure I can walk that far."

Rebecca chuckled and reached for a needle loaded with white thread. "You'll be fine. Give yourself a minute." Naomi dragged her braid across her shoulder and clutched it with a death grip. She exhaled another shaky breath.

"Here, help me for just a minute," Rebecca said, fighting with the bustle. "The reverend's not going anywhere. Hold this ruffle out of my way."

Naomi obeyed, stepping behind the dress form and lifting most of the bustle up into the air. But her nerves were jangling like she'd had too much coffee. After a few minutes, Rebecca burst out laughing. "You're fidgeting like ants are crawling up your legs. So, go. Go!"

Forcing herself to stick to a walk, Naomi listened to the hum of conversations on the boardwalk as she weaved her way through the flowing crowd of beards and plaid and leather. A few men leered, several tipped their hats and smiled, some with friendly intent, but no one said anything inappropriate or tried to touch her.

A pleasant change from this time last year. By now, her reputation was pretty well established and, more importantly, she was *McIntyre's woman.* She'd overheard the description used by customers at the restaurant and, Naomi had to admit, she rather liked it. No one would dare touch the intended of someone as powerful and prominent as Charles McIntyre. Tom Hawthorn's recklessness and consequent humiliation had most likely succeeded in cementing the concept.

The wagon with Silas's body passed by her, going in the opposite direction, and she turned to wave at her family.

"We'll see you tomorrow, Naomi!" Hannah hollered. "Don't get married without us."

"Then don't be late!" She regretted those last words as she resumed her march. Sarah would be devastated, while she could only think of getting her sister back in time for the wedding. But she trusted that if Hannah felt Sarah needed her more, she'd stay. A foul odor assailed her, snatching her thoughts back to the walk. Holding her breath, she gently pushed her way past two miners reeking of whiskey and unwashed stink, and hurried the final few yards to the stage office. Reverend Potter, neat and starched in his black suit and white collar, reached for his leather valise as Jim, the driver, eased it down to him.

"Reverend Potter, it's so good to see you!"

A short, pudgy, older man with a round face and twinkling slate-gray eyes, one would have never guessed his tenacity or courage. Potter took the gospel into the wild-and-wooly mining towns of Colorado. He was a one-man Christian army. To him, no soul was too lost, no town too remote.

He greeted Naomi with wide arms and a wider smile. "My dear Miss Naomi. Wonderful to see you again." He hugged her in a grandfatherly way. "I have missed my precious flock in Defiance."

"And we've missed you. Thank you for coming on such short notice."

He dropped his gaze down to his dusty shoes. "Yes, about that, Naomi." She heard him take a deep breath.

"What is it, Reverend?"

"Are you quite sure about this? I don't mean to cast aspersions on Mr. McIntyre's character and I do appreciate that he has attended preaching my last few visits, but . . ." Concern lined his wrinkled brow. "Well, he's got quite a reputation, young lady. How well do you really know him?"

"I know him well enough, Reverend. And I'm not going into this with blinders on." She tugged his sleeve and pulled him a few feet away from the entrance to the stage office. "He is a changed man. He grows in his faith every day. The way he grieves over his past, he doesn't understand that's evidence of change right there." The Reverend's mouth settled into a worried line. Naomi laid her hand over her heart, hoping he'd understand the suggestion to search his own. "I love him and I believe in him."

"You think you know what you're getting into?"

She dropped her hand and straightened her shoulders. "Yes, sir, I do."

"Well, I've heard the story of how he got shot, several different versions as a matter of fact." They both smiled at the way legends and tall tales sprouted in the mountain towns. "But they all had one common element." He pointed at her. "He was ready to give his life for you. There is no greater love. I merely wanted to be sure you were aware of things."

"I am."

"All right then, where is the groom? I'd like to go ahead and spend a few minutes today with both of you, if we could."

"Oh, he should be right across the street in his office."

———

A familiar perfume wafted across the ledger page and McIntyre's mind froze. His fingers went slack and the pencil fell from his hand. The devil was a woman and she had walked through his door.

McIntyre rose and, inch by inch, absorbed the curvaceous, captivating creature standing before him. Amaryllis Dumas—the one woman who had evoked such a carnal, almost primal, passion in him over the years that it was frightening to recount. Scores of soft gold and copper curls fell around her elegant, petite face. Ice-blue eyes flashed him steamy reminders of their past and dangerous ideas for their future. Her dress, the same blue as her eyes and unabashedly low-cut, left nothing to his imagination. It served to recall uncomfortably explicit memories.

To his chagrin, he heard the Scripture from some time ago echo in the back of his mind, especially the part about a stranger's bosom. He blinked and tried to pull himself out of all the steamy, erotic memories that Amaryllis invoked . . . but there were so many.

Why didn't she stay in Tent Town?

"Amaryllis, it's been a long time." He sounded steady enough, but in truth, her unexpected appearance rattled him. Over the years, bedding Amaryllis had been as natural as breathing, almost a ritual one might say, no matter how long they had been apart. Their way of saying hello . . . and she could say it well.

Her grin widened, as if she could read his mind, and she glided over to him like a cat slithering up to be petted. "Charles McIntyre." Her arms went around his neck and her generous bosom pressed against him. "How I have missed you, *chérie.*" The heavy Creole accent poured off her tongue like Southern honey. McIntyre instantly disentangled himself from her and stepped back as if she had transformed into Medusa. Her face went slack with shock and she left her arms hanging in the air.

McIntyre couldn't believe the strength it took to keep away from her. He was well aware of this woman's power . . . but not his unexpected weakness.

A petulant groove formed in her brow as she lowered her empty arms. "Not exactly the greeting I was expecting, *chérie.* It has not been so long you have forgotten me, *oui?*"

"Quite frankly, Amaryllis, a lot has changed since you were here, what, two years ago?" She batted those lashes at him, normally a weapon to be respected. The shock of her arrival was wearing off, however, and he felt stronger. *Lord, keep me strong . . .* "I thought you heard. I have become respectable."

She burst out with a laugh, but bit it off quickly when his expression didn't change. "It is true then?"

He didn't take offense at her shock, but suddenly his office felt claustrophobic. He brushed past her, eager for a larger room. "Here, let me get you a drink."

"I think I need one," she muttered, sounding perplexed.

Brannagh, as was his habit, had left the pitcher of water, a bottle of good whiskey, and several shot glasses waiting at the end of the bar. McIntyre was tempted to toss back some of the alcohol, but instead poured one for her. He knew better than to offer her water. Amaryllis came up behind him, pressed her curves against him. She was warm, soft—and so very willing.

He swallowed his obscene thoughts . . . but it had been so long since he'd been with a woman.

Telling her to hit the road wasn't going to be the easiest thing he'd ever done, but he knew he could. He had to. He wouldn't lose Naomi over something as meaningless as animalistic pleasure. He turned and handed Amaryllis the glass. She took it with a smile that reminded him of a she-bear—a very hungry one.

Stiffly, he stepped away from her again. "I am a legitimate business man now. I've closed the saloon, sent my Flowers on their way with a little seed money . . . and I am engaged to be married."

That part of the statement stopped the whiskey at her lips. For several seconds, Amaryllis's expression stayed perfectly still. Slowly a smoldering fire filled those ice- blue eyes and she set the drink down. "I heard. Anyone I know? I have always liked a little healthy competition."

She moved a touch closer and, for an unfathomable reason, he didn't move back. Her captivating gaze, the sweet smell of her perfume, somehow managed to hold him still. Before he realized it, Amaryllis had slid her hands up his chest, grabbed his face and brought her lips up to his. His senses roared to life, rational thought abandoned him. She tasted like raspberries and her bosom pressed against his chest so invitingly. Of their own accord, his hands moved to her small, delicate waist, just like old times.

I am a new creation in Christ.

The Scripture exploded in his mind, along with an image of Naomi.

His tongue burning with desire and guilt, he pushed Amaryllis away and held her at arm's length. Disgusted with himself, he shook his head and whispered, "You don't understand. I've changed."

Movement over her shoulder drew his focus to the door. His gut twisted when he realized Naomi stood in the entry, her face stricken with horror and heartbreak. Beside her, the Reverend, looking almost as devastated, closed his gaping mouth. McIntyre quickly stepped away from Amaryllis, but the damage was done. Naomi spun on her heels and fled as if wolves were chasing her.

CHAPTER 46

*P*anic stabbed McIntyre in the heart. God, how would he ever explain? First, he had to catch her. He couldn't let Naomi go one second more with that vision in her head. She'd hate him. The pity on the Reverend's face said even he had doubted McIntyre's conversion. He couldn't stand it if Naomi lost her faith in him, too.

He brusquely shoved Amaryllis aside and raced to the door, but a tall, dark form blocked his path. Beckwith grabbed his shoulder. "The daughter of that peddler. She's been spotted over near Engineer Pass with One-Who-Cries and his renegades. We've got to ride."

McIntyre knocked his hand away. "I've got to see Naomi."

He started to push past the marshal, but Beckwith shoved back. "You don't seem to understand." He turned slightly and lowered his shoulder, as if he was ready to block McIntyre again. "The girl's alive and this might be our only chance to get to her, if we can catch One-Who-Cries between us and the soldiers." For an instant, McIntyre contemplated shooting Beckwith as the fastest way to get past him, but the urgency of the situation finally seeped into his brain. Beckwith chucked his thumb over his shoulder. "I've already got a horse out here."

McIntyre muttered a curse and instantly regretted the coarse language, which surely wouldn't help his cause. He grabbed the Reverend's arm, intent on making the man believe him. "Reverend, tell her it's not what she thinks." He turned his head slightly so Amaryllis could hear. "I don't care if I ever see *her* again, but I can't live without Naomi. Tell her she can still believe in me." *God, let her still believe that.* Desperation tightened his grip. "Promise me you'll tell her.

Reverend Potter stared back with a dubious expression. McIntyre's knees nearly buckled with relief when the man nodded. "I'll tell her, son."

Nodding his thanks, McIntyre walked out to the horse waiting for him. He was none too thrilled to discover he was riding after One-Who-Cries with Marshal Beckwith *only.* "You and I don't make much of a posse, Marshal. The only thing we'll make is a funeral."

Beckwith swung up into the saddle. "Wade is going to deposit Black Elk into a nice warm cell then ride out after your friends. Remember, that was your idea." He backed the bay away from the hitching post as McIntyre seated himself on a big sorrel. "Besides, all we need to do is herd One-Who-Cries toward the soldiers."

McIntyre shoved his hat lower and shook his head. A third man probably wouldn't have made much difference. If they ran into One-Who-Cries, they'd be wishing for ten. At least he and the marshal were heading in the opposite direction of Sarah's farm. He gained some comfort from that, knowing that Hannah and Mollie were out of harm's way.

As the two men galloped out of town, McIntyre looked back over his shoulder. He didn't expect to see Naomi, especially in the fast swirl of traffic, but hoped he might. Instead, he saw Reverend Potter make the sign of the cross for him. McIntyre touched his hat in thanks and turned back around. Beckwith's black coattails flapped in the wind as he quirted the bay. Kicking his horse, McIntyre hunkered down in the saddle and followed. The faster his sorrel went and the farther he got from Defiance, the more an inexplicable sense of dread settled over him. He was going in the wrong direction and knew it, knew it as well as he knew his own name.

But a young girl's life was on the line. He prayed he was doing the right thing. He prayed for protection.

He prayed Naomi would forgive him.

---

*M*atthew walked stiffly down the boardwalk, cursing the noon sun that made his head ache as if a herd of horses had stampeded over him. The stench of unwashed bodies assaulted his nostrils, declaring war on his guts. The wound in his ribs throbbed with his heartbeat and he hoped this trek down the sidewalk would be worth the effort.

As he shuffled forward, Matthew pondered the possible outcome of his plan if Amaryllis could manipulate things. He'd slogged to within about a hundred feet of the stage coach office before he realized the noon stage had already arrived. He was confused for a moment, seeing passengers climbing *on,* and he stopped. He was late. So where was Amaryllis? Had she even bothered to show up?

A few choice words from some men in front of him drew his attention. He grinned with delight when he saw Naomi pushing through the miners, storming toward him. And the shattered look —oh, *beautiful!* Matthew could have danced a little jig as he prepared to intercept the clearly furious, clearly devastated woman. Somehow, Amaryllis had pulled together the perfect timing and earned her thousand dollars.

Matthew waved at Naomi. "Hey, what are—" He stopped, letting well-practiced compassion sadden his countenance.

"Naomi, darlin'." Eyes blazing, jaws clenched, she meant to stomp past him, but he grabbed her arm. "Hey, hey, what's the matter? Something happen?" Naomi looked up at him with an expression of such deep heartbreak that guilt twitched in his soul—just a twitch, not to be repeated. For a moment he saw her turmoil, a longing for the past, for John, and he spoke gently to her. "Naomi, talk to me. What's the matter?"

She opened her mouth but no sound came out. A flood of emotions cascaded over her face and, for an instant, he had hope. She gazed on him with yearning, love, even desperation, but like a sudden afternoon thunderstorm, she let go. Tears welled up and he saw mindless fury replace the pain. "Don't touch me!"

She jerked her arm away and sprinted toward the hotel.

Matthew leaned on his cane and scratched his chin. While he hadn't appreciated that last change in her, he figured he could wander back to the hotel in a bit and console her. She needed a shoulder and his was all hers. She'd come around. He felt sure of it. In the meantime, he wanted to see Amaryllis, if she wasn't still entertaining McIntyre.

Pounding hooves caught his ear and he turned as Marshal Beckwith thundered by on his bay mare, pulling a rider-less, antsy sorrel. The lawman practically rocketed toward the Iron Horse then leaped from the saddle like it was on fire.

Concerned his plans might go awry somehow, Matthew hurried forward through the crowd, peering over miners and pushing past lumberjacks. The marshal had stopped at the front door of the saloon and was engaged in conversation, but Matthew couldn't see with whom. A moment later, he *and* McIntyre headed for the horses. Scowling as if he was contemplating the marshal's murder, McIntyre jammed his hat on his head and jumped on the sorrel. The two pulled out and McIntyre cast a glance backward. A man in a black suit stepped out on the boardwalk and made the sign of the cross after the two riders.

Well, now . . . Matthew scratched his head. *What has happened here?* He wondered if he could be so lucky as to have McIntyre called up for posse duty again.

The old man in the suit started toward Matthew. Flustered, he turned and peered intently into the window of the saddle shop, rubbing his neck for cover. He caught a glimpse of the white collar and wondered if the Reverend had been a witness to Amaryllis' concocted play. Anxious for details, he hurried to the Iron Horse where he found her leaning on the bar, her hand wrapped around a drink.

Matthew appraised the dress she was wearing and smiled to himself. The gal hadn't come to lose this battle, that was for sure. He sauntered up to her with as much grace as he could muster, considering his condition. "Well, Amaryllis, I think you've earned your money."

Angry blue eyes flashing with displeasure hit him like a blast from hell's furnace. Something had gone wrong. Fiddling with the St. Jude medallion around her neck, she positively fumed. "You did not tell me Charles McIntyre has gone respectable. And," she straightened up, "you did not tell me he is *engaged to be married.*"

Matthew chewed on her disapproval for a second, puzzled as to why any of that mattered to her. "True, I didn't mention any details. Didn't think you needed 'em. It was worth a thousand dollars to me to have Naomi catch you with him, as I explained. Did you accomplish that or not?"

Her full, pink lips turned into a shaky pout. "He pushed me away. He's never done that before. *No one* has ever done that. But I know she saw us kissing."

"She did indeed." And Matthew was going to savor every beat of Naomi's broken heart. He rubbed his chin to hide a pleased smile. So pleased, he was dang near tempted to swing Amaryllis around like they were at a square dance, but he would contain himself.

"I thought she was merely another one of his girls." Amaryllis paused. The quiet drew Matthew's gaze back to her. "He loves her.

318

I saw it in his eyes. I am superstitious, Matthew." She let the medal slide from her fingers. "There is a curse upon us now. Love is a strong force that will have its justice."

Matthew started to laugh, but cut it off when he realized she was serious. To hide a niggling of worry in his brain, he snorted with contempt. "You were down in New Orleans too long."

"Maybe, but I am going to get a room at that hotel, take a bath, and get on the first stage out in the morning. Defiance is no good for me now."

Matthew decided he couldn't care less about her plan. His was the one that mattered. "What was all that about with the marshal?'

"He wanted Charles to ride with him, something about an Indian and a captive girl."

Gratified with the way things had turned out thus far, Matthew poured himself a glass. "Amaryllis, when I met you, I knew you'd come in handy." He raised the glass to her, but she didn't offer hers. He shrugged off her disdain and took a sip. "We'll have to walk into the hotel separately. Wait here a few minutes before you come down. And remember," he reached into his pants pocket and produced a leather drawstring bag filled with coins, "you don't know me."

Smiling, Amaryllis took the payment and pressed it to her bosom. "I've never seen you before in my life."

CHAPTER 47

eeling like the King of Siam, Matthew headed back for the hotel, an almost lively bounce in his step as he flowed with, and sometimes against, the men of Defiance. His size pretty much kept the conflicts limited to nothing more than dirty looks. As he walked, he could see Naomi weeping in her room, Rebecca consoling her. He would slip in, sit patiently and listen, rub her arm sympathetically, softly offer his condolences. Eventually she'd see Matthew . . . really see him.

And maybe, on second thought, he'd keep Amaryllis around long enough to make *sure* Charles McIntyre's stripes were in full view. After that, the little missy could hit the trail. Matthew waited for a hotel guest, a fella with a saddle bag tossed over his shoulder, to come through the front door before he went inside and headed toward the stairs. Rebecca startled him by coming out of the kitchen, an apple in one hand and her reticule in the other. "Rebecca, how's Naomi?"

She stopped short. "What do you mean? Is something wrong with her?"

Matthew thought quickly. If Naomi had avoided Rebecca,

maybe he could just waltz right on into her room and play the hero. "No. I mean have you *seen* Naomi?"

"No, not since she went to fetch the preacher." She polished the apple on her sleeve as she strolled toward the door. "I have some things to pick up at the mercantile. If anyone comes in for a room, just tell them to sign the register and take a key. Do you need anything from the store?"

A slow, easy smile crept across his mouth. "Nope, not a thing."

He waited for her to clear the building before he took the stairs to Naomi's room. Her door was partially ajar. He listened for a moment but didn't hear the expected sound of muffled sobs or even sniffling. Puzzled, he pushed the door open a hair. "Naomi, are you all right?"

Only silence answered. He opened the door and surveyed her neat, simple room. The bed was made, her shawl rested on the footboard. Irritated that the only decoration was a wedding photo of her and John by her bedside, he crossed to her window and searched the back yard below. She wasn't in the garden, she wasn't down by the water.

He breathed a curse and wondered where else she could have gone. At a complete loss, he surveyed the room again hoping to spot a clue. Nothing tipped him off. The woman had disappeared. After a twinge in his side, he decided a quick swig would clear his mind. He'd keep the visit to Tent Town short, since Naomi was around here somewhere and she needed him.

---

*M*cIntyre had to hand it to Beckwith. The marshal had a sixth sense about tracking men. He squinted at the rider coming toward them. Except *that* was no Indian. Through the long evening shadows that reached across the rutted dirt path, they could make out the silhouette of a soldier. The marshal nudged his horse out on to the trail and McIntyre followed. Seconds later, the cavalry scout jerked his horse to a halt in front of them.

"Are you the sheriff from Gunnison?" The scruffy boy's dubious expression deepened as he scanned the road behind them. "I thought you had a posse."

"No, we're out of Defiance." Beckwith's jaw tightened with suspicion. "Your C.O. wired and asked if we could ride up the south side of Engineer Pass, maybe drive One-Who-Cries toward you."

"Well, I'm trying to find that posse from Gunnison. Colonel Wilkes thinks the renegade may have doubled back and is heading north again."

A bolt of fear shot through McIntyre. That would put the renegade on the other side of Defiance, and Sarah's spread right in the middle of the trail.

"How did he slip through?" Beckwith asked, his voice carrying a none-too-subtle accusation.

The scout stiffened but apparently chose to let the insult go. "That's what One-Who-Cries does best. Anyway, I don't have orders for you. I'm supposed to tell the crew from Gunnison—"

"We're heading back." McIntyre had heard enough. He shot Beckwith a disgusted glare. "Or at least I am."

He turned his horse and took off in a cloud of dust. Even riding hard, he wouldn't make it to Defiance before midnight. Still, he would check on Naomi, maybe at least gauge things between them. After that, he could change horses quickly and get out to Sarah's.

He needed to keep his mind on his business, but the devastation in Naomi's eyes haunted him. The past six hours had been hell for him. Questions and accusations rained down like a hail storm. What Naomi must think? What Matthew might be trying if he knew about this rift? And why the Sam Hill had Amaryllis come back to the Iron Horse? More importantly, why had he let her get that close?

Because he was still that weak.

He slowed his horse down to a trot, taken aback by the thought. He wanted to shoot himself for putting Naomi through this. He'd warned her about the women, but had been arrogant enough to think none of them would have an effect on him.

Again, he saw her face, the shock, the heartbreak—her trust in him completely shattered, and his spirit died. From the moment he'd met her, he'd put Naomi through so much, from Hawthorn threatening to kill her to Amaryllis breaking her heart.

God, I love her too much to do this to her.

And he knew what he had to do now. It would rip out his heart, but if he loved her, *truly* loved her, he should give her what was best for her—her freedom. Freedom to find and marry a respectable man who would never put her in such contemptible circumstances.

The decision, however, did not allay the sense of disquiet haunting him from the moment he'd ridden out of town. It roared to the surface again and screamed at him to hurry back to Naomi. The urgency pounded in his brain like a stampede and he kicked the horse back to a gallop that transformed into an all-out run.

CHAPTER 48

*N*ight had long since settled when McIntyre, Beckwith on his heels, crested Red Mountain Pass. He had expected to be met with the sight of Defiance, tents and buildings glowing serenely on the valley floor. Instead, flames from the west end of town lit the night sky like a giant torch.

The hotel!

His heart stopped and a bone-chilling dread seared his mind. He kicked the sorrel and raced toward town, trying to outrun the nightmarish scenarios that hunted him like a pack of demons.

But the nightmare was real. Before he reached the hotel, he heard the deafening cacophony of crashing, splintering wood. Men screamed warnings as the ravenous flames devoured the fuel. McIntyre raced down Main Street in time to see the second floor of the Trinity Inn collapse into the burning jaws of the first floor. Flames and sparks clawed angrily at the sky.

Stunned, he raced up to the fiery skeletal remains and skidded to a stop. Through the flames he could see three lines of bucket brigades stretching down to the stream. Dozens of men, yelling back and forth, scurried about like ants, frantically tossing water on the hotel. The building, though, was a loss.

Fear and smoke strangling his lungs, he scanned the mayhem of men moving in every direction. A beam let out a final burst of flame and with its light, McIntyre spotted Rebecca and Ian tossing water on the remnants of the front porch. He hollered their names as he jumped off the horse, but they couldn't hear him over the roaring flames. He ran to Rebecca and spun her around. Grimy, covered in soot, she blinked as if she didn't recognize him, then her eyes glazed over.

"Where is Naomi, Rebecca?" She didn't answer immediately and panic stole his reason. He shook her violently. "Where is Naomi?"

Ian stepped in, gently pushing McIntyre back. "Lad," he moved between him and Rebecca. "We've no' found her yet."

McIntyre's brain stopped. He couldn't comprehend the meaning of the words. "Wha—what do you mean? Where is she?"

"We dunna know."

McIntyre heard the veiled pain in Ian's voice and stepped away from him, trying to distance himself from what he was implying. "No, she's here somewhere." He swallowed his panic and pointed at the charred hotel. "She is not in there." Rage erupted in him, a rage so strong it frightened him. His teeth clenched hard, to the point of hurting his jaw. "She is not in there!" He commanded it to be so. He railed against heaven. Ian reached to grab hold of McIntyre but he jerked away. "She's not in there."

"We have a body!" a man yelled. McIntyre swung toward the voice. Two men had ventured into the back of the hotel, where the kitchen was. Together, they used shovels to heave a smoking beam out of the way. Heaving and grunting, they stood the stove upright. "Yeah, could be a woman!"

Rebecca screamed, the agony in her cry vibrating through every fiber of McIntyre's being. His limbs went cold and he didn't think he could move them. He stopped breathing and wasn't sure if he'd ever start again.

*S*omehow, McIntyre found himself at Doc's, staring out the window into the night, holding his hat in a death grip. He had no recollection of the walk over. Behind him, Ian consoled Rebecca in soft, gentle tones. McIntyre could hear her agonized whimpers. She'd collapsed at the hotel, moaning inconsolably about losing Ben and Gracie and now Naomi. At the moment, she seemed to have faded into shock. Off to his right, Wade huddled in a rocking chair, a sooty gray bandage encompassing the top half of his head.

Black Elk had hit the deputy over the head with a bed leg. For reasons still not clear to McIntyre, the deputy believed the Indian had gone over to the hotel and started the fire, perhaps as a diversion to make his escape from town easier.

Had Naomi walked in on him? Had they fought?

No.

McIntyre knew that Naomi was not dead. He wouldn't grieve. He wouldn't give up. If she was dead, he'd know it. He'd told her once he was bound to her. This connection was not something he could explain, he could only feel it. When Naomi died, he would die, too.

She was not dead.

She was not lying on that bed in Doc's examination room.

The door behind him opened and Doc stepped out, tucking his glasses into his pocket. Haggard and bent, he shook his head and stared at the ground. "We have a female, between the ages of twenty-five and thirty. Approximately five-foot-three. Small-boned." McIntyre caught his knees before they buckled. Rebecca started weeping softly into her hands. "That's all I can say for sure."

McIntyre rushed to him, jabbing his finger in his chest. "So you're not sure it's her, are you?"

Doc cast a pleading glance at Ian and ran his hands through his cropped, yellow hair. "Do you know another young woman who meets that description and who would have been at the hotel? I understand Mollie and Hannah took Silas out to Sarah's." He rested a hand on McIntyre's shoulder. "I'm sorry."

McIntyre stared at nothing and crushed his hat in his hands. The belief that Naomi was not dead kept him standing. He wouldn't listen to that other voice, the one telling him to accept the facts. He heard only the prophecy of death in that voice, for if Naomi was dead, he couldn't live.

But she was not dead. If he repeated it enough times, he could make it true. So where was she? He didn't know where to start looking for her. Slowly, McIntyre slipped his hat on. "Who was the last person to see Naomi?"

Doc rubbed his chin. "Matthew, I believe."

Ian nodded. "Matthew said he saw her leave your saloon and head toward the hotel, no one has seen her since then."

CHAPTER 49

*H*olding Little Billy with one arm, Hannah hugged Sarah tightly with the other. Slowly, reverently, Billy and Emilio lowered Silas into the black hole. This new grave lay forlorn and lonely, with only one other for company, in a vast, grassy plain. Hannah had offered the most hopeful words she knew, reminding Sarah that she would see Silas again and that God wept with her over this loss. Sarah had nodded and prayed silently while Hannah spoke.

Now, Sarah stared down at the grave, her soft, round face twitching as she fought for control. The bun at the nape of her neck had lost much of its shape with her auburn hair poking every which way. Trembling and quite disheveled, a quiet peace still emanated from her. Even so, the woman's shoulders jerked and heaved as the first shovel of dirt thudded on the pine. More tears slipped down her pudgy cheeks.

Hannah looked at the small grave beside Silas's. The headstone said Marcus had gone to be with the Lord at the age of five, over ten years ago. First a child and now a husband. Sarah had taken everything the West could throw at her. Would this break her? Or was she the kind of woman who could throw it right back at the devil? Filled with gratitude for the baby in her arms, Hannah let her own tears flow.

On the other side of Sarah, Mollie had her head bowed, eyes closed. And beyond her, Naomi stood staring at the coffin, trance-like. She'd been like that most of the day, from the moment she had run and jumped onto the back of the wagon. The move had struck Hannah as panicked and irrational, scaring the daylights out of her, but Naomi wouldn't talk about it. She would, eventually. Hannah wouldn't let her suffer alone.

Several minutes later, Billy, Emilio, and Lucas, the gangly young man who panned for gold on the ranch, finished off the grave with rocks plucked from the surrounding pasture. Mollie reached an arm around Sarah and patted her on the shoulder. "Would you like to go back to the house now, Sarah?"

"No, dear," she patted the girl's hand in return. "I'd like to stay here a while. We were married thirty years, seems only right to stay by his grave for a bit."

The comment made Hannah look across the new grave to Billy. Their eyes met and held. Sweaty, his face smudged with dirt, he smiled slightly when she shifted Little Billy on her hip. Hannah prayed she would never have to stand over his grave.

"All right, Sarah," Hannah said without taking her gaze off Billy, "take your time."

God, please don't make me have to bury my husband until we're all old and gray and bent with age. Please . . .

---

*N*aomi hugged the rough-hewn cedar post on Sarah's porch and leaned her forehead against it. A breeze, the chill of winter still in it, drifted down from the mountains and wafted over her. In the distance, she heard the soft lowing of cattle, a horned owl announcing the advancing twilight, and the faint yipping of a coyote.

She tried to concentrate on them. Not the wail that had escaped Sarah when they'd told her the reason for their arrival, not the wail that wanted to rip free from her own breast. She felt foolish and stupid for being upset about Charles. After all, *he* at least was still alive and Naomi would heal. Sarah would never see Silas again this side of heaven. That kind of pain was like a searing brand on your soul.

But the image of Charles in that woman's arms—she clamped her jaws down tight to stop the sob. Her fists clenched. She would not cry, she would not cry—

"Naomi, please talk to me." Hannah's tender plea jolted her out of her miserable thoughts, but only for a moment. Naomi shook her head, not trusting her voice. If she broke, if she started crying, she might not stop, and she hated to cry. "Please, Naomi." Before she could stop her, Hannah had wrapped her in a hug. "It's going to be all right, whatever is breaking your heart, Naomi. It's going to be all right."

No it isn't. And the dam broke. "I caught Charles with another woman," she wept into her little sister's arms. Hannah stroked her head and kissed her hair and held on while Naomi emptied herself of the tears, till she clawed her way back to solemn footing. It took a while. Naomi didn't know she could cry so much. This was grieving, but differently than what she'd gone through for John. In a way, it hurt more, because of the betrayal involved.

After what felt like an eternity, embarrassment got the better of her and she pulled away, drying her eyes. "Oh, gosh, I'm so stupid." Naomi raised her fists to her forehead and wanted to pound Charles out of her mind. "How could I be so stupid?"

"I can't believe you are. Naomi, that man loves you. I'd bet my life on it. Are you sure of what you saw?"

"Oh, yes, indeed." She choked on the last word. "Maybe he does love me, Hannah, but if I can't trust him, if I can't believe in him . . ."

"I wish you hadn't jumped on the wagon with us. He'll be sick with worry and so will Rebecca."

Yes, Naomi did regret that. As for Charles, she'd love to think of him in misery and torment, but it seemed he was capable of finding comfort. *What was it he had said about these other women? I am done with them?* And she'd believed him. Oh, if he was standing right in front of her, she would shoot him, she was sure of it. John had never hurt her like this.

The grief and fury blazed through her chest, burning her hope to ashes. How she ached. "Hannah, I need to be alone."

She stepped off the porch and wandered toward the furthest point of Sarah's yard, the edge of the corral, fifty or so yards out. The Maddens had a neat, one-story adobe home on five hundred acres with a hundred head of cattle. One side of the house grazed the forest that swept down off a long hill, the others opened to a sweeping valley. The towering mountains in the distance and carpet of rolling pasture, like all the spectacular views in the Rockies, made Naomi feel small and easy to overlook, but she knew God was near. She stared up at the deepening purple sky, the last rays of the sun fading, and wondered how she would survive this.

God, I hurt so badly. I just want to curl up and die. How could he do this to me? She smacked a fence post and almost cursed the name of Charles McIntyre. She hated that he could make her feel this way. Foolish tears welled up again. She sniffed and fought them back with steely determination. *I can't forgive this. I can't forgive it because I can't forget it.*

Despite her best efforts, Naomi hugged her ribs and crumpled to the ground. She cried as quietly as she could and asked God over and over to take away the pain. After a while, the reservoir of tears empty and full dark upon her, she lost herself in the night sounds. The horned owl hooted again, this time closer to the house. His mate answered from the barn, or so it sounded to Naomi. The horses in the corral grumbled then whinnied nervously. The coyote yipped again, and he sounded closer as well. Uneasy, Naomi climbed to her feet and listened.

She was being silly, of course, except that the horses were stirring about more restlessly now. Silly, maybe, but not stupid. A plethora of creatures could be out here. Mountain lions, bears, even wolves prowled ranches. Time to go back—

A hand snaked out of the darkness and clutched Naomi's face. Instantly she was pulled back against a lean, sinewy body. The acrid smell of sweat and bear grease filled her nostrils. She elbowed the person with all her might. As her captor flinched, she wrenched her mouth loose and screamed with every ounce of terror she had shooting through her. She turned and saw the flash of war paint, glimmering black eyes, and feathers. Her scream turned to growling as he tried to wrestle her back into a hold. Out of her mind with rage, Naomi clawed and scratched, gouging flesh with her nails. She kneed the man like she was fighting with Satan and kicked at his shins with merciless blows. He tried desperately to gain control of her flailing, clawing hands, while dodging or absorbing the kicks.

A rifle shot split the night, followed by the sudden explosion of multiple, chilling war cries. Out of the corner of her eye, Naomi saw the fist coming down on her like Thor's hammer.

And the world turned black.

CHAPTER 50

*M*cIntyre tried not to think about anything but finding Naomi as he worked his way down the dark trail back to the hotel. At first, he followed the smell of smoke, his mind numb. Enough glow remained from the embers to bring him the rest of the way. As he drew closer, he saw a lone figure tossing water on the dying flames. Flames that, now starved of fuel, would die soon anyway. Still, the man worked, wearily, methodically, mindlessly. When he straightened up after throwing a bucket of water, McIntyre recognized him.

Matthew. He's grieving, he thought, and wasn't sure at first how that made him feel.

Quickly, though, the anger resurfaced and he clenched his jaw. *Let him grieve.*

Something tugged McIntyre's eyes to the heavens. Through the haze of smoke, and to his dismay, a still, small voice whispered *But if ye do not forgive, neither will your Father which is in heaven forgive your trespasses.*

You ask too much, God, especially right now. Just help me find her. That's all I care about. I'll do anything, give You anything later . . . Let me find her alive first.

Resisting the nudge to show Matthew any mercy, McIntyre approached him. He meant to ask where he'd last seen Naomi. Instead he blurted out, "She's not dead."

Matthew snapped his head around. Soot streaked his face and hair. His hands bled, no doubt from blisters formed from carrying the buckets, his black-and-white plaid shirt was pockmarked with burn holes from sparks. He didn't seem to know McIntyre.

His forehead wrinkled in confusion. "They pulled a body out. It has to be her."

"I don't know who it is, but it is *not* Naomi."

Matthew shook his head, as if trying to get his brains to settle in place. "It has to be her."

McIntyre's hands clenched at the delay. "Doc said you were the last person to see her. Where did you see her . . . and how was she? How did she look?"

Matthew's expression changed, darkened. "She was upset." His stare drilled into McIntyre, accusing him. McIntyre realized Matthew knew about Amaryllis. As if the memory clipped the man at the knees, he stumbled back, tripping over his bucket. Reflexively, McIntyre reached for him but missed. Matthew sat down hard, sending up a cloud of ashes.

Wearily, he dragged his legs up to his chest and rested his beefy arms on his knees. He wagged his head back and forth as if in misery, and stared off into the darkness. Matthew groaned, "It's my fault, all my fault. Look what I've done. I only wanted to get her out of here."

A feeling of dread pressed down on McIntyre. "What's your fault?"

Matthew sighed, a long, forlorn exhalation that seemed to clear his mind. "I paid Amaryllis to . . . compromise you."

McIntyre's blood felt like it screeched to a halt in his veins. Holding back his rage took every ounce of self-control he had ever used. He rubbed his jaw and stepped away from the giant before the urge to kill him won. The image of pummeling the jackass rampaged through his mind. But he realized that could wait, had to wait. *One goal*, he told himself. *Keep one goal in mind: find Naomi.*

He absently massaged his aching thigh and tried to think. Naomi was upset. She ran toward the hotel. How far did she get? "Where did you see her, Matthew?"

"In front of the saddle shop."

"Did you see her enter the hotel?"

Silence, then a slow, "No . . . I didn't. I saw you ride off so I went into the Iron Horse to talk to Amaryllis. I came back to the hotel, but couldn't find Naomi." He paused. "I saw Rebecca." Hope wound its way into his voice. "She said she hadn't seen her either. Since I couldn't find her, I went over to Tent Town for a drink. When I came back, the hotel was on fire." He scratched his head, trying to make sense of the web of details. "Maybe she never came back to the hotel." Matthew climbed to his feet and looked at the charred ruins. "But if she didn't, where is she? And whose body . . .?"

McIntyre rubbed his eyes. For years, staying up all night had been a way of life. Now, seeing four a.m. felt like torture. He took a calming breath and thought back over the day. Conversations, people. He didn't have far to go to ponder the coincidence of Black Elk *and* Naomi missing at the same time. Had he taken her? Where would he go? The questions started his heart racing as a stomach-turning possibility wound its way into his brain.

Would Black Elk try to meet up with One-Who-Cries? Would he take Naomi to him? Somehow, the three of them were tied together, he was sure of it. He *felt* it. The Army scout said the renegade had doubled back. If One-Who-Cries was trading women for guns, Naomi might have been tempting to Black Elk. And what if the Indians came across Hannah and Mollie?

What if One-Who-Cries had them all?

*B*illy heard Naomi's terrified scream and bolted from Sarah's house like he was on fire.

He and Emilio burst into the yard, stunned to find rampaging Indians *everywhere*. They rode in a whooping, hollering circle just outside the glow of the porch lamp. Rifles fired and wood splintered on Sarah's porch.

Thank God Emilio had the presence of mind to grab rifles on the way out and he tossed Billy one. "Shoot!" Together, backs to each other, they fired their weapons at the invaders.

Boldly, the Indians raced around the boys, cutting them off from the house. *If only Lucas hadn't ridden off for his camp*, Billy thought, lamenting the absence of a third gun. Arrows flew through the air like streaking meteors. Emilio howled as one hit his foot. Caught in the open, surrounded, Billy knew they were going to die if they didn't make it to cover.

The water trough appeared through the swirling tornado of Indians and horses. Closer than the house, they had to make a run for it. He hesitated for a split second, though. The girls were in the house . . . and Little Billy. Another arrow zinged past him, making the decision for him.

"The trough," Billy yelled, cocking the Winchester. "I'll cover you." As the words left his mouth, he heard the whoosh of another arrow, felt it strike deep in his thigh. He looked down, marveling over the lack of pain.

In front of him, Emilio hobbled frantically toward the trough, shooting at the circling, flashing targets. An Indian leveled his weapon on them. Acting on instinct, Billy fired first, the shot hit the barrel of the other gun. The bullet made an odd *zing* sound as it ricocheted off. Startled by his rider's strange jerk on the reins, the Indian's horse reared. Billy took advantage of the moment to lunge for the trough.

The next few minutes were a nightmare of rifle shots, war

cries, and choking dust. Then, like ghost warriors, the renegades suddenly faded into the night and disappeared.

He and Emilio fired a few more shots but the Indians were gone. In the tomb-like silence, he and Emilio waited, needing to be sure they weren't coming back. The stillness of the night was suffocating.

Billy raised his head. The porch lamp still glowed and he could see dead bodies, two dead *Indians* to be precise, littering Sarah's front yard. Emilio stood up and limped quickly toward Sarah's.

A throbbing in Billy's leg drew his hand down, but he didn't look. He felt the shaft of the arrow protruding from his leg and flinched. He explored further and discovered the tip, fiendishly sharp, poking out the back of his leg. Sucking in a breath, he clawed his way to his feet, only to stagger drunkenly. White-hot pain shot from his thigh to his brain. Sweat popped out on his forehead and he held on to the trough, trying to get a handle on things.

"They're gone."

Billy whirled at the sound of Emilio's voice. Fear burned in his belly and his throat dried up. "Hannah? Little Billy?"

"Little Billy and Sarah hid in a secret place under the floor . . . but . . ." Emilio shook his hair back and crammed his hat on. His tan shirt was smeared with blood around his left shoulder. "One-Who-Cries took the girls."

CHAPTER 51

*L*ivid, McIntyre threw his hat across Beckwith's office. "I have never seen such a bunch of chicken-hearted, yellow-bellied cowards!" He wanted to strangle someone, namely, the men in Defiance. How could they be so gutless? He and the marshal had covered both ends of town separately, knocking on every door and tent pole. They hadn't found one volunteer for a posse. One-who-Cries had them scared spitless.

As far as McIntyre was concerned, there would be hell to pay for these cowards when this was over.

"They don't have a dog in this fight," Beckwith said evenly, rising from his desk. He strode to the door, plucked his hat off the hook near the entrance, and sighed. "I'm a little tired myself, but let's go get those girls. We can rest when they're safe."

McIntyre appreciated Beckwith's undying devotion to his job, but they stood a far better chance of recovering the girls in one piece if they had help. "Somehow, we've got to force them to help, Marshal. We have no idea where the Army troops are or where that posse from Gunnison is. We're on our own."

Beckwith's eyes narrowed. "McIntyre, the men in this town are some of the laziest, greediest, and most shiftless—"

He cocked his head to one side as if listening. After an instant, McIntyre heard it, too, horses coming at a gallop. They hurried outside and in the silver-gray of dawn met Billy and Emilio riding in from the west end of town. McIntyre stepped down into the street, and grabbed a hold of their horses as they reined in.

"One-Who-Cries attacked us at Sarah's," Billy told them, his voice raspy, as if talking was a huge effort. "They've got Hannah, Mollie, and Naomi."

The relief and vindication that surged through McIntyre nearly dropped him to his knees and lifted his hope at the same time. "Thank You, God," he whispered. The simple prayer carried more weight than he could have ever imagined. He knew, without a doubt, God heard it. He cleared the tightness from his throat. "How long ago?"

"They hit us right at dark," Emilio said, his somber tone acknowledging the substantial lead.

Their blood-stained clothes and bandages told the rest of the story. "Kill any of 'em?" the marshal asked.

"*Si.* Two," Emilio exchanged a disappointed look with Billy, "but we think that could still leave six or eight."

Ian, Wade, and—to McIntyre's displeasure—Matthew rode up beside the boys, the deputy leading two horses. Their grim expressions melted to confusion when they saw the boys. "All right," Beckwith said, marching toward one of the fresh mounts behind Wade. "You two git on over to Doc's—"

"No." Billy shook his head defiantly. "We're going."

His determination stopped the marshal cold. The law man studied the bloody strip of cotton wrapped around Billy's leg, working his jaw as he thought. "All right, go to the livery and get fresh horses." Beckwith switched his gaze to Ian. "Why don't you go tell your new wife her sisters are alive? I expect that's news she could use." He swung into the saddle. "When you're done, gather up Billy and Emilio and meet us at Silas's farm, and be quick about it. We won't wait long."

Ian jerked his horse away from the group. "Ye willna be waiting on me." He spurred the horse and headed toward his cabin.

McIntyre climbed up on the other fresh horse and met Matthew's wary gaze. He really didn't want the big ape along, but they needed all the help they could get.

As if reading his mind, which McIntyre knew wasn't hard, Matthew shoved out his hand. "I know I'm a double-dealing four-flusher, but I do care about Naomi. I'll do what it takes to get her back."

What it takes to get her back? He suspected Matthew was talking about more than fighting Indians, but he shook the man's hand anyway. "Fine."

Beckwith took off down the street, and the posse launched after him. Now that McIntyre knew for sure Naomi was with One-Who-Cries, his relief didn't mean much. The blistering hate he bore for the savage melted into a suffocating fear. The Indian was short-tempered and most likely wouldn't take to a feisty white woman like her. That was putting it mildly. McIntyre's stomach constricted at the reality of this nightmare.

One wrong move, one smart remark, and the Indian might well cut out her tongue.

---

*T*he first thing Naomi became aware of was a gentle rocking motion, and then the strong odor of horse. She opened her eyes and frowned. Dirt. Pebbles. Why was the ground where the sky should be? And were those *her* hands tied with rope?

Disoriented, panic seized her and she tried to wiggle to a sitting position. Something slapped down firmly on her bottom with a good sting and she swung her head to the right. A leg, a leather-covered leg, with a moccasin on the foot, trailed down the side of the horse. A sense of foreboding clenched her stomach.

"Naomi . . . Naomi, are you all right?"

Hannah's voice came from somewhere behind her, or more accurately, on the other side of this horse. She tried again to wiggle around to see something but the Indian on the horse slapped her again, harder. That was going to get old. "I'm fine," she said through clenched teeth. "What happened? Where's Little Billy?"

"I think he's fine. Sarah hid with him in a secret place underneath the living room."

Oh, thank You, God.

Relieved about that at least, she tried to assess the situation. "Mollie? Is Mollie here?"

"Here . . . and praying."

"Your God will not save you." The deep, vaguely bored voice came from the Indian practically sitting on top of Naomi.

She turned and twisted enough to manage a skewed view of him. A young man with a large nose and beady, angry eyes stared down at her. Wearing a buckskin shirt draped in several bear claw necklaces, he sneered at her as a single feather in his hair danced in the breeze.

Huffing, she went back to her original position, which, now that she was awake, made every part of her ache. Her head, her shoulders, her hands . . .

She wiggled and rolled her wrists for a few minutes, testing the knots. Gruffly, an arm slid under her stomach and before she could even gasp, the Indian had her sitting astride in the saddle. The sudden change in position sent the blood draining from her head and he had to hook his arm around her again to keep her from her toppling out of the saddle.

Naomi bit her lip and squeezed her eyes shut, waiting for the dizzy feeling to subside. When she felt more like herself, she looked around. They rode along a wide trail heavily forested on both sides with aspens. On her right, Hannah shared the saddle with another brave, a handsome young man so lean and muscular he could have been strung together with rawhide. And to Naomi's left, Mollie rode with an Indian who verged on paunchy and wore a scar down his right cheek that started above his eyebrow and finished below his jaw.

Naomi twisted and saw four other riders trailing the group. She gasped when she realized one of them bore a captive as well. A young girl, all of about fourteen or fifteen, rode with them. She was pretty and petite with hair the color of fresh cinnamon. Dirt stained her face and her long, bountiful hair hung in tangled knots and rats' nests. Her once blue-checked dress was a filthy, tattered gray now and fear filled her wide brown eyes. Naomi had to turn away and shut hers again to gain a moment of calm. These men were cowards to attack defenseless women. She longed for the real men she knew.

"Hannah, what about Billy and Emilio?" she asked, moving from thoughts of Charles to the boys.

Though the question was directed at Hannah, the Indian behind her answered. "We didn't take the time to kill them. They were fortunate we were in a hurry. If we had taken you in Defiance, they would be dead." Relief warred with her mounting animosity. At least if he left the boys alive, they'd go for help. As if to purposely dash her hopes he added, "They won't be riding anywhere for a while."

Naomi sagged against him, realized she was touching him and jerked away as if she'd leaned on a hot stove. He laughed, a low chilling sound. "I do not want you, white woman. I want her." He motioned to Hannah. "I saw her riding one day, on a black and white pony. Her hair shined in the sun like gold." He nudged his horse closer to Hannah's, so their legs touched. "Black Elk was supposed to bring you to me." He reached out and stroked Hannah's loose, messy braid, which hung down the front of her shoulder. "But things worked out better this way."

Before she could jerk away, he groped her. Hannah gasped and all the Indians laughed at her outrage. Reacting to the offense, Naomi brought her head back against One-Who-Cries' nose as hard as she could. She heard the bone crunch and he roared in pain. Howling, he grabbed Naomi's braid and used it like a rope to snatch her from the saddle, slamming her to the ground.

The horses whinnied and pranced about with fear. Hannah and Mollie screamed, their cries echoing down the desolate trail.

CHAPTER 52

*N*aomi broke the fall with her shoulder, the impact jarring her teeth in her head. The Indian leaped down off the horse and sat on her, using the full weight of his body to press her to the ground. Horses dancing nervously about them, he grabbed her wrists and pinned them above her head with one hand, squeezing the fragile bones to the point of breaking. Amidst the raucous laughter of his braves, he used his free hand to wipe blood trickling steadily from his nose down Naomi's left cheek. Grimacing, she rolled her head back and forth trying to avoid his touch. He wiped again, and this time dragged his bloodied hand across the front of her pink calico, lingering on her bosom.

She stopped rolling and looked up at him, surprised by the hate boiling up within her. If she had so much as a butter knife, she would surely use it to carve out his heart. She saw hate in his eyes, too, but a more ancient kind and it chilled her. He carried a dark, malevolent evil in his very being that she'd never come face-to-face with before, and fear gripped Naomi's soul. This man was capable of unspeakable acts.

Oh, God, please protect us. Please send Charles.

"My name is One-Who-Cries," he hissed, drawing nose to nose with her. Blood dripped on to her lips and she had to fight the urge to vomit. "You are alive because you are worth three rifles, but if you do that again," he pulled a knife from somewhere and pressed it to her throat, "you will watch me hang one of them," he inclined his head slightly toward the girls, "and I will gut her like a deer."

Naomi knew without a doubt that he was capable. As he jerked her off the ground by her braid, a Scripture leaped to mind. Holding her hair so he wouldn't rip it from the nape of her neck, she began whispering, "He that dwelleth in the secret place of the Most High shall abide under the shadow of the Almighty." One-Who-Cries stopped dragging her toward his horse and turned on her. "I will say of the Lord, He is my refuge and my fortress: my God, in Him I will trust." As his eyes narrowed, a peace settled over Naomi. She spoke louder, for Mollie and Hannah to hear. "Surely He shall deliver me from the snare of the fowler and from the noisome pestilence." She couldn't help the contempt that colored the last word.

With stunning force, One-Who-Cries backhanded Naomi. The force of the slap almost lifted her off her feet. Pain rocketed through the bones in her face. She cried out and staggered, but stayed on her feet. The coppery taste of warm blood filled her mouth. Understanding the little tyrant's game, she met his steely gaze with her own, though the stinging slap and her fear had rattled her.

She'd break before she ever bowed to someone like this.

The darkness within him lightened to unveiled admiration and he smiled. "Perhaps I have picked the wrong woman."

No, you've picked three *wrong women.* This time, she had enough sense to keep her mouth shut. Holding Naomi's hands, One-Who-Cries retook his seat on the horse then dragged her up into the saddle with him. Mollie and Hannah had watched all this unfold with horror-stricken expressions. For their sakes, Naomi tried to purge herself of her anger. She couldn't think clearly if all she wanted to do was rip out this man's heart. Continuing to pray, she spit out blood as the group trotted through a formation of huge rocks.

Gaining some peace and focus after a while, she decided to ask the savage some questions. "You said your name like I should know it."

"Know it? Maybe not. Fear it?" He moved his lips to her ear, "yes."

Quite the pompous peacock, but maybe that ego was a weakness. Wincing from the pain still throbbing in her left cheek, she asked, "Why did you attack us?"

"I trade you for guns."

"Where? Where will you trade us for guns?" If they managed to get away, this could be helpful information for getting their bearings.

"Cochetopa Pass. You whites call it Redemption Pass."

"The person you're trading us to, what will he do with us?"

She felt his chest puff up behind her, as if he was quite gratified by the answer. "He will take you all to brothels in Mexico."

CHAPTER 53

*B*illy hugged his son one last time and savored the **moment.** Refusing to think of the danger that might lie ahead, he handed the child back to Sarah. "The next time you see me, Little Man, I'll have Mama with me." He ruffled his son's hair then quickly turned away before his boy, Sarah, or Rebecca could see his tears.

Ian had brought Rebecca with him, thinking she might be of some help to Sarah. Since the hotel was smoldering ashes, she had insisted she could do more good here than in town. Sarah could handle herself and a baby. Rebecca, owl-eyed and frightened look-ing, her hair a dark, tangled mess, was the one who needed the company. She needed her sisters. Clearing his throat, Billy remounted and trotted up to where the others waited.

He needed Hannah. And he *would* get her out of the clutches of that crazy Indian.

One reason was right in front of him. Emilio had his sore foot propped on the horse's neck while he studied the ground with grim determination. He had done this before with amazing skill, according to McIntyre. Seven horses running across a pasture left a trail a blind man could follow. But up in the mountains, when the renegades tried to lose the posse by following a stream or crossing over rocky ground, Emilio would sniff them out. In part because he was clearly gifted, but mainly because he was in love with Hannah, too.

Still wearing torn and bloodied clothes, Billy glanced down at his bandaged leg. It ached ferociously. He assumed Emilio didn't feel much better. But those Indians had picked the wrong girls to kidnap. Billy reckoned he and Emilio would ride through Hell covered in kerosene to get them back. Judging by the hard expression on McIntyre's face, so would he.

They rode hard for two hours before Emilio raised his hand and pulled them to a stop near a stream. He dismounted and limped along the water's edge for several minutes, first downstream then he crossed the water and went back up. The group dismounted as well and let their horses drink while he continued his hunt.

Ten minutes later and a hundred feet upstream, Emilio knelt and plucked something from the stream's edge. Billy watched closely as his friend examined the item. When Emilio hurried back to the group, Billy mounted his horse.

"They went upstream," Emilio said, grabbing Cochise's reins. "This is where they got out, up there at those rocks. I found a feather." He held it up, a broken, rather innocuous brown section of plumage.

"Birds drop feathers all the time," Beckwith pointed out.

"Not with marks on them from a rawhide string."

Emilio dropped the feather and the rest of the group saddled up. Over the next few hours, the trail turned hard to the south and the going slowed. Emilio meticulously searched the rocky, shale-covered ground every few yards to make sure he was following the right path. Finally, in the midst of an aspen forest, he stopped abruptly. Here, even Billy could make out the trampled grass and trail of dirt clods thrown by shoeless horses.

Emilio turned his horse around so he could face Beckwith and McIntyre. "I think I know where they are going and I know a shortcut. But the trail, it is very rough." He removed his hat and swiped his wrist across his forehead. "It is an old trail, a secret one the Spanish missionaries cut. They walked or rode small donkeys so there are many low trees."

"First, where do you think they're going?" Beckwith asked, leaning forward.

"Redemption Pass, there is an abandoned toll gate and shack there."

"That's most likely where they're trading."

McIntyre traced the stitching in his saddle horn, thinking. "They're meeting someone who will be armed to the teeth, maybe several someones." He swung his gaze up at Emilio. "There's high ground in that pass. It'll be like shooting fish in a barrel for whoever gets to it first."

"*Si.*"

Billy inched his horse forward. "Can we get there first?"

Emilio sighed. "It will be close, but I think we can make it." The body of men turned to Beckwith and McIntyre for a decision. The marshal stared off into the woods. McIntyre swished his reins back and forth and studied the ground. "For what it's worth, if it was up to me," Emilio raised his chin, "I would take the shortcut."

---

*M*cIntyre exhaled as he and Emilio dismounted again. The boy shrugged apologetically. The trail was so overgrown it was almost invisible. Everything from chokecherries to junipers had laid a claim to the path. And every time they had to dismount so they could shoulder their way through thick, evergreen branches or side-step a briar patch, they lost more time.

Two hours into this mess, his temper flared. "Emilio, this isn't a trail, it's barely a rabbit path—"

The boy whirled on McIntyre with a finger pressed to his lips. He didn't say a word, but wrapped his horse's reins around a bush and slipped off into the brush. McIntyre turned and passed the hand signal back. They all waited in tense silence, interrupted occasionally by the swish of a tale or the stomp of a hoof.

How close were they to One-Who-Cries? McIntyre realized his hands were sweating and he wiped them on his trousers. His throat was dry, too. He knew he should move on from the hate, put it behind him like a good, church-going man, but he wanted revenge so badly he could taste it. Justice for three of his best friends, redress for Naomi. Today, maybe the scales would finally balance.

But he had made a promise and it stirred uneasily in his soul.

I'll do anything, give You anything . . .

Then give Me your hate.

He pushed the request to the shadows of his heart, to be dealt with later, when he found Naomi.

A good half hour passed. McIntyre had resolved to go retrieve Emilio when the boy soundlessly slipped back among them. "I found One-Who-Cries. I . . ." His voice wavered, "They had a guard watching the trail. I killed him."

McIntyre saw that Emilio doubted his course of action and felt for him. "You did the right thing, son. They've got three women down there."

"Four." He nodded at the surprised looks. "*Si,* another girl, but I've never seen her before."

"The peddler's daughter," Beckwith said.

"How many braves, lad?" Ian asked, checking his revolver.

"I counted six braves, and then four *banditos* with a wagon rode up. They are all at the old tollgate."

The men exchanged knowing glances. *Time for the fat to hit the fire*, McIntyre thought, and started to offer a plan. "If we can get to that high ground—"

"No good," Emilio shook his head. "There was a rock slide. The whole pass is different."

All right, McIntyre breathed. Think of something else. *God, help me think of something else.* "Are they keeping the girls in the cabin or out in the open?"

"In the cabin. I saw them take them in. One Indian stands at the door. The other five, they are . . ." Emilio struggled for the right words and drew circles in the air, "in different places around the . . ."

Matthew shouldered into the group. "He's trying to say they've established a perimeter, but they don't know their main guard is down."

"Which should allow us to get closer than they'll expect," Beckwith reasoned.

"Aye, but ye're forgetting about the four new men. We have to assume they are armed and we can't make a plan till we know where they are."

Frustrated, McIntyre removed his hat and scratched his scalp through dirty hair wet with sweat. If he had just married Naomi the other night, maybe none of them would be here now. They could be doing something mundane and safe, like drinking lemonade down by the stream. If this all fell apart, the guilt would consume him.

"All right," he replaced his hat. "Emilio, do you think you and Billy could sneak up to the cabin, maybe slip the girls out if we cause a diversion? Is there any cover for you at all, brush or a woodshed, something?"

"*Si*, there is scrub brush and junipers that come close to the cabin."

"What kind of a diversion?" Billy asked.

"Well, I've got three sticks of dynamite in my saddle bags."

Every head twisted toward Wade, whom McIntyre had all but forgotten.

"What are you doing with dynamite?" Beckwith asked irritably.

"I thought it might come in handy."

CHAPTER 54

*H*annah shuffled into the cabin behind the girls and grimaced. A one-room structure, it was barely bigger than a small bedroom, one that had been abandoned for years. It only had two small windows, both missing their glass, and a warped door in the back wall that, judging by the dust, had not been opened this decade. Cobwebs reached floor to ceiling and covered the rusty, dilapidated stove. One splintered chair forlornly occupied a dark corner and the rest of the room was bare. Dust, an inch thick on the floor, swirled around the hem of her skirt. The lean Indian shoved Hannah hard between the shoulder blades and sent her crashing into Naomi.

Both girls turned, fists balled, daggers in their eyes, but held their peace and watched him leave. As the door closed, Naomi groaned, rotated her right shoulder and sank to the floor. Hannah thought her sister would die if she could see herself, left cheek red and puffy, blood smeared on her face and dress. But the beating the Indian had given her could have been so much worse. Grateful it wasn't, she dropped down beside her and took over gently rubbing her shoulder. "Sore?"

"Uhmm. It was kind enough to break my fall."

Beside them, the new girl sat down and took a deep breath. "I'm scared." It was the first sound she'd uttered.

"Oh, sweetie," Mollie sank to the floor beside her and leaned in, raising her tied hands to show her she'd hug her if she could. "It'll be all right."

The poor thing looked terrified, the way she hunkered down into herself. Hannah wanted to ask how long she'd been a captive, but thought the question could wait. She needed something more positive on which to focus. "What's your name?"

"Terri."

"Where are you from, Terri?" The question from Naomi drew the girl's gaze. She took one look at her blood-covered face and burst into tears.

As Mollie tried to comfort her, Naomi leaned into Hannah. "What? What did I say?"

"Nothing. Nothing. She's just exhausted." There wasn't a thing they could do about Naomi's appearance right now, so why mention it?

Conversation effectively snuffed for the time being, Naomi stared up at the ceiling. After a long while, a tear rolled down her cheek, cruising right across the dried blood. "I overreacted again, Hannah." She shook her head, clearly disgusted with herself. "I should have given him a chance to explain. Now I may never know—"

"Don't think like that. Charles is on his way. So is Billy. We're going to get out of here."

Hannah smiled with pride as Naomi squared her shoulders and shook off her moment of self-pity. "You're right. We're not giving up."

Terri's crying dried up and she wiped away the tears. "I'm sorry. It's been hard. They killed my family."

Mollie took the girl's hand. "We are going to get out of here. You'll see."

A picture of hopelessness, the girl rested her head on Mollie's shoulder, and Mollie did the best she could to pat her on the knee. Hannah's own hope wavered because of the fear and hopelessness Terri exuded. She whispered to Naomi, "Truth be told, I am a little afraid too."

"I wasn't, until I saw his eyes."

Hannah turned inward and waited. God would give her something to strengthen them. A moment later, she had a verse. "Blessed be the Lord, my Strength, which teacheth my hands to war," the other girls bowed their heads, "and my fingers to fight. My goodness . . ." She spoke the list slowly so they could savor the promises, "and my fortress, my high tower, and my deliverer, my shield, and He in Whom I trust, who subdueth my people under me. Heavenly Father, we give You glory and honor. We know no weapon formed against us shall prosper. No enemy shall have victory over us today. Please, God, I ask that You would deliver us from these evil men and send Your angels to protect our loved ones who even now draw near. Thank You, Lord. We pray this in Jesus' name."

She looked up and Naomi was staring at her. "Why did you say they're near?"

Had she said that? Yes, and she knew it to be true. "Because they are."

Naomi's gaze shifted suddenly from Hannah to something behind her. She sucked in a little breath and Hannah turned to see what had her sister's rapt attention.

"See? In the dust there."

Hannah slid closer to the wall. At first she didn't see it then she recognized the potential tool all but hidden in the dust. She picked up the rectangular piece of glass, about two inches long and one inch wide, one end broken into a sharp point. Breathless, she held the piece of glass up for them to see.

Smiling, Naomi raised her bound hands. "And the truth shall make you free."

*B*illy's heart pounded so loudly in his chest, he was afraid the sound might give him and Emilio away. Slowly, silently, rifles in hand, they crawled on all fours through tall grass, and short, twisted junipers toward the back of the cabin. The tollgate and house sat in a wide, long ravine, a high pass between two colliding mountain ridges. The floor of the ravine and the lower part of the mountainside was spattered with these clusters of dense scrub. A broad, lazy stream cut through the pass, leaving one side just wide enough for the road, the tollgate, a small corral holding the Indian's horses, and a one-room dilapidated cabin. Across the water, a hundred feet or so from the gate, a large rock formation, like a whale's back, tore itself free from the mountain. It trailed the creek for a good four hundred yards, forming a cliff along one shore twenty to thirty feet high.

Where the cabin sat, a finger of scrub grass and junipers came down off the mountain and reached almost all the way to the back door. Billy guessed the gap they had to cross in the open was maybe forty feet or so. He wished it was less. Aware that there was a guard on the cliff, as well as one somewhere farther up on the mountain, they kept low and took their time moving.

They had not had a chance to scout the area and were clueless as to where the other Indians or Mexicans might be. They were trusting that their friends did. Stiff and sore from their previous skirmish with the renegades, not to mention the fight with each other, their goal was to avoid confrontation, if at all possible, and quietly slip the girls out the back door. McIntyre, Beckwith, and the others would attempt to draw the Indians' fire if it became necessary.

That was the plan anyway.

Crawling on their bellies, the boys slithered to the edge of the brush. A low, twisted juniper gave them the chance to rise up on their knees and study the back of the cabin. It didn't have a window on the back wall, but there was a door. "I don't know." Emilio sounded hesitant. "That door, who knows how long since it was opened."

"I doubt it'll open easy as a church door on Sunday morning."

Emilio stared at him through the evergreen's needles. "We'll have to use the dynamite to cover the sound."

This meant they had to use their one stick for getting *to* the girls, rather than for getting them out of there. Billy didn't see an alternative. They needed a diversion now, something to cover the noise, and there was no way to signal Wade.

Unexpectedly, he felt a cold wind blow through his soul, a wind that threatened to break him with panic. Empty and afraid, he peered at Emilio through the needles. His friend lowered his head and quickly mouthed a silent prayer.

Billy pondered his part in all this, everything that had happened to bring him to this moment, and wondered why he was here. Initially, he'd believed he'd made a grand mistake coming west. After all, he'd been covered in blood and bruises practically since he'd left home. And, he'd made only the slightest headway with Hannah.

Yet, if he hadn't come, would Emilio be making this stand alone?

At that instant, he knew he had been placed here by *design,* and the revelation terrified him because nothing felt certain to him except that. He had no idea how things were about to unfold but he knew beyond the shadow of a doubt his presence here was planned.

For such a time as this, a voice whispered to him.

God, he prayed with everything in him, *I know—I KNOW—You have Your hand on this situation. I don't know if I'm supposed to live or die today, but please don't let this be the end. Let it be a beginning for Hannah and me. Please. I'll give You anything You want, do anything You want, just, please, help me, use me to get us all home safe.*

Before his prayer had finished, an explosion on the other side of the cabin shook the ground, bringing a trickle of rocks down from the mountain behind them. Stumped as to why Wade was already throwing dynamite, the two boys took advantage of the ensuing chaos, overrode the pain warring in their bodies, and charged for the cabin.

---

*M*cIntyre almost cursed when he saw Wade light the dynamite and toss it . . . until he realized the deputy was trying to stop four riders who had come up from the south side of the pass, men wearing sombreros like the four down there gathered at the wagon. Beckwith, Ian, Matthew and McIntyre had positioned themselves in rocks almost roof level with the cabin, but on the opposite side of the rock-outcropping, where Wade was, across the stream. Not the high ground they had wanted, but they could see most of the yard, and the front and one side of the cabin.

Wade had ridden far to the north over rough terrain so he could circle back and come in on the rock escarpment. His vantage point had allowed him to see the four new riders cross the stream and trot toward the gate. The deadly throw had eliminated the new threat before they'd gotten off a single shot, but all hell had broken loose. The brave on the look-out in the rocks spun and fired at Wade. From somewhere above McIntyre and his group, another rifle fired.

The four Indians below had been chattering and gesticulating wildly at the Mexicans, striking the wagon with their hands. A sign the negotiations weren't going well. They heard the explosion and started shooting frantically as if they were at Custer's Last Stand.

After a few indiscriminate rounds, they located Wade's position and opened fire, screaming their bone-chilling war cries. The deputy leapt behind some rocks for safety and McIntyre, Ian,

Beckwith, and Matthew brought their guns into the fray with a deadly, thunderous barrage. Instantly, the men below whirled on them. The brave atop the rocks went down with a screech, the rifle flying out of his hands and bouncing over the cliff into the water. Rifles and revolvers fired in deafening chaos. Gunsmoke and expelled cartridges filled the air. McIntyre tasted sulfur. A shot came from behind him, up the mountain, shattering rocks beside his group. "Ian, there's someone in the woods above us!" he shouted over the cacophony of gunfire.

His friend spun and scanned the tree line, waiting for the man to give away his position.

Returning fire in frenzied confusion, the sombrero-wearing men below and one Indian lunged for cover behind the wagon. The other three braves dove to the side of the cabin McIntyre couldn't see. *He* couldn't see them, but Wade should be able to, if he could raise his head long enough to fire.

Looking down his rifle sight, he saw Billy and Emilio charge for the cabin's back wall, but lost sight of them as well. He realized the two boys had no idea the explosion had driven the guard at the front door of the cabin back inside with the girls, or that there were now three other braves using the cabin's exterior for cover. Wade had the high ground on that side of the cabin and it would only be minutes, if not seconds, before the three renegades realized they also needed to take cover in the cabin.

McIntyre knew they had to keep the Indians and bandits pinned down. Otherwise, Billy and Emilio were in a real hornet's nest. Shots zinged back and forth in the pass. Lead bounced off the rocks behind McIntyre. Pieces of slate shattered next to his head and he hunkered lower, recalling the bullet hole in his Stetson. Ian fired and they heard a muffled grunt in the woods above them. Below them, screams erupted from the cabin.

Billy and Emilio were fighting for their lives.

"We've got to get down there!" McIntyre shoved his hat down tighter. "Ian, did you get the one above us?"

He watched the tree line for a moment more then nodded. "I believe so."

"All right, you and Beckwith try to work your way around to the corral and draw the fire from those men at the wagon." He leapt to his feet, kept his head down and hollered over his shoulder, "Matthew, come with me!" Matthew cocked his rifle and followed.

Bullets whizzed past McIntyre's head, ricocheting off the rocks and pines as he ran. He heard gunshots, screams, and a piercing war cry from inside the cabin. Then, the screeching, splintering sound of wood as a big, heavy warrior crashed through the front door. He flailed wildly for two steps but momentum carried him off the porch and he fell backwards into the dirt, a red stain spreading on his chest. That left four Indians and their four trading partners. The boys still apparently had no idea there were three renegades holed up against the exterior wall.

McIntyre zigzagged through the scrub brush to the spot where Billy and Emilio had crossed to the cabin, likewise stopping at the juniper. The back door opened and Billy, his Winchester raised, peered outside, checking for enemies. As he turned his head, an Indian leapt out from the other side of the cabin, rifle at his shoulder. McIntyre snatched up his .30-30 and fired. The Indian stumbled back and collapsed. Billy pressed himself against the door post, eyes wide as full moons. McIntyre waved his rifle at the boy and nodded reassuringly.

One more down . . .

Knowing that he had compromised his position by shooting, McIntyre motioned for Matthew to get ready. He eyed the side of the cabin for more movement. Nothing, either the other two were waiting or had run and joined the men at the wagon. A burst of gunfire seemed to argue in favor of that theory.

Aware that Ian and Beckwith couldn't see him or Matthew, he prayed Wade *could* and sprinted for the open door. Matthew followed, moving like the injury to his side was only a bad dream. Nearing the entrance, a shot rang out, followed by a garbled howl from the other side of the cabin. Wade had hit someone, thank God. McIntyre dove through the door and landed on his stomach, followed almost simultaneously by Matthew. Relieved they'd made it this far, McIntyre gazed up into a face smeared with blood.

CHAPTER 55

*cI*ntyre scrambled to his feet and snatched Naomi away from the girls who were clutching her. "My God, are you all right?" he asked, his relief nearly choking his voice.

Naomi threw herself into his arms and hugged him so tightly he couldn't breathe. "I knew you'd come for us." She kissed him like she hadn't seen him in a hundred years. For a moment he held her just as tightly, gripping her like she might keep him from going over a cliff.

But this reunion had to wait. He pulled away. "We have to get you out of here." He didn't want to think about why she was smeared with blood, and whether it was hers or someone else's.

The three other girls hunkered down in a corner, while Billy and Emilio crouched at each entrance. A bullet whizzed through the open window, spraying splinters on the girls. "Down! Everyone, down," McIntyre ordered as he released Naomi and shoved her toward the girls. He cocked the Winchester, turned and joined Billy at the back door. "Any second now an Indian on the other side of this wall is going to charge in here to get away from Wade." He nodded at Emilio, alone at the front door. "Get ready."

Out of the side of his mouth, he told Matthew, "Get these girls out of here. We'll bring up the rear, maybe get the one on the outside."

The big man nodded and quietly gathered the girls. "When I say run, ladies, run like a pack of wolves is after you." Wide-eyed like frightened children, they nodded and let Matthew bunch them closer to the door. With the injuries to this party, McIntyre knew they wouldn't move like greased lightning, but between Billy, Emilio, and himself, they should be able to give the cover necessary to get the girls into the brush so they could scurry up the mountain.

A storm of gunshots started up again. McIntyre could tell it was Ian and Beckwith firing and it sounded as if they'd made it to the corral. Rifle blazing, a brave exploded through the cabin's front door. McIntyre saw a blur of buckskin and fringe. He and Emilio and Billy fired. Guns roared, wood splintered. The Indian jittered like a convulsing bug in the hail of bullets. Before he fell to the floor, Matthew yelled, "Go, go, go!" shoving the girls out the door.

In a flurry of calico, they scurried like mice, followed immediately by the men. As he hurried toward the exit, McIntyre glanced down at each of the dead. One-Who-Cries was not among them. A battle still raged between the men hiding behind the wagon and Beckwith and Ian. Perhaps if he could make sure the girls were getting away, he could get in position to help them.

As McIntyre stepped outside the cabin, Billy and Matthew glanced over their shoulders at him, but their gazes jerked to something behind him. While Matthew almost smiled, Billy's eyes rounded in shock. The hair on McIntyre's neck stood up.

"Where did *he* come from . . .?" Billy whispered. McIntyre started to turn. "Look out!" Billy lunged for McIntyre, spinning him around as a rifle fired. Eyes rounding in confusion, the boy clutched McIntyre's lapels and slid to his knees. Sounding far away and almost surreal, Naomi screamed the boy's name. An instant later, Hannah screamed. As Billy fell to the ground, McIntyre saw the spreading bloodstain on the boy's side.

Horror turned to fury as the sound of a rifle cocking brought his gaze up to One-Who-Cries. Smoke wafted from the end of the renegade's rifle and he glared at McIntyre. Matthew had seen the Indian, too, yet he hadn't uttered a sound.

Sneering, the Indian started to raise the rifle for another shot. In a blur of motion, McIntyre lowered his Winchester and whipped out his revolver. Before One-Who-Cries could blink, the Colt was pointing at his head. The Indian froze.

Finally . . .

The hunger for revenge raged in McIntyre's heart. The blood on Naomi. The bullet in Billy. Friends from long ago, skinned alive and hung out for the bears to eat. "Ned Bess, Leo Frey, and Warren Cornelius. Three good men you butchered." Squeezing the rifle in his left hand with a death grip, he cocked the .44 and picked a spot in the middle of the brave's forehead.

His finger tightened on the trigger . . . the steel was cold and eager to kill.

But the will to pull the trigger suddenly left him.

And he knew why. The answer shined before him as brilliantly as the sun that burns away the clouds after a hard rain. If he killed solely for vengeance, then he was a murderer and nothing had changed. But he *wasn't* the same man. God *had* changed him. He had forgiven him. He felt it in his soul, finally. Now McIntyre had to forgive himself, let the past go. Staring down the barrel at his enemy, he could make that choice now.

You said anything, the Lord reminded him. *Give Me your hate.*

The moment hung between them.

One-Who-Cries was imprisoned by his past, shackled to his hate. But McIntyre wasn't anymore. "I will not murder you." Filled with an amazing sense of peace, he dropped the hammer, holstered his gun and let his hands fall to his side.

A muscle in One-Who-Cries' jaw ticked. His eyes darkened

and he smiled, a dark, bitter thing better left under a rock. "Fat Buffalo, Two Moons . . . Hopping Bird. My family, butchered by whites."

The muscles flexed in One-Who-Cries' shoulder as the Indian jerked the rifle up. McIntyre snatched the .44 free from the holster faster than lightning arcs from sky to earth. Fire exploded from the barrel. The fatal bullet knocked One-Who-Cries back a dozen feet. The Indian landed spread eagle on the ground, staring up at the sky with cold, dead eyes. McIntyre took a step back from the once-vicious warrior and lowered his gun.

---

*H*annah, Mollie, Terri and Naomi scrambled into the safety of the brush like panicked rabbits. Refusing to think about what might be happening behind them, Hannah surveyed the scrub and juniper ahead, trying to determine the fastest path to the tree line, only fifty or so feet beyond them.

She turned to the girls following her: Mollie, marching with determination; Naomi, skirt gathered in her hands, fully poised to run; and Terri, on her feet but quivering wildly with fear. Resolute, she grabbed Terri's hand. "Come on, we need to make it to the trees." She spun, prepared to lunge for the cover when an Indian rode out of the forest above them. Joseph Black Elk sat atop Cochise, Emilio's horse. Freezing all four of the girls in their steps, his baleful glare sent slivers of ice through Hannah. Slowly, he raised his bow and aimed the arrow at her heart.

She heard the gasps from behind her, but for Hannah, the moment hung in eternity. No fear, no thoughts. In the back of her mind a prayer drifted heavenward, but she was entranced by his eyes, dark orbs of pain and hate . . . and weariness. She heard the gunshot down near the cabin, followed by Naomi's scream, "No. Billy!" Now, heedless of the brave and his arrow, Hannah whipped her head around and saw Billy fall.

No, no, God, please, no!

Determined that whether an arrow was flying toward her or not, Hannah was going to get to Billy. But she had to know. She turned back to Black Elk.

He hadn't moved. The arrow hung in the bow, poised for death. She thought of the man whose back Black Elk had filled with arrows. It didn't matter. He would not stop her from getting to Billy. Hannah shook her head and spun away from him, flinching, ready for the arrow. Mollie and Terri stood transfixed. After a moment, Hannah heard pounding hooves fading off into the mountains.

"Billy," she skidded to a stop and dropped down on her knees. Shot in the side, bleeding profusely, he lay facing the sky, his breath coming in hitched exchanges. She didn't know if she should move him or even touch him. Her hands hovered over him. "Billy, hold on. Everything is going to be all right." Tears choked her voice and the stark terror that he might die froze her mind . . . except for the realization that she didn't want to live without him. "Oh, Billy, I'm so sorry. Please forgive me for being so prideful."

His mouth worked, opened, closed, finally he managed, "I love you, Hannah." He swallowed, flinching as if something hurt. "Emilio . . ."

"He's right here."

Emilio touched his arm. "*Si*. I am here."

"If I don't make it . . ." Billy struggled to speak, his voice weakening with every syllable like a child dozing off. "If I don't make it, promise me you'll take care . . . take care of them."

"No, Billy," Hannah squeaked. "Don't you say that." Her tears gushed. "Don't you say that!"

Emilio leaned closer to Billy and whispered, "You have my promise, but you don't need it, my friend. You will make it."

He will *make it.* Anger swallowed Hannah's fear. She was a nurse and she was capable of more than crying like a simpering fool. Billy needed her. She slapped her hand to his side and closed her mind to the warm liquid seeping between her fingers. "We have to stop the bleeding. Emilio, rip a piece of cloth from my skirt."

Please, God, make it stop.

---

*S*hots rang out again on the other side of the cabin, reminding McIntyre of the lives still on the line. He knelt down to the unconscious Billy and touched his shoulder, grateful for the boy's sacrifice. "You came a long way to take a bullet for me," he whispered. "Thank you. Now, hang on and we'll get you out of here."

Wondering if Billy had heard any of that, McIntyre pulled the stick of dynamite from the boy's pocket and inched along the outer wall of the cabin. He glanced around the corner. He could see movement behind the wagon, but no clear targets. "Wade, can you hear me?" he shouted at the deputy.

"Yessir!"

"We have these boys surrounded on three sides now. Let's end this. Move in and toss a stick of dynamite at them with your previous accuracy." What was that in Spanish? "*Lanzala . . . dinamita!*"

"Yessir!"

Quick, shuffling sounds and anxious mutterings came from behind the wagon. McIntyre peered out once more and scanned the bloody, obliterated remains of the four men and their horses, a strong argument for these banditos to give up the fight. Shortly, from behind the wagon four pairs of hands rose toward the sky and someone yelled, "*¡No más! No más!*"

CHAPTER 56

"Near as I can tell, the bullet hit a rib and bounced off," Hannah said, leaning close to the hole in Billy's side. The men had laid Billy on the back of the wagon where she cleaned the wound with whiskey from the gun traders. Billy had hissed and told her that hurt worse than getting shot. She hoped his sense of humor was a good sign. "He's got a good, clean exit wound and the bleeding has stopped." She peered closer at the injury. I don't think it damaged anything too important."

"I'm glad you're so sure," Billy said, stopping her hand from its not-so-gentle-probing.

She tightened her lips, unhappy with his sarcasm. "It could have been much worse." Taking a deep breath, she straightened up and turned to the group watching her so keenly. "I've never done this but I think I should sew him up before we move him."

What she wouldn't give for Doc Cooke to be here to do this.

"You people don't need Wade or me for this," Beckwith said, sizing Hannah up with a respectful nod. "But you might can use this." He tossed her a small, leather case. "You should find everything necessary for fixing a bullet hole in that." Quickly, his eyes sought out Mr. McIntyre. "Since you need the wagon, you see those rifles make it back to town. And take care of digging the graves." He pointed a bony finger at Emilio. "You come with us, to get these banditos back to town. *Si?*"

Emilio's shoulders sagged, but he nodded. "*Si.*"

Beckwith tipped his hat to the group and marched off. Wade started to follow, but Mr. McIntyre touched him on the shoulder. "Wade, you saved our a—" He stopped, and then started over, "You saved us today. Thank you."

Everyone else muttered their thanks and Hannah grinned at the blush that crept up the deputy's neck all the way to his forehead. When the men were gone, she turned to Mollie. "I could use your help."

"Nobody starts anything until I get a few shots of the liquor," Billy pointed at his mouth, "in here this time."

———

*N*aomi moved Terri away from the surgery, figuring the poor thing had seen enough blood. She gazed up at Naomi as they walked. "You really should wash all that blood off."

Naomi touched her cheek, felt the dry, crusty blood on her cheek. She had completely forgotten what a sight she must be. Eager to get the Indian's blood off her, she tucked Terri under the porch roof of the cabin and smiled reassuringly at her. "They found some jerky in that wagon. I'll get it and a canteen of water. That should fix us both up."

She headed back to the wagon and saw Charles leave Ian to intercept her. She was so relieved to see him and so confused. After all of this, she just wanted to forget the vision of him in the arms of another woman and pretend it never happened. But could she?

"Naomi." He approached her carefully, hands behind his back. His white shirt wasn't white anymore and grime filled in the small lines around his eyes and on his neck. Unspoken thoughts flitted across his face, every muscle in him tensed. After several seconds of searching for the right words, he settled on, "You didn't see what you thought you saw. I swear it. And it's that simple."

Willing to accept that, but not willing to discuss it at the moment, she took a deep breath. "Charles, I feel so overwhelmed right now. We'll talk about it later."

He raised his hand to her cheek, the one her captor had slapped, and a moan escaped her. The flesh was tender and no doubt several shades of black and blue. "One-Who-Cries?"

She nodded.

The battle between who Charles McIntyre was, and who he wanted to be, played out in his eyes. She touched his beard, stubbly, less than perfect, and then let her fingers drift to his chest. "Let the dead bury their dead."

He swallowed and touched her hand. Sadness filled his eyes, but he blinked it away. "Speaking of which, Ian and I are going to bury these dead." He lingered a moment longer, opened his mouth as if to add something, but pulled away from her instead. Naomi watched him as he rejoined Ian. The storm of emotion raging in him troubled her. She supposed it could be a million things. Regret over the incident with the hussy in the saloon. Disappointment he hadn't protected her from One-Who-Cries.

But it had looked like good-bye.

CHAPTER 57

O nce back at Sarah's, Naomi cried over the reunions.
She cried willingly and without shame. Rebecca threw
herself into Ian's embrace, nearly knocking him off the porch. He
spun his new wife around like a precious treasure dropped into
his arms.

Sarah met the wagon in the yard so Little Billy could greet his
parents. His arms went out to them and as Billy crawled slowly,
gingerly off the tail gate, they all heard, "Dada."

Billy froze, gazing at his son with stars in his eyes. Grinning,
Sarah handed the boy to his father. Hannah and Billy hugged their
baby till the child must have thought his parents were going to
smother him.

As Naomi watched from beside the wagon, a hand slipped into
hers, fingers entwining. Deaf and blind she would've known him
and she squeezed his hand in recognition.

"Naomi . . . we need to talk."

Charles' smooth, velvety voice was filled with misery. Dirty,
untrimmed, a bit disheveled, he stole her heart all over again. She
nodded, and he pulled her away from the group. They wandered
for several minutes through a field of sweet-smelling timothy.

Beneath a canopy of emerging stars and a rising, sliver-of-a-moon, he stopped and turned to her. The western sky still held enough light that she could see him well. She was startled by his troubled brow and tight lips. "Naomi, I can't marry you."

Her jaw went slack and her knees almost buckled. "What? Why?"

"Because I love you too much." He clutched her hands between them. "When I looked over Amaryllis's shoulder and saw what I had done to you, the pain I caused, I . . ." he trailed off and shook his head. "I can't—I won't—do that to you again."

Angry, Naomi snatched hers hands away and stepped back. "Say it plain. You want that trollop instead of me.

"What? No. God, no, I don't care if I ever see Amaryllis Dumas again. Actually, I hope I never do." He grabbed her shoulders. "I won't make that mistake again, but Amaryllis won't be the last woman to come looking for me. And what of men like Hawthorn? I can't keep putting you through that."

Naomi folded her arms and turned away from him to think. Was this the truth? Would he walk away from her to save her? For the millionth time, she saw Rose point her gun at him, saw Charles, unarmed, lunge for the weapon . . . *to save her.* Truthfully, she had no doubt there wasn't any sacrifice he wouldn't make for her. So how could she let him go? She loved him, she needed him, but she couldn't beg him—wouldn't. Absolutely would not. Ever.

Such a firm refusal tugged her conscience. Pride, more often than not, had been at the bottom of Naomi's biggest mistakes, like running out of town the other day. Occasionally, it should be set aside. Knowing when—that had always been the bane of her existence.

"She kissed me, Naomi, but I kissed her back." A misery welled up in Naomi that threatened to break free in a humiliating sob. A knife in the gut would have been less painful. Her throat felt like she'd swallowed a bandana. No, she definitely wouldn't be doing any begging. "For a moment I forgot who I was. And then I heard . . . a Scripture, and I saw your face."

Naomi's shoulders sagged. She knew she couldn't let him walk away. If she did, it would be because of her pride. She felt the Lord telling her to believe in Charles. God had forgiven his sins. Now, together, they had to try to forget them and build a life together. She was called to be his helpmeet and denying that would be nothing but disobedience. Besides, how did she know she wouldn't have had the same moment of weakness if Matthew had managed to kiss her?

"What happened next?" she asked, buying time to think.

"Well," he sounded surprised by the question. Perhaps he thought she wouldn't want the details. But she *needed* them. "I pushed her away and started to run after you. Beckwith grabbed me at the door, though. Said he needed me to ride in the posse after One-Who-Cries. I asked Reverend Potter to tell you it wasn't what you thought. But you never saw him."

Pride goeth before a fall, she thought, kicking herself. "No, I ran as fast and as far away from you as I could. I jumped on the wagon and rolled out of town." She turned around and dropped her arms to her side, surrendering to him and God. "Instead of believing in you the way I promised I would." Her eyes locked with his. She took a slow step toward him and he matched it, though the half-smile on his lips said he was stuck somewhere between hope and confusion. "Charles McIntyre, I am not some hothouse orchid. I can take a little pain." Another step, that he again matched, bringing them a breath apart. "I'm willing to risk my heart if you can swear you'll be faithful to me."

He took both her hands in his, smiling as if she had no idea how easy that would be. "You cannot imagine the hell I went through when everyone was telling me you were dead. I knew you weren't. I *knew* it. I told God I couldn't live if anything happened to you." He exhaled a long, deep breath, as if he had narrowly avoided a cliff. "And I told myself that if I loved you, I'd let you go because it would be the best thing for you. I want what will make you happy, Naomi."

She touched his hands, desperate for a kiss, eager to start a life with him. "Do you hear yourself? You don't sound like much of a scallywag to me. Not anymore."

A hesitant smile tipped his lips. "I believe I'm coming to agree with that."

What came over Naomi, she'd never be able to explain, but at the same moment Charles folded her into an embrace, she squealed with joy and leaped into his arms, knocking him to the ground. Giddy, exuberant laughter bubbled up in her and infected him. Together they laughed and hugged and drank in the freedom to live without fearing the past. Breathless, Charles spun Naomi beneath him in the timothy. He pressed his lips to her forehead and waited for his self-control to squash the laughter. After a moment, he spoke, his voice low and serious. "We are done with the doubts and the second-guessing?"

"We are."

He pulled back to look at her. "I assume my suggestion that we call off our wedding has been denied?"

She reached up and trailed her finger over his lips, wishing for a kiss. "Very definitely, sir. You asked me to marry you. I'm going to hold you to that."

aomi thought she was prepared for the sight of the hotel, but nothing was left. She surveyed the cold, black ruins, stunned by the devastation. A few pieces of its blackened skeleton pointed defiantly at the sky. Everything was gone, the building, her clothes, their furniture, everything. She had the bloodied, pink calico dress on her back and that was it.

"Don't worry. Your guests have found other accommodations," Charles squeezed her shoulder for reassurance, "and you and your various, assorted family members will stay at the Iron Horse till we rebuild. I understand that Ian, Rebecca, and Matthew managed to save a few things. Those are at the Iron Horse as well."

She couldn't imagine what they would all do now. She didn't want to go back into the hotel business. The certainty of the thought surprised her. "I don't want to work in a hotel anymore, Charles." A little frightened by her lack of direction, she turned pleading eyes on him. "What should we do?"

He slipped an arm around her and turned toward the ruins of the Trinity Inn. "Take it one day at a time, princess."

*M*cIntyre made sure to extend his offer of hospitality to everyone in Naomi's party, including, and especially, Matthew. While the ladies were out back enjoying his luxurious bathhouse, he sent Emilio and Billy off to get dinner from Martha's kitchen. That left him alone with the giant. Stepping behind his bar, McIntyre reached for his finest bottle of Irish whiskey.

"Let's have a celebratory drink—you and I, Matthew."

Tension singed the air between them as it had ever since Redemption Pass. Now it was time to get things out in the open. The big man casually sauntered up to the bar. Both of them still wore their dirty, grimy clothes. They reeked of sweat and smoke. Matthew's eyes glittered with resentment—and defeat.

McIntyre poured the drink in front of him. "Tell me something, Matthew. If you were willing to let someone shoot me, why didn't you just do it yourself?"

He fingered the drink for several seconds before slamming it back. "Because I'm not a murderer." He set his glass down on the bar and stared at it.

"Which is why I don't think you killed Amaryllis." Matthew's head swung up and McIntyre tossed him the St. Jude medallion, melted by the fire, but still recognizable. "The patron saint of lost causes. Her idea of a joke." McIntyre regretted not having had more kind words for the woman, words of a more eternal nature. "O'Connell found it in the ashes. It was her body they found in the kitchen." Matthew stared at the twisted, partially melted medal.

"I suppose we'll never know what happened. Perhaps she walked in on Black Elk lighting the fire. Perhaps he thought to kidnap her." He poured Matthew one last drink. "You'll be leaving us. On tomorrow's stage."

Matthew sucked on his cheek as if holding back any comments. A moment later, though, he opened his hand, and showed his palm in surrender. "What will you tell Naomi?"

McIntyre wanted to be a better man, and he definitely wanted to be a better man than this charlatan standing before him. "Nothing. I will leave her faith in you intact."

*H*annah laid Little Billy across the feather bed and wrapped his bottom in a fresh diaper. Running back into a burning hotel for a few of their belongings had been a foolish, foolish thing to do . . . but she would be eternally grateful to Rebecca. Even with the losses added up, she was blessed beyond measure. She dragged her fingers along the ornate brass headboard and hoped the former Flower who had occupied this room could say the same.

As for Hannah and her sisters, Mollie, and poor lost Terri, they had bathed last night in the most decadent bathroom she had ever seen, slept in luxurious brass beds beneath warm, soft blankets, and woke this morning to Mr. Brannagh preparing breakfast. Charles McIntyre knew how to take care of the ones he loved. Sighing with contentment, she lay down beside her son and lightly danced her fingers down his nose and across his little pink lips. He giggled excitedly and the sound of his innocent laughter convinced Hannah the day was, indeed, filled with hope and promise.

"Hannah," Rebecca called from downstairs. "Could you come help me with something?"

Hannah swooped up Little Billy and marched downstairs. The saloon was empty, except for her sister rifling around behind the bar. Enjoying the show of it, Hannah bellied up to the bar. "Sarsaparilla, bartender, for my pard and me." Rebecca smiled, but it was only half-hearted. She continued searching for something. "What are you rooting around for back there?"

Exasperated, Rebecca dropped her hands to her hips. "Everything we rescued from the hotel wound up back here in a pile."

She moved something aside with her foot. "Matthew promised me he got it."

"Got what?"

"Unless *this* is it . . ." She reached down and dredged up a huge carpetbag, slinging it on to the bar with a sizable effort. She laid the bag on its side, opened it, and hauled out a wrinkled heap of white silk.

"Ooooh, Naomi's wedding gown."

"Shhhh." Rebecca scolded. "She's upstairs. I don't want her to know we saved it yet." She dragged the gown the rest of the way out of the bag but kept it hidden behind the bar as she inspected it. An envelope had caught in the bustle and Hannah snagged it, immediately recognizing Naomi's handwriting. "Let me see that," Rebecca said, reaching for it. She studied the front and pointed at the date. "This is the second letter. He said he never got this one." A troubled groove in her brow, Rebecca's gaze drifted up to Naomi's room. "Matthew has been lying to us the whole time."

CHAPTER 59

*N*aomi sat on the bench outside the Iron Horse, amidst the bustle of traffic, but alone with her bitter disappointment. She pulled the letter out of the envelope just to make sure—again. The second letter. The one letting Matthew know they were all right. Things in Defiance weren't so bad after all. She might even like the place.

Shaking her head, she tucked the letter back inside as a shadow fell across her. She didn't look up. She never wanted to look at him again. After a moment, he set his bag down on the boardwalk and joined her on the bench. She tried to remain seated, but found she couldn't bear being this close to Matthew. Jaws clenched, she rose and crossed the boardwalk to lean on a post. She heard his frustrated sigh.

"I suppose you hate me."

"No." And that was true. "I feel betrayed, disappointed . . . but I don't hate you."

"I did it all for the right reasons."

She choked off a disbelieving gasp and turned to him as he rose. "You mean selfish reasons." Heat rushed her cheeks as her anger escaped. "I was right the first night you came here. You haven't changed a bit."

The hope in his eyes flickered and faded out. Suddenly, his anger flamed to life. He crossed the distance between them and grabbed her shoulders. "I'll tell you what I am," he growled. "I am sick of coming in second." His fingers dug into her flesh. "You cannot choose a pimp and whoremonger over me!"

The night he'd grabbed her and torn her wedding dress came screaming back to Naomi. The fear, the vulnerability, Matthew's desperation to bend her to his will. Well, no more. Snarling, she wrenched free and shoved him with every ounce of determination she could muster. He took a step back, propelled more by surprise than by her strength.

Chest heaving, she grabbed a handful of her skirt to keep her hands from clawing out his eyes. "Charles McIntyre is twice the man you'll ever be . . . and he would never force me." As the words left her mouth, understanding exploded in her heart. She knew why God had sent Matthew here. Her muscles relaxed and she sagged a bit. "I'm done." She heard the disbelief in her own voice, but couldn't deny the certainty of the feeling. She let go of her anger and relaxed her fingers. "I've been holding on because you're his brother and you look like him. And because I pitied you." His face hardened. She didn't care if the truth hurt. They both had to hear it. "I'm done, Matthew."

Moving quickly, before she could second-guess herself, she yanked off her wedding ring, grabbed his hand and thrust the gold band into his palm. "I'm turning toward the future, like John wanted me to. And you're not a part of it." She folded his fingers over the ring and walked inside.

*M*cIntyre ran his hand over the skip-peeled pine arbor that Billy and Emilio had built and nodded. The boys had done a fine job. It framed a majestic view of the Animas River backed up by Red Mountain Pass. The snow-capped mountains all around were turning warm shades of purples and oranges as sunset washed his valley in the fading light. He would never get over the beauty of it.

"She's almost ready."

Reverend Potter's voice startled him and he turned to the small crowd. Beckwith, Wade, and Doc Cook stood to one side, Mollie, Emilio and little Terri waited on the other, creating an opening for the wedding party. Behind him somewhere, Bud struck up the Bridal March on his fiddle and McIntyre swallowed. This was real. Fear and excitement coursed through him and he allowed himself a smile.

Ian and Rebecca marched toward him, followed by Billy and Hannah. Grinning like fools, the couples parted at the altar, revealing Naomi. McIntyre gasped. She was wearing a shimmering, curve-hugging, white satin *wedding* gown. Her hair flowed down her shoulders like a golden waterfall, and a woven chain of fresh buttercups sat lightly upon her head like a halo. In her hands, she held a colorful bouquet of pink wild roses, columbine, and violets.

She was breath-taking. And she was his bride.

Naomi smiled shyly up at him, her eyes glistening like polished emeralds, and the ground shifted beneath him.

Ian clutched McIntyre's shoulder and placed a hand on his back. "Steady, lad."

McIntyre realized he couldn't feel his legs and Ian was literally holding him upright. Embarrassed, he cleared his throat and found his footing. But he didn't take his eyes off her and extended his hand as she approached. "Naomi, I am speechless. You are the most beautiful . . ." His throat tightened up and he had to stop speaking, stunned that he had become *emotional*.

"This isn't the first time I've worn it," she bit her lip and added softly, "but it feels like it."

Enormously pleased by that, he squeezed her hand but couldn't manage a reply.

Together, they faced the Reverend, who smiled tenderly at them and began the service.

CHAPTER 60

*H*annah's face hurt from smiling. Surprising the ladies, Mr. McIntyre had arranged for the ceremony to be performed on his ranch. The wedding had been a private affair, with only a few people outside the family invited, such as Doc Cook, Marshal Beckwith, Wade, and little Terri. After the vows, quite a party had started up. Mr. McIntyre, with the help of the other men, had provided a deer on the spit and Shorty and Bud playing their fiddle and banjo. The girls had cooked plenty of side dishes and promised not to turn down any dance request.

Now, leaning on the porch rail of her sister's new home, Hannah took a breath. The smell of fresh pine, the torches' warm glow, and the toe-tapping music brought her a sense of peace. Homes, hearths, and families gathered near. No matter what the future held, she and her sisters would always be close. A burnt-out shell of a hotel couldn't change that.

Tapping her fingers in time with the music, she surveyed the crowd below, dancing and swirling in the flickering light. The love-struck gaze between Ian and Rebecca as they shared apple pie made her laugh out loud. They weren't going to be at this party much longer, that was a safe bet. And the nervous way Mr. McIntyre kept tugging at his collar and casting dreamy glances after Naomi tickled her to no end. The big, tough man of Defiance, so in love he was fidgeting like a ten-year-old boy about to sing in church.

When her gaze fell on Emilio, though, her amusement died. She tilted her head and pondered his feelings for her. Shoulders drooping, head bowed, he leaned into Mollie as they danced haltingly owing to his foot. Hannah had never meant to hurt him, and she felt guilty for the way she had sort of tossed him aside. He deserved better from her. He had been such a good friend—could have been more, maybe, but she was meant to be with Billy.

The thought still scared her, but she'd prayed and prayed and finally realized that giving him a second chance was, well, at the core of her faith. God gave her second chances all the time. Besides, God had gotten her through the first broken heart and would do it again, if necessary. But Billy had been noble enough to tell her to marry Emilio if he didn't make it. Maybe, if he'd known he wasn't mortally wounded, he wouldn't have made that statement, but he had and it revealed volumes about what was in his heart.

"Well, if you aren't the picture of deep contemplation."

She started at Billy's voice as he limped up the porch steps toward her. "Don't sneak up on me like that."

He lifted his crutch. "Yes, in my present condition, I'm as stealthy as a cat." They laughed, but it died quickly, replaced with a silence that begged for something real and deep to be spoken. "I'm going to buy Boot's Mercantile."

"Oh, really, that's wonderful. You'll be putting those Page business skills to work."

She hadn't meant that as an insult, but Billy suddenly found his shoes fascinating. "Funny, the one girl my pa said *I* was too good for turns out to be the one girl too good for me."

"Well, aren't you lucky?"

He frowned. "What?"

"Aren't you lucky I'm not a snob like your pa? Besides," Hannah moved closer to him, "I don't think you're the snob you used to be."

He clenched and unclenched his fingers, licked his lips, and finally rested a hand on her waist. She didn't move away, but held his gaze. Once upon a time, Billy's blue eyes had been able to stop all communication from her brain to the rest of her. Now, she could think past the love she saw in them and keep things in perspective.

"Hannah," he straightened a bit more, leaned his crutch on the rail, and placed his other hand on her waist. "I love you. I want to be with you. I want to be a father to Little Billy. I want us to be a family. I want—" He stopped short, exhaled, and grinned sheepishly. "What do *you* want?"

She nodded slightly. "The same things."

"Then will you marry me?"

Her lips twitched with a teasing smile. "In six weeks."

His whole body sagged. "Six weeks?" She waited to see which way he would go with that. She knew what the old Billy would do, but what about this new man standing before her? His face fell and he sighed. "Six weeks, six months, I'll wait as long as you want. But, why six weeks."

"Wade took the Reverend back to town right after the ceremony so he could catch the last stage." She batted her eye lashes. "He's halfway to Animas Forks by now."

He swiped a defeated hand across his mouth. "I've got to talk to McIntyre about getting a full-time preacher in this town."

<hr />

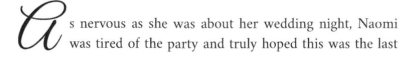

s nervous as she was about her wedding night, Naomi was tired of the party and truly hoped this was the last event of the evening. Giggling, Hannah gently tied a bandana over her eyes and whispered, "Now, Naomi, don't peek."

Rebecca came to one side of her and Hannah stayed on the other. Slowly, carefully, they walked her off away from the cabin toward the water. She could tell that by the fading chatter. The sound of the river got louder as she struggled with her wedding dress, trying to hold up her skirt and walk blind in the tall, thick grass. "What are you all up to now?" she asked, on the verge of losing her good humor. She wanted to tell everyone to please go home.

"You'll see," Hannah sang. "Now don't move."

They whispered behind her for a second. Naomi thought it sounded as if one of them walked away. The rustle of a dress faded before it disappeared altogether. "Which one of you is still here?"

"Me."

Hannah. "So what's happening? Tell me something."

"Well," her voice faded, came back closer to her ear. "I can tell you that you're definitely going to like it."

"You're not doing something awful like a shivaree?" *God, please, no.*

"No, Mr. McIntyre forbade it."

Naomi fell silent and tried to listen for clues but the water made it difficult. Once or twice she thought she caught the odor of a candle perhaps, and maybe heard the jingle of fading wagons, but wasn't sure. Finally, Hannah shifted, giggled, and kissed Naomi again.

"Stand right here and don't move a muscle." From a few feet away, she called, "I'll see you tomorrow, Naomi. Maybe."

Naomi harumphed. She'd already been standing here so long her feet were beginning to hurt. Suddenly, Charles' arms slipped around her and he lifted her off the ground. She clung to his neck, excited and nervous. "I don't remember anything about carrying the bride across the threshold *blindfolded.*"

He chuckled. "There's something I want you to see all at once, not bit by bit—an unveiling, so to speak."

As he walked, Naomi was surprised by the butterflies cavorting in her. She was deliriously happy and yet terrified. "Charles, I love you." Saying it made her feel better.

He slowed his walk, but carried on. She was slightly surprised he didn't say it back. What was going on here?

"Now, take off the blindfold."

She did as he commanded and removed the cloth. Positioned in front of their cabin, she immediately saw the dozens of glowing candles that lined the stone path on both sides, trailed up the porch stairs and down the porch in both directions, and led into the house. Full-on dark now, the glow was warm, inviting and . . . she frowned. There were *a lot* of candles, *dozens* and *dozens* of candles, maybe *hundreds*.

He carried her into the cabin where candles sat in the windows and in groups on the small table, lined the hearth, mantle, cook stove and dry sink, and formed a wide ring around their massive, pencil-post bed. The cabin, their home, spartan and in need of a woman's touch, glowed with the warm, inviting light. Surveying the large, one-room structure, her gaze traveled up the bedposts to the roof's beams where she realized her new home had no roof! An infinite host of stars twinkled and shimmered above them. A shy quarter moon peeked between the rafters.

"We ran out of time, but it will have a roof soon."

She brought her gaze back to him and her heart started pounding. All the trouble he'd gone to make this night so special . . . so pure. In a little while he would be all hers and she blushed at the promises of romance and passion. "It's beautiful."

"There is a candle burning for every day that I have known you." In the glow from these lights, the tender look in his eyes had the power to make her weep or faint. She wasn't sure which might happen first. "You are the light of my life, Naomi, and you pointed me to the eternal Light." He kissed her lightly. She tightened her grip on him and their hunger deepened. After a moment, he pulled away. "Can you believe," he asked, laughing, "that I am nervous?"

She rubbed her cheek along his beard, kissed his neck, nibbled on his ear. "Is that going to be a problem, Mr. McIntyre?" She felt a shiver shoot through him.

"Ohhh, no, Mrs. McIntyre." A wry grin tilted his lips as he reached back with his foot and shoved the door closed. "No problem at all, your ladyship."

"I'm going to hold you to that."

"I expect you will."

EPILOGUE

A horse's impatient grumbling filtered into McIntyre's dreams and his eyes fluttered open.

The open roof overhead and slate gray sky streaked with orange bewildered him for an instant. He lifted his head and remembered with delight that the luscious, naked creature partially wrapped around him was his wife. Their bare limbs were entangled wildly with each other as well as the sheets. And somehow they'd wound up at the opposite end of the bed.

Then it all rushed back. White satin slipping to the floor, soft caresses, and tantalizing sensations, a wondrous night of pleasure. The mere memory started his heart pounding.

Grinning like a love-struck fool, he lightly kissed the top of Naomi's head and dared to recall a night so perfect and pure he had no words to describe it. Naomi's surprising *zeal* had left him speechless and enthralled. She'd wanted him, and wanted to please him. She'd loved him with a passion and abandon that had ignited almost insatiable fires within him—

A horse whinnied, snatching his thoughts back to earth. He

hadn't imagined the sound after all. Apprehensive, he quickly but carefully, worked his way out of the bed, rummaged through a jumbled pile of clothes on the floor, and came up with his long johns. Hopping across the floor as he dressed, he grabbed his gun from the holster hanging beside the door and lurched to a window. One hand feverishly worked his underwear up to his waist while the other used the revolver to move the lace curtain aside.

Relief swept through him.

Chief Ouray sat atop a sorrel and stared stoically at the cabin door, as if time had no meaning. Beside him, a young boy, not much more than ten or twelve, dozed fitfully on a pinto's back. Sensing McIntyre, the chief's gaze moved to the window. The men nodded and McIntyre dropped the curtain. He looked back to make sure Naomi hadn't stirred, deposited his gun in its holster, and slipped outside.

"Chief. It's good to see you," he said, stepping down off the porch to reach his friend. The two shook hands, but McIntyre was instantly taken aback by the great sadness in Ouray's face. Lines that told many stories had deepened noticeably since their last meeting and his leathery brow puckered with misery. His coal black hair had gone gray and he looked thinner, his shoulders more bent. He and the boy both looked exhausted, as if they'd been riding for days. "What is it? What's happened?"

"Hopping Bird is dead," Ouray answered solemnly. The boy's head jerked up. Unveiled rage flared in his young, dark eyes when they lit on McIntyre.

Puzzled by the glare, McIntyre took a step back and let Ouray's loss sink in. He hadn't given the chief's daughter any serious thought in years. She had been his squaw for a short time, before he'd had enough sense to realize the path to destroying One-Who-Cries could not go through Ouray, not if he called the man his friend. The girl had been a pawn, another woman to use and throw away. McIntyre had made amends with her father for that, but not with her. Until this moment, it hadn't occurred to him he should even try.

"I am very sorry for your loss, Chief. She was a good woman."

McIntyre let his gaze drift to the boy. He reminded him of Hopping Bird. Slender, black hair cropped at his shoulders, he had soft, round features like his mother, near as McIntyre could recollect. But gray circles smudged the skin under his eyes. He was clearly weary from travel. And, yet, the lad held on to that venomous scowl. Trying to shake off a sense of foreboding, McIntyre motioned toward his cabin. "Come down. I'll fix us all some breakf—"

"I have come because of your promise."

There was much history between the chief and himself. And he owed the old man. No matter what he was about to ask, McIntyre knew he couldn't refuse. He tightened his jaw, furled and unfurled his fingers, but in the end, nodded, freeing the chief to continue.

"White Mountain is a bad place now for the Utes. More trouble is coming. The new agent Meeker fusses like an old woman and only causes hardship for my people."

"One-Who-Cries is dead, Chief." At the news, the old man's eyes darted to the boy, as if looking for a reaction. The child didn't flinch or waver in his hate-filled stare. A little unnerved by its steadiness, McIntyre shrugged and continued. "Maybe things will settle down without his rabble-rousing."

The chief sighed, the sound weary and hopeless. "Others will rise up to take his place. There will be no peace on the White Mountain Reservation. In the end, there may be no Utes." He turned to the boy, who still hadn't taken his eyes off McIntyre. "This is my grandson, Two Spears . . . so named," Ouray swung back to McIntyre, "because he comes from two worlds."

The intensity of the Chief's somber gaze explained his meaning . . . and the favor. McIntyre felt light-headed.

Surely, he's not asking—

"I cannot lose any more to the blue coats. I want my grandson to live—" Ouray, his voice strangled, clenched his jaw until he regained control. "Hopping Bird did not want this, but it is my decision now. If Two Spears is to live, I fear he must do so as a white man. I give him to you to raise in your world, Charles McIntyre. He is your son."

―――――

*D*ear Reader, if you were moved by the story of my sisters and their men in Defiance, I humbly ask if you would consider leaving me a review? Authors live and die by your kind words. I would be more grateful than you can imagine!

More importantly, I hope you've come to realize nothing can separate you from God's love. So accept it, ask His forgiveness for your sins, and move on. His mercies are new every day!

If you don't know Jesus, it's so easy to meet Him! Please follow this link to discover the simple steps to Salvation and a relationship with Christ. You'll never regret it. http://peacewithgod.net/

―――――

SNEAK PEEK

And now, here's an excerpt from *A Promise in Defiance, Book 3* in the Romance in the Rockies series...

"I don't know, Matthew." Delilah rose from her desk and carefully swished her large, enticing bustle over to the bar. She felt the man staring, no doubt with lust. His eyes glittered with the hunger men never seem to conquer. "Defiance is done, I suspect. Once Diamond Lil left and McIntyre closed the Iron Horse," she turned two shot glasses up and uncapped a bottle of whiskey, "that sealed it for me."

Matthew leaned the chair back on two legs. He was a big man, about the biggest she'd ever been acquainted with, and the wood protested under his weight. She handed him his drink, ignoring that handsome, square jaw and broad chest, and strolled to the window to look out over the streets of Salt Lake City.

"You know, you are a fine figure of a woman," Matthew observed. "That curly auburn hair of yours shimmers like honey. You could pass for a respectable woman—if you'd dress right."

Annoyed by the assumption that she *wanted* to be respectable, she turned sideways so he could get a better view of at least half her curves, and the low neckline on the verge of overflowing. Slowly, she swept a sultry glance over him. Such were her weapons. And she was well-trained in the art of war. "Save the flattery. Defiance is dead and I'm comfortable here."

Salt Lake City was going to keep her well-heeled for quite some time, but she didn't smile at the traffic below. This town turned her stomach. She couldn't run this brothel like she wanted. It had to be quiet, almost respectable. No shows. Nothing raunchy, nothing that might draw attention to the house. A bunch of pious hypocrites, these Mormons couldn't hand over their money fast enough, but it all had to be hush-hush. Which proved the old adage: no matter how many wives a man had, he still wanted a little forbidden fruit.

She did smile at that—a dark, bitter reflection of her revulsion. *Saints, my eye . . .*

But at least a simple brothel might not get her run out of town. Her last place had pushed the boundaries . . . and a moral citizenry had risen up against her.

Prudes.

Behind her, Matthew gulped down the shot and sighed with satisfaction. "Delilah, any woman who can run a cathouse in the middle of Salt Lake City ought to be able to restore a two-bit mining town to its former glory."

She snickered softly at the joke and shook her head. "It hasn't exactly been hard. Give a man a poke or a bribe in this town and you can get by with a lot."

"And that's my point. Nobody stops you. Once upon a time, McIntyre owned the finest brothel west of the Mississippi. Men will talk about the Iron Horse for generations." He raised an eyebrow at her. "Unless you give 'em somethin' else to talk about. Come on, I know you want to open another Fox Den. And you can. Bigger. More . . . entertaining."

That brought her head up slightly. She swallowed her own drink, tapped pretty painted nails on the rim. "Oh no, I don't doubt I could rival him. But fancy furniture, pretty gals," she looked over her shoulder at Matthew, "girls with no *boundaries*. It all takes money."

"You sell this place. I'll fund the rest."

Delilah narrowed her eyes at him. "That is suspiciously generous." She wandered back to her desk, settling in the chair, all but burying it beneath her huge bustle, and rested her elbows on the blotter. "What do you want out of this? And don't lie to me. Men are worse gossips than women. I know McIntyre ran you out of Defiance."

His face puckered up like she'd shoved a lemon in his mouth. "True—he did. Because I wasn't prepared to stay." He laced hands the size of bear paws over a flat stomach and shook wavy blond hair off his forehead. "Now I'm ready to settle down in Defiance." Suddenly, he leaned forward and pressed a hand down on her desk. "And I want it wilder and woolier than it was before. 'Cause that's the kind of town that suits me . . . and he'll hate it."

I hope you'll grab your copy of A Promise in Defiance today and finish reading about Logan and Delilah!

AFTERWORD

... Final thoughts:

To craft a story, sometimes an author plays with the facts a bit. For example, I take a few liberties with Colorado geography. But I wanted to mention a bit more about Chief Ouray, a real Ute chief who worked hard to protect his people from extinction. As a result, some Utes loved him and others hated him.

A dismal failure, the White River Reservation did, indeed, breed unrest and a rebellion broke out in September of 1879. Indian Agent Nathan Meeker and ten male employees were killed by renegades and Meeker's daughter and wife were kidnapped for ransom. Ouray and his wife Chipeta negotiated their release. If you'd like to learn more about this event and the pivotal role Chipeta played, please check out my blog at http://ladiesindefi ance.com/2014/08/06/like-a-phoenix-queen-of-the-utes-rose-from-the-ashes/

And thank you for reading about all the *Hearts in Defiance!*

ABOUT THE AUTHOR

"Heather Blanton is blessed with a natural storytelling ability, an 'old soul' wisdom, and wide expansive heart. Her characters are vividly drawn, and in the western settings where life can be hard, over quickly, and seemingly without meaning, she reveals Larger Hands holding everyone and everything together."

MARK RICHARD, EXECUTIVE PRODUCER, AMC'S HELL ON WHEELS, and PEN/ERNEST HEMINGWAY AWARD WINNER

A former journalist, I am an avid researcher and endeavor to skillfully weave truth in among fictional storylines. I love exploring the American West, especially ghost towns and museums. I have walked parts of the Oregon Trail, ridden horses through the Rockies, climbed to the top of Independence Rock, and even held an outlaw's note in my hand.

I grew up in the mountains of Western North Carolina on a steady diet of Bonanza, Gunsmoke, and John Wayne Westerns. My most fond childhood memory is of sitting next to my daddy, munching on popcorn, and watching Lucas McCain unload that Winchester! My daddy also taught me to shoot and, trust me, I can sew buttons on with my rifle.

Currently I reside near Raleigh, NC, on my farm with my three boys and lots of dirt, some dogs, and a couple of horses. Oh, and a trio of cats who are above it all. And did I say dirt? #FarmLife

Heather Blanton

Please subscribe to my newsletter by visiting my website at
authorheatherblanton.com
to receive updates on my new releases and other fun news. You'll
also receive a FREE e-book—
A Lady in Defiance, The Lost Chapters
just for subscribing!

ALSO BY HEATHER BLANTON

A Lady in Defiance (Romance in the Rockies Book 1)

Charles McIntyre owns everything and everyone in the lawless, godless
mining town of Defiance. When three good, Christian sisters show up,
stranded and alone, he decides to let them stay—as long as they serve his
purposes...but they may prove more trouble than they're worth.

Hearts in Defiance (Romance in the Rockies Book 2)

Notorious gambler and brothel-owner Charles McIntyre finally fell in
love. Now he wants to be a better man, he wants to know Christ. But all
the devils in Defiance are trying to drag him back to the man he was.

A Promise in Defiance (Romance in the Rockies Book 3)

When scandalous madam Delilah Goodnight flings open the doors to the newest, most decadent saloon in Defiance, two good men will be forced to face their personal demons.

Daughter of Defiance (Thanksgiving Books & Blessings Book 6)

When you hit rock bottom, you have a choice: seek the light or live in the darkness. Victoria chose the darkness. Can someone like her find redemption?

Hang Your Heart on Christmas (Brides of Evergreen Book 1)

A marshal tormented by a thirst for vengeance. A school teacher desperate to trade fear for courage. They have nothing in common except a quiet, little town built on betrayal.

Ask Me to Marry You (Brides of Evergreen Book 2)

Here comes the bride…and he isn't happy. With her father's passing, Audra Drysdale accepts she needs a man to save her ranch. A mail-order groom will keep her prideful men working and a neighboring rancher at bay. What could go wrong?

Mail-Order Deception (Brides of Evergreen Book 3)

Intrepid reporter Ellie Blair gets an undercover assignment as a mail-order bride and heads off to Wyoming where she discovers her potential groom isn't what he appears to be, either.

To Love and to Honor (Brides of Evergreen Book 4)

Wounded cavalry soldier Joel Chapman is struggling to find his place in the world of able-bodied men. A beautiful but unwed woman may be his chance to restore his soul.

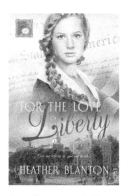

For the Love of Liberty

Novelist Liberty Ridley experiences an ancestor's memory from the Autumn of 1777. Stunned by the detail of it, she is even more amazed to find she's intensely drawn to Martin Hemsworth--a man dead for two centuries.

In Time for Christmas

Is she beyond the reach of a violent husband who hasn't even been born yet? Abandoned by her abusive husband on a dilapidated farm, Charlene wakes up a hundred years in the past. Can love keep her there?

Love, Lies, & Typewriters

A soldier with a purple heart. A reporter with a broken heart. Which one is her Mr. Right? A Christmas wedding could force the choice…

Hell-Bent on Blessings

Left bankrupt and homeless by a worthless husband, Harriet Pullen isn't about to lay down and die.

Grace be a Lady

Banished and separated from her son, city-girl Grace has to survive in a cowboy's world. Maybe it's time to stop thinking like a lady...and act like a man.

Locket Full of Love (Lockets & Lace Book 5)

A mysterious key hidden in a locket leads Juliet Watts and a handsome military intelligence officer on a journey of riddles, revelations, and romance.

A Good Man Comes Around (Sweethearts of Jubilee Springs Book 8)

Since love has let her down, widow Abigail Holt decides to become a mail-order bride, but with a clear set of qualifications to use in choosing her new husband. Oliver Martin certainly doesn't measure up...not by a long shot.

Made in the USA
Coppell, TX
03 August 2024

35557878R00246